PRAISE FOR HOLLY BOURNE

To C,
This book grew into being as I grew you into being.
Every day I'll fight for a better world for you.

First published in the UK in 2023 by Usborne Publishing Limited, Usborne House, 83-85 Saffron Hill, London EC1N 8RT, England. usborne.com

Usborne Verlag, Usborne Publishing Limited, Prüfeninger Str. 20, 93049 Regensburg, Deutschland, VK Nr. 17560

Text © Holly Bourne, 2023

Author photo © L. Bourne

A CIP catalogue record for this book is available from the British Library.

ISBN 9781474966832 J MAMJJASOND/25 05375/6

Printed and bound using 100% renewable energy at CPI Group (UK) Ltd, Croydon, CR0 4YY.

holly bourne

YOU COULD BE SO PRETTY

USBORNE

YOU COULD BE SO PRETTY
is a work of fiction but it deals with many
real issues including eating disorders,
domestic abuse, pornography, misogyny,
sexual harassment and assault, which some
readers may find distressing or offensive.

THE DOCTRINE

states that the Bad Times are
over and True Gender Equality
has been achieved.

The Doctrine has issued guidance
on how women and girls can
best integrate themselves into
this new world of Empowerment.

Of course, the Doctrine is
only guidance. It is not law.
It is every individual's choice whether
they want to embrace it or not.

We must celebrate every girl's
choice, without question.

That is what we all fought for.

BELLE

I'll never forget the sound of my mother's scream.

It woke me with a shrillness that pierced my bones and I scrambled up in bed. I was initially too terrified to move, my heart a frantic hummingbird in my chest, until I heard a wail that soured the air of our house. I kicked my covers and teddies off, ran to the door and listened at the crack, waiting to hear intruders, but the house was still apart from my mother's quiet sobbing. With shaking hands, I reached up to twist the doorknob and padded out into the corridor.

"Mother?" I whispered.

I found her in the corner of the bathroom. A huddled mess on the bath mat, bent over like a dropped doll.

"Mother?"

She flinched and looked up, the moonlight hitting her beautiful tear-streaked face. She reached out an arm, and I went to her instantly. My mother clutched me to her ribcage and wept onto my shoulder. "Oh, Belle," she gasped.

I tried to pat her back. I didn't know how to help. I was only seven years old.

"Mother, I'm scared. What's wrong?"

"I can't...I can't...Belle, what am I going to do? They're going to...they're going to make me an Invisible." She let me go and reached up, holding out a thin hair on her head. "Do you see it? Oh, Belle..." In the night's shadows, it took a second to make out the source of her scream. There, in my mother's manicured fingers, was one stray grey hair. It was the same pale colour as the moonlight glowing through the window. I took it between my fingers, not understanding at first. It felt different to the rest of my mother's hairs. Wirier, denser, and stripped of all pigment. A howl erupted from her throat and she collapsed in on herself again.

I sniffed up my own tears, feeling the most desperate helplessness. I didn't fully understand what an Invisible was yet. I wished my father was there, but he was never there. Always away, working, doing his part for the Industry. And even though I was young, I knew she wouldn't allow herself to be like this if he was around. Then a solution occurred to me. I told my mother to wait and I ran into my room, raiding my desk drawer for my colouring pens. I returned and paused in the bathroom doorway. My mother was still crying, while holding out her strand of grey hair like it would contaminate the others.

"Mother."

I sat cross-legged next to her and she seeped into my shoulder again.

"I don't want them to make me an Invisible, Belle. I can't."

"Mother, this might help."

8

I took the pen lid off with my teeth. She watched me take the offending strand between my pudgy fingers.

"You're not invisible, Mother," I told her, as I held the felt tip to the hair and started to colour.

It was an awkward job. The strand kept dropping from my fingers and I'd have to rummage to find it again. And it was a crude solution; the colour was hardly a perfect match. But the ink took to the hair surprisingly well, sinking into the porous texture, transforming it back to vitality, until it fell back, blended, into the other hairs.

"There we are, all done," I said, using the voice she used on me when I grazed my knee and needed a plaster.

My mother gathered herself from the floor, slowly rising until she was level with the sink. She leaned towards the mirror, examining her reflection. Even with her tear stains, even in the bad light, even without her Mask on, she was so beautiful. She turned her head this way and that and then smiled before twisting back to me.

"My beautiful girl," she said, bending down to scoop me up into a hug. I wrapped myself around her like a spider monkey. "Thank you," she whispered into my hair. "Thank you, my beautiful, *beautiful* girl."

JONI

I clung to Mother's leg while we both watched my father leave. She stood like a marble pillar, her eyes following him around the house, as he packed his things and told her all the reasons why she was disgusting and pathetic and how no one could blame him for leaving. His New One loitered by the front door, her arms crossed defiantly, shooting my mother looks of repulsion, her young, sculptured chin jutting out, all like, *I don't blame him either*. But Mother stood resolute, her hand shaking on my shoulder, and gave him nothing back. It was safer that way. He might want to inflict one final blow as a parting gift.

She did flinch, however, when he slammed the door behind him, leaving us in an empty house. But she recovered, squeezed my shoulder and stood motionless again, waiting…waiting…

Only after half an hour did she trust he'd actually gone. Her legs caved and I fell to the floor with her. "It's going to be okay," she whispered, kissing my cheeks, stroking my hair. "It's going to be okay, it's going to be okay."

I started crying, relieved and yet missing him already, and she hugged me to her, rocking me until I was calm again. Then, out of nowhere, she stood resolutely, a look of determination carved into her face.

"Mother?"

She walked upstairs, and I followed at her feet like a hungry kitten, until we reached the bathroom. The floor was littered with bottles Father had flung down in his haste to leave his family. Mother located a vial of Mask Remover in the corner, emptied it onto some cotton, and I sat on the toilet as she slowly, carefully, wiped her Mask off. I gasped as unseen parts of her revealed themselves. My mouth dropped open as she wiped and wiped, until a pile of coloured cotton clogged the sink. Then, smiling at her reflection in the cabinet mirror, she opened the door and took out a pair of scissors.

"Mother, no!"

She ignored me and stared ahead as she hacked off all her hair, letting it fall on top of the stained cotton.

When she was done, my mother's new face turned to me and everything about her was different. It wasn't just the lines I could now see that I hadn't before, or the shape of her skull through her new haircut...but her eyes...they were bright and dancing.

She brought me in for a kiss, and there was a lightness in her touch. A fresh way of holding herself, like she'd lost stones of Sin.

"We're free, Joni," she whispered to me. "Now we are free."

TEN
YEARS
LATER

BELLE

I wake up how I wake every day – exhausted and hungry, with the ghost of my mother's scream vibrating around my head.

"Belle?" she calls up the stairs – happy and energized and not screaming on the bath mat. "Are we doing Body Prayer together or not?"

"Coming." I allow myself thirty more seconds to lie back and fully rid myself of my recurrent nightmare. I hate waking up. Sleep's my only distraction from the gnawing in my stomach. I imagine a breakfast of scrambled egg, yellow and rich with melted butter seeping into thick white bread. Then I chastise myself. I am so greedy, so disgusting. I should not desire such things.

"Belle? Come on. You need as much time to Mask today as possible."

I'm so grateful to my mother for keeping me in line. I jump out of my bed and into my Body Prayer clothes. I sync my Device to the Ranking as I run downstairs, so everyone can see how much Sin I burn. It's particularly important to post today, it being the Selection and all. There are only eight weeks of lessons left before the Ceremony, and today at school everyone is voting to select the shortlist of potential winners. As Mother has reminded me for months – years, even – this is the most important day of my life. I feel light-headed as I jump off the last step and clutch the banister for a second. Sometimes I eat a banana before Body Prayer, but it's such a waste to do that when you can burn off more Sin on an empty stomach.

"Honestly, Belle, come on."

My mother marches into the hallway, her arms crossed over her hard torso.

"I said I'm coming."

She smiles and strokes my cheek, softening. "Sorry, my Bella Donna. I just want to make sure today goes perfectly for you. Remember, I've turned down two Mask appointments so I can focus solely on you today."

"I know, I know, thank you." Like I had any choice in that.

"Come on, let's sweat out that Sin. It's the most important day of your life to date."

"I know."

She picks the hardest intensity prayer and, as the world wakes up around us, Mother and I fall into perfect synchrony, the spring air seeping through the open windows. Sweat pours from my skin until I'm slippery with it. My legs burn like fires are raging inside of them. We jump so far and so high that the house shakes and it's just as well Father isn't here, like he usually isn't. He's constantly away, driving long distances to help the Industry. Once our Sin has been suitably burned, we turn to Muscle Pulling, leaning over in an array of stretches

16

to yank our sinews as lean and long as possible.

"Have you picked your final Look?" Mother asks, reaching down to touch her toes.

"I think so. It's a bit warm for the denim but I reckon I can pull it off."

She flips herself upright, takes me in and smiles again, touching my cheek once more. "Oh, I'm so excited for you. I'd do anything to relive my Just Right years."

"Let's just hope I get Nominated."

I ride another nausea wave at the thought of not getting enough votes today and failing to fulfil the Doctrine's destiny for me. I must win The Ceremony. I must be the Prettiest. I must Have It All.

"Of course you will. You're my daughter after all." She wrinkles her nose. "But you can never be too careful. Come on, I'll let you shower first."

Everyone always wants to know my morning ritual so they can copy it, but, as today is so busy, I'll explain briefly. I wake up, I do my Body Prayer, I wash, scrape off my top layer of skin, then scythe off any new bodily growths. I strip my hair, apply colour balance and nourishment mask, then rinse. After drying myself off, I brush my body to stop Sin Dimples forming, then I apply my creams. There's the compression one, then the nourishment one, and finally I apply skin camouflage. While they're settling in, it's time for my face. I pour acid onto my fingers and dab it on, then face nourisher, then light-blocker, before adding a pre-Mask. Then it's back to my hair, which takes another forty-five minutes to sculpt perfectly around my face. Mother comes in to do my Mask today. She blends three different colours of face camouflage and begins to artfully dab it on, painting a new face over mine, and adding illuminator so I glow out light. Then it's onto my eyes and eye framers, rosy cheeks, more illuminator. We will do lips after we've had breakfast. God, I'm so hungry. After a small meal that hardly touches the sides of my stomach, I get into my chosen Look, set up the Halo and let Mother take photos for the Ranking. It's the Selection Day, so I have to get my poses perfect. I squeeze every muscle in my body so they're taut, and then arch my back, point my toe forward, hold my breath till I'm practically blue, and ensure my hand is on my hip with my arm bent away from my body. The Doctrine insists this must look effortless, so I arrange my Masked face into a relaxed smile and look off to the side, hiding my wince of discomfort. We finally upload, deleting any visible Sin that crept in, then we sit together on my bed and refresh our Devices, seeing the Validation come in, counting it up, working out if I'm getting the most. Very quickly it's clear we've totally smashed it. I'm Number One in my class's ranking so far, and very far ahead. Vanessa, my best friend, hasn't uploaded her Selection Day Look yet, but it would take a *lot* to beat me.

"We did it!" I shriek, feeling the familiar mixture of relief and self-esteem flood through me. I am the Prettiest. I got it right today. I have the crown for another twenty-four hours, and these twenty-four hours are the most vital.

My mother high-fives me, jubilance radiating from her face

– or maybe that's just the Halo I've left on. "A team effort. I have no doubt you'll be selected for the Ceremony today, but still…it's always better to smash it." She strokes the curl flowing down across my forehead. "You're so lucky," she sighs. Her face falls – though only metaphorically, due to all the Immobilizer in it. "So young still. I used to have hair this silky, before I had to start covering it…"

My stomach twists under my cropped top, tugging out last night's nightmare.

"…but, hey, your mother still hasn't become an Invisible, has she?"

I shake my head. "You're still the most beautiful mother in town."

And we hug delicately so as not to ruin each other's hair.

I start the torturous process of walking to school in my Selection-worthy shoes. Mother offers to drive me in on her way to appointments, but agrees that would make my Look seem too high-maintenance. Walking is taking much longer than usual though, as I can only take tiny steps in these high heels.

My Device goes and I pause for a moment, leaning against someone's garden wall, resting my feet.

Damian:
DAMN GIRL, your upload this morning was
HOT

Blue Balls Belle strikes again
Just casually editing the pics so your mouth
is open...
Xxx

I feel an initial ripple of discomfort before I remind myself this is a compliment. The Doctrine says I am lucky to receive such attention. Especially from Damian, *especially* on Selection Day.

Belle:
You are too gross

He sends back a tweaked version of my Look with a penis leading to my mouth. I should be flattered. The Doctrine says I should be flattered. I *am* flattered. I check nobody is looking and then bend down to rub my aching feet. I must get my reply just right. Unoffended, up for it, a laugh, carefree, fun, sexy, not too serious.

Belle:
I feel sorry for you that Deep Fakes are your only sexual outlet.

Damian:
BURNNNNN. YOU'RE SO SMOKIN' HOT
YOU BURN GIRL.

I smile at myself. That seems to have done the trick. Just as I'm about to keep walking, a notification pings in. Vanessa's just released her Look to the Ranking. Dammit. Not bad. She looks amazing. I feel a funny mixture of rageful fear that she'll outperform me, combined with joy because she's my best friend and I want her to get Nominated too. I send off my Validation and put my Device back in my bag, eager to get to school to see the Selection all play out. People simply *must* Nominate me when they see me in real life.

Ergh. *Joni's* walking ahead of me, on the other side of the road. She doesn't walk, that girl, she *lollops*. Her arms swinging, legs open, her disgusting rucksack jiggling. I find the disrespect she shows herself and the Doctrine so repulsive. It's also quite scary, like she's a contaminant. *Lollop lollop lollop.* If there's one thing I can count on today, it's that Joni's NOT going to be Selected. She'll claim not to care, of course. Along with the rest of the pathetic Objectionables. All Joni cares about, it seems, is beating me to the Scholarship, which I don't have time to worry about until next month as I'm so preoccupied with the Selection. She's got a good chance at beating me too, with all that spare time she has due to her lack of personal grooming, wandering about, walking like a man who just sat on a cactus.

It's her choice, I remind myself, as rage blooms through me.

I repeat the Doctrine's mantra until it calms me down to the bones.

It's her choice. It's her choice. It's her choice.

I am so grateful to the Doctrine, for helping me navigate this world now the Bad Times are over. For giving us these

Rules to help us acclimatize to our freedom. But they are only *guidelines*, I remind myself. If someone as repugnant as Joni wants to waste her freedom by rejecting them, that's *her choice*, and I must celebrate her choice because we are *so lucky* to have all these choices. I just wish she could respect MY choices a bit more, rather than always making wild claims at school that we're all brainwashed if we don't want to be as disgusting as her.

I sigh and let the anger evaporate off my skin, soothed by the Doctrine. I totter along, excited to see Vanessa and scream at each other's appearances. In fact, I'm so calm, I don't initially notice the car that's slowed down next to me.

JONI

I wake up feeling gloriously well rested. It's late. I should probably have set my alarm for half an hour earlier, but who cares? Sleep is so wonderful and restful. Long live sleep, that's what I say. I smell slightly, so I take a shower but can't be bothered stripping my hair. I'm sure the Doctrine will cope with one more day. Well, actually, the Doctrine can't cope at all with such things. If Belle turned up today with Day Three hair, I think everyone would pass out with shock. But everyone will be looking at the Pretties today – exclusively so. Literally nobody is going to notice me on Selection Day.

"You're going to be late," Mother says as I thunder down the stairs. She's sitting at our kitchen table, which is covered with placards and other protest paraphernalia.

"I'm never late. I've timed it perfectly." I plant a kiss in her wiry hair and grab two slices of white bread and shove them into the toaster. Then I lean against the counter and point at the pile of signs. "What's the fight against today?"

She sighed. "There's still no regulation at the Empowerment Centre. Anyone can call themselves a technician and carve

23

someone up. I heard they agreed to see a twelve-year-old last week."

"*Twelve?* Jeez."

"With parental consent. Which all the brainwashed Pretties will happily give, of course."

"Twelve is…" I try to remember myself at twelve. I hadn't even started my bleedings yet. "…quite an extreme age."

"But *it's their choice*, remember?" Mother puts on her Doctrine voice.

"But of *course*." I laugh. "Totally. Can't go around questioning logic like that."

She stands up and kisses the top of my head. "That's my girl."

I eat my toast and watch Mother whirlwind around the house, clutching her activism leaflets, before finally leaving with a rushed goodbye.

"Enjoy Selection Day," she calls on her way out. "Or, should I say, endure it?"

I laugh out some toast crumbs. "Only eight weeks left until I can hopefully get the Scholarship and escape."

"Exactly. Getting into the Education is the only Selection that matters, remember? Right. Time. I must go."

The house is eerily quiet once the door closes, and I inhale it, enjoying the calm. Living with my mother is like living with a constantly combusting firework – beautiful, but noisy and exhausting. Despite myself, I use the quiet to run through the likely Selection that day, placing silent bets on who'll get through. I hate that part of me's still vaguely interested. I hate that I'm

24

tempted to check my Device and see what's happening on the Ranking. I wish I could be stronger like Mother. But, then again, Mother isn't seventeen. She reminds me of this often.

"It will be much easier once you're out of your 'Just Right' years," she's said countless times, when the Doctrine gets too much. "The noise will never be louder than it is now."

I bring my empty plate to the sink, wash it, check the time on my Device, and realize I could actually be late if I'm not careful. I dash upstairs and clean my teeth, not bothering to check the mirror, and then close up the house and make my way into school.

I think about Mother as I rush along. She seems so strong, so certain, so unbothered by it all. I wonder if she gets moments of doubt, like me. Or if she really, truly doesn't mind being so hated. The Society generally tolerates and ignores Invisibles until they try to be seen and heard. Then it *hates* them. No decorum in that. Our whole town despises Mother and her ilk. She faces daily disgust. I've heard her be called "an abomination of a woman" and yet she claims it's funny. How? Maybe she's right. Maybe it will get easier for me in time.

My musings are interrupted by an annoying clip-clop sound behind me. After a while, I turn around to see if I'm being stalked by a horse, but no, it's Belle of all people. She's teetering to school in the world's most ridiculous heels. She does it vaguely effortlessly. Everything about Belle appears annoyingly effortless. She's lost in her Device as she clops along, no doubt triple-refreshing the Ranking as the Looks come in, worrying if she's Masked enough to fulfil her true life's purpose. I wrinkle

25

my nose and keep walking. It's *good* for me that she looks so Pretty. Any moment she's committing herself to the Doctrine is a moment she's not studying for the Scholarship. Because she's annoyingly smart, Belle, as well as being annoyingly beautiful. I have to put up with her in all my First Set classes. Not content with being the Prettiest Pretty, she's determined to get into the Education too. She hardly needs to sleep, from what I can tell. Totally superhuman. How else does she find time to get such good marks in school while looking like that?

I plod on, checking the time on my Device again, wondering if I'm going to make the first bell, when I notice the clip-clopping has slowed almost to a stop. I turn back to see a car inching along beside Belle. Her face has changed. She's no longer absorbed in her Device but is smiling nervously at the driver. "Honestly, thank you but I'm happy to walk," I overhear her saying in a diabetically sweet voice. I slow and wait for the car to drive off, but it doesn't. It keeps kerb-crawling and Belle's trot is a wobble now. "Honestly, you're being very generous, but I want to walk." I hear her say it a little louder this time.

Then something changes. The car stops.

"Stop being such an ungrateful slutty bitch," a man's voice shouts from the window. And I'm running back, threading my house keys between my knuckles, joining Belle's side.

"Is everything okay here?" I ask, trying to sound like my mother at her most scary. "Belle?"

Her eyes are wide. Maybe she's shocked I'm here? I look into the driver's window to see a youngish man with a red-tinted face, glaring at me with acute disgust.

"Who ordered the monster?" he asks.

"Excuse me?"

"I wasn't speaking to you," he says.

I turn back to Belle. "Are you okay?"

She's shaking. "I'm fine."

"Hear that, you Objectionable mess? She's fine. There's nothing wrong with offering a Pretty girl a lift to school."

"Unless she says no and then you won't leave her alone."

"It's a *compliment*," he says, quoting the Doctrine. "Come on…into the car." I can't believe it. The man's taken off his seat belt and is walking around towards us. Belle grabs my hand and my body floods with adrenaline as he gets closer. I take in his rosy face. He's calm. That's what makes it worse. He's going to drag Belle calmly into his car like that is a totally normal thing to do.

"Honestly," Belle says, "I just really feel like walking. I need the air…" Belle can't stop herself following the Rules and trying to appease him, even as he takes a step closer. I scan around to see if anyone's going to help us, but the street's empty. He lurches forward and grabs Belle's waist with both hands. She shrieks, just as my fist flies out and I punch him in the eye, then sink my keys into his leg. He lets out an animal roar and staggers back against the car. I move forward and kick him hard in his groin and he lets out another howl and collapses onto the pavement, while Belle stares at me wide-eyed.

I turn to her. "Run. Now."

"But…but…" She's shaking. Frozen and shaking.

"But what?"

27

"It's…it's…a compliment."

"No, it's not, it's an attack. Run. Now!"

I drag her with me, and it's like she suddenly gets it. She grabs my arm and lets me lead her away, while a stream of abuse and threats erupts from the man's mouth. I twist back and he's trying to get himself up, staggering on the pavement, leaning against his car, clutching his groin. If he catches up with us, we're doomed. I spy an alleyway and tug Belle towards it, but she's slowing us down, hardly able to run in her stupid heels.

"Lose your shoes," I shout as we start down the alleyway.

"*What?* No. They're my—"

"Do you want to actually die? Lose them now."

I crouch down and go to tug her heels off. She lets out a noise of surprise but then her survival instinct must override the Doctrine, and she bends over and whips them off herself. We leave them behind as we pelt along, fear pulsing through my blood.

"I'm coming for you," he yells from somewhere behind us.

"We have to get out of the alleyway or he'll catch us up." Adrenaline's made my brain quietly calm and I race through exit routes with strange clarity. If we jump over some fences, he may think we've run out the top of the alleyway, and we could lose him. I can't hear his footsteps yet but there's no man faster and stronger than a man angry at a girl. Belle's slightly ahead of me now, her breath coming out in even pants. Of course she's faster than me, she does Body Prayer every day.

"We need to scale the fences," I gasp out.

"What?"

I point at the garden fences on either side. "We need to climb over a few of these. He won't think we've done that. Then we can hide in someone's garden, wait for him to run past."

"What? I can't."

I hear his yell again closer behind us, coming towards the alleyway entrance. "Where are you bitches?"

Belle turns white under her Mask.

"It will throw him off. It's the only way."

"Okay."

I easily scale the fence, but Belle can't. She's hardly able to lift her leg up in her skintight denim. I clamber back over and give her a leg-up, but she's uselessly stiff. In the end I have to push her over, and hear her topple to the other side. I vault over too, landing in a bush beside her.

"What the hell?" she's complaining, trying to get up, her clothes covered in mud. "You just pushed me—"

"Shh, we need to keep going."

I scarcely take in the garden we've landed in. I'm too busy sizing up the height of the opposite fence. "I'll give you another leg-up."

"Umm, no thanks."

"You won't get over it otherwise."

And she can't argue. We race across the lawn and I give her another leg-up, pushing her over the next fence, and the next, before we collapse in a random rose bush – panting, scratched, terrified.

"This is actually madness—"

"*Shh.*"

A few gardens away I hear his heavy footsteps thud down the alleyway. Belle grabs my hand and we stare at each other, suspended in total fear, as we listen to him grunt in pain and anger. Sick bubbles in my throat now that I've done all I can. *How can this be happening? Why won't he give up?* How can I be eating toast and then, half an hour later, be about to be attacked by a total stranger? The footsteps pause. Has he figured it out? Belle's eyes meet mine again and we stare at each other, breathing in one another's breath, our entwined hands damp with sweat, shaking in the thorns of the rose bush, awaiting our fate…

And then…mercifully, his footsteps pick up again, and he races down the alleyway, chasing our ghosts.

We wait five minutes and hear nothing more.

We are safe. For now, we are safe.

My ribcage releases and I roll out of the bush onto some stranger's lawn, gasping quietly up into the blue sky. I try to take deeper breaths, but they arrive short and sharp and mostly useless. I feel Belle shaking by my side. She starts weeping and we stay like that a while. Both of us sprawled out on the lawn, stunned, scarcely believing it's over. Trying to take in that it happened at all.

Once fifteen minutes have passed, my breathing's better and the reality of our situation grinds in. I start assessing our surroundings – working out what we should do next. I look up at the house, wondering why they've not noticed two girls in their Just Right years land in their gardens like fly-tipped rubbish. But the curtains are closed. They're either away, or still asleep.

I manage to find my voice. "Are you okay, Belle?" This is essentially the first civil conversation we've ever had, despite growing up in the same class our whole lives. She regularly sniggers at my appearance and I snigger right back at hers. But today we're united by fear. She staggers up, wiping the mud off her clothes, examining the scratches across her bare stomach. She tries to wipe away the black bits of Mask from under her eyes and I notice how her tears have carved rivers of paler skin through it. Her hair looks, quite rightly, like she's been dragged through a hedge backwards. But she's safe. So am I. Somehow.

She looks up at me and I can see she's still shaking as she smooths down her ruined clothes. I expect her to acknowledge what just happened. To thank me. For saving her. For rescuing her...

But this is Belle we're talking about so, of course, instead, her face sets, and all she says is, "You've *ruined* my Look."

BELLE

What a complete disaster. I don't even know where to start with what a disaster this is. My hair? I can feel an actual *burr* in it. My Mask? Ruined. I whip out my Device and use reflection mode to assess the damage, but, even with Halo-mode on, I am a mess. On Selection Day of all days. How can this be happening to me?

Joni, of course, is focusing on all the wrong things.

"I just saved your life and you're worried about your Look being ruined?" She looks even worse than me, unsurprisingly. Her face is red, and she's got an actual snot trail smeared across her cheek from crying. I shudder.

"It's Selection Day," I remind her, glancing down to see if my manicure's ruined and noticing my hands are shaking again. I fold them into my muddy lap. "I know that means nothing to you, but excuse me for having a life to be proud of."

"Are you forgetting you'd have no life at all if I hadn't just saved you?"

"Oh, stop being so dramatic."

My words aren't quite matching how I feel though. In truth,

my heart feels like it's been squeezed in a vice until it almost exploded. Whenever I blink, the man's face flashes behind my eyelids, and I want to scream and cry for about ten years. The way he went from friendly to violent so fast. The feel of his hands on my waist. What would he have done to me? Despite the wisdom of the Doctrine, his attention didn't feel like a compliment...

I push all this from my brain and focus on things I can control. How do I get out of this garden? How do I mend my Look before school? I'm already late. I've missed my Grand Entrance. Oh, this is such a nightmare. I decide it's all Joni's fault and glower at her, but she has the audacity to look at *ME* in disgust? She staggers to her feet and sweeps mud off her vile T-shirt. I'm surprised she's shown even that ounce of respect for personal grooming. Then she starts trampling around the garden, muttering to herself. "Okay, okay, what to do...call Mother? No, she's... The Protection Agency...do I call them? No, they're not safe..."

"What are you doing?"

"Figuring out how to get to school safely. Oh, brilliant, there's a gate." She points and, sure enough, there's a gate onto the street.

"Get to *school*?" There's no way I'm going to school before I mend my Look. Maybe I should call the Protection Agency? When the compliment gets dangerous, you're supposed to call them. Those are the guidelines. More importantly, I can use their mirrors and undo the worst of the damage, then I can arrive at school before lunch and the final hour of voting.

"Maybe we *should* call the Protection Agency?"

"No, they're not safe. And *we're* not safe until we get away from this madman and into school," she says.

My breath catches. Was he really a madman? There it is again – his face behind my eyelids. He was so calm as he grabbed me. Oh God, if Joni hadn't come…

If Joni hadn't come and made him angry by randomly attacking him…

I let out a laugh and get to my feet. "But of course you feel the actual *Protection Agency* isn't safe. That makes total sense."

"How do you know he wasn't a protection officer?" Joni shoots over her shoulder, trying the gate's latch and finding it unlocked.

This is too much. She's ridiculous. I know her mother's a gross conspiracy theorist, but I thought Joni would have more intelligence. She's my main competitor for the Scholarship after all, and is always trying to put her hand up before me in classes.

"Because they're here to *protect* us, not drag us into cars?" I scramble up properly and wince as I follow her, my feet stinging on the gravel path, reminding me that I've lost my shoes. What was I playing at, letting Joni rip them off me? It all feels dreadfully embarrassing now. Though, when I glance at the windows of the house, I feel another involuntary shudder. Nothing feels safe. The thought of the attacker still lurking around here somewhere has me breaking out in a new sweat.

"I'm not calling them. You can. But I'm getting to school. We'll be safer there."

"And if we happen to bump into the man on the way?"

"We won't. School's only five minutes away." Her voice betrays her, breaking on the last word. Our eyes meet again and we can't look away for a moment – both of us united in how totally terrified we are. Then I shake my head, dislodge it, and tussle with what to do. I can ring Mother, but she'll go nuts if she sees the state of me. Or I can run to school with Joni and arrive a total mess and ruin everything. No…I just need to convince Joni that she's wrong and…oh no, where's she going?

Joni pushes through the gate, crouching low, looking side to side. Then, without turning back, she runs ahead, the gate crashing closed behind her, not even waiting for me.

"Joni? Joni!" I whisper as her footsteps get quieter. She's left me. I push through and catch her up. She's hiding behind a parked car and doesn't acknowledge my presence, just mutters to herself.

"Okay, so the alleyway ends there to the right. That's the way he went. If we go left, through that other alleyway, we should come out near the school gates…"

My brief respite from fear vanishes, and I nod, taking in her plan.

"Let's go." Joni darts across the road before I even have a chance to think about it. I speed after her, scuttling past a few houses, before running into another alleyway. For a second, I think I see the man, standing there in the middle, waiting for us with a smug grin, and my body freezes in terror…but the alley is empty, and I run through my ghost of him, and feel fresh tears fall down my face, ruining my Mask further. We run and run, my feet burning as they trample over pebbles and gravel and filth and rubbish. At every turn, I think we'll see him, but soon enough we're outside school, bent over and panting.

"We're here," I say, glancing for one last time up the road.

"We made it."

We smile at one another in a quick, unacknowledged truce. Relief surges through me, settling my breath for the first time since the car slowed down next to me, and I almost drown in it…before something cold kicks in. A guilt. A feeling of me-being-silly. An irritation…

I glance down at my demolished feet. "You owe me a new pair of shoes."

Joni laughs harshly. "Still no 'Thank you for saving my life, Joni'?"

"He was only being friendly," I find myself saying in an odd robotic voice. I turn and hobble off towards the school gate, suddenly not wanting to be near her a second longer. "You're the one who attacked him and got him angry."

"Are you being serious? I stopped him attacking—"

"You stopped him offering me a lift to school." I interrupt her, still not sure why my voice is so robotic.

She laughs again. "Oh well, sorry. I must've just been jealous he didn't pick me to abduct."

"Well, he didn't, did he?"

She's lolloping behind me and I can feel her anger radiate off her body. "Oh my God, you actually think that, don't you?" she says. "That he was just offering you a nice lift to school, and I'm jealous?"

I narrow my eyes. Maybe that is what I think? I need some kind of story to distract everyone from why I look so Objectionable.

"I forget how…totally brainwashed you are."

Irritation rips through my skin. Joni and her stupid conspiracy theories. Almost as ugly as her.

"More like *hair* washed," I shout back, triumphant in my insult. "Something you don't seem to understand. Tell me, when was the last time you stripped your hair? Back in the Bad Times by the looks of it."

The insult doesn't land. As I glance back, I see her face looks mildly amused. Like I've done exactly what she predicted I'd do. And her arrogance morphs my fear into anger. She thinks she knows me?

We turn onto the school's drive.

"Your heels," she says quietly. "They're like that for a reason, you know."

I turn back. "Like *what*?"

"Impossible to walk in…to run in."

We're now at the school gates and I really don't want anyone to see us. Nobody can see the state of me. Or see me standing alongside Joni. I should flounce off and not indulge her deluded programming, especially as someone could be looking out the window right now. But something holds me still a moment too long.

"What do you mean?" I find myself asking.

"I'm just saying. Everything about how you're dressed today for the Selection, about how you dress every day… You think it's to make you look Pretty. But it's actually to make you weak."

"*Excuse me?*"

"Those shoes." Joni points at my dirty bare feet. "You wore them because they make your legs look long and slim. You think they complement your body and finish off your Look. But have you ever thought why shoes like that get the most Validation?" she asks. "It's because they weaken you. They're bad for your health. Your mobility. It's because they make it harder to function. To even go from A to B, and live your life to its fullest and without pain. Those shoes make it harder to run from danger. Just like those ridiculously tight denims you're wearing made it impossible to scale those fences. Again, it's about making you physically weaker…especially as you have to be hungry all the time in order to fit into them." Joni looks at me with pity. *SHE* looks at *ME* with *PITY*. The world turns upside down. Also, how does she know I'm so hungry? "You think following the Doctrine gives you power," she says, "but it's all designed to weaken you, to make you compliant."

For a moment, her words staple me to the ground. My mouth hangs open. For a second, everything is forgotten and my brain feels buzzing and cluttered and—

The bell goes, jolting me back. And before I have a chance to mend my Mask, our whole year group pours out of the assembly hall, finding me a total mess and standing next to the worst Objectionable in our whole school.

* * *

I'm so angry. So unbelievably angry. Everyone's seen me looking like a total train wreck the day of the Selection and it's all Joni's fault. If she hadn't dragged me through the mud and then held me up trying to radicalize me to be as disgusting as her, everything would've been perfect. Fixable. But no, out everyone poured, seeing me breaking all the Doctrine's Rules. I'd rather everyone had seen me nude than without my proper Mask on. We've been the gossip of the whole school all morning.

"Did you see? Belle? Without a Mask on, I know."

"They almost died."

"Well, Belle did. I think Joni was just there."

Thankfully, nobody thinks Joni and I were hanging out of Free Will. And I've worked very hard to spread the official storyline, which is that the attacker came after me because I looked too good and he couldn't help himself. This is, thankfully, corroborated by the Protection Agency when they turn up to interview us individually. I called them to piss Joni off. Also, I wanted to ensure everyone knew just how serious it was, hoping that would deflect from my temporary Masklessness.

"I hope we're not taking up too much of your time," I told the protection officer, as I sat in the head teacher's office, hoping I could leave soon. I was missing all the gossip about the Selection and hadn't had one chance yet to check my Device.

"Your friend seems to think this man is very dangerous," the officer said. He had a notepad out on his knee, though I noticed he hadn't taken any notes.

"She's not my friend," I clarified.

"Yes, she said the same." He smiled at me. "I must say, you don't look like you're the sort to spend time together."

I smiled. I'd managed to cobble together a replacement Mask and mend my Look and thankfully it was holding up okay. Vanessa's Mask was too dark a match for me, but she had lent me the spare pair of heels she kept in her locker, and I'd found a drying pot of old Mask at the bottom of my bag.

The protection officer smiled again. "So, talk me through it once more. You say this man wanted to offer you a lift to school?"

I nodded. "Yes. He kept telling me how Pretty I was. But he got...umm...aggressive when I wouldn't get into his car."

"That's a shame," the man said, like my attacker had left a banana peel on the road that I'd accidentally slipped on or something. He looked me up and down, taking in my tight denim, new heels, my torso on show. Something prickled inside me, but I must have just still been in shock or something. "And were you wearing this when it happened?" he asked, gesturing to my Look.

"Umm, yes?"

"Well, you're a very pretty Pretty, Belle. Maybe he just couldn't help himself?"

The prickling in my stomach got stronger. "He did seem quite dangerous," I found myself saying.

"Oh, I'm sure he was. Sadly, when you're such a Pretty, Belle, you're going to incite a lot of this." He winked. "It's a curse sometimes, as well as a blessing, looking like you."

That's when I realized the Protection Agency wasn't going to do anything. That they didn't think this was a problem. Just like Joni said. And though I'd only called them to get my story straight, and I knew I should trust their judgement, a small chill ran through me knowing that man was still out there. How was I ever going to walk alone again if they didn't catch him?

But it's Selection Day, and I can't allow myself to be distracted. Especially after such an abysmal start. I don't want stupid Joni to get into my head with her mad conspiracies. Anyway, the whole drama seems to be working out in my favour.

"Belle," Damian calls, when I get into the recess room at lunchtime. "I heard you're so Pretty today that you're inciting boners in random members of the public and they simply must attack you."

I smile as I make my way over, walking carefully in Vanessa's slightly big shoes. "And there you were, thinking you were special."

He laughs reluctantly and puts an arm around me, drawing me to our corner with the rest of the Pretties. As we're walking, he reaches down and pinches my buttocks. I startle, but when I look over, he's grinning and acting like he didn't. I laugh, to let him know I find it funny, like I know I'm supposed to.

Colin is all set up with his polling booth and there's a queue of about five students casting their votes for the Selection. We glide past, pretending we're not hugely invested in who everyone is voting for, and I feel Colin's eyes on me. He's wanted to Link with me since childhood because he is delusional. "You need to be more careful," Damian says, as we

reach the corner of Pretties. "Your whole Blue Balls act, Belle…
well, it has consequences. Of course men are going to get
violent. If only you were more *giving* with your beauty, like
Vanessa here."

"Hey," said Vanessa, who sits swinging her legs on our table
next to Ben, her long-term Link and Damian's best friend.

"Giving is one word for it," Ben says, and they high-five each
other. "Though Nessie here really loves taking it too. Don't
you, gorgeous?"

"Ben! Shut up," she shrieks, reaching out and hitting him.
It's hard to tell if she's genuinely angry or not. Vanessa and I
have been best friends since we were fledglings and were the
first in our year to get into On The Cusp Masks. I felt I really
knew her until she fell madly for Ben and Linked with him.
Now I find her harder to read. He doesn't always seem very
nice to her, but it only seems to make her love him more.

"What? Come on, we're all friends here."

Damian laughs. "Can I join your friendship circle, please?
I'm stuck with Blue Balls Belle here."

Everyone laughs while I feel myself stiffen up. Damian
came up with the nickname Blue Balls Belle only last week and
it's sticking. Hard. I'm starting to worry it will really spread and
become a problem. I've refused multiple dates with Damian,
always with good humour, but this new "Blue Balls" joke feels
dangerous. Inspired, the boys load some Smut onto their
Devices and stream it to the recess-room screen. This is their
favourite thing to do – as in, they do it almost every day – and
we all twist to watch, everyone but me pointing and laughing.

42

My stomach dives, like it always does when Smut comes on.

"Don't worry about Damian," Vanessa whispers as the boys wander over to the screen to point out all the flaws of the Smut actress.

"Hmm."

"It's your choice, remember?" she says, parroting the Doctrine. "Stay a Vanilla for ever if you really want."

"Hmm."

To tell the truth, I've been dreading this day coming. I knew there was only so long I could hold out on not doing anything with all the male attention I attract. Being a Vanilla was aspirational in my younger years, but, as other girls have renounced their Vanilla status, I'm starting to look stuck-up. And the Doctrine states I mustn't be a Vanilla by the end of the Ceremony.

Everything's going wrong today. It feels like the tall tower I've spent so long building is toppling over and crumbling to dust. I've worked so hard to follow the Doctrine, and to be the Prettiest and now that power feels like it could be snatched away. I've been counting down to Selection Day for months, and now, with hours to go before the results, I'm dreading it rather than looking forward to it.

Laughter ripples across the recess room, and I jerk my head around to see the cause of celebration. The Smut actress looks like she's in real pain, and Damian and Ben keep rewinding it, adding their own dialogue to it.

"If only I had a bigger mouth."

"Please don't stop until I bleed."

The other boys start laughing in a howling, wolflike way, and I scan the room to see who else is watching. A few people have turned away, including four Beta Boys in the corner who Damian frequently accuses of being Fairies. But everyone else is finding the clip hilarious. The Try Hards are, predictably, right near the screen, copying everything Damian and Ben are saying, one of the girls laughing with a closed mouth and sort of swooning around their company. They're so pathetic, really. I think I find them harder to stomach than the Objectionables. The Smut actress yelps and the boys erupt into more laughter, rewinding the clip so they can watch it again.

"Put it on slow motion," a male Try Hard calls, and Damian nods, no doubt making his day.

"I love it when they get spat on," Damian adds, putting it on super slow motion.

I force myself to look away, arranging my face into bored disinterest. I cannot show Smut getting to me, especially after the mess of today. It will make the rumours worse. There have been mumblings since the "Blue Balls Belle" inception that I'm secretly a Frigid, and that will ruin my chances of being Selected. My eyes flicker to the polling station again. The queue is even longer now, Colin looking a bit frantic at the table. I scan everyone's faces as they bend over to make their Nominations. Do they look like they're writing my name? My stomach tightens. I want this so much. If this morning's drama and my temporarily Maskless face stops me getting Nominated…I don't know. The humiliation would be too much to bear. I'd never forgive Joni Miller.

44

And, like she knew I was thinking of her, in sails Joni. Lollop lollop. Yuck. She's making her way to the Objectionables' Corner with one of her even more repulsive friends. Seeing her again ricochets me back to that morning. Her hand in mine. Pulling me away from danger, and pushing me frantically over the fence. Our eyes locking, our breath suspended. My heart starts racing again.

Joni flops onto a chair with her legs wide open, her hair falling into her face. One of her gross friends – the one who looks like a dead fish – leans towards her, to console her by the looks of things. What's going on? Joni never needs consoling. I wonder how her interview with the Protection Agency went. What was it she said this morning? That you can't trust them? More memories swarm in.

"It's like this for a reason, you know."

"It's all about making you weaker."

My head starts to throb. A choking noise echoes from the screen followed by more laughter, and I look over at Damian's face, which looks fully alive. He's so handsome but, boy, there's a darkness behind his eyes. He's pointing out the Sin on the Smut actress and the Try Hards practically vibrate the carpet with their laughter.

Damian's officially asked me out three times now. And I know what's expected of me if I Link with him. My eyes go to the screen. I should be immune to Smut. It's basically played at least once a day at school and Damian regularly sends me clips to enjoy. I should enjoy it, like the Doctrine tells us to. Everyone else does. I should think it's both sexy and funny. The Doctrine says Smut is fun and healthy and only Frigids take issue with it because there's something fundamentally wrong with them. The Doctrine says it's the ultimate celebration of our freedom, and only broken girls don't want to celebrate their freedom. I can't be a Frigid, can I? If I am one, nobody can ever find out. As I glance at the screen, the attacker's face flashes in my mind and I start shaking. I want to be anywhere but in this room. In this school. In this body. In this Society. I hate it, I can't breathe, I'm so hungry, I'm so frightened, I'm so ugly, I hate... I hate...

I actually hate Joni Miller.

She's noticed the Smut playing and she's straight up, of course, bouncing out of her chair. She marches right over to the screen, and, without any fear or anything, she switches it off. A tidal wave of groans echoes around her.

"What the hell did you do that for?" Damian asks.

"It's disgusting and you're disgusting," she replies, crouching down and ripping the power out. "And it's not allowed in school. So unless you want me to tell Ms Blanche..."

"You know that means nothing. The teachers all watch Smut at home anyway."

"You can explain that to Ms Blanche's face then, can't you? When I tell her you're playing it? Which I'll do if you dare turn it back on."

"You're such an ugly, foul killjoy..." Damian launches into a tirade of horrifying expletives but Joni's already walking away, like his words are vapour.

"Objectionables like you shouldn't be allowed in here,"

he calls after her, as she retakes her seat and picks up a book of all things, while everyone watches.

"The only thing Objectionable in this room is you."

"Just because I wouldn't make Smut with you in a million years."

I flinch. We all flinch. This is the worst of the insults. The worst thing a boy can say out loud. But, yet again, Joni is unmoved.

"Bless you for saving me from a venereal disease." She keeps her eyes on her book. "That's so kind of you."

For a second, the hate in Damian's face twists into something ugly. "A *what?*"

"Maybe spend less time being a disgusting misogynistic cretin and go look up some big words in the dictionary."

I have no idea what "misogynistic" means, and neither, clearly, does Damian, or the rest of us. He declares he's bored and wants to play Rage Ball. He nods his head towards the door, and we all stand, ready to follow. Vanessa pulls down her tiny skirt.

"You coming?" she asks, noticing me dither.

I look back at Joni and thick hatred courses through me. *How dare she?* How can someone be so gross and yet so confident? Isn't she ashamed of what she looks like? And yet, here she is, telling me what to do, what's wrong with my Look, telling Damian he's wrong and not even caring about his opinion... I narrow my eyes and a plan falls into place like it's been parachuted out of the sky. Joni needs to know her place.

"In a second," I say. "With all the drama this morning, I've totally forgotten to make my Nomination."

Vanessa nods and grins. "You can't Nominate yourself, remember?" She jabs me with her delicate elbow.

I laugh. "I'll vote for you, of course."

She screeches and gives me a hug. "And I'll totally vote for you too."

I'm not sure I believe that. We love each other, but Vanessa has always been my main competition, and I'm hers.

"I'll catch up in a second."

The Pretties filter after Damian and the energy in the room feels off now they've left. The Try Hards look put out, but everyone else seems to sigh in collective relief. I glare one more time at Joni, who's now eating a sandwich. In public. *An egg sandwich!* My stomach twists at the sight of it. She truly is the most disgusting person on earth.

Colin's shocked when I approach him at the booth. He half wilts into his chair under my presence.

"Hi, Belle." His voice squeaks while I smile my best smile at him. "Umm, is everything okay with your Nomination form?"

I lean over, so my chest is level with his face. His eyes bulge. "Colin, you are just the person I need to see."

"Am I?"

"Of course." I lean back and his eyes follow my chest, then scan down to my stomach and the low cut of my jeans. I reach up and playfully flick his chin, forcing him to look up, and he blushes. Caught out.

"…Now, I was wondering if you could do me a tiny favour."

JONI

Today has been objectively terrible. I just want to go home, climb into bed, and scream until my throat is hoarse. I feel broken in every bone and I want Mother to tell me it's going to be okay, and that it's all worth it in the end, and it's *not* easier to just put a Mask on and follow the Doctrine like everyone else. But fighting is so tiring, so lonely, so seemingly pointless. So endlessly humiliating. And I can't go home because, of course, today's bloody Selection Day and I have to sit through the whole goddamned Nomination Ceremony first. Just add an extra hour to school, like today hasn't been hellish enough.

Honestly, I thought saving someone's life would be more rewarding.

A ridiculous concept, really – believing that putting myself in danger to protect Belle Gentle might be karmically rewarded. Instead I've had grief all day. She only went and ignored my advice and told the Protection Agency. She seems to be *getting off* on the storyline she's so beautiful that the attacker couldn't help himself. While I got hauled out of classes to be grilled in the head's office by two protection officers who clearly hate me.

"We know your mother," was how I was greeted. "In fact, we had a run-in with her this morning at one of her 'protests'."

"Apple doesn't fall far from the tree, does it?" the other officer said. His lip curled with the familiar disgust I'm used to inciting. Honestly, you'd think I rubbed faeces onto my face rather than just quietly refusing to wear a Mask. How can a face, a naked human face, be so repulsive? It's a face! We all bloody have them under our Masks. And it's not illegal to show them...well, not yet. Give it a decade or two.

"They don't have to make things illegal," Mother always said. *"If Society punishes you enough, then laws aren't needed, and they can continue this delusion of choice."*

I crossed my arms and scowled to make my face even sourer. "As far as I'm aware I've not done anything wrong," I said. "I just helped someone not get abducted."

"Belle told us you punched this man, and kicked him in a private area?"

"To give us time to run away, yes."

"But you don't know this man was a danger."

"He was pulling Belle into his car."

"She said he was offering her a lift to school."

My hands started shaking with acute rage. "But when she turned him down, he got violent and nasty."

"Sounds like *you* got violent and nasty."

"Well, if you find this poor victim of mine, see if he wants to press charges."

I soured my scowl even further, and jutted my chin out. They hate it when you show open defiance and I needed to feel

50

a tiny bit powerful. To score a point. Just one. Against them. Against this hell mouth of a day. Every interaction I've ever had with the Protection Agency has been like this. They exist only to protect the Doctrine, not us. I had learned that lesson in various, painful ways. How they never helped Mother when she rang them in fear at what Father would do. How, on the rare occasion they turned up, with her face bleeding and body shaking, they'd act the same as they're doing to me now. "*Your husband says you hit him too*," they'd say... Father with not a scratch on him and Mother openly bruised and bleeding. "*Sounds like you both need to learn how to control your tempers.*" In time, we learned to stop bothering to call them at all.

Eventually, they let me go back to classes. Me having done nothing wrong and all. But it meant I missed my whole Political Sciences lesson. I grabbed a sandwich with my friends, Darnell, Sita, Hannah and Jack. Or "The Top Tier Objectionables" as we're otherwise known. Darnell was annoying me slightly with how exciting she found everything.

"So, what was Belle *like?*" she asked, eyes wide, like I'd spent the morning with a celebrity. "Does she smell nice? Everyone always says how nice she smells."

"She was everything I'd thought she'd be and more," I deadpanned, striding to the recess room to recover a bit from this whole goddamned morning. But, of course, the recess room was atrocious too. With that awful polling booth set up. And then, of course, disgusting Damian putting on yet more Smut.

"I can't believe he's put it on again," Jack whispered, acting totally grossed out but not actually going over and saying anything. That was Jack all over. Hovering around me, telling me how great I was for confronting the Doctrine, but not actually confronting it much himself. It's always nice to have people onside, especially boys, but I do wish I didn't have to end up doing everything myself.

"It must be a day ending in the word 'day'," Sita added, taking a bite of her sandwich, "because those are the days Damian puts Smut on."

I waited a moment, seeing if any of them were going to take the hit. But, as the groans from the screen grew louder, they all hid in their sandwiches.

"I guess I'd better turn it off," I sighed, getting up and dealing with the inevitable verbal abuse and further social annihilation.

And after all that, here I am, stuck at the back of the dumb Selection Ceremony in the school hall, waiting to see who's been Nominated for the Royal House of Shallowness.

Colin can hardly contain himself, he's so high on his own self-importance. It's pathetic how the Pretties boss him around, and even more pathetic how much he loves it. He's sat at the front with his envelopes, chest puffed, craning about to ensure everyone's looking at him. Our class head, Mr Simmons, strides to the front, a big grin on his stupid face, and starts his spiel about how the countdown to the Ceremony is his favourite time of the year. I turn to Darnell and mime making myself sick – feeling marginally better when she sniggers. I did see her checking all the Looks on the Ranking earlier when she thought I wasn't watching, however. Then again, I almost did the same myself this morning.

"Hello, everyone. Well, isn't this exciting?" Mr Simmons claps his hands. "You've been voting all day and now the time has finally come to find out who is in the running to win this year's Ceremony. I know there's been some shocking twists today…" The whole year turns towards Belle, who pretends to blush at the attention. I take her in. She's managed to save her Look, it seems, though she doesn't look quite as perfect as she did this morning.

Darnell whispers in my ear. "Did he just call the attempted abduction of a female student a 'shocking twist' like it's an entertainment show?"

I roll my eyes. "Haven't you heard? It wasn't an abduction, just a legitimate response to Belle's tight denim."

The rest of my little gang hear me and we all snigger quietly until a Try Hard shushes us.

"Right, let's start with the boys first…"

Mr Simmons takes an envelope from Colin, opens it, and then makes us sit in silence for way too long to make it all more ceremonious. He parrots out the obvious male Nominees, and we all clap as the worst boys in our year get up and are rewarded for their terribleness. Damian is first up, of course, pounding his arms into the air, making sure his biceps are bulging. Ben too, who basically copies everything Damian does. People cheer and whoop, but the mood is still tense with anticipation. We all know it's the girls' Nominations that matter the most. They are the ones who have worked the hardest. Made the most sacrifices. I bet Belle hasn't eaten a pleasurable forkful of food in two months at least, if she even did before then. I peer through the sea of heads to look at her again. Her face, with its Mask on, reveals very little.

"And now, the moment we've all been waiting for. The girls' Nominations…"

I keep watching her blank and beautiful face. Her fists are clenched, but she's otherwise apparently calm. It seems a lifetime ago her hand was in mine, her breath on my face, our eyes locked on each other. Then the room cheers and her Mask is splitting into the most perfect smile. Belle gets up gracefully, tugging down her top, and weaves towards the front. Everyone's acting like she's won the whole Ceremony already. She's spun the trauma of this morning into the most stunning gold thread, making us think, maybe for a moment, that the best Pretty in school wouldn't be Nominated. I mean, she did have a slightly smeared Mask for a whole ten minutes this morning, and there is still dried mud on her denim… Over the wild applause, Vanessa's also chosen. She pulls a rehearsed smile and goes up to join her friend, hugging Belle when she reaches her. I'm tuning out as the remaining names are called, assuming the worst is over. I'm wondering about Mother and her run-in with the Protection Agency this morning. She won't be in Custody again, will she? Surely they would've told me? It is ridiculous that Mother's been arrested four times for her campaigning, while Father was never arrested once…

"…and now, we're almost there. The final Nomination for this year's Ceremony is…Joni Miller."

There's a collective inhale. I'm tugged towards the mention of my name. Twisting towards Darnell, my eyes asking her, *Did that just really happen?* Her wide-open mouth indicates that it did. Hannah, Sita and Jack all look like equally gaping fish.

"Joni?" Mr Simmons asks in faux innocence, like this isn't clearly some kind of terrible wind-up. "Congratulations on the Nomination. Come on up here."

There's a stunned silence. I have no idea what to do. Sweat breaks out across my body and I know I should storm out, or protest, or make a joke, but shock has rendered me compliant. So I find myself standing up and making my way towards the front, my whole body shaking. "Come on," he says. "Stand with the other Nominees."

I'm shepherded next to Belle and the two other girls shortlisted. And now I'm effectively in a line-up with them, the collective penny drops, and laughter starts engulfing the crowd as everyone else realizes this is a planned stitch-up. A few giggles trigger a wave of snorts, and soon the whole room is in hysterics at the ridiculous notion that I would be Nominated at all.

Mr Simmons, of course, ignores the mass hysteria and continues to act like everything is perfectly above board. He's always hated me. Hated how I speak back in class, how I campaign against discriminatory uniform policy, how I once muttered "Perve" under my breath when he was complimenting a twelve-year-old student on her Look. "Now, a round of applause, everyone," he says, raising his clapping hands, encouraging everyone further. They whoop and cheer and wolf-whistle with an overexaggerated loudness, making it perfectly obvious that they know I don't belong here. I keep blinking to try and wake up from this nightmare. I'm still too stunned to run away. Instead, I do something I rarely do. I stand there and I take it. I allow it to bury me. To silence and stupefy. *Who did this to me?* I look at my fellow Nominees and everything becomes exceptionally clear. Damian's hyena-laughing, Ben is whooping like a dolphin, Vanessa is giggling attractively, but Belle...she's gone red. She won't look me in the eye. It's her. She must've whispered sweet nothings into Colin's ears until he agreed to add me into the envelope. But why? She must know this is my worst nightmare and yet she's done this even though I saved her life this morning. It doesn't make any sense. I can't...

The jolting unfairness unravels me. I lose a total grip of who I am, and what I stand for, and what matters, and how I don't care. I turn again to the Nominees, everyone's laughter raging in my ears, and, for the first time in a long time, I see what they see. A line of stunning young women in their Just Right years with an utter aberration standing next to them. In juxtaposition next to these Pretties, I can only be seen as truly ugly. Even though my face is totally typical. It has two eyes in the right place, a nose, lips, chin...everything is where it's supposed to be. In fact, they are even symmetrical. I don't even have blemishes or scars. My hair isn't wild or tangled. It's just hair, hanging from my head. My body has two arms, two legs, it works. It keeps me alive, it walks me to school each morning. My body is body-shaped, down to the simple fact I feed it and move it. I'm *not* ugly. I'm just a person. A person in a girl's body. But compared to these girls, these Masks, these starved and contorted bodies, honed to perfection through gruelling regimes and ice-sculpting at the Empowerment Centre for the bits that won't bend to their regime…I am disgusting. Gross. A shame to myself. I am nothing but a disgrace.

It's my choice, I find myself saying, in their words.

And, to some extent, it's true. They're not arresting me. They are not carting me off in the night to be euthanized. But they are ridiculing me. Shaming me. Laughing at me. Even though I am the smartest girl in this year…they do not care, they cannot see it, they can only see my natural ugliness compared to the Pretties' synthetic attractiveness. And, for the first time in so long, I feel shame. A buckling of myself. Standing there, being laughed at. My friends just shrugging at me in shock, too scared to defend me.

I'm being punished for daring to help someone.

I look one more time at Belle. Her blush is making its way through her Mask and she still won't look at me.

And I hate her. I hate Belle Gentle so much.

BELLE

It's been a week since the Selection and I'm still haunted by that day. I'm a twitching mess whenever I walk anywhere alone, worried that the attacker will jump out from nowhere. And I'm also haunted by Joni's face when my prank was revealed. I'm at work, standing in a Choosing line-up, Mask forward, trying not to look at the other Chosen Ones alongside me, and I get another flashback to that day. She looked so… broken, and I can't dislodge it from my head. It's joined my nightmares alongside Mother's scream. The sleeplessness is almost impossible to hide with my Mask, and Vanessa keeps asking me if I'm sick. Last night, Joni's face plagued every dream. I've never seen her face like that. She's always so cocky and confrontational in lessons – spewing her anti-Doctrine propaganda to whoever's unlucky enough to be sitting near her. The truth is, I split her open and let her vulnerability spill out and, I'm not going to lie, it felt terrible. I still feel terrible. Nothing about how I behaved that day makes any sense, but it's happened now and what can I do? It's too late to change anything. And it serves her right, doesn't it? Mouthing off against the Doctrine like that. Just because she's too ugly to do anything other than try and steal the Scholarship off me.

The photographer walks up and down the line-up, staring solely at our lower halves. I suck in my stomach as he passes and give him my very best smile. He ignores me.

"Okay, turn around so I can see your buttocks," he commands, clapping his hands, and I turn slowly with the other girls, facing a blank wall. "Too flat," his voice says, somewhere to my left. He flaps a Chosen One away and I sense a girl leave, but can't see which one it is. I try to stand so my buttocks stick out more, worrying he'll tap my shoulder next and insult my body. I've not eaten properly for two days for this Choosing and I'm low-key worried I might faint. I mustn't. I really need this job. Well, I really need the finance from this job. I feel the photographer's hot breath on the back of my neck and I stand to further attention.

"You have a nice one here." He squats down, so he's eye-level with my buttocks, and then, without warning, he prods them several times. I close my eyes. It's the same with most Choosings, and I don't know why it makes me feel all weird. I'm lucky to even be here. I shouldn't be wishing the denim was thicker. "Perfectly juicy. Turn around."

I rotate back and he straightens himself and starts examining the whole of me. He pauses for a long while on my breasts, and then reaches out again and takes a measurement of my hip with his hand. "The denim fits you well. But your face…" I flash him a smile again. "I'm not sure. You're a bit guarded. Unapproachable…"

I'm not sure if I need to respond. I widen my smile.

"Hmm…better…maybe. Go stand over there."

I wilt with relief as I'm ushered to the corner, and, one by one, a few other hopefuls join me for the second inspection. I hate Choosings at the best of times. Though I'm ashamed to admit it, I find it challenging being around other Pretties who are as, or Prettier, than me. I know I'm supposed to celebrate their beauty. But instead I cut my body into parts and measure all my parts against the other Chosen Ones' parts, and hate myself for not winning every category. Even when I get a job, I come away feeling broken. Though obviously I can't talk to anyone about it. Working as a Chosen One gets me so much Validation, and I know Mother needs the Finance. Especially this week. Father's home after a super-long-distance driving trip, and she can't run her Masking business while he's here. She's too busy ensuring she looks her best for him and gets him everything he needs, the moment he needs it. He sits in a chair mostly and barks orders, and then tells us how Pretty we both are to make up for it. I'm already spending the Finance for this job in my head, which is stupid because the girl to the left definitely has peachier buttocks. But I'd give half my earnings to Mother, to help with the house, and the rest I urgently need to buy supplies. I'm running out of Eyelash Extender, as well as Inner Glow, and they're my most expensive necessities. Inner Glow is my most important Mask ingredient.

"Remember, Belle. Women need to glow, otherwise nobody will see us," Mother has always said. *"Only men are allowed to be matte."*

I also need to go to the Hair Ripper to be re-smoothed. The rest of my earnings, if there are any, will go towards my mediocre savings. I'm naively trying to have some Finance stashed so, if Joni beats me to the Scholarship, I could maybe still go to the Education. Which I know is pointless, as Education is way beyond my means, even with my Chosen One work.

Joni.

Even thinking her name stirs up emotions. Look, I feel bad, okay? It's not like I can take it back. And she almost ruined my chance at winning the Ceremony. I bet she did it deliberately. She knows the Doctrine states how important it is to Have It All, and just because she's too disgusting to win the Ceremony *and* go to the Education, she was trying to sabotage me.

I'm shaken from my thoughts as the photographer plods over, sizing up the final candidates. There's only three of us left, and he shouts orders to rotate slowly, to bend over and back up again. He tells the girl to my right her "tits are too small" and she walks off with a smile still cemented to her face.

"Right, it's between the two of you. Let's size you up."

I know not to flinch when his hand gropes my buttocks again. I'm so close to getting the job. I glance over at my competitor, who's also standing forward, like her groped body isn't attached to her. She keeps blinking and staring at the wall ahead, and I copy the coping strategy as my flesh is kneaded, distracting myself by going through everything I need to do this weekend. Two more Body Prayer sessions. Help Mother care for Father. Do all my extra reading so the Scholarship doesn't go out the window. Book an appointment for Hair Ripping. Plan my Looks for the week. Go through my Device and check my Validation statistics and ensure they keep going up, rather than plateauing. I need to Body Pull too, to keep me lean. And I should probably try and buy some Nutrient Sachets, as I really haven't been eating properly lately and don't want my skin to suffer. Then I should try and see Vanessa. She's really pushing me into Linking with Damian. And try not to think about Joni… And homework. *And try not to think about Joni…*

"Mother?" I step through the door, clutching my Booking Form, ready to celebrate. "Mother?"

She appears at the top of the stairs. "Shh, your father's sleeping."

"Oh sorry." I copy her whisper and wave my form in the air. "Hey, I got the Booking. I shoot next week. It's good pay for the Home Pot, plus I get five free pairs of denim."

Mother's Mask stretches into a proper smile and she descends the stairs to hug me.

"Oh I knew you would. Well done, my Bella Donna. Oh my beautiful girl. Thank you." She hugs me tighter. "Right, we really do need to be quiet, he's having one of his days."

I raise both eyebrows, heeding the warning, and we tiptoe into the kitchen, which is furthest away from their bedroom. I leap onto the counter. I feel so much lighter since getting the Booking. The worst Choosings are when they strip and grope you and then you don't even get the job. Mother tells me that's all part of it and I should be grateful to have such opportunities, but still…my stomach always hurts when I'm grabbed like that. By photographers in the Choosings, by boys in school when they want to thank me for a great Look. There's no one I can admit this to but…I'm terrified of the touch of boys. Of men. Every time a boy touches me, I feel this strange urge to strike them away. It's a madness. I don't know what's wrong with me. I should be desperate to Link with Damian, but all the Smut he plays makes my stomach drop out. If anyone finds out I'm potentially a Frigid, it will ruin my reputation. The Doctrine is very clear that I need to stop being a Vanilla by the end of the Ceremony. With Damian circling, I'm going to have to face my fears soon. Blue Balls Belle is running out of time. I should be excited about fulfilling the Doctrine and Having It All, so why do I feel so sick and scared?

"Is Father okay?" I ask, to jog my mind away from it.

Mother's tight smile reappears. "He's fine. Sleeping it off always helps. Flat Tummy Tea?"

"That would be great, thank you."

I watch her fuss around with the kettle, wondering what Father's said to upset her. He's been super grouchy since he got back, and he's taken on another long trip because we need the Finance. While we wait for the tea to stew, I imagine all the things I want to drink more than Flat Tummy Tea. I picture a banana milkshake with whipped cream on top. Or a thick hot chocolate, with a film of melted marshmallows. Even a fresh orange juice would be amazing, but Mother says you so often drink your Sin. I wilt into the counter – craving subsidence and nourishment and fun…

"We should try to have three of these each day," Mother says, handing me my mug. "With the Ceremony coming up. I'll do it with you. They actually don't taste that bad, do they?"

"Not that bad, no."

"In fact, they're nice even."

"Mother, I wouldn't go that far."

I expect her to laugh but she bristles. "Well I think they're nice. And they weren't cheap either, mind. I got them for you as a present."

"I know, sorry. I'm just…you know what Choosings are like. It's not fun, lining up like that."

Like I made Joni do…

She tilts her head to one side and blows on her tea. "But you were Chosen?"

"Yeah, but…"

"So it's worth it, isn't it? Because you were Chosen."

"I guess."

There's a sludge of silence. I force myself to drink the disgusting tea and picture my stomach flattening with each sip. I plan the Looks I'll be able to wear with a stomach like mine. If I had a banana milkshake, my stomach would wobble over the tops of my denim. A clear signifier to everyone that I lack willpower, that I'm weak and gross and can't be trusted. I'd look like *Joni*, who regularly bulges out of her denim with no shame. It's her *shamelessness* I find the hardest…

"There's something I want to tell you actually," Mother says, putting her cup down.

I readjust myself on the counter. "Oh, yeah?"

"No big deal. I've just booked myself in for a Mask Graft at the Empowerment Centre in a few weeks' time, when your father's on this next big trip. I might need you to hold the fort on meal prep and stuff."

My eyes flicker upwards, to where Father's sleeping.

"You're having a *Mask Graft*?"

"Yes. No shame in that."

"I know, I know." I put my mug of disgusting tea down. "I just…I thought you said you didn't need Cutting yet?"

"Everyone else my age has had one."

"Yes, but they're not as Pretty."

She genuinely softens at that. "You're very sweet, Bella Donna. But I think I've delayed it long enough. There's only so much Immobilizer and Mask alone can achieve. And your father mentioned I'm drooping slightly…"

"He did, did he?" My stomach swoops and I feel a small blodge of dread. This means Father really is in a bad mood. We can read him this way. If we're his gorgeous girls, it's a good day. If there's a stinging comment, it's a day to tiptoe around carefully.

Mother sips her tea, her mouth scrunched up defensively. "I'm lucky he's looking out for me," she says. "That he wants me to be the best version of myself. It only came out harshly because he needed a nap." She tilts her head. "Plus, he pointed out that I could lose Mask clients if my own Mask isn't up to scratch. It's bad advertising."

I pull a face. "Since when has he wanted you to have more Mask clients? He hates it when you work."

"Honestly, Belle, what is wrong with you today?" She pulls my tea away before I've finished. "All boastful because you've been Chosen for this job."

"What? Hang on, I'm just—"

"We're not all in our Just Right years, you know?"

"I know that, I—"

"Because soon it will be your turn, Belle, and let's see how long you go without needing Cutting."

"Mother, I—"

"It's my choice, anyway." She juts her chin out and flounces from the kitchen.

"I know it's your choice," I call after her.

But I can't help thinking that we use that phrase a lot. That the Doctrine demands we use it, we believe it. That we will fall back into the Bad Times if we don't support each other's choices. But the words are starting to mean less and less. Especially since my run-in with Joni.

Joni.

Why do I keep thinking about Joni?

JONI

You know what? It's okay. I'm over it. I'm back, baby. I will never let Belle or any other brainwashed lemmings make me feel like that again.

I walk into school this morning with a determined air of unattractiveness, just to piss them off. I've deliberately not stripped my hair for four days even though it's actually bothering me. I'm dirty protesting. I am Ugly protesting. I will not let them get to me. I will get to them. I'm going to be the best in class, and win this Scholarship, and go to the Education, and use that to eventually become a Leader and actually end the Bad Times, rather than everyone pretending they're over. That will show them. I'm going to show everyone.

…Though, of course, this is school, so my wilful defiance is largely ignored. Nobody particularly looks at me as I stride through to classes. What's important is I know inside that I am powerful and awake…not them. They actually think the Bad Times are over. They think how we live is healthy. They think it's normal.

God, I'm so lucky I have Mother. Where would I be without her?

She luckily wasn't charged on that awful Selection Day. They'd arrested her, as usual, but hadn't been able to charge her, as usual. Much as Mother's existence feels illegal to most people, it isn't. There's nothing in our law about being over forty-five, female, and shouting about something you believe is wrong. They let Society punish women like Mother, rather than the law.

"Don't you worry about me," Mother had said, when I'd come home the other week, wilted and broken, and also terrified she'd been arrested. She had a graze across her face.

"Did they hurt you?"

She batted me away. "I just fell over resisting arrest. It's no biggie."

"Mother!"

"What? It's just a graze. Anyway, what's wrong with you… you're all droopy."

I'd actually been too ashamed to tell her about the Selection. This never happened. Since everything we went through with Father, we tell one another everything. We have to trust in each other after he so consistently made us distrust everything else. But, after feigning a stomach bug for two days, Mother caught onto why I was missing school and out it all came. I curled into a ball and wept as I described the whole year laughing at my faux Selection. She stroked my hair, hushing me, like she used to when Father was still here.

"Oh my darling," she said, dabbing at my eyes with one of her hankies. "I wish you'd told me sooner. You know what I'm going to say, don't you?"

I'd snorted hard to try and stem the snot running. "What? That I'm better than them? That I'll show them when I win the Scholarship and make something of myself? That I'm beautiful in my own way?"

"Well those things, obviously. But don't you see? What happened to you was proof of why the Doctrine exists and how and why it works. You said you'd told this girl, Belle, about her shoes, and why they're designed to stop her running?"

"Yeah, I told her after *saving her life*. And how does she repay me? By doing this."

Mother pulled a hair away from my face where it had stuck to my cheek from my tears. "But you got her to question it, didn't you? By the sounds of things? You say this girl is smart?"

I nodded. "Annoyingly so."

"Well, if she's smart, then what you said must've landed. And the Truth you spoke no doubt made her question everything and that made her scared. She would've been attacked if it wasn't for you. She was confronted with the horrors of the Doctrine for once, rather than just enjoying the benefits of keeping to it. You made her doubt her own reality, her whole *identity*… People don't like that. So they hit back."

I sat up, wiping my eyes. I knew all this. Deep down I knew all this, but it felt so much better with Mother confirming it. "She didn't have to be so cruel. I mean, technically, I'm supposed to attend the Ceremony now I've been Selected." I laughed. "Can you imagine? Me? At the Ceremony?"

"Aren't you supposed to attend regardless?"

"*It's my choice*, remember? That get-out clause works both ways."

Mother laughed and hugged me and I clutched her tight, wishing she could always be like this. She isn't cold, but she is distracted, always so consumed with her protests and running the Centre for Discarded Women.

She held me at arm's length, forcing me to look into her eyes. She had so many wrinkles etched around her face, marking every smile and sob, triumph and trial. Wearing the story of her life on her face, proud of every moment.

"You've got to remember why the Doctrine exists," she told me. "Remember, it's not about what you look like, or how Pretty you are. That's the Big Lie. It's all about…"

"…*behaviour*." I nodded. "Yes, I know. I know."

"Do you? Because it sounds like you've forgotten. The Rules prescribe behaviour, not Beauty. The end result isn't a Pretty Face, but compliant girls. Weakened girls. What this girl did to you wasn't anything to do with exposing how Ugly you are. She did it to try and stop your *behaviour*. To get you out of her ear, trying to change things. If you let this get to you, it's worked."

Mother's words, always a medicine. I wish she wasn't an Invisible. I wish more people would listen to her. I can't wait to get out there into the world and start waking more people up and changing things.

I jutted my chin out. "Well it's not going to work," I said.

"Of course it won't."

"And it's made me a million times more determined to beat her to this Scholarship."

Mother rubbed my hair before stepping away, and I knew our magical moment had passed. She was needed elsewhere, by girls more desperate than me.

"That's my girl."

So, yeah, Belle can go to hell, quite frankly. She won't win. I won't let her get to me. I have only a few months of school left. If I can get this Scholarship, I'm out of here. Mother says it's much better in the City. Still bad, but the Doctrine is less strictly followed and people feel much more free to be themselves – whether that's to go barefaced, or use Mask for creative expression rather than just to be Pretty. *"You'll notice so many differences away from this Town of Doctrine,"* she promises. *"People are less scared to look how they want, love who they want. It's not perfect, but better, especially at the Education."* Getting this Scholarship is everything and I refuse to be derailed.

I keep striding through the halls, unashamed, making direct eye contact with anyone who dares look at me with disgust. I take copious notes in lessons and tell Damian to go to hell when he flicks a spitwad into my dirty hair. There are so many dreadful things about Damian, but the worst is he's very clever and therefore I can't ignore him as he's in all my top tier classes. Despite spending most of the time making everyone watch Smut on his Device, he soars through exams, sometimes even beating me. When the bell rings, he stands blocking the door.

"Damian, get out of my way."

"Joni, please, wait. There's something I want to say."

I glance up to see our teacher has left, but most of the class has stayed, obviously knowing what's about to happen.

"Get out of my way."

Damian drops to one knee and swishes out his arms. "Joni, my love. This enemies-to-lovers thing is taking too long. As you've now been Selected, as you always should've been, I want to cordially invite you to Link with me for the Ceremony." He whips out some plastic Ownership Flower and holds it out like he's proposing. Everyone cracks up while Damian looks up at me earnestly.

I smack his arm and the flower goes flying. "You're hilarious," I say, stepping past, trying to keep myself from blushing.

"Is that a yes?"

"What do you think?"

"I'll pick you up at seven," he calls after me. "I mean, as it's the Ceremony and all, I'd really appreciate it if you'd strip your hair for once."

More hysterical laughter. I push past the gaggle of Try Hards gathered at the door.

"And I wish you'd strip your *soul* for once, but I'm not sure there's a strong enough soap."

I wince and flee through the corridor. What a ridiculous comeback. Stripping your *soul* for once? I should've at least made a joke about him stripping his penis or something. I was just so thrown. I dart to the cafeteria, face in flames, grab a sandwich, and scuttle out to the fields. This lunchtime I'm supposed to be studying with the others, but I don't want to see anyone right now. Hannah, Sita and Jack will just tell me not to care, which is fine for them as they never take the full hits. And Darnell will probably find it all way too exciting.

The field's already full of students enjoying the spring sunshine. Girls arranging their limbs daintily and not eating lunch, while watching the boys play Rage Ball. I skirt around the edges until I find my entrance hole in the surrounding shrubbery. Then, checking nobody's looking, I duck in, and weave my way through the undergrowth until I find my spot. There's a space where the bushes have grown a sort of canopy and I collapse to the mud and lie against a branch, taking breaths until my heart returns to normal. It's so much easier to be brave in my head. This morning, I'd been up for a fight. Glorious in my defiance. But one practical joke from Damian and I want to cry again. I replay my mother's words to soothe myself.

They go for me because I upset the order.

They go for me because I scare them.

It's nothing to do with what I look like, and all to do with how I behave.

I could look like the Pretties but that life is a self-created prison. I get out some reading, take a bite of my sandwich, and ensure I'm still several chapters ahead for that afternoon. My stomach doesn't want to digest food yet, so, as I chew, I calm myself by imagining what Belle will be doing this lunch while I'm getting ahead. She'll spend some significant time in front of a mirror, topping up her Mask. Then her and Vanessa will no doubt be making the most of the sunshine and the chance to show off the results of their Body Prayer in minimal clothing.

I predict they're in the fields, taking multiple images for the Ranking, and then comparing their Validation counts. She clearly won't be eating lunch, making her hungry and weak for this afternoon's lessons. I will beat her. I will win. She can't be both. I deserve it more. God, I hate that girl… I wish I could stop thinking about her.

The bush next to me rustles and I sit up, but it's just Darnell, who emerges with some twigs in her hair, her eyes brightening when she finds me.

"Joni, I thought you'd be here."

I pat the space next to me. "Sorry I bailed on lunch with everyone. Damian was being a dick and I just needed some space."

"Yeah, I heard in the cafeteria that he asked you to the Ceremony."

I roll my eyes. Of course everyone knows already, and of course Darnell has already found out. She really is a quiet little gossip. "Wow, so it's gone around school already."

"Just ignore them."

"Hmm."

"Sita and everyone said they hope you're okay."

"I'm fine."

"Jack said Damian is pathetic."

"Did he say that to Damian himself?"

Darnell shifts from side to side in the dust and blushes a bit. "Well, no…"

"Didn't think so."

"He…he tries."

74

I've always suspected Darnell's got a slight crush on Jack, but even she can't pretend he'd ever say anything to Damian. She sits down and pulls out her own sandwich and we maintain a comfy silence while we eat. This is what I like about Darnell. She knows when I need a moment. I do wonder if she'd be a Pretty, or even a Try Hard, if she was able to. People are horrible about how she looks. I've heard Belle and Vanessa refer to her as "The Fish Girl" several times, though, mercifully, I don't think Darnell knows that's her nickname. They're so awful, and yet, the fact she was eavesdropping in the cafeteria just now, listening to the Pretties debrief on their shaming of me… it makes me wonder if part of her is drawn to their light? Secretly wants to be them?

After a while, Darnell swallows a bite of her sandwich and twists towards me. "Ms Blanche was looking for you."

"Oh yeah?" Ms Blanche is our head teacher.

"She told me to tell you to come to her office after school."

I pull a face. "Weird. Did she say why?"

Darnell shakes her head.

"Maybe they've got an update on that attacker guy?"

"Maybe."

That couldn't be it though. The Protection Agency was so unbothered by the whole thing, it couldn't be that. I chew the rest of my sandwich and I wonder.

The afternoon isn't much better. After Damian's proposal, I'm subjected to unwanted whispers and stares and giggles. It's a relief when the final bell goes. I pack my bag with some extra reading, still feeling very fired up about the Scholarship. I have a shift at the Centre for Discarded Women but, if it's quiet, I may be able to cram in a few chapters. I whistle on my way to Ms Blanche's office, but when I find Belle there, my tune comes to an abrupt halt. She's sitting on a chair awkwardly so she doesn't show her knickers in her tiny skirt.

"What are you doing here?" we both ask the other at the same time, with identical levels of disgust.

"I was told to come," I say. "And you? Do you need a deadline extension after breaking a nail or something?"

"You're hilarious. I was told to come too."

I realize then it must be something to do with the Scholarship and I hate Belle even more. It's not fair. She's ruined my last term at school, she shouldn't be allowed to go for the Scholarship too. Plus, what the hell would she study at the Education? Anal bleaching, so she could go into business with her mother? One of them sorts the top end, the other the bottom?

"What's so funny?" Belle asks, noticing my laugh.

"Nothing. Well, just you."

She bristles, but doesn't fight back. We sit and watch the closed door in silence. I follow the second hand on the clock, and hope this doesn't take too long. I've got to be at the centre by half four.

"Did the Protection Agency call you?" Belle asks finally.

"What? No."

"They rang me last week. About the guy. They say they've

followed it up but can't find anything on him. They're closing the case. They say it was probably just an isolated incident."

I let out a hack laugh. "Violence against us is never an isolated incident."

I expect her to scoff, like she did the other week when I talked to her about her shoes. Instead, she tilts her head. "What do you mean?"

I shrug, though I'm thrown. That sounded like a genuine question, not an invite to further tease me. "I'm just saying… violence towards us…it's all day, it's everywhere," I say, finding myself talking to her like she's a genuine person, rather than the girl currently ruining my life. "Violence like what that guy did. It…he…he's not a one-off. Someone like him is part of the pattern."

She listens, clearly puzzled. "I'm not sure I know what you mean."

"How could you? Being friends with boys like Damian? Thinking it's hilarious whenever he puts Smut on."

Again, I expect a rebuttal, but her eyes widen. "You think Smut is violent?"

I scan her face again, but, again, I get nothing but a feeling of genuine earnestness. In fact, Belle seems almost nervous to be asking.

"Er…yeah…Smut is violent," I say. "Most of the actresses in it aren't having a nice time. They're just pretending, even if it hurts them. They get paid more Finance for the more violent stuff."

"Are you…?"

77

She cuts off and Belle's head falls, her Mask disappearing behind her long sheet of hair. I take a moment to take in that day's Look. It's very hard not to be drawn towards Belle's beauty, like she's an enchanted spinning wheel. Her tiny skirt just about covers her muscular, lean legs. Her dainty feet are slid into a delicate pair of leather sandals, and she matches the skirt with a white, perfectly cut, short-sleeved blouse that ties at her tiny waist. Every centimetre of her skin glows, as if lit from within. There isn't one blemish to be found, or one bulge; everything fits perfectly. Her hair also has a sheen of health to it – all falling to one perfect length, the different colours of her blondes meshing together into a trio of honeys. It's hair you want to reach out and touch, to take a strand to your mouth to feel how smooth it is against your lips. So beautiful – yet she's such a bitch.

"Am I…what?" I ask.

"Are you…do you…never mind," she says from behind her hair.

And that's when I get my first inkling. Something I've said has gotten to Belle. I've found an entry point. When she heaves herself up, I can see the conflict dancing across her eyes, the confusing thought that *Everything Joni says is wrong, so how come it feels right?* It's the same look Jack and Sita and the rest of them got when they first approached me, asked me why I reject the Doctrine. Oh my God, imagine if I could Awaken Belle against the Doctrine! If I can get to her, I can get to anyone.

I find myself reaching out, putting on my kindest voice – which she most certainly doesn't deserve. "Belle, are you…"

The office door opens and Ms Blanche appears on the threshold, a warm smile on her face.

"Belle! Joni!" she welcomes, as we both jerk up. "So glad you could make it. Enter."

We traipse in behind her, and I notice how much longer it takes Belle to get into and out of a chair. As we stand, she's tugging her skirt down, rearranging bits of her Look so they all fall into place. She twists her ankle slightly in her heeled sandal as we step into the office, and then has to tug her skirt again as she re-sits, checking it covers everything, that it's tucked under her thighs to stop her legs sticking to the leather. She reties her blouse at the stomach as it needs to be at a slightly different length in this new chair. I collapse into my chair and open my legs to make a point and I see her shudder. I grin. Oh, trying to Awaken Belle could be fun…

"I'm sure you want to find out what this is about," say Ms Blanche. "Thanks for coming. As you two know, you're our two female students with the highest grades this year, which means you get put forward to apply for the female Scholarship at the Education."

I sit up in my seat, not wanting to miss a word.

"Now, we haven't had the best history of our students getting picked. We've only had one girl win it over the last decade. Which, quite frankly, isn't good enough, as there's only three schools in our district. So, this year, we thought the two of you may benefit from some special preparation sessions to give you both a better chance."

Belle and I share a look – one of interested horror. I'm

excited by the prospect of coaching sessions, but not with her.

"I know there's only one Scholarship to go around, but I hope you girls will enjoy learning together. I've arranged a timetable of two afternoons a week. You're the only ones who can really help the other revise…."

No. Not one-on-one time with Little Miss Shallow. Not after she rigged the Selection. She'll make my life even more of a hell.

But hang on…this might be a hidden opportunity to Awaken her…

Ms Blanche smiles and I find myself smiling back. She tries, Ms Blanche. I mean, she's a typical Invisible and dresses according to the Invisible Rule Book. She wears appropriate length suit dresses with flat, orthopaedic shoes. She clearly tongs her short grey hair into her daily bouffant. And she wears the Invisible Mask: pearly pink lip enhancer, some blobby extra eyelash, some face camouflage that sinks into the creases around her eyes. Unprovocative. Unnoticeable. Inoffensive, which is the main thing an Invisible should be. Just to prove my point, her eyebrows furrow.

"I must say, this may be one of the last years we have a chance at the Scholarship," she says, leaning forward over her desk. "It's becoming increasingly controversial. Madame Rebecca Harkness, the woman who established the Scholarship, had some quite…*old-fashioned* views when she set it up. She believed girls benefited from an Education 'free from the violent eyes of males'."

Without meaning to, Belle and I share a look, reminded of the Smut conversation we'd just been having.

"…that's why she made this Scholarship for female identifying students only. But, as you can imagine, since the Bad Times were abolished, this all seems reductive. This really might be our last year to go for it." She smiles again. "We'll have to see how this plays out. But, are you girls willing to put the work in?"

I share a glance with Belle again. She looks horrified.

"Shall we start sessions on Wednesday, hmm? It might be good if you swap Device numbers."

She watches us refuse to acknowledge each other for a while. If Belle thinks I'm asking for her number, she is even dumber than I thought.

"Girls? Is there a problem?"

Belle blinks first. "No, of course not. Great idea." She's using the sugary sweet voice she often uses to bedazzle and distract. I notice it's the same voice she used when trying to placate the man in the car. "Joni? Can I have your number?"

"Sure, Belle," I say, mimicking her voice. "That would be *super*."

She rolls her eyes, but compliantly stabs my Device code in. I feel a swell of sickness seeing my numbers on there. She could now easily pass them onto Damian and Vanessa and have them ruin my life with prank calls.

"Could I get yours too?"

An equally panicked look shadows her face. Or is it disgust? I tilt my head and realize it's that. She is actually *sickened* at the

81

thought of giving me access to her. Like I'd want it! I put on her voice again. "Maybe we should call each other every night? Check in with how the other is doing?"

Ms Blanche claps her hands. "You see! That's the spirit. See each other as helpers, not adversaries."

"We could even have revision sleepovers?" I start to enjoy myself. "You can come over to mine. Then I can give you a Transformation if you'd like?"

There's a moment of horror on Belle's face until she realizes I'm winding her up. "That sounds wonderful. I'll bring snacks."

"Sin-free ones, if possible. You know how much I value my figure."

We're dismissed and our fake civility dissolves the second we're out of Ms Blanche's door. I notice Belle crossing her arms and stepping away from me as we make our way to the school gates. We both seem to be walking in the same direction, and though I can't bear to be near her, why should I change my route? So I hold firm, walking faster to lose her. This, it turns out, is even more annoying, as it's like being stalked by a horse. The stupid *clip-clop* of her stupid sandals right behind me. We must live quite near each other, and I wonder if I'm going to be stalked the whole way back. The clip clopping stops and I lumber on a few paces, thinking, *Ha, I won,* until a weird instinctive nudge makes me turn back. Belle's frozen, leaning against a wall, her Mask a painting of panic. Her mouth's open and she's making this weird hissing sound, like she's been possessed. I run back and wave my hand in front of her.

"Hey, all okay in there?"

She doesn't notice me. There's a gurgling in her throat. Her eyes seem unable to focus. Then she shakes herself, meets my gaze.

"Hey. Yeah. Sorry. I…I don't know what just happened to me."

I look around and realize we're on the road where the alleyway comes out. We're retracing the path of the attack.

"Are you having a Panic or something?"

"I…my heart hurts. I…"

She collapses and I have to step in to catch her, and steady her down to the pavement so I can lean properly against the wall. She's ridiculously light in my arms and I get another uncomfortable twinge of jealousy – at her lightness. If I ever swooned, nobody would be able to catch me. I'd land on top of them like an elephant and smush them to a pancake.

"Put your head between your legs," I command. Many women have Panics at the Centre and Mother's taught me the best way to treat them. "Try and breathe into your stomach. You're okay. You're safe."

She's shaking so hard she's basically turned blue. And I'm reminded again that her Beauty is also her Frailty. Her body can't handle this minor malfunction.

"I can't breathe…"

"Yes you can. If you couldn't, you'd be dead by now. You are breathing, you just don't think you are."

My words have an effect and her skin slowly turns back to its usual peaches-and-cream. Her fingers are no longer blue. I wonder if it's my destiny to be Belle's bloody rescuer all

83

the time. And now she's sitting up better – a bit befuddled, but ultimately better – my sympathy fades.

"You okay now?"

"Hmm? Yes, I think so. I…er…that was weird."

"What happened?"

"I don't know. I was fine…and then…suddenly I couldn't breathe and…"

"I told you, it's a Panic. It makes sense. We're right near where we were when that man came after you. Have you not walked this way since or something?"

"No, I've been too scared…I…" She looks up at me like she's just remembered who I am. An Objectionable rather than a Good Samaritan. If school wasn't long finished, I'd bet she'd be pelting away in her heels rather than risking being seen with me. "…I mean, he was only paying me a compliment." Her voice comes out like a robot programmed her.

"Of course he was."

"Why are you being so weird, Joni? You're always so weird. I…"

"…I'm always somehow looking after you. Yet again, you are welcome."

Belle pushes her hair off her sweaty face, her eyes not knowing where to land. Now she's feeling a bit better, I'm finding this mildly amusing. Seeing her fight instinct with weird Doctrine logic. "I…you're making me late. I…I need to go home."

I laugh. "I'm making *you* late? I'm the one late for work now."

"You have a job?" She wipes more sweat away.

"Yeah. I help my Mother at the Centre for Discarded Women."

"The what?"

"It's for women who have to leave home because it's not safe to stay. Or just for women who have no home because their husbands cast them out."

"Because they let themselves go?" she asks, as she tries to get herself up off the pavement.

I step back and roll my eyes. "Yep, it's all their fault, really. The women," I deadpan. "We should really make it a shelter for men. *The Refuge to Hide from Your Ugly Wife Who Dares to Age as She Gets Older and Follows Natural Scientific Order.* They're the REAL victims in all this. Sorry."

"I…okay, so I'm being stupid."

"Wow, she admits it."

Something in the air softens and we laugh at one another as I perch on the wall next to her. Belle has a different smile when she's laughing naturally. It cracks her face open, and makes one eye much smaller than the other. It's beautiful…much nicer than the delicate grin she usually parades as she wafts about school. I get out my Device to check the time and realize I really am late. I fire off a message to Mother to explain, then I glance over at Belle again, to see her glance over at me.

"So…" I prompt. "Do you have anything you want to say to me?"

She's quiet as she plays with her fingers. I'm about to stomp off in protest, when, sensing I'm about to leave, Belle says sorry in a tiny voice.

"What was that?

"I'm sorry," she whispers again.

I almost wilt with shock at the apology and she looks as shocked as I am. She even puts her hand to her voice box like it has possessed her mouth. I pretend to be calm. "Sorry for *what?*"

"Umm…for putting you into the Selection," she says, still holding her throat. "And for all the grief Damian gave you about it. It was wrong, and I'm sorry."

I wasn't expecting her to actually apologize. She means it as well, I can tell. She's looking right into my eyes again through a film of tears. With an apology this genuine, it's hard to not let her off the hook instantly.

"I just don't understand why," I say. "I mean, I wasn't expecting a medal for helping you. But I wasn't expecting to be thrown under a bus."

She shakes her head. "I know. I'm such a bitch sometimes, I swear. It wasn't even anything to do with the man, but the stuff you said. Outside school. I felt…shamed in some way."

"*Shame?*"

"Yeah, like you were saying it would be my fault if that man caught me, for wearing those shoes."

"Oh…"

"You implied I could've outrun him if I was wearing ugly shoes like yours, and therefore it would have been on me if he'd caught me."

"Oh." I'd never thought of it like that, but I can sort of see where she got that from. I believe she genuinely felt judged,

86

and she was truly scared of him if the Panic was anything to go by. All the nonsense she's spun about the attack being an inconvenient side-effect of being so Pretty is clearly just that... nonsense.

"Also...well...I was so stressed about the Selection, and angry at you for ruining my Look," she continues. "Whereas, you're right. You did rescue me. And what's the point of being Selected but dead?"

"I'm sure there are lots of girls at school who would make that trade."

She laughs and doesn't deny it.

"Anyway, I'll try and get Damian to back off. If it helps any, he's awful to everyone. You should see the state of the messages and photos and Smut clips he sends me. I think I've seen his penis more than I've seen my own body."

She's expecting me to laugh along, but I don't. "That's disgusting. He shouldn't be sending that sort of stuff to you."

"It's a compliment, isn't it? The Doctrine says—"

I leap off the wall to stop her. "Oh God. I am too late for work to get into this...come on." I hold out my hand to pull her from the wall. "Let's take you home."

She hesitates and, yes, she does look side to side to see if anyone is watching. Or maybe she's checking for the guy. It's so hard to know.

"Thank you."

I can't believe it. What a breakthrough. Belle has not only apologized, but asked me actual questions about my thoughts on the Doctrine. I can almost feel my fingers fizz with excitement at the prospect of turning her. If she's Awakened, that could change so much, open up so many other people to hear the truth. We start walking home, and her hand's warm in mine. It takes us both a moment of walking before we drop our entwined fingers.

BELLE

Last night I heard Mother and Father arguing about Finance again. They started in whispers, like they always do, but soon escalated to yelling, like they always do. And it was the same argument it always is.

"What's all this crap in the kitchen? Flat Tummy Tea? How much did this cost?" Father's angry voice. The one that jeers a little.

"It was a present for Belle. You know her Ceremony is coming up."

"Well, I've had to take an extra-long drive to pay for it, so I hope it's worth it. Seven thousand miles. Two weeks. I swear I'm never in this house. I only come home long enough to see the Finance you've wasted with all your Mask nonsense."

"That's for Belle. It's all for Belle. You know how important her Just Right years are."

I'd turned over in bed, trying to drown it out with my expensive silken pillow that stops my hair from frizzing. I winced at Mother's lies. She blames all Mask paraphernalia on me or her business, keeping up this pretence that she isn't the one using most of it. Father veers between complimenting Mother on how he's got the most beautiful bride in town, and then teasing her about becoming an Invisible one day. I know the Doctrine states that it's important not to ruin the illusion of how we make ourselves Pretty. It's a woman's choice, after all, to want to be beautiful. But just because we're Empowered enough to make that choice, doesn't mean we need to burden men with the effort required. It ruins the mystique for them. It's not men's fault they become handsome Silvers while women become Invisibles – it's just nature. They shouldn't have to be burdened too with our bad luck. With that all said, I do wonder how deluded Father is, sometimes, thinking his wife is naturally so ageless and stunning. Surely part of him must know Mother needs to do some things to look so good? And, when he enjoys it so, why does he endlessly complain?

Finance. It always comes down to Finance between those two. And Finance, and my family's distinct lack of it, is very much evident today during my first study session for the Scholarship.

Mr Mitchell is our tutor for these sessions and he's droning on about how vigorous the entrance requirements are.

"The Education accepts only the brightest, most critical minds. It's hard enough to gain entry if you're applying through the usual system, but for a Scholarship place the bar is set even higher. You must impress them with your exam results, your extra-curriculars, your…"

I'm distracted by an annoying chewing sound, and reluctantly turn towards Joni, who's sat next to me, slurping on the end of her pencil like some kind of feral child. Ergh. Does literally everything she does have to be lacking in decorum?

She interrupts Mr Mitchell by raising a hand, and he grinds to a halt. "Yes, Joni?"

"It's just not very fair, is it?" she says, taking the moist end of her pencil from her mouth. "That only, what, five per cent of girls who get in are on Scholarships? If they want to promote equality, shouldn't that extend to wealth too? Rather than having the majority of students be Well-Financed ones?"

I see him fight the urge to roll his eyes. It must be a nightmare teaching Joni. She likes to use the word "unfair" about twenty million times a day. In fact, if she got a penny every time she used the word, she wouldn't have to apply for a Scholarship. She could just pay and go the usual way and let me have it instead.

"I'm not here to discuss what is and isn't fair," Mr Mitchell shuts her down. "I'm here to explain the process to you."

"Well, will it help my application if I tell them how unfair it is?"

"Unlikely."

She sighs. "This is so rubbish."

I hold up my hand but don't wait to speak. "If you're against the process, feel free to withdraw."

Joni smirks and I get this strange jolt at having amused her, although I was being mildly serious. This process would be much easier without having to endure her, compete against her.

"What a surprise," she mutters. "Belle Gentle doesn't see any problem with the concept of inequality."

"That's enough, girls." Mr Mitchell holds up his hands, but glances my way to reassure me I'm not the problem. "We don't have much time as it is. Now, if you look at these sheets…" He rummages around the top of his desk. "…hang on, I thought I had them. Wait a moment. I've left them in the teachers' quarters. I'll be five minutes."

He strides out, leaving us alone. Being alone with Joni always makes me edgy. I try to ignore her for a while, sketching out a possible Look for the Ceremony in my notebook. Five minutes turns to ten, to fifteen. I'm determined not to look at her, though her breathing is so heavy and gross, it's very hard not to. And, when I do give in and look up, she's grinning at me again.

"What is it?"

She tilts her head. "I've just had this marvellous idea."

"What? To experiment with wearing shoes that don't make people's eyeballs bleed?"

Joni doesn't even glance down at her gross, industrial shoes, and keeps grinning. "Why don't you just sell all your Mask stuff?" she asks. "Or just not buy any for a while? Then, surely, you'll have enough Finance to not need the Scholarship?"

I know she's just sparring, but it hits too close to home today, after hearing last night's argument. "Can you just *not*?"

"Not what?"

"Whatever it is you're trying to do. Can you please desist? I know it's very opportune for you that Mr Mitchell's taking a while, but please leave me alone. You can't recruit me into whatever saddo club you've made."

She's still smiling and has started sucking her pencil again. "Have you not thought about it, though?" she presses. "How much it costs to be you?"

"I get paid very well, actually, being me. With all my work as a Chosen One."

"Yeah, and I bet you spend most of that Finance on Mask products so you keep getting Chosen. Seems a bit circular."

I strain around to the door, wanting Mr Mitchell to come back and rescue me.

"I mean, how much is a pot of face camouflage? Twenty? And you get through, what? Twelve pots a year? That's two-hundred-and-forty annually, just to cover up your perfectly normal face…"

She's wrong, I think, still staring desperately at the door. A pot actually costs thirty, and I use three different types blended together. And that's not also counting the pots of light-blocker and nourisher and pre-Mask I also use.

"And all these new Looks. How much do you spend on updating your clothes all the time? A hundred?"

On a tight month, maybe a bit more than that.

"…and all your Body Prayer classes, and equipment, and clothing…I bet that adds up."

I flip then, twisting around. "Will you just please leave me alone?" I practically spit. "I don't want to talk about Finance with you."

"But don't you ever tot up how much it costs to be you?"

"This is none of your business."

"Well, it is, actually, if you're also applying for the Scholarship when you might be able to pay for it yourself by selling your eyelashes or something."

Selling my eyelashes? Despite myself, I laugh.

Joni catches my laugh and we end up giggling together. "Nobody sells their eyelashes," I say.

"Not yet. But I wouldn't be surprised if it becomes a thing under the Doctrine. An eyelash black market."

I snort again, and try to make it into a cough so she doesn't get the satisfaction of knowing I find her funny. She's giving me a knowing smile and I get another strange blast of warmth through me, before remembering all my current circumstances and shaking my head.

"Even if I sacrificed all my Mask products, it wouldn't come close to paying for the Education," I say. "But nice try." I sigh. "Having no Finance is so shit, isn't it? Like, having your future be decided by a Scholarship rather than being able to buy one?" I know I'll have to endure many more arguments through my floorboards, endure more weeks of Father being away for ages for work, endure the awkwardness of sharing my Finance from Chosen One work with my Mother. I know I'll only get good Finance through my Just Right years before I'm dropped. I'm hoping I can help them more long term with an Education.

Joni nods with her jaw jutting out. "That it is."

We sit in silence for a moment, awaiting the late return of Mr Mitchell and his important sheets of paper. I'd never given much thought to Joni's Finances, but it seems strange, that someone so seemingly strong has such a weakness like being poor. I guess it's one tiny thing we have in common. I can imagine it doesn't sit easily with her – needing something so much, the way she needs this Scholarship. And, as if she senses my sympathy, she jerks, like she's uncomfortable in her skin, and puts her stupid smile on her face again.

"Want to start an eyelash black market together?" she asks. "I feel like we'd make great business partners."

I throw a pencil at her, and laugh yet again.

JONI

I think I'm going to do it. I'm going to Awaken Belle Gentle. What brilliant payback it will be for her entering me into the Ceremony. I mean, ultimately Awakening anyone is a good thing, but part of me will, admittedly, enjoy watching the unravelling of her life that will occur when it happens. A little bit of revenge combined with doing something for the greater good. It's deliciously tempting.

"No way," Sita says, when I announce my plan. "Belle IS the Doctrine. It would be easier waking a dead bear from hibernation." A student passes our stall and Sita tries to hand them a leaflet, but they put their head down and pretend they've not seen her. This is how most of the student body is reacting to our table. I campaigned for months to get Ms Blanche to let me do a lunchtime fundraiser for the Centre for Discarded Women, but it's proving quite fruitless. Mainly as we all seem to be too Objectionable for anyone to want to be seen near our table, let alone donating Finance to our cause. Our natural faces apparently don't make people feel very charitable.

I shake my arm out. It's hurting from trying to hand out rejected leaflets. "I'm telling you. The girl has weak spots. She actually listened to me the other day when I was talking to her about the cost of the Doctrine. And she laughed, not only at my jokes, but at herself."

Sita and Hannah shake their heads, but Darnell gives me a supportive tap. "If anyone can do it, it's you."

I put my hand on top of her hand. "Thank you."

"I still can't believe you have to spend so much time with her. I mean, what's she like? Really?"

I raise both eyebrows. Darnell is so quietly obsessed with the Pretties, bless her.

"She mostly refuses to talk to me still, in case my ugliness is contagious. And we're studying for most of it. But…Belle…" Images of her flicker through my head from the two study sessions we've had together so far. "She spends so much time checking her reflection on her Device, or her Ranking. I don't think she realizes how much time. It's like a nervous tic or something. But she's got depth. She got better marks than me in our Assessment Rehearsal yesterday, even though I have no idea where she finds time to revise. I can't deny the girl's clever. And, well, she must be clever because I'm getting through to her. I can tell."

The rest of our lunch hour drags by, as time really slows down when the whole school are ignoring you. Our collection bucket only has a few coins in, and I keep looking into it forlornly, dreading telling Mother how badly it's gone. Funding the Centre is a constant source of stress for her, and I regularly don't let her pay me for my shifts. We urgently need more bedding, as we can't really take donations of used linens, but my fellow students clearly don't care. Or just don't want to get too close to our table for fear of contamination.

If I were to wake Belle up though…imagine how much Finance she could earn us?

As if she knew I was thinking of her, Belle and her lot appear at the end of the corridor towards the end of lunch. Damian keeps grabbing her arse and she keeps shrieking playfully and batting his hand away.

"You stink from playing Rage Ball," she complains as he puts his arm around her, wiggling away from him.

"Always with the excuses, Blue Balls."

They're coming closer, and my table of friends freeze, slightly scared, as you never know what you're going to get with Damian. But I'm feeling emboldened by the time Belle and I have spent together, and how she's laughed at my jokes. Because I am clearly stupid.

Just as they approach, I lean right forward, so a leaflet is basically blocking their path, and I say loudly, "Help us fund the Centre for Discarded Women. They desperately need your help to stay warm this winter."

Damian stops, so the rest of them stop too. Vanessa and Ben even break off their canoodling to see how he's going to respond. I see him size me up, see the inevitable disgust register on his top lip, his eyes scanning over the rest of the table. My heart starts thumping as I wonder if I've made a mistake. His eyes land on Darnell, of all people, and she stiffens –

either with fear, or excitement, or both.

Then, miracle of miracles, Damian takes his arm away from Belle's shoulder and starts digging in his pocket. Everyone gets more upright as he rummages – our table, the Pretties, the groups of students watching. I panic for a second that he's going to put some rubbish in the collection bucket as a joke, and literally gasp as he pulls out a crisp Finance note of incredibly high value. He holds it out to Darnell, who's staring at him with her mouth open, practically quaking.

It's too good to be true, surely? Or maybe Belle's been telling him about me? About our work? Maybe I'm already wheedling my way in and making positive change...

"I'm making this very generous donation for a very important cause," he says, speaking directly to Darnell.

"I...thank...y—"

He cuts her off. "Now, I want you to take this Finance and use it to buy some Empowerment Procedures." Ben, behind him, lets out a bark of a laugh. "See it as a Finance-saving investment for the Centre. Because let's face it, if you don't get some work done, darling, you're definitely going to end up in that Centre before you're even out of your Just Right years."

Laughter ripples around him as the note lands in Darnell's bucket. She's frozen by the attack. I make eye contact with Belle, all *What the hell?* Surely she's going to say something? Surely after I helped her with her Panic the other day. But no... She doesn't laugh with her friends, but she doesn't stop him either. She just shrugs at me, at our table, and then tugs Damian's arm.

"I'm hungry," she says. "Buy me a cookie?"

They all swan off without glancing back. The second they're at the end of the corridor, we flock around a shaking Darnell.

"Are you okay?"

"He's such a prick, ignore him."

"We love you, Darnell," I say.

There's pain all over her face, that even a hug from Jack doesn't dislodge. I feel hatred froth between my teeth at how needlessly cruel Damian is. And at how needlessly compliant Belle is in the face of his atrocious bullying. She probably believes Darnell deserves it for not following the Doctrine or something.

"I'm fine," Darnell says, not looking it. "I'm fine," she repeats, sounding surer this time. Then, bless her, she reaches into the bucket and pulls out the note, putting a grin on her face. "Now, I don't know exactly how much linen this will buy, but it's certainly a lot."

I bury her in a hug and tell her she's brilliant. As she pats my back, I think it again.

I will Awaken Belle Gentle.

She has no idea how much I'm going to wake her up and unravel everything.

BELLE

I go over to Vanessa's after my denim photoshoot because I don't want to waste my Look. Mother may be one of the best small-time Maskers, but her skills are nothing compared to the super professionals. The shoot itself was a bit strange. They'd failed to mention that they wanted to shoot me with the buttons undone and putting my hands down there, leaning forward like a Smut star.

"You're so stiff," the photographer complained. "What are you, a Vanilla?"

Was that word going to haunt me this whole term? Was there a memo out or something? So I threw my head back and pretended to be like the women I see in Damian's Smut clips. It felt hugely ridiculous, but the photographer said, "That's better," and hopefully he'll book me again. I've already spent my Finance, even though it's not come through yet.

"That was great," the campaign manager told me as we took a break. I allowed myself a few sips of water while they touched up my Mask, but only tiny ones so I didn't bloat. "Do you want to see some of the shots?"

I nodded and was led over to the Varnish deck, where I immediately realized my mistake. Images of me were already up on a giant screen, while Varnishers mended all my imperfections.

"You're doing great," one said, without taking his eyes off the screen. He deep-zoomed in on my face and I watched as he made my eyes bigger, my nose a bit thinner and thickened my lips. I know *all* images get Varnished, but to watch it in real time felt pretty shaming.

"Sorry about my nose," I found myself saying. "I hope you don't have too much work."

He batted the comment away. "Everyone's got something."

It struck me as mad that even I, a semi-professional Chosen One, was still made to feel not Pretty enough. How could I not be enough when I'd hardly eaten, had muscle definition that looked like I was an illustration, long hair, perfect skin under my Mask, a symmetrical face? *And* with the best Maskers covering my face. Yet I still needed Varnishing? If I wasn't Pretty enough, then how could *anybody* be? I felt an urge to slap him but stopped myself and shook my head. I was definitely spending too much time with bloody Joni at our dumb prep sessions.

Joni…I'm still smiling at a memory of her when Vanessa opens the door. In our last prep, Joni had been trying to get me to add up all the Finance I spend on Mask products. I'd refused so she'd started trying to figure it out for me – getting all the prices of my products wrong… But Vanessa's Look brings me back to the present.

"Vanessa, wow, you look stunning."

"You too. How was the shoot?"

"Oh you know." I try to shrug it off. "Shall we go to the woods while there's still good light?"

"Yep, I'll just grab my stuff."

As she's closing her front door, I take in Vanessa's Look again. It really is stunning. I wouldn't be surprised if she'd spent all day on it. Her Mask is flawless, her hair piled high in an elaborate style, and her dress hugs her perfect curves like it's been drawn around her. A prickle of annoyance rumbles through me. I'm supposed to be the Best One today. I'm the one with the professional Mask and hair, who has just come from a Chosen One shoot. I hadn't mentally prepared for Vanessa to equal me today, let alone maybe outshine me. I've been so busy preparing for the Scholarship and trying to Have It All that I've not noticed Vanessa sneaking up on me. She's really upping the ante with the Ceremony looming.

"Okay," Vanessa says, as we struggle to walk through her garden in our heeled shoes. "I think I've got everything."

"Did you bring the big Halo?"

"Yep."

"I had four pointed on me at the shoot earlier. *Four*," I tell her. "And yet they still Varnished me." I feel a bit odd, sharing that.

Vanessa smiles in half sympathy. She always gets a bit funny when it comes to talking about my Chosen One work. "Bastards," she replies. "Why Varnish perfection?"

I smile back, relieved. "Exactly... Shall we take off our shoes?

I keep sinking into the mud."

Vanessa's house backs onto a small wood, and even though it's been super hot recently, the dense forest means the ground's still damp. She gives me a strange look in response. "What if we see somebody?"

"In the middle of the woods?"

"Well…yeah. You're right."

As we take off our heels, I realize that we don't only put on full Looks for when people see us, but also for the *anticipation* of being seen at any given moment. I put on Mask even if I'm alone at home, just in case. *Would someone think I'm Pretty right now if they could see me?* I ask myself when I pass the mirror on the landing. Then I inevitably do a shoot for the Ranking, so people know just how Pretty I am even when I'm alone… I've never really had thoughts like this before, and realizing it all is terribly exhausting. I wish Joni would stop getting into my head and trying to make me Objectionable like her. It's unsettling how much I keep thinking about her.

Vanessa and I venture further into the woods, towards this little glade we've used for previous shoots. It has a tree with a low-hanging branch that looks like a swing seat, and it's an effort not to use it for every shoot we take together.

We arrive at the glade and start setting up. "Are you looking forward to tonight?" Vanessa asks. The light's falling through the tree canopy beautifully, like we're living in the middle of a wooded disco ball. I pull out the legs of Vanessa's giant Halo and push it into the soil.

"Yeah, I guess."

We have plans to meet Damian and Ben in the park tonight. I'd actually forgotten about it and feel a heavy dread land in my stomach at remembering.

"It will be nice to all hang out. I swear we never see you these days."

"It's these stupid Scholarship sessions," I say, checking the focus on the camera.

Vanessa, meanwhile, is struggling to put her heels back on. "It's so weird to me that you're going for this Scholarship when you could be a full-time Chosen One."

"I…"

I'm not sure how to answer that one. Thankfully, Vanessa moves on.

"I must say, the more you stay away, the more Damian likes you. Who knew hanging out with Joni of all people would make him jealous?"

"Oh…"

"In fact, I think he's definitely going to ask you to the Ceremony tonight."

"Right…"

"Isn't that great? We can get a carriage all together. Anyway, do you want to go first?"

"You can go," I say, my voice thick. Vanessa grins and hops up onto the tree branch, getting into her first pose. I allow myself to get distracted by the fun of the shoot to stop myself spiralling. I direct Vanessa into different positions, crouch down to get the best angles, and even risk ruining my own Look by climbing a tree to get some downward images. I tell her to pout, and I laugh as she pulls the occasional funny face. This is us at our best – messing around for photos. We've done it together for years and it's my happy place. I take around four hundred, which should give her enough to choose from.

Vanessa eventually leaps down from the tree. "Okay, your turn, Miss Chosen One, come on."

It's Vanessa's turn with the camera, and I jump onto the branch and go through my familiar poses. I ensure my right side is always facing the camera. I suck in my stomach and arrange my arms in a way that any excess skin at the top is tucked into my armpits. I make sure my toes are always pointing so my legs look their thinnest. I keep my chin lowered so it doesn't look chubby. I pull up my jeans to just the right place on my hips where my stomach doesn't bulge, though it shouldn't anyway, not as I've been hungry for a fortnight. All these poses come effortlessly to me. I've been doing them for years now – since Vanessa and I first started doing this.

Since I was eleven, I would obsessively go through the Ranking of older Pretties and forensically examine their images, to see how they posed, what they wore, what Looks worked well. In fact, this is how Vanessa and I became friends. We've spent years dressing up together for the Ranking. It's our main bonding activity. I feel the light of the Halo on my face, the dappled sunlight sprinkling itself across my stomach, and I relax into this familiarity. Of the fun of getting the best shot, of the anticipation of seeing how well it will do on the Ranking, of the joy of having a friend who knows your best angles. The earlier, horrible part of the day fades, and I twist around in the tree seat, and smile back at the camera over my shoulder. In fact, I feel positively great, until Vanessa brings it up again.

"So, what's going on with you and Damian?" she asks, with the camera held to one eye.

"What do you mean?" I lean against the tree, looking off to the side, grateful I don't need to make eye contact.

"Why won't you Link with him?"

"I wasn't aware I had to."

"I mean, you don't, of course. *It's your choice.* But he's so good looking. And he's smart. And rich. The Try Hards would positively die just to have him glance in their direction."

I raise my arm above my head and pout into the lens. "I don't know. He's quite…full on, isn't he?"

"Are you scared?" She lowers the camera, her eyes wide, and I drop my pose. I can't meet her gaze.

"Scared of what?" I put on a breezy voice.

"You know? Of the Rules of the Doctrine… About needing to not be a Vanilla by the end of the Ceremony."

Dread starts racing through my veins. The same urgent fear I felt when that man grabbed me to pull me into his car. I hold onto the rough bark to steady myself, and Vanessa, sensing it, puts the camera down and leaps up next to me on the branch. She puts an arm around my shoulder. "It's okay to be scared," she soothes. "I was."

I twist towards her, meeting her brown eyes. "*Really?*"

This is the first time we've ever spoken about this. When she Linked with Ben, she seemed to take in her stride all the requirements of that. I thought she was happy, because Ben told everyone she was one of the Prettiest girls he'd ever seen even though she had dark skin. He made a real public thing about it. "Lucky me," she always said, though was I right to take that at face value? But, then again, whenever Smut is played at school – which is daily – he always puts his arm around her and says, *"We've done that, haven't we, sweetie?"* like it's a lovely play they've attended together, rather than something I watch and then need to go to the toilet and put my head between my legs after. Vanessa's always seemed so relaxed about it all until now…

"Of course I was nervous," she says. "It's a big deal. Why do you think Damian's chasing you so hard? He likes the fact that it's all new to you."

"Doesn't it all…" I almost don't say it. I'm so scared she will tell Ben and that it'll get out that I'm a Frigid. But I need to know and I have nobody else to ask "…*hurt?*" I manage.

I expect Vanessa to reassure me. To tell me my worst fears are stupid, but she winces. "Of course," she says instead. "It really hurts sometimes, especially the first time. In fact, Ben likes it the most when it hurts."

"He does?"

"Yeah. But the Doctrine says it's Empowering, doesn't it? To have men get so excited by us? To have that power? To make them so happy?"

"But…the pain…"

Something passes across her face, something I can't explain. Something that hurts to watch. "I mean, obviously please don't tell anyone it hurts me sometimes, yeah?"

108

"Of *course* not."

"I guess it's part of being Pretty, isn't it?" she asks, like she's trying to convince herself. "It's not like walking in heels isn't painful. Or Hair Ripping isn't painful. Or our Piercings. Or a particularly hard session of Body Prayer… I've never really thought of it as a *different* pain."

I blink away the soft light of the forest. "Isn't it worse though, cos it's…you know? Intimate."

She changes suddenly, crosses her arms. I've pushed too far. "Ben wouldn't do anything I don't want to do."

"I know but… You want to…you don't mind being in pain?"

"I don't want to be a Frigid."

"No, of course not."

"It's my choice."

"I know it is."

The conversation tumbles out of control and runs loose in the woods. I've offended my best friend, though I'm not sure why. Panic hits. I'd hoped Vanessa would reassure me, but she seems quite muddled too, though she's making it clear she doesn't want it to seem that way. I hope she doesn't tell Ben that I'm scared – he'll certainly tell *everyone*. And I hope she's okay. All of her uncertainty is news to me.

I look at the forest floor and imagine lying down and burying myself in the mulch so nobody can see me or touch me. "Maybe I'll say yes to Damian…" I say, feeling so exhausted at the thought of accepting my destiny.

Vanessa's voice brightens immediately. "Really?"

"I mean, I can't date much, not with the Scholarship."

I'm already wanting to backtrack, or at the very least buy myself more time.

"But you'll go to the Ceremony with him?"

I gulp inwardly. "Yeah, I guess." Then I worry I'm not being enthusiastic enough. Not Belle-like enough. "If he's not going with Joni, that is," I add, feeling a bit odd as I make a joke at her expense.

Vanessa snorts and leaps off the tree, wobbling in her shoes as she lands. "Wasn't that hilarious?"

"I guess…"

"That girl is going to die a Vanilla. No boy in their right mind will ever go near her."

I dangle my leg down and use my foot to draw in the muddy dust, scuffing my shoes. I feel it's more the other way around with Joni. She won't go near any boy she thinks is beneath her.

"Look, it's natural to be a bit scared, Belle," Vanessa says, putting her hand on my shoulder. "I was too. But it does feel nice, seeing them get pleasure. Powerful. Damian's the best-looking guy in school. And being with him after the Ceremony sounds like the perfect way to fulfil the Doctrine. You're perfect for each other. I mean, you can't avoid it for ever, can you?"

I shake my head, and she holds out her hand to help me down. As we make our way back through the trees, the sun low and casting a golden spell around each branch, I think maybe the point of getting the Scholarship wouldn't just be about Having It All. That, maybe, it *wouldn't matter* if I was Blue Balls Belle at the Education. That at least there I'd have my brain up for scrutiny, not just my body. That's why I'd rather study tonight than try to stop Damian's hand crawling up my leg. But I don't feel I can make that choice, even though the Doctrine promises me I can.

We change our Looks again before we meet the boys and I'm sort of sick of staring at myself. The second we get back to Vanessa's, we pore through our shots, choosing the best. Then we upload them to the Ranking and put some music on while we lie on her bed, our hair mingling on the pillow, laughing and giddy as the Validation rolls in. Ourselves again. As the likes and comments bloom and grow, I can't help but feel soothed. All of Joni's weird comments fade to white noise as I imagine how many girls are wishing they could look like me.

Vanessa brings up a dinner of chopped vegetables and fresh dips, alongside a big pizza. We take more shots of ourselves for the Ranking, dangling the pizza into our mouths without actually swallowing one bite. We eat the carrots though. The pizza haunts me as I start getting ready. It smells so good, the cheese the perfect shade of golden brown. My mouth waters, my stomach twists. I want to eat the whole thing, and then another one, and then have ice cream, and then cake, and then more pizza. I want to cram so much food into my body that I can't do up my ridiculous new denim. I want to eat until I feel nothing, and until Damian thinks I'm so disgusting that he doesn't want to come near me and touch my body and make it hurt while I pretend that I like it. Nobody can know this about me. Nobody. I must get over this, I must fulfil the Doctrine, I...

There's a sudden screaming over the loud music. I stop my Mask application and twist towards Vanessa. She shrugs. Another scream.

"It's not fair. It's not faaaaaaaiiiiiiirrr!" The shouting gets louder, as Vanessa's little sister, Hope, storms past the door into her neighbouring bedroom.

"I hate you, I haaaaaate youuuu!" we hear her add through the wall.

I raise an eyebrow at Vanessa in the mirror. "What's all that about?"

Vanessa laughs, unbothered, and runs Clamps over her dark hair. "Oh yeah. Ignore Hope. She's just freaking because Mother won't let her have her hair Corrected yet."

"Oh." Hope was only twelve. "Is there an age limit or something?"

"Not technically. The Empowerment Centre do it, but Mother has this thing about making us wait until we're fourteen."

"Oh…how come?"

Vanessa chews her lip as she clamps down a section of her hair. It hisses and sputters under the heat and she smothers it into straightness. "It's this whole thing. When you're too young it can mess with your hairline… She'll cope."

She clamps another section of her hair and won't meet my eye in the mirror this time, making it clear she doesn't want to talk any more.

We fall into awkward silence, both of us focused on redoing our Masks. I never know what to say when it comes to things

112

like the difference between Vanessa's and my hair and skin. She gets all rigid and it's one of the few things that never feels easy between us, but I try and follow her lead when it comes to talking about it. And her lead is to never go there. The sobbing next door dies down, and there's a tapping at the door.

"Go away," Vanessa shouts.

Hope's voice is small and pleading. "Please let me come in and watch. Pleeeeeeease."

"Ergh, you're so annoying."

But Vanessa nudges the door open with her foot and Hope runs in like a hyper puppy, seemingly quite recovered. "Wow," she says, taking me in. "You look beautiful." She stares up at me like I'm a star in the sky.

I smile and reach out to tickle her soft cheek. "Thank you. I just have a super nice Mask on today. I had a shoot earlier."

"It's so cool that you're a Chosen One. I hope I can be when I'm older. Can I watch you do your Mask?" She sits cross-legged at my feet, staring at me, enraptured. "I want to be a Chosen One, but Vanessa says you have to be twelve times as Pretty to be one with our skin. She says it's not fair. That she could be a Chosen One too if it wasn't for—"

"Hope, shut up," Vanessa says, cutting her off. "Stop being a brat because you're mad about your hair."

"But it's NOT FAIR. Mother won't let me."

"Hope, she'll let you," Vanessa says, her voice bored. "Just not till you're fourteen. That's when I had it done."

"It's not fair. I don't want to be an Objectionable. I hate my stupid hair."

"And I hated my hair. But I had to wait, and so do you."

"Argh!" She kicks her legs out in sheer frustration while I take in her Look. She's wearing some On The Cusp Mask products, as most of them do at that age. Blotchily applied with the cheap stuff they can afford with their pocket Finance. Hope's gone for a shade too light, and I see the tide marks on her neck, where Mask meets skin.

"Let's put some music on," Vanessa says, giving me the eyes again. The *I don't want you to ask about what was just said* eyes. I follow her lead again, though my stomach feels funny after what Hope just said. I didn't know Vanessa wanted to be a Chosen One...that she thinks her skin has stopped her. Does she really think maybe the Bad Times aren't over for everyone? That True Equality might not be ours yet? I hate how she's never wanted to share that with me. I've always thought she believes the Doctrine but...but...my head hurts. I try to respect her silent guidance and drop it. She switches on her Screen, and our favourite music channel comes on, acting like a pacifier for Hope. She settles down between my legs as the young Stars gyrate along to their songs. I immediately feel less Pretty. I may be a low-grade Chosen One, but Stars are something else. Their bodies almost defy belief, as they dance in their leotards, stroking themselves while they sing.

"*Put your hands around my neck and show me that you love me.
Leave your mark. Show me that you care.*"

They mime choking themselves during the chorus and, below me, Hope copies the dance moves, knows them by heart. I feel my ribcage contract again, the panic rising. If I go to the

Ceremony with Damian, I know what will be expected of me afterwards and how it's going to hurt. I watch the whole song, feeling deep shame settle into my bones at my secret Frigidity. Maybe Vanessa's right? Maybe it's not so bad. Maybe it can be fun, can make me feel powerful? But I don't know…

I look down at Hope again, whose little hands are still clasped around her neck, singing along, and yet again, I find myself thinking of Joni and what she'd make of all of this.

JONI

It's a tricky shift at the Centre and I'm run off my feet from the moment I come in.

"Joni, it's a nightmare. Good luck," Mother says, leaving as I'm arriving. She's off to the Council to continue her protest against the Empowerment Centre.

"Cheers, Mother."

"It's all in hand. But stay hydrated."

Two women have arrived overnight, both with children, traumatized and homeless. As I hang my bag up and get myself ready, my duty manager, a wonderful Invisible called Carol, fills me in on what's needed.

"Do you mind being chief babysitter?" she asks, holding a clipboard and trying to maintain an air of togetherness. "One of the mothers is in bad shape. I need her to get checked out by the medical team. She left last night after the beating when he was asleep. I need to ensure Security's activated, as he's definitely the type who'll come looking. The other mother is freaked out about us rooming them together. I need to calm her down and let her know it's not for long. Seriously, I'd sell my hair for a few extra rooms. Not that it's worth anything, it having lost its Pigment and all."

I nod. "I can babysit."

"Thanks, Joni, you're amazing, as always. I can't wait for you to get into the Education and make us all proud. Actually get some power to do something about all this."

I bite my lip. "That's the plan."

I steer my way through the Centre, saying hi to some of the women I've got to know. They wave. Some come over for a hug. I pass the newbies, sitting uncomfortably in the corner, eyeing everyone nervously as they clutch their documents and wonder how the hell this has happened to them. Carol's already comforting the really bad one, whose face is marbled with bruises. A strange coldness trickles down my spine, as it always does when I see the women's bruises. I blink away freeze-frames of my mother's bruises and how she used to cover them with Mask. I leave them to it and find the new children in their shared bedroom – three little girls, all of them sitting on their beds, staring at the walls, looking lost and unkempt. One's still wearing pyjamas, I'm guessing from her flight the previous night.

I knock lightly and they all flinch. I keep my voice bright and approachable. "Hi, girls, I'm Joni. I work here. How are you doing? I thought you may want someone to come play with you? Shall we get some toys?"

They all eye me curiously, not moving from their beds. I step in delicately and open the toy chest in the corner. "I can't believe nobody's shown you this yet. Sorry. It's been a busy day."

Their interest is definitely piqued by the mention of toys.

Their heads raise higher, straining to look.

"There's some really good stuff in here..."

That's a lie. All the toys are sticky, with bits missing, and were donated many years ago. I grab the toys, assessing the ones I think may land with these poor girls. They are all, unsurprisingly, wearing some kind of Princess paraphernalia, even on the pyjamas, and I know now's not the time to challenge them on that. I pick up the dolls and lay them on the floor.

"Now, there's not much time to prepare for the Ceremony," I say, in a high-pitched doll's voice. "And I've not got any idea what dress to choose. I hope somebody helps me."

The pyjama girl is instantly at my side, picking up the doll, making it hers. "Can she choose whatever she likes?" she whispers.

"Of course." I make my voice louder. "And there's plenty of beautiful dresses here for all the dolls if anyone else wants to play?"

An hour later, and the dolls have all attended the Ceremony, won, and are now wondering what to wear next to the After Party.

"I want the pink dress," Dominique says, still in her pyjamas. She brazenly tries to pluck it out of the other girl's hand.

The other girl, Delilah, bats her off. "Not your turn yet."

"This isn't fair." Dominique's face starts quivering, on the brink of a tantrum.

"Shh, it's okay," I say, stepping between them. "There's

another pink dress in the toy trunk next door. Hang on, let me go get it."

I leave the girls playing dress-up with the dolls. I've asked Mother many times why we allow such toys in the Centre when I know how she feels about them. But she always says you've got to give these children what they're used to, to help them feel safe. "And, sadly, for most of them coming to this shelter, they come from homes where they follow the Doctrine quite strictly."

In the common room, things have calmed down somewhat. The bruised lady is just back from being checked in the medical room, and the other mother is filling out forms with Carol, who's patiently talking her through each page. The older residents are getting dinner ready. Women are crammed into the communal kitchen, laughing as they chop and stir what smells like spaghetti bolognese. There's a mixture of Pretties, Invisibles, Try Hards and a few like me…wearing no Masks whatsoever. The Centre's the only place where I see these divides crossed, and it still makes my heart warm. I cough next to Carol and the new arrivals look up.

"Sorry to interrupt, but just wanted to introduce myself. I'm Joni," I say. "And I'm looking after your daughters tonight. They're doing fine, just to reassure you. The dolls have all just had the best Ceremony ever."

Both of them smile – although the one in her nightdress, I'm assuming Dominique's mother, looks like she may cry. "Are you sure they're alright?"

"They're having the best time. Well, not the best, obviously.

But they're calm. We'll be eating soon too. I can stay as late as you need."

"Thank you." They both give me that look the women here often do when they first arrive. Like they can't believe the kindness and, even then, don't feel they deserve it. It makes me angry every time. I feel the itch in my fingers. The one so strong it makes me want to shake my limbs out to dislodge it. It's the itch that I want to change things. Make things better for these women. Reminding me that, in order to do so, I have to do well in this stupid regime and somehow clamber my way to the Education and get qualifications and power.

I check in on more of the regulars, and return to the new children, who now want to play Transformations.

"Do you have any Cusp Mask?" Delilah asks. "Do you? Please say you do."

I squeeze her shoulders. "Why don't we play something else? We could play superheroes?"

My suggestion's greeted with three unimpressed faces. "No way. Boring. We want to do Transformations," Dominique says.

"I'll see what I can do."

I grumble out of the room and make my way to the Pretty Cupboard, which is unusually well stocked this week. It's one of Mother's other strange contradictions – that she uses so much budget on buying Mask products for the women here. Outside the Centre she's campaigning against their very existence, but inside she happily deposits them, and doesn't say anything when the women flock to the cupboard and clutch the products like precious jewels. There's a small bin of On The

Cusp Mask – lip enhancers that have already been snapped by other children here, or eye colour palettes that don't suit anyone. I bring the bucket back to the room with a "*Voila*" and the three girls rummage through it, shrill with delight. Half an hour later, when the new mothers come to collect their children for dinner, they find their highly-decorated children.

"Mummy, Mummy, look at my eyes. Look at them. They're purple." Dominique runs over and flutters them at her mother, who laughs and coos and hugs her to her chest. "You look so Pretty," she exclaims. "I have such a Pretty girl."

The other girls twirl for their mother and are met with similar acclaim. "You both look gorgeous."

"The nice lady gave us a Transformation."

I smile again at the new arrivals. "Is that okay? I'm not very good at Masking, but they don't seem to mind."

Dominique's mother tears up. "No, it's lovely. She looks lovely. I wasn't able to take any of our stuff with us…" Her voice catches, and I watch her struggle to regain control of her emotions. She crouches down. "We've got ten minutes before dinner where we are going to meet everyone. Do you want to help mother be Pretty for then? I want a Transformation too."

Her child smiles and hugs her. "We can both have purple eyes."

"Perfect." She twists back to me. "Is it okay? For us to join in with the game?"

"Of course. We have even better stuff for the adults in the cupboard. I can show you?"

I watch as the women shuffle over to the Mask cupboard

and get practically tearful when I tell them the products they choose are theirs to keep. Then we return to their cramped bedroom and play Transformations until dinner. I watch these two women, who are strangers, start complimenting one another on various parts of their face and body – swapping tips about how to Mask, and carefully teaching their daughters how to apply things. As Dominique pokes a brush at her mother's closed, bruised eye, a serene bliss descends on the mother's face. The Doctrine finds her, soothes her, brings her back to herself. I watch this poor, lost woman sighing with bliss as her hair is kneaded at by pudgy fingers, with her child saying, "*Mother, you look so beautiful.*"

It's dark by the time I'm walking home, and I tuck my ponytail into my top so nobody can reach out and yank me somewhere. I tell Mother I'm on my way but get no reply and I half jog, my heart lurching whenever I have to walk past a bush. I may've shown strength around Belle when I walked her home, but what happened to us is still etched on my mind. Knowing he's still out there is very hard to forget.

"I'm home," I call breathlessly as I push through our front door. "What a shift. How was the meeting?"

I'm greeted with eerie silence. Tension paints my skin as I walk into the hall. "*Mother?*"

She's home. I saw her bag by the door. She never doesn't greet me. I walk towards the kitchen with a thick sense of dread.

"Mother?" She's sat at the kitchen table with her face cradled in her hands. There's an envelope on the table, pushed artificially forward so it's impossible to miss.

"You've got a letter," she says, still not looking up.

"I have?"

"It's your father's handwriting."

"Huh?"

My legs half buckle and I stagger over and liquefy next to her, staring at the envelope. I wouldn't have known it was his handwriting if she hadn't said. It's been years since he left, and it's not like he's ever written to me before. I wonder how it would've felt to have ripped it open innocently, if I'd arrived home before she did. I most likely wouldn't have told her that he'd written. Anything to do with my father makes Mother like…well…this. Floppy, non-communicative, broken.

"I…I don't have to open it," I tell her. "I don't know if I want to, to be honest."

She sighs and pushes herself up. Her eyes are wide and white. "I'm afraid we have to see what he wants. I never thought he'd be in touch again. I thought we were…"

Safe. That's what I know she's not saying.

We never moved when Father left. He'd made it so abundantly clear how totally irrelevant we were to his life with His New One that was the best outcome. We didn't need to go to the Centre and seek emergency housing. Father left quickly, efficiently and permanently. He'd taken what he needed, told Mother that he couldn't be blamed when she was such an Objectionable pathetic mess anyway, and that was that. Door

123

slammed. His reign of fear over. Mother changed the bills to her name. We didn't have the Finance to move anywhere new, but at least we were free from him. But this letter undoes all that. I want to run over to the windows and close the curtains. I hate him. I don't care what he has to say…and yet now…this envelope taunting me on the table… I also really want to know what my father's written. Has he…missed me?

"Will you…stay with me?" I ask. "While I read it?"

Mother lets out a grunt and I'm not sure if that's a yes or a no. She takes a sip of water from her glass and the liquid sways madly in her shaking hands. I haven't seen her like this in years. Long dormant memories arise, filling my chest. I rip open the envelope, wanting this suspense over.

My darling Joni,

Sorry it's been so long since your old Pa got in touch. I've missed you terribly, my beautiful girl. I didn't mean for it to be so long. I just didn't trust your mother not to have poisoned you against me. I hope she hasn't, as I would love to see your face and see how you are doing. I've thought about you every day since I had to say goodbye, and it would be wonderful if we could reconnect. You were such a beautiful young girl. I can't wait to see the stunning young woman you've no doubt become. Here's my Device number and address. Please get in touch. Let's not let the past spoil the present, eh?

With all my love,

Father x

BELLE

Damian's hand snakes around my bare waist and I can smell the sweet alcohol on his breath as he leans too close to my face.

"You're feeling a bit scrawny, Blue Balls," he comments, pulling me towards him on the wall. "What brand of jeans were you shooting for today? Twig Leg Denim?"

He and Ben erupt into laughter and his spit speckles my face. I try to contain my wince.

"If my body's so repulsive to you then why can't you keep your hands off it?" I quip.

Ben laughs even harder. "She's got a point there, Dame."

Damian shrugs good-naturedly and takes a long sip of his drink. "I'm just a concerned bystander, Belle. What can I say? I worry about you. So rigid and uptight these days. You need to relax. Let yourself go. Enjoy life!"

I sip my low-Sin alcohol from my straw so it doesn't ruin my lip enhancer, and wonder if I could kick him off the wall without consequences. Then I startle at my own thought. "I *do* enjoy life," I insist.

"Oh yeah? When did you last do anything wild?"

Vanessa lets out a shriek of laughter, way too late for any of the jokes. She's on her fourth drink and she's glazed and useless, her head dropping onto Ben's shoulder. She doesn't usually drink like this. Like me, she worries about the toxins. But tonight she's clearly decided to let herself go a bit and I wish I could do the same. I need to learn how to relax. The Doctrine says being Uptight is a waste of our freedoms.

"I'm here spending time with you, aren't I?"

Damian throws up his hands. "Oh my, Belle has had one drink on a wall. She's so totally out of control, this one. She may put a jumper on later when it gets cold. Watch out, everybody."

A group of girls from the year below walk past us, distracting Damian. They slow a bit, noticing him, and start walking in a more posed way, showing off their blooming Just Rightness. Damian acts disinterested, swigging from his drink, but watches them until they round the corner.

"A seven, a six and a five," he announces. "Ben, would you agree?"

"I came out with a four, a seven and a nine."

Vanessa paws his face. "And what would you give me?" she slurs, wrapping her arms around his neck.

"An eight and a half," Ben says, matter-of-factly.

Vanessa's face caves in, while Damian bursts out laughing.

"What?" Ben asks, his chest puffing out in defiance. "I was just being honest, Nessie. You know I think there's always room for improvement." He tries to kiss her, but she ducks out of the way, shame hunching her body over. I wonder if she wants me to check she's okay or will be more annoyed if I draw

126

attention to her. "Come on, don't go all Angry Melanated Girl on me. I thought I had one of the chill ones…"

Damian laughs again as a blank look takes over Vanessa's face. She reaches out and takes her drink, downing it in one, not looking at Ben. "Honey, babe, gorgeous…come on…an eight and a half is great. That's really high. I never give out tens, you know that."

"That's true," Damian says to me. "He doesn't. Not even for you."

"Babe. Come on, babe. Smile for me, gorgeous. You're so Pretty when you smile. That's it. See? Hey, I got it wrong. You're a nine when you're smiling like that."

A terrible silence descends as Vanessa seemingly forgives Ben and they start kissing. Silence is replaced by their groans. The whole night has been excruciating and I just want to be at home studying, but then I also don't want Damian to go off me. Even though I don't like him. He's the most good-looking boy in school. The Doctrine states that winning his affections is the ultimate goal – the pinnacle of Having It All. I wonder for the fiftieth time what's wrong with me.

"They putting you in the mood, Vanilla?" he asks, bumping my shoulder.

"I wish you'd stop calling me that. I'm not…"

"Vanilla?"

"No! I'm just…"

"A Frigid?"

This really is getting increasingly hard to play. I'm being outmanoeuvred every time it comes up. "I just know my worth, that's all. Come on, Damian, name one romantic thing you've done to win me."

He sighs. "I send you all those photos of my penis."

"You're such a prince."

"I am! I trim beforehand."

"Oh my God, you're so gross." I can't help but laugh, and he, surprisingly, laughs with me. I can like him like this. When he's being a bit more self-aware. I feel less trapped. We sit giggling on the wall and I let myself relax a little, taking another few sips of my drink, until Damian leaps down all of a sudden.

"You know what, Belle?" he says, face weirdly serious and resolute. "You're right. I've *not* done any of this properly."

"Damian, what are you doing?"

He clambers down onto one knee, wobbling slightly from intoxication.

"Belle, you really are the Prettiest girl in school," he declares, holding his arm up. "I know I give you a hard time, but it's only because you make me nervous."

I start giggling from the shock, behaving like my IQ has just plummeted. When I look over, I see Vanessa and Ben have pulled apart and are watching, smiling. In fact, Vanessa's filming it on her Device. She's doing me a favour – I should be grateful she's recording this for everyone to see – yet at the sight of the blue light in her hands, I feel like I'm choking. "Damian, get up!"

"Not until you agree to go to the Ceremony with me. You know it makes sense. You and me. In fact, I won't go at all if you won't come with me."

Vanessa gasps, like Damian just suggested a suicide pact or something.

"Yeah right." I try to style it out.

"I'm being serious. Link with me or I won't come at all. I'll miss my own Ceremony. Think about what that means. Please, Belle, that's how serious I am. I promise I'll stop joking around. I think about you all the time. Please go with me."

Suffocation descends, especially as I know I'm being live-streamed onto the Ranking. I disassociate for a second and wonder if Vanessa's getting my best angle. I suck my stomach in so it will be flat in this video that will no doubt be circulated everywhere by midnight. I can't say no. Not to this. A *romantic* Damian. Every girl in school wishes this would happen to them. I should be flattered he's picked me. It means I've won. Yet I know what's expected of me that night…afterwards… I've seen the Smut he watches.

"Okay, get up, I'll go with you."

"Yes!" Vanessa and Ben shout, while Damian clambers to his feet, visibly relieved and delighted, which throws me a bit. He goes to kiss my lips but I push him away. "But I can't date much before," I warn him. "I have the Scholarship to prepare for."

His face scrunches up. "What Scholarship?"

"The Rebecca Harkness Female Scholarship to the Education. I'm up for it with Joni."

"It's just for girls? That doesn't sound very fair. What if I want a Scholarship?"

I shrug, glad he's not kissing me. The thought makes my

mouth water, like I'm on the verge of vomiting. "Well go get one. You just can't get this one. Anyway, I've seen your house, Damian. You don't need one."

"What do you need a Scholarship for anyway? Aren't you a Chosen One?"

"Yeah, but I want to Have It All...I want to...I don't know... *learn*..."

Ben holds up Vanessa's floppy arm. "Vanessa can't have it all, can you, babes? Not smart enough."

"Oi," she says, giggling again. "Excuse me, but I'm in all the same classes as Belle. I'm just stupid enough to not want to move far away from you."

They laugh with their heads together then start kissing again. I know it's her choice, but I don't understand why Vanessa has no interest in leaving this town. She claims she doesn't want to leave Ben, but he isn't always terribly nice to her, especially if our talk earlier is anything to go by. Has it always been like this, and bloody Joni is making me see it? I'm starting to realize it's more relaxing to not notice things, and to just submit.

Damian's hand slithers around my waist again. I let out a sigh, like I'm totally relaxed and breezy, and turn back to him. "Anyway, the interview date is going to be announced any day now and I'm totally slammed with preparing for it. So, Damian, yes I'll Link with you. But I can't...much...until..."

He wiggles his eyebrows. He knows what I'm saying. He knows I'm just buying myself time.

"So you're going to make me wait?"

His naming of it draws the suffocation nearer. My skin crawls. Lungs squeeze in. I want to hit him and run and keep running and never stop running. But all I've run out of is excuses.

I wink and make myself what the Doctrine demands – sassy and confident and excited. "Hey. Damian. It's going to be an amazing night."

"Really?" He wiggles his eyebrows again. "Okay, Vanilla. But let's just say, you better be worth the wait."

And it's only later that night, when I can't sleep because my heart's going so fast, that I realize he was making a threat.

JONI

Today is Candid Day, so naturally the whole school is hysterical. Candid Day is some stupid charity initiative, the brainchild of Belle and the Pretties, designed to make girls feel even worse about themselves under the guise of "helping others". The collective stress leading up to this was so acute, I could probably have snorted the air and increased my heart rate. I've overheard about ten million frantic conversations about Ritual Cleanses, emergency Eyelash Transplant appointments and whether or not it's cheating to carry a Halo around with you at all times.

This morning, as every day is Candid Day for me, I woke when I normally wake and got ready like I always do – with minimal effort. What's less normal is I ate my cornflakes in total silence, as Mother's gone catatonic since the letter arrived. She'd grabbed it out of my hands the second I'd finished reading it, and then put her face right into mine and said, "You're not going to reply, are you?" For reasons I don't yet understand, I hesitated before answering, and she walked away, saying, "I can't believe it," and now's hardly speaking to me even though I haven't replied to him yet.

Anyway, Candid Day. Over our terrible breakfast of silence this morning, I did find myself logging into the Ranking and checking out Belle's All Natural Look. I'm not sure why. Boredom perhaps. Of course, her uploaded Candid Shot was perfection. I do marvel at her ability to curate perfection under any circumstances, even Candid ones. Her skin was porcelain, her eyes bright, her cheeks blushed, her hair falling perfectly, undone and slightly roughed up, around her shoulders. She must've had at least three Halos on to achieve such a shot, and I looked forward to comparing this image with how she actually looked in real life at school later. I wondered yet again how she finds the time to do all this and yet still match my grades in our extracurricular sessions. It's so enduringly annoying.

As I'm at my locker, I hear Ben's voice waft past, deliberately loud and arrogant. "It's actually quite a worry how Objectionable so many girls are behind their Masks," he yells out to Damian, to upset as many passing girls as possible. "Like I know going All Natural today is for charity and all, but maybe it's more charitable for y'all to put your Masks back on?"

Damian lets out his gross macho laugh. "It's fraud, that's what it is," he agrees. "False advertising. Imagine getting some of these girls home and realizing what's underneath? We should be allowed to litigate."

His voice fades as he strides down the corridor. As I scan the locker block, I see the boys' words had the desired effect. At least six Candid girls look on the verge of tears, getting Reflection mode out on their Devices and checking their faces.

Candid Day passes in a blur of contagious anxiety. I try not to buy into any of it, and try not to judge anyone. But it's hard not to examine how the different girls have interpreted the brief. Some have clearly worked as hard as possible to be Natural Beauties without their Masks, but with a huge amount of prior effort to pull this off. Skin facialized within an inch of its life, fluttery lashes implanted at the last minute as Lash Build is against the Rules. I see many girls pinch their cheeks, hard, to invoke a natural blush. Whereas others have gone down the route of still wearing Mask, but trying to make it a Natural Mask. Piling on face camouflage but in a dewy formula, and using so much Outer Glow I'm basically blinded as I walk past them. The choice of Candid Looks all involve variations on the theme too. Some have carefully curated sexy twists on Leisure Wear by cutting them into cropped tops or shorts. Whereas others are still determinedly wearing their Everyday Looks, claiming loudly that, "Actually, this is what I wear around the house. I like to be glam at all times, just for me."

At least it's raising Finance for charity, I suppose. Although it's disheartening how much the school has supported this fundraiser when we hardly earned anything for the Centre the other week. At lunchtime I chuck some coins into the bucket that Belle parades past – slightly annoyed I have to pay for the privilege of looking how I look every day, and that she pretends not to know me. I also try not to get vexed that the charity is called "Masks Without Borders" and is an initiative to deliver Mask products to women in developing countries, where, sadly, "Every day is Candid Day."

"Some of them have never even been given the opportunity to wear a Mask," I overhear Belle preaching as she shakes her bucket, while Vanessa raises an eyebrow behind her. "They don't even know what one is. Isn't that terrible?"

"I reckon they'd much prefer an Ebola vaccine," I mutter to myself, but only quietly, as I can't quite be bothered to get into an argument about how Masks are actually just as important as vaccines, because Feeling Beautiful is a universal human right. I've had less energy for most things since Father's letter arrived. I know it word-for-word. I mean, clearly the obvious thing to do is to ignore it and think, *What a scumbag, how dare he get back in touch?* Yet, weirdly, that's not where my heart has gone. A small part of me feels…good that he's written to me. The little abandoned Joni is excited her father is back, even after what he's done. I'm so confused and Mother's silent treatment isn't helping. She's acting like it's my fault he wrote to me or something.

"Are you going to see him?" she asks me each morning.

"I don't know yet."

"It's your choice," she says, sounding like the Doctrine.

"I just wonder why he's getting in touch," I ask aloud, for the hundredth time, desperate to be able to talk it through with her.

Mother never replies though. She just presses her lips together and I can hear her brain screaming, but she never shares. Her eyes just glaze over and we have yet another breakfast in silence.

* * *

I'm distracted all through our Scholarship tutoring, where Mr Mitchell is going through interview protocol with us. I take notes but nothing he says sinks in. Belle seems super focused, as always. Putting her hand up, asking loads of questions, making four sets of notes to my one.

"Do you have any idea what the questions will be?" she asks. "Or is it different every year?"

Mr Mitchell leans back in his chair and raises both arms behind his head. "It's different every year but they tend to follow the same topics." He yawns. "They're very big on it being a girls-only college, even if they are under pressure to allow boys to join. Which makes sense to me really. Seems a bit old-fashioned now the Bad Times are over, but definitely don't say that in the interview. They're not just interested in your academic record either, but your general *gumption*. They'll ask questions about your passions, your beliefs, what you stand for and against, and why. You will not get this Scholarship if you come across bland."

For the first time all session, Belle looks slightly depleted. "Oh…" she says.

"So think about your charity work and your beliefs. You raised a lot of Finance for charity today, didn't you?" he asks only Belle. "And you organized Candid Day? I saw your announcement at lunch. Very impressive. Make sure you tell them about that."

"Yeah, I guess." She doesn't seem that enthused by today's success though.

We are left for the final hour to make notes on what

motivates us and our extracurricular activities. Belle starts scribbling like mad, her hair spilling onto her paper, while I sigh and stare up at the ceiling and wonder again about Father. *Why* did he get in touch? What does he want? I…I remember everything he did to Mother. The slaps, the sobs, the silence afterwards. But what did he do to me? Father technically never did anything to me. Surely it won't hurt Mother if I see him but she doesn't? It wouldn't put her in danger. Maybe he even wants to apologize? The fact he's missed me…it feels good… But Mother…what he did to her… Argh, my brain.

"Argh!" Belle shouts, mirroring my thoughts, and she throws her pen across the table. I have to dodge it, and she apologizes, but then yells "Argh!" again, up to the ceiling. She throws her arms up too, before folding over and banging her forehead on the desk. She then lurches up, eyes panicked because she's publicly malfunctioned, before glancing over at me and no doubt reminding herself my opinion doesn't matter. "This is just pointless," she tells me, seeing me watching. "This is so stupid and pointless."

I raise both eyebrows. "You've only *now* come to that conclusion about Candid Day?"

"Oh shut up, you – *Mrs I Care About Freaking Everything and The Interviewers Will Have Died of Old Age by The Time I Finish Answering Most Questions.*"

I'm jerked from my thoughts of Father and smile. I've never seen an angry Belle before. I can imagine she'd think it's most unbecoming, but it's quite fun. "Calling me Joni is just fine," I say.

"Oh, and she makes jokes." Belle puts her forehead back on the table. Up close, I can see she isn't wearing any Mask that I'm aware of. She really does have the best skin.

"What's your problem?" I ask. "You worried they're not going to ask you about how many squats you can do in the interview?"

"Well, yes, I am sort of worried about that actually."

"You didn't really think—"

She thrusts herself upwards. "No, of course I don't think that. But, yeah, okay, you think I'm a shallow idiot, that's fine. Your opinion has literally no impact on my life whatsoever. But these people do, and what if they…what if they…"

"…what if they're not bowled over by how Pretty you are, even when you're Candid? Well…" I smile. "I guess, maybe I do have an edge on you."

She sort of wilts, and I can see I've gotten to her. I feel a bit bad actually, I hadn't meant to. "Yeah, well, *LUCKY YOU* with your job at the Centre For Discarded Women. I bet the Education will lap that up."

I shrug. "Only reason I do it."

God, her face is sour. What is wrong with Belle today? "Yeah, well, maybe it is."

I'd been finding this entertaining for a moment, but when she says that a part of me snaps. "Or maybe," I yell at her, "I care about these women because my father beat my mother to a pulp every day of my childhood. And maybe I felt totally helpless to do anything about it and I want to make up for it now. Maybe," I practically screech, "some people don't do things because of what they look like, but because they actually care, unlike YOU."

It's all out of my mouth before I'm even aware. I clap my hands over my lips, stunned at myself. Belle jolts too and we both sit in the aftermath of my revelation, neither of us knowing how to proceed. There goes my chance of Awakening her, screaming at her like that.

"Shit," she sighs, after some time. "Sorry."

She's apologizing. It's a miracle. But my heart is still beating rampantly. I can't believe I've just told her about my father. *Belle.* My sworn enemy. The most powerful girl in school. "Look, I didn't mean to blurt that out," I say, arms up. "Please don't tell anyone. About my father, I mean."

"What?" She looks genuinely aghast. "Of course I wouldn't."

"No. Sorry. Where did I get that from? You've always been *so nice* to me."

We share another of our many awkward silences. Belle's face is red, highlighting that she really isn't wearing a Mask today.

"I really have been awful to you, haven't I?" she mutters, staring down at her wad of notes.

I wave my hand. "Nah. Entering me into the Ceremony was joyful. Being hounded by Damian is great. I'm lucky to get such attention."

She sighs. "I just find you so...annoying."

"Wow, you just keep getting nicer, Belle."

She twists round to look at me. "No. Sorry. I don't mean to be horrible. Honestly, I just...everything you are, everything you stand for…you don't care… I don't understand how you don't care…I find it hard to be around…" She wipes her eyes and no Mask comes off. "It gets to me. That's all. Because I don't understand it. You have all these strong opinions and you don't care that they rub people up the wrong way and it's never made sense until now…" She trails off for a second. "Your father…no wonder you want to fight so hard."

I cannot actually believe what I'm hearing. I'm getting through to Belle? I get under her skin? It seems totally unimaginable. I'm everything she hates, everything she's disgusted by, everything she fears.

"That's why I want to go to the Education," I find myself telling her. "To get Qualified, so I can change things. I was too young to do anything to help then, but I'm not too young now."

Belle looks up and, before I know it, she's reaching over the table and taking my hand, squeezing reassurance into it. "I can't even imagine. That sounds awful. So scary."

"It was…"

I find I'm about to tell her about his letter, weirdly. It feels safe to, in this moment, in this empty room, away from everyone to see and judge us. Then my protective instincts coil into action, I remember who I'm with, and I spring my hand away. "Why do you want this Scholarship, Belle?" I ask her. "I don't get it. I mean, yeah, you're smart and all. But you fit in so well here. Why do you want to go miles away to the Education?"

She pulls her rejected hand away and shakes it, like she wants to dislodge any of the Objectionable atoms that landed on it. "I don't even know sometimes," she admits. "For ages, it's just been about Having It All, you know? Like the Doctrine says I should. But now…things are… It's just this feeling. That I need to get out." Her eyebrows furrow, creating a fault line down the middle of her perfect forehead.

I raise both mine, noting what she's just said. She really is displaying signs of having an Awakening. Her dewy face looks shocked at what she's just admitted. Am I getting through to her? The only problem is, the more Belle wants to get the Scholarship, the more she'll fight me for it.

"Get out of what?"

"I…I'm not sure. I just…at home…well, my father has never hurt me or Mother, but there's a lot of pressure at home. To be Pretty, to win the Ceremony. To Link with Damian. To help Mother with Finance. It's like everyone wants a piece of me, and not the real me, but this exhausting performance…" She stops and gulps. "I…I really think we should carry on with our work." Even without her Mask on, her mask is back on. She tilts her chin, almost defiantly, marking in the sand that our bonding time – or whatever the hell just happened – is over. I shrug, mainly just relieved she's not going to tell the whole school my secret, and we both return to our notes in silence till past five-thirty. In fact, we both enter a frenzy of competitive note-taking, attempting to psyche each other out with just how seriously we're taking our applications. When Mr Mitchell returns, saying our time's up, we pack our bags in more silence, but, yet again, find ourselves walking in the same direction.

We step into the spring sunshine, the sun still hours away from setting, and I chuck my backpack over my shoulder and start lolloping home, trying to ignore her ignoring me. We continue this ridiculous game until we reach the road the man was on. At that point I notice Belle slow slightly behind me and get a bit shaky. She's muttering to herself, and I overhear, "*You're safe, it's been weeks, he still hasn't come back.*"

I stop and she almost bumps into me – her eyes jerking wide as she's jolted.

"Joni." She startles like she's only just noticed me.

"Are you okay?"

"I'm fine."

"If it helps any," I say, "I think, if he was going to come back, he would've done it by now."

"I'm fine. Honestly." Even though she's clearly not fine. We're only metres from where it happened and her gaze keeps flitting to where the car stopped.

"I'm being serious. He was likely just a chancer. To be that brazen…I really do think he was just passing through. Nobody who lives nearby would behave like that."

"Do you really think so?"

I nod. "I do think so, yes. I have a good radar for understanding violent men, unfortunately. With…you know…what I told you."

She wraps her arms around her thin, candid frame. "I hope you're right. I don't know what's happened to me recently. Since that day, I find it hard to be alone. To walk this way alone. My head's a mess. I'm second-guessing everything…"

I smile, though not at her pain. Is now the best time to nudge? Just a gentle push in the right direction? I decide to go for it.

"My mother would say you're having your Awakening," I say.

"My what?"

"Awakening. She gets very excited about girls having their Awakening."

"Awakening about what?"

I gesture all around me. "About all this. About how messed up it all is. The Doctrine. The consequences if you don't follow it. Realizing that you're never safe, no matter how closely you follow the Rules. Realizing that you're exhausted from following them. Starting to realize that they exist to exhaust you…"

Her nose crumples. We start walking again. We turn the corner and my stomach sinks, wondering if I took it too far too fast.

"You're doing it again."

"Doing what?"

"Being annoying."

I smile again. "Hey. It's your Awakening. You do it in your own time. But being angry is a very normal phase of it."

"Stop saying I'm having an Awakening. I don't want to have a fucking Awakening."

She's angry but she laughs. And I laugh with her. We look over at one another, and that sets off another ripple of laughter. And I know I'm safe. That I pushed just the right amount. In fact, Belle can't stop giggling. She hiccups for two whole roads, everything seemingly setting off fresh hysteria. "Fucking Candid Day," she says, before erupting again. "*Candid Day*. Do you know I've spent as long prepping for today as I probably will have to for the Ceremony."

I faux-gasp. "You mean, you didn't just roll out of bed this morning looking like that?"

"Shut up."

"To be fair, you have no Mask on by the looks of things."

She sighs. "No Mask. But I've used up all my Finance on deep cleanses, Lash Implants, and semi-permanent Mask around my eyes."

My eyes widen. "Woah, she admits it."

"Yes, well…" She laughs. "No offence, but nobody listens to you."

"You do. You're having an Awakening."

"Stop it." She gurgles with laughter again and mock-hits me, in what can only be a gesture of fledgling friendship. My stomach feels warm. I catch her laugh and we take our time walking the rest of the way home, enjoying the sun on our faces, the non-stop giggling. I haven't laughed this much with, well, anyone really. Darnell and that lot are so earnest. It's lovely and all, but it feels good to be taking the piss with someone. To have that ease. In fact, we're getting on so well that I dare joke about Damian.

"I heard you've stolen my date for the Ceremony," I say, nudging her with my shoulder. It's been all around school that they're Linked now.

It's a misstep. The joke falls flat on its face on the pavement between us. I feel the happy spell get vanquished. In fact, Belle stops for a second, and it takes me a few steps to realize and turn back.

"Sorry. I was joking…"

"No, it's fine. I mean…I deserve it."

I tilt my head. "I thought you'd be thrilled to be going with Damian?"

Her face goes totally blank. I see a portcullis shutter down. Her arms cross. She won't make eye contact. My time's up. "Of course," she says, like she's reciting lines. "It's great. I'm so lucky to be going with him."

"Belle, seriously? Are you alright?"

But she's closed again. Gone. In fact, she says, "You know what? I'm really late for something…thank you for…bye…"

Then she's off, practically at a run, which she's able to do in those suitable shoes for Candid Day.

BELLE

I take the day off school for Mother's Procedure. She doesn't ask me to – she doesn't need to. Father can't know she's having it done, and she needs someone with her. She's manic as I eat my tiny breakfast, bouncing around the kitchen like a child excited to open birthday presents.

"I've not been allowed to eat since six last night," she says. "Not only am I going to look fresher, I'm going to lose Sin too. Two for one, eh? Isn't that wonderful?"

I nod and push the tasteless OatMix into my mouth where it cements up my throat.

"Be careful with the Fig Syrup," she says, as I pour more in. "There's more Sin in that than you realize."

I sigh and put the bottle down. I'd added two drops. Two. On top of the three whole drops I'd initially put in. We only go through about one bottle of the stuff every six months. I swear she never used to be this…much, did she?

We get a carriage there, as she won't be able to drive home, and Mother bounces both knees as we drive to the Empowerment Centre. "Oh I can't wait," she keeps saying, still brimming with excitable energy. "I've been putting this off for too long. We need to plan my new Looks once I'm healed up. Oh, we're here, we're here."

I've been to the Empowerment Centre many times before, escorting Mother to her many Injectable appointments. Yet it seems more daunting today, especially as we push the lift button to take us to the top floor, where all the Cutting is done. Several posters smile at me as we ride up, all Chosen Ones staring vacantly out at us, telling us how much the Empowerment Centre has changed their lives and built their confidence and saved their careers and made them better people. In the bottom left-hand corner of each is a small shot of them Before, when they were either Objectionable or Invisible, or both.

People see me again, one poster tells me. *They listen when I talk now. It's been incredible.*

A strong smell hits me when the lift door opens. A sterile itchy stench of iodine. Everywhere's painted white, and the receptionist desk is slick and sleek, but there's a different energy to this floor. A…desperation, maybe? Mother dashes over to announce her arrival and the receptionist raises one finger to tell her to wait while she finishes a call. I take her in, biting my lip nervously. The receptionist is clearly very Empowered, but almost to the point of looking like a Try Hard. Her lips are too puffy, her face too tight. I try to age her, but she looks like a haggard schoolgirl, if that makes any sense.

It's then that I start to worry about Mother.

"Thanks for waiting. Madame Gentle, you said? Ah yes,

you're all booked in. Welcome. Let's take you through to your Preparation Room where Dr Gill will talk you through the risk assessment. Is this your daughter?" She grins at me with her puffy fish lips, her skin straining over her tight cheeks.

"Yes, isn't she beautiful?" Mother hugs me.

"Stunning. Well, we won't need to see you for a few years. Lucky thing."

It isn't all luck, I think to myself, as we sit in the waiting room. *I do not sleep. I hardly eat. My whole body is tight and sore and tired and hungry and plucked and I'm so exhausted, but maybe it's worth it because of what you've just said.* I rub my eyes, and wish I could stop having thoughts like this. They're only adding to my exhaustion.

A Face Nurse comes to collect us and tells us what a wonderful day we are going to have together. She carries a clipboard and we weave in and out of more white corridors, studded with doors containing portholes. A lot of moaning sounds seem to be creeping through the cracks. We're taken to a little room with an imposing bed full of levers, pulleys and computers, and a little en-suite. It is very *hospitally,* I notice. Much more than the Injection floor, which feels more like an exclusive nightclub. I mean, downstairs even has a cocktail bar. But this room has the iodine smell, and a heart rate monitor, and a pair of paper knickers and a gown Mother's told to change into before they come back for her blood. Even with the slick brochure on the bed, *Welcome to the First Day of the Rest of Your Face*, with an evening menu to choose from, there's very much a vibe that Mother's going to be put to sleep, cut

148

open, bleed, bruise, need to heal… It's all quite gruesome. But she's not bothered.

"Oooh, a menu," she says, picking up the brochure. "I hope they have some low-Sin options. Especially if I can't do any Body Prayer while I recover."

She flicks through, reading the testimonials like they're a gripping novel, while I check out the en-suite – noticing the bars around the shower to grab, the giant stack of stickable pads to soak up seeping blood…

"Do you mind staying in there while I get changed?" Mother calls. "Cripes, these gowns are disgusting. I can't Go Under wearing these."

"Mother!"

"Don't worry. I'll put it on, but I'm wearing my silk gown over it. Honestly, what are they thinking with this colour?"

When I step back inside, I hate how she looks in a gown. She suddenly looks so frail and small, even with her silk tied around her. She's also had to put on a pair of gross thick compression stockings and it hits me then. My mother, who I love so dearly and need so very desperately, is about to have a Cutting. That's a big deal. That's a *huge* deal. If she was having a Cancer removed or something, we'd all be worried sick. Instead we're pretending this is some kind of extreme Spa Day.

Dr Gill knocks and Mother jerks, like she's expecting a hot date to arrive.

"Madge, you wonderful lady. Look at that silken gown. I love it." He hugs my mother like she's an old friend, which, in some ways, I guess she is. He's been doing her Injectables for years. He looks so much more surgeony today, in a green gown and plastic cap. "Now, shall we run through what you've decided? You added some Empowerments on after our previous consultation, didn't you?"

"What? Mother?" I ask.

She ignores me and simpers while Dr Gill starts drawing over Mother's face with a purple pen.

"So we're trimming your skin away here, here and here. Beautiful. All that Sag's going to tuck nicely behind your hairline. And your nose? We're thinning it, aren't we? Great suggestion. A thicker nose just ages a woman, don't you think? You've been able to get away with it until now, but it's a good thing you've come."

"Mother? You're getting a *Nose Shave?*"

"Shh, Belle, we're concentrating."

Dr Gill has given her a hand mirror and she's staring intently at her face, which now looks positively clown-like.

"And, as discussed, Madge, it does seem pointless doing a full Mask Graft if you're going to leave those eyebags like that. Immobilizer can only do so much, after all. So, if we make some incisions under the eyeballs here…" He draws on her again, sketching two smiling faces under her eyes. "…we can then lift the excess skin. Slightly longer healing time, but an overall better effect."

"Perfect. Thank you, Dr Gill. You're so generous."

"Don't you mention it. Right, I'll see you afterwards. The nurses will come collect you when it's time for your Sleep Injection."

We're left alone and I stare in horror at my mother. There's more ink on her face than skin. She widens her eyes that are about to be cut open. "Stop looking at me like that."

"Mother, this isn't what I thought…"

"The doctor is being very generous squeezing all this in. He only wants the best for me."

"But…how can we afford it?"

"He's given me a good deal, with a great payment plan. He cares, Belle. He wants us to be happy."

Does the doctor care about us? I never used to question it. But with my mother's whole face about to be sliced open, now I'm not so sure. He makes more Finance the more Procedures he performs.

"Don't look at me like that. If you can't be supportive, just leave."

"Mother!"

"Seriously, stop making me feel bad. It's okay for you, in your Just Right years. You have no idea the pressure I'm under. Well, just you wait. You'll see one day. Then who'll be judging?"

My eyes itch with tears. "Mother," I say again, almost in a whisper.

"*What?*"

"I'm…sorry."

Her face is still sour under all its ink. "You are?"

"I was just surprised, that's all. It's going to look amazing. *You* are going to look amazing."

My words are the calming balm she needs. She becomes my mother again, forgives me, and beckons me to her for a hug.

"Thanks, my darling. I know you understand. And you'll understand even more when your Just Right years are over."

"Isn't long now."

"No, they go so quickly."

I climb onto the bed with her, resting my head on her bony shoulder, and we curl up and choose her meals, discussing which ones have the best nutritional ratios. She gets stiffer and stiffer under me, her eyes flicking to the clock more often.

"Are you nervous?"

"No. Just excited."

Eventually the nurses arrive, with beaming smiles and an expensively friendly bedside manner. "We're ready for you," one says. "Are you ready to have your whole life transformed?"

"More than ready." Mother lifts her arm so they can apply numbing gel. I stumble off the bed, feeling out of place, and watch them set her body up for her big Sleep and Cut. She chatters away, asking them if any Stars have ever been in, making friends.

"Right, off I go. See you in a few hours, my Bella Donna." Mother waves her fingers as they wheel her out, like she's about to go for a mudbath.

"You're free to stay here," the nurse tells me, as she's pushing Mother through the door. "Or come back in three hours. She'll be coming around by then."

The door swings shut and leaves me alone with the stink of iodine and an empty hospital room to stare at. I feel dread inside every one of my bones but try to tell myself everything will be fine. Empowerment surgeries are everyday, commonplace, totally normal, expected even… Most women I pass on the street have been put to Sleep on this very floor and done what they needed to do. I have three precious hours without school or work. I should make the most of it.

It feels wrong revising on Mother's hospital bed, so I perch on the chair to one side, open my book and try to read the next few allocated chapters. I startle as I hear a trolley being pushed outside, and I get up and peer through the porthole. A slumped body is being wheeled past, bloodstains all down their gown, a nurse holding multiple bags of liquid attached to it. I gasp. The body looks practically dead, and the nurses treat it as such, slamming it through the next set of doors, feet first, with a loud clatter.

I can't concentrate on my book after that. I try but sigh a lot, wondering what Mother's going through, what her peeled-back face must look like. I can't stay in this room, so I follow signs to the refreshment area. Another lump of a body is wheeled past on the long walk there. This woman's almost conscious. She makes a deep, guttural moan, like her very essence is in pain. There are bandages across her breasts, more dried blood everywhere. "It hurts, it hurts so much," she groans.

"Shh, shh. You look stunning, Fiona. Stunning. Just wait until your husband sees."

"It hurts."

"Yes, yes, we know it hurts."

She twists her head around as I pass and our eyes lock. She widens them at me. She looks quite mad. I step closer to the wall.

153

"Help me," she croaks with a rasp.

I stop where I am and press myself against the wall, but the nurse laughs. "Ignore her. Sleep injections make them say the funniest things. Come on, Fiona, let's take you back to your room." She pushes the groaning body past but looks back to me. "Everything okay, lovely? Are you lost?"

"Just…refreshment area…where?"

"You're almost there, it's around the corner."

I order a cup of tea and watch it go cold, the steam rising and waning as I stare out the window, trying to ignore everyone around me. There are a few women around, waiting like me for their loved ones to be wheeled out, bloodied and bruised and Empowered. They seem jovial though. Two women discuss just how proud they are of their shared friend.

"*I can't wait to see what she looks like.*"

"*Me neither. I'm so glad she talked herself around.*"

"*Thank God. It was getting awkward, her being so Invisible. She really let herself go. Hopefully she'll be less resentful now.*"

I stand, leave my cold tea, and take the lift down to head outside. I clop around the precinct to try and clear my head but it's hard to walk far in my shoes. I resist a sudden urge to take them off and run barefoot, for as long and as far as I can. I start thinking of the Education, and how far away it is. The distance feels glorious, which makes no sense, as I'm so close to Having It All here.

My Device goes and I leap on it, expecting an update from

the nurse. But it's just Damian. A reminder of how great my life is going.

Damian: Missing you at school today. But still
thinking about you.

It accompanies a photo of him in the school bathroom with his hand down his pants. I know this should be funny. I know this is a compliment. But all I feel is my skin closing in on me, the feeling of choking in my own body. I'm trying to formulate a suitable breezy response, but can't stop myself typing out, *Leave me the fuck alone*, then erasing it, worrying it may accidentally send before I delete it. My Device goes again.

Damian: Sorry. I'm only winding you up. I really
am thinking about you though. Can't wait for the
Ceremony.

"Huh," I say out loud, not sure what to make of the U-turn. The softening of his crassness. I feel mildly safer for about two seconds until my Device goes a third time. This time a nurse.

Your mother's coming round.

Nothing prepares me for the state of Mother when I step into her room. There is no Mother really, just a pile of bandages where her face is supposed to be, with drainage needles sticking out of her, pumping out rank liquid into two hanging bags.

"She's sleeping it off," the nurse tells me. "But she'll wake soon."

"Did everything go okay?"

"Dr Gill will happily chat things through with you."

That's a strange answer. The nurse won't make eye contact. "I'll come and check on her soon. Take a seat. She was asking for you when she came round."

I'm left alone with the bloodied mess of my mother. Her eyes peek out from the bandages. They're closed, but I can already see giant angry bruises swelling up all around them. Her mouth and nostrils are the only other things visible, apart from the thick stitches peeking out along her hairline. She looks like some kind of Frankenstein monster. Her eyes start to flutter.

"Belle?" she murmurs, her voice the same low groan of the body I walked past earlier.

"Mother? I'm here. It's okay. I'm here. It's all over."

She lets out a throat rattle, her eyes still closed. She reaches out from her scratchy hospital blanket and starts pawing at her face.

"Mother, be careful."

"What are these? What are they? I don't like them."

"They're just draining your face. Mother, how are you feeling? Not too sore?"

With effort, she opens her eyes, which are red and dry, and finds my face. "Belle."

"It's me."

"My Belle."

She reaches over and clutches my hand, and I try not to look at the cannula poking out of her. "I'm here. It's all over."

"Am I Pretty again?"

"I'm sure, once you heal, you will be."

A peace finds her face, softens the parts of it not covered. "Good," she breathes out. "Good."

Her eyes flutter shut again and she finds sleep once more.

I'm two chapters further along when Mother wakes again, the hot air smelling sweet and rich as it comes through the hospital window.

"Look who's back with us," I say, in a very chirpy voice, putting my book to one side. "It's only the most beautiful woman I've ever seen."

"Who are you?" she asks, trying to sit up, looking positively distressed.

"Mother, it's me. Are you alright?"

"Why are you here? I don't like you. You're too Pretty. Go away. I hate you."

"Mother?"

"Everything hurts. It's so hot. What's going on? Why won't you leave me alone?"

"Mother? You're scaring me."

I leap up and lay my hand against the part of her forehead where I can find skin. I feel a deep heat radiate from her before she smacks me away.

"Mother, you're boiling."

"Get away from me. Don't touch me."

I step back, stabbing the panic button as I do. "It's okay, Mother. Help is coming. Not long now."

"I don't like you. Can't…hate it…*you*…" She lurches up in a frenzy and starts trying to pull out her cannula.

"Mother! Stop! You'll hurt yourself."

Then she's retching, her head falling forward as she vomits all down herself, all over her bandages. More and more of it coming. Thin and liquidy as she's not eaten all day.

"Help!" I scream. "Can somebody please help!"

Mother's body starts shaking, the drains in her head vibrating violently. One dislodges. I scream again. Her eyes roll back into her head, her mouth froths with bubbles of spit and sick.

"Help," I scream helplessly until my vocal cords almost tear. "Help!"

Then my mother is still and all I can hear is the dull beep of her heart monitor crashing.

JONI

I find Belle folded in half on the steps of the Empowerment Centre. Her skin's touching the hot concrete in her tiny shorts and I wonder how she's not burned herself. Her shoes have been kicked to one side and, when I call her name, she looks up with no Mask left on her face. It's all cried off.

"You came," she croaks in a voice I've never heard before. "I didn't think you'd come."

"I didn't think I would either." I stare at my feet, which are swollen and red in my hot sandals. My big toenail is slightly yellow, which even I find unseemly. "Your mother, is she…"

"She's alive. Just… They need to keep her in."

"Wow. Phew. So, what happened?"

"She had a few more Empowerments than initially planned and her body is overwhelmed. It can happen sometimes, the doctor said. They think maybe there's an infection? Some people just don't take well to Cutting, he said. We didn't know she was vulnerable before, because she's never needed to be Cut until now." Belle raises her chin defiantly, like she's proud of this achievement.

"Okay. I'm glad she's alright."

I tap one of my feet, unsure what to do. It doesn't seem right to go sit next to her. I'm still not even sure why she asked me here. I just got this panicked, awful call from her where she could hardly breathe, begging me to come.

Belle's still babbling. "These reactions are rare, they say. Super rare. It basically never happens. Empowerment surgeries are really safe."

I bite my lip. "Until they're not," I say.

I expect her to fight me, but she nods, thoughtful. "Until they're not."

I keep tapping my foot, unsure what to say. I have a dim and dark thought that this happening is one of the best ways to Awaken her, then feel ashamed of myself for thinking it. Belle is Belle – bitchy and shallow – but she's still a human, and she looks so broken right now. I make myself try and see the human rather than the project.

"Is she going to, like, recover okay?" I ask.

She sighs and nods hesitantly. "They think so. She flatlined, so her body has gone through a lot. But they say it's mostly about rest now, and keeping the infection under control."

"Have you called your father?"

Belle's eyebrows draw up. "Hell no, why would I do that?"

"Because your mother's in hospital."

"He can't know. Honestly. She'd kill me if I told him."

"I think he needs to know. It's his wife."

She stands, dusting her legs off. "No. He can't. The Empowerment is supposed to be a secret. It will be a nightmare

160

if he finds out. He's on a long job anyway. She'll be fine by the time he gets back."

I know better than to press further. I've learned from working at the Centre that you don't push women to speak until they're ready. It's just never occurred to me Belle would be someone I'd need to use that training on. A few red flags flap in the breeze regarding the way she talks about her father. I get a tingle of a memory of how my mother used to have to hide all the work she did on her face. How Father would attack her if she didn't look perfect, but also attack her if he saw her doing anything to make herself look perfect. How she was supposed to just fulfil the Doctrine without making any visible effort, taking any time, or it costing any Finance. I tilt my head and take in Belle. Her daily Mask seems to cover up more than just her natural face.

She starts walking away, barefoot, and I dash after her, still not sure why she called me and not someone like Vanessa. I'm also not sure why I came.

"Where are you going?"

"I don't even know."

"I'll take you home, if you'd like? Make sure you get there okay?"

Belle pauses, her face unreadable. Then, without warning, she hugs me.

"Thank you," she whispers into my ear. "That would be wonderful."

* * *

I should be less surprised than I am by the drab exterior of Belle's house. I knew she lived near me, so couldn't be in the Nice End of town, but still, when she walks through her garden gate, still barefoot and beckoning for me to follow, I gawp at how...*not very nice* her home is. It's much the same as mine. Small. Ugly. A concrete block more than a house. But if the outside surprises me, the inside downright shocks me.

"Sorry it's a bit of a mess," Belle says, shoving her heels on top of a packed rack filled with every footwear imaginable. "We were in a rush this morning."

"It's...you have a lot of stuff."

"Do we? I guess we do."

There's clutter everywhere. It looks like many attempts have been made to tidy and contain it, but it's impossible to hide the sheer volume of Doctrine paraphernalia that this house contains. The coat rack's practically falling off the wall under so many different jackets, coats, shawls, scarves, hats... multiple different clothing options for every possible variation in weather and temperature. The sitting room's more like a Sinposium than a sitting room, the corners stuffed with Body Prayer mats, weights, Muscle Pulling blocks, belts, different training shoes for different functions.

"Do you want a drink or something?" Belle asks.

"Umm, sure."

I follow her into the kitchen, which is also piled with towers of stuff. I've never seen so many jars of Enhancers before. They line the clogged countertop, bottles upon bottles of special pills, honeys, powders and fluids. There's a mixer in the sink, covered in some dried-on super-concoction paste Belle must've had for breakfast that morning.

"Do you want a detox tea? We have loads of flavours." She yanks open a cupboard and has to catch two boxes that fall out. "We've got a cleansing one, or a calming one, or this Flat Tummy one acts like a magnet and attracts all the Sin in your stomach onto its molecular structure and stops you absorbing it and then it comes out in your urine. It doesn't taste great though."

"Total cons never do," I mutter.

"What was that?"

"Umm, do you have just normal tea?"

Her nose wrinkles. "Are you kidding?"

"What's wrong with normal tea?"

"The toxins. I don't even want to see the state of your thighs."

I roll my eyes, but do quietly worry about what drinking tea has apparently done to my thighs. This prickly moment reminds me of the sheer surreality of me being here, and it frustrates me that she can't be nice to me when I've come out to look after her. Is it worth it, trying to change this girl's mind?

"Belle? Why did you call me?" I ask as she pours water into a kettle. "You have lots of friends, like Vanessa and stuff. And, well, you don't like me."

"I don't *not* like you."

"Oh."

Her saying that releases a strange warmth in me, although it's hardly a compliment.

"I couldn't call anyone else. Mother will be too humiliated. She doesn't want anyone to know she's had a Mask Graft."

My head's still swimming from her saying *I don't not like you*. Does that mean she *does* like me? Or just doesn't hate me? Why do I even care? Why am I even here? Yet I stay and keep asking questions. "Why not?" I ask.

"Because she wants people to think she's a Natural Beauty, obviously."

"But all women who don't become Invisibles have Mask Grafts. That's literally the only way to stay visible. You can't, like, defy science. Defy time…ageing."

"Oh my God, there's *loads* you can do before Cutting. Loads."

"Yes, but *eventually* you have to get Cut. Why pretend this isn't a total requirement?"

I'm handed a cup of foul-smelling tea, and I suspect, if I swallow any, its molecular structure isn't going to do much except taste bad. I take a sip anyway and almost spit it out, whereas Belle perches on the clogged kitchen counter, sipping hers religiously like it's going to revive her from this day.

"I…well it isn't for everyone…a total requirement, I mean. *It's our choice.*"

I let out a "Ha".

"It is. Nobody forces anyone."

"Don't we?"

I can't take another sip of this dreadful drink. I put it carefully on some space I clear on the counter.

"It's like the Doctrine says, we're so lucky to live in this time. Women are free now. Free to do what we like to ourselves and our bodies. We should celebrate every choice a woman makes and…"

I lose it then. How can she spout this deluded parroting of the Doctrine considering what's just happened?

"Seriously, Belle, I know you're in shock, but this is actual rubbish. We all know that if your mother hadn't had this Cut, that has now almost killed her, she would've become an Invisible. That's not a true choice, that's a…oh, sorry. Shit."

I've made Belle cry. She puts her tea down and weeps into her hands, her shoulders jolting. I go over and pat her back, feeling guilty. Today really isn't the day to make any points. Why can't I help myself? Me coming down on her as heavy as the Doctrine is going to have the opposite effect to what I want.

"I really thought she was dead," Belle sobs. "I don't know what I'd do…she's all I have."

Another red flag that she doesn't seem to be able to trust her father.

"She's going to be okay."

"She might not. If the infection doesn't clear."

"I'm sure it will. She's being well looked after."

…*by the same people who did this to her.*

"I don't want Mother to die."

"She's going to be fine. It's all going to be alright."

I pat and shush her for ages until she finally calms down. Her face is a total mess when she eventually looks up. She's been crying so hard, her face has an actual rash. Her voice breaks on every word.

"And I'm stuck here alone. I'm…I'm…too scared to be alone

at home. So close to where the man attacked me…I can't…"
Belle starts shaking and her crying kicks in again. She's a
complete state. I can't leave her in this house like this. When
the inevitable solution descends into my brain, I almost push it
away. It's too strange. Too much. There's trying to Awaken the
girl that humiliated me, and then there's drawing a target on
my face and saying *I'd really like it if you practised your axe-
throwing on me*. And yet, somehow, weirdly, I shock myself
by saying… "You don't have to be alone, okay? Do you want to
come stay at my house? My mother is always happy to take
people in."

And I'm even more shocked when she looks up, relief all
over her face, her tears already stemmed, and says, "Are you
sure? That would be great."

Belle's room is even more of a surprise and I've finally figured
out the ball she drops to keep everything else so together. It's a
mess. Her room is foul. I almost laugh. Clothes and Mask
products litter the carpet. Her wardrobe vomits up its excess
clothing into piles on the floor. Her dressing table, where I
guess she applies her Mask each day, is chock-a-block with
bottles and contraptions that baffle me even more than the tea
with the special molecules.

"Let me just grab a few things," she says, picking her way
through the mess. "Are you sure it's okay if I come?"

"It's fine." I remember what day it is and hold up a finger,
a bit worried. "However, my mother is having an event at ours

166

tonight which is pretty hard to dodge. It's quite anti-Doctrine, and you may have to sit through it."

"I don't mind," Belle says, clearly too desperate to defend her beloved Doctrine. She starts emptying her dressing table into a bag. Apparently she will need everything there for a few nights' stay. We're going to have to hire a packhorse. "I just really can't be by myself."

It still strikes me as weird that she'd rather stay at my house than ring her father. As she adds clothes to her vast bag, I notice the pristine, designed corner of her room and smile to myself. This is the part of her bedroom I actually know, as it's the background for all her pictures on the Ranking.

I message Mother to give her a heads up.

Joni: Is it okay if Belle comes to stay for a few
days? Her mother is in hospital and she's too
scared to be home alone.

Mother must be home and setting up rather than at the Centre, because she replies right away.

Mother: Isn't that the girl who was awful to you?
I mean, the door's always open, you know that.
But why are we being nice to her?

Joni: I honestly don't know.

Mother: Well, she's welcome. Just be wary of

letting people into your life who have hurt you.

I'll see you both when you get here.

I know right away she's talking about Father and the letter. Mother's as subtle as a brick fired out of a cannon. She can't talk to me about it upfront, so she has to resort to some kind of code. But Father's letter is the last thing I want to think about right now – with the Prettiest Pretty in school currently packing to come stay at my house. The world is too surreal for me to take on any of it.

But as Belle finishes packing her things, Mother's words bury in.

She's right. Why am I allowing this to happen? I'm considering meeting my father, and I've essentially invited my bully to come live with me. Surely that's not healthy? Surely I should tell both of them to do one?

But Belle's face is so hopeful as she zips up her bag. She looks like an abandoned child who's being rescued, and I don't know how to say no to that face, especially with her Mask off.

"Okay, I'm ready, you ready?" she asks, lugging a bag onto her shoulders.

I gulp. "I'm ready."

BELLE

There is only one obvious conclusion to be made about today: I am clearly hallucinating. My OatMix must've got spiked at breakfast somehow. I pinch my skin, hoping I will wake up and discover it's this morning again, with Mother's Cut still to come, and I can talk her out of it and then she won't practically die in front of me... But no. This is my life. My mother's half dead, and I'm walking, Maskless, in broad daylight, towards Joni's house to stay with her.

Joni's house.

Surely I've been spiked and I'm on drugs?

Her home is only two roads away, which is just as well as my bags are so heavy I'm practically staggering. Joni's gone all quiet to my side, which isn't like her. She got a message just before we left and it seems to have freaked her out. I wonder how she reacted when I called? I still don't know why I called her. Is it the drugs I'm most certainly on? Or is it because, rather devastatingly, I realized I had literally no other options, even though I'm the most popular person in Class? As I lay crumpled on the stairs outside the Empowerment Centre, frantically looking through my Device for someone to contact, none of the names felt safe. Not even Vanessa's. They'd all judge Mother for having a Cut, and no doubt tell everyone. Weirdly, it was the most judgemental girl I knew who I could trust not to judge...*Joni*.

"We're here," she announces, stopping outside a house that looks pretty similar to mine. Concrete, grey, small. I wonder if it has the same inside layout. "Look, a warning. My mother's incapable of not being herself. I know you've been through a lot today, but she means well, alright? And she'll probably make you come to this thing tonight."

I think of all the many times I've crossed the street to avoid Joni's mother yelling at me through a loudspeaker in town, but beggars can't be choosers. "Honestly, it's lovely that she's letting me stay," I say, meaning it, because it is. "Though what's this *thing* you keep bringing up?"

For the first time since we left my house, Joni smiles. "You'll see."

The inside of their house is a surprise. It's a lot, *lot* tidier than mine. I expected it to be a mess, considering the state of Joni's mother, but it's clean and clear, and smells nice and looks quite...chic really.

"Mother, we're here," Joni calls, and I brace myself as I hear her approach.

"Girls, *Belle*, welcome." I've forgotten how jarring she is to look at. I almost step back as she comes over to hug me. I've never got this close to her before. I've always seen her from afar, making a fool out of herself. She really makes *no* effort.

Joni can just about get away with it as she's in her Just Right years, but wow, *wow*, is her mother a mess. I let her hug me but hold my breath. Her face…the lines…it's like they've been carved out of melting butter. Her skin sags around her jaw. Her eyes are buried in wrinkles and puffiness and she's not wearing *any* Mask products, so they look piggy and small. Her hair's that silver grey colour that made my mother scream me awake as a child. A whole head of it. Dead and wiry. She looks so old. I have this urge to strike her. To push her away so she doesn't touch me and contaminate me.

"It sounds like you've had quite the day." Her voice is like honey that relaxes me and changes my opinion instantly. "You can stay here as long as you need to, okay? We're happy to have you." She hugs me again, and already I don't want to flinch. Her voice is so calm, I feel so held. I have a fleeting thought of how I never feel like this with my own mother – soothed and nurtured. She's always so suffocating with her ambitions for me, always wants me to be the compliant Bella Donna. Then I feel sick for thinking such a thought. "I'm sorry for everything you've had to go through today," she says. "Now, your mother…I have a friend at the Centre. If you send me written permission on your Device, I can ensure she sends me updates as soon as she has them so you don't have to chase. Is that okay?"

Okay? It's the biggest relief ever. More of my bones melt. "That's amazing, thank you."

Joni watches us as we hug again. She's seen my initial distaste, I can tell. Nothing gets past that girl. I gulp in further shame and make a pact to be as respectful here as I can be.

171

No bitchy Belle. Not when I'm being shown such undeserved kindness.

"Right, food. You need food. You must still be in shock." Her mother wanders to the kitchen. She has the same unattractive lollop as her daughter.

"I'm fine, honestly," I call after her. If there's one good thing to come from today, it's that I've been too stressed to eat.

"Don't be ridiculous. You're eating. Look at the state of you. I can count your ribs. If you don't eat, you can't stay."

My mouth drops open as Joni shrugs at me. "She means it," she says, smiling. "Anyway, you won't be able to avoid eating later. The food's too good."

"What's this bloody mystery event?"

She smiles again. "You'll see."

And I wonder if I've made a mistake, coming to stay here.

Joni's mother feeds me four pieces of toast, loaded with scrambled egg and butter, and I must say, it's bliss. I tell myself it can't hurt if I've not eaten all day. And, boy, these eggs, the butter, how it seeps into the toast…heaven. I want to cry. I feel the protein hit my stomach, mending my aching muscles.

She watches me with a small smile, noticing every chew and swallow, and, without asking, gives me the second two pieces of toast. Her face is still distressing and yet there's something about how she's looking at me. Proud that I'm eating, watching the nourishment hit my exhausted body… I feel *mothered*. Then I remember the current state of my own mother and the eggs curdle in my stomach.

She takes my empty plate away. "Right, people aren't arriving for two hours, so that gives you time to settle into your room and have a rest. I'll check in with the Centre while you sleep."

"Thank you. Truly, thank you."

"Joni? Can you show Belle where she's sleeping? I've made the bed up."

Joni, who's only had two pieces of toast and was reading one of our set texts while I stuffed myself, puts it down and nods. "Yep. Sure. Do you need any help setting up?"

"None at all. Go prepare for that Scholarship interview. You've missed most of the afternoon."

I feel guilty that I've taken Joni away from her studies, sabotaging her preparation. But, as the eggs hit my bloodstream, I feel remarkably tired. Hit-by-a-sledgehammer exhausted and incapable of feeling difficult emotions. I sway when I stand, and almost trip up their stairs with my big bag of stuff.

"The spare room is pretty cramped," Joni explains as she pushes the door open to my temporary home. "But it's quiet and the bed's okay."

"Thank you." This is all so awkward and surreal. She points down the hall. "That's my room. I'm going to go work some before everyone arrives. Knock if you need anything." She points out the bathroom too, then she leaves me to it.

So this is where they keep all their crap. My room looks how I expected the whole house to look. A small single bed is made up in the corner, with a pillow cover and duvet set that doesn't match. The rest of the room's packed with old placards and posters, loudspeakers, rucksacks full of Christ-knows-what, bottles of water, boxes of badges and whistles and all sorts. I let out a "huh" noise and seep into the bed, climbing under the covers like the posters are monsters I need to hide from in my sleep. The painted slogans scream across the room.

FREE THE FACE.
WE AREN'T UGLY – THE DOCTRINE IS.

My fingers twitch with an urge to take a picture on my Device and send it to Vanessa. She'd find these hilarious. I can imagine her rebuke already.

"*I need freedom from the sight of your face.*"

I laugh at my imaginary piss-take, then the guilt rushes right back in. What the hell is wrong with me?

Sleep will help. I lean up and pull shut the flimsy curtains, which leaves orange wisps of sunbeams leaking in around the edges of the window. I lie down and try to release my body to unconsciousness. To give it the rest I know it needs. But whenever I close my eyes, all I can see is my mother's heartbeat flatlining on the screen. Tears bleed silently into the unfamiliar scent of this unfamiliar pillow until, eventually, I find peace.

My Device jolts me awake, trilling me upright, and it takes a while to find the off button as my body's not ready to be up yet. I must've only got twenty minutes or so, and the exhaustion has found my limbs and filled them with lead. The sun's still leaking around the curtains but I feel like I've woken in a different year – like a bear who's come out of hibernation too early. I long to lie back down but I only have an hour until all these mystery people arrive and I'm a total state. An hour's hardly going to be enough time to get ready as it is.

I find towels at the end of my bed and take one to the bathroom, turning on their shower, which isn't as good as ours. The water pressure is weak and spluttery, which Mother would change immediately. I lean my head away, reckoning I can get away with a volumized ponytail tonight rather than stripping it and starting from scratch. I scrub the smell of iodine and sickness and panicked sweat off my body, glad I brought my own wash as Joni's looks basic and pointless. Definitely not even nourishing. I do wonder how that girl copes. I wrap myself in the small towel and panic when I realize I left my Nourishment Cream at home. There's a bottle of gross-looking stuff in the bathroom cabinet, with some of it dried around the lid, but I slather it on regardless, then pad back to get ready. I have no idea what Look to go for.

Joni erupts into laughter when she sees me an hour later.

"What? What is it?"

She's still giggling. "Oh my. I just…didn't expect…wow. Tonight's going to be interesting."

I smooth down my cropped top. "What's wrong with my Look?"

She lets out another honk. "Nothing. It's just…er…the first time a Look has ever been to Sister Circle, that's all. Never mind. There's a first time for everything."

"*Sister Circle?*"

The doorbell goes downstairs, and I hear Joni's mother rush over to open the front door. The house smells wonderful, like it's been bathed in jasmine. Sounds of excited, friendly voices echo up as the guests are greeted. Whenever the door shuts, the bell goes again.

Joni grips my shoulder. "You're going to find tonight strange," she warns me. "But please keep an open mind, and please don't tell anyone at school about this. It's…a safe space. I'm trusting you to keep it that way." She lets go of my shoulder and I sort of miss her physical contact. Joni tilts her head, very serious. "I still don't get why you called me, and I reckon you're just as confused about why as I am. Which is okay. I think. But…well…look, this is me being kind to you. I don't ask for anything in return other than you protect tonight, and you protect the people here. It's only fair as I'm protecting the secrets that are important to you. But, if you don't think you can hold your tongue, then please call Vanessa and leave."

Woah, she's getting very stern all of a sudden. What the hell's about to happen downstairs? A sacrificial ceremony? Is everyone going to get naked? Oh no, I bet everyone gets naked. Getting naked is such an Invisible thing to do… But, annoyingly, Joni's reading me just right. It's like she knows I almost took photos of the spare room. I close my eyes for a second and ponder, yet again, why I'm such a terrible person sometimes. I always thought I was quite a nice person, as being nice is part of Having It All. The Doctrine demands we are as Pretty on the inside as on the out. But Joni has made me feel quite internally ugly since I've been forced to hang out with her.

"Sister Circle is safe with me," I say. I mean it. I want to mean it.

Joni grips my shoulder one last time, making it tingle. She believes me.

"Okay. Well come on then, *Miss Look*, let me introduce you to the sisters."

My mouth falls open when I enter Joni's living room. In the past two hours, it's been transformed into a cave-like, mythical, ethereal place of wonder. A giant cluster of candles sits on a large plate in the middle, emitting the gorgeous jasmine scent in big wafts. It's like an inside campfire. Around it, there's an array of comfy cushions, blankets and beanbags with women and girls already choosing their places. At the back stands a table laden with the most lovely looking buffet – foods chock-a-block with Sin, arranged on plates in circles, alongside an urn to make fruit teas.

Girls and women. Wow. I wasn't expecting both. But I'd say the split is about fifty-fifty. There's about ten here in all, chatting like they know each other very well, while Joni's mother flits around, offering cups of tea. She spots us traipsing down the stairs.

"Wow, look at you, Belle," she says, hugging me. She's changed into some floaty gross sack of a dress, but she smells comforting, like fresh laundry. "I hope you slept some? I rang my friend and your mother is stable and sleeping."

"Oh, wow, that's amazing."

"They say you can call for a full update tomorrow but no reason to worry tonight. And you're allowed to visit her right after school."

"I...I..." I'm so relieved I may collapse into a beanbag. "Thank you."

Joni's mother reaches out and squeezes my shoulder in the same caring way Joni does. "It's lovely to have you with us tonight," she says. "I know you've been through a lot today, but I do hope you'll find this really nourishing." Then she turns away and claps. "Right, sisters, it looks like we're all here. Shall we?"

Everyone arranges themselves around the candles, and Joni leads me to two spare cushions in the corner. I'm definitely the most overdressed person here in my skirt and crop top. And definitely the only one wearing a Mask. It's never been this way around and I feel stupid, wanting to cross my arms to cover my bare waist. All the Invisibles look much like Joni's mother – they are of varying ages and races but all are in matching states of disrepair. Almost all of them have the dreaded silver hair and they wear frumpy sacks that cling around their soft, sagging bodies. I've never been around so many Invisibles close up. It's quite startling. They look so...old. And then there's the younger Objectionables. Weirdly, Joni's the only one here from our school. I was expecting that strange fishy girl who follows her everywhere to come. The one Damian was so mean to. Has Joni kept her away to protect her from me? Am I really that dangerous? Maybe I am... Whatever the reason, I'm the one who stands out here.

"Welcome, welcome, everyone," Joni's mother says, with her honey-sweet voice again. "Oh, it's just so lovely to be here all together, isn't it? Bathed in light. Bonded by sisterhood." I raise my eyebrows. I've heard some woo-woo things said by Muscle-Pulling instructors before and it's always vaguely tolerable coming from instructors that are stunning and lithe. Yet, this sort of magical language seems improper coming out of an Invisible's mouth. Disgust writhes in my guts again. "Shall we all take some breaths together, as one?"

I find myself peeking as we take our deep breaths. I sneak a glance at Joni, expecting her to be mocking this, but her eyes have fluttered closed, her hand moving with her breath on her ribcage, her face soaked with candlelight. She seems at peace, uncynical. She looks almost beautiful and this strange tingling rolls through me. I close my eyes properly and attempt to join in.

"There, isn't that better? Now, you may have noticed we have a newcomer tonight." I prickle as everyone's eyes land on me. "Please welcome Belle, who's our guest for the evening. Belle, we hope you greet us with an open heart and mind."

"Yes, sure, of course."

"Belle, to explain a bit about this evening – I've been running Sister Circle for five years now. It aims to build bonds between the generations of women and girls, to pass on our knowledge, love, power and insight, so we are stronger united."

"Right. Okay."

"Sadly this 'free' society deliberately grooms young girls such as yourself to fear women older than you. To find us

179

disgusting, distasteful, boring, irrelevant…or Invisible, which I think is the word you use, right?"

It's not just the heat from the candles making me go red. Why is she focusing on me so much? Surely everyone uses the term "Invisible"?

"Do not blame yourself, Belle. There are strong forces at work, with a clear purpose. To prevent us from uniting and loving each other. To keep us scared, and docile, and filled with hate, and self-hate. We are weaker when we're turned against each other, and much stronger together – when wisdoms can be passed between generations. At Sister Circle, we pair younger girls with older women as mentors, to rebuild these essential bonds. It's truly magical. You'll see."

The whole circle smiles warmly at me, even though they've basically been told I think they're gross. They do not seem to mind my obvious initial judgements, which I'm trying very hard to hide from my face.

"Now, shall we start by all sharing a statement? Something to bring us together, and make us feel strong? The theme for tonight's circle is loss. About how we have to lose and let go of things in order to be free. How about we complete the following statement? *When I lost my Mask, I also lost my…* Let's acknowledge our grief, rather than pretend our way of life doesn't come with huge sacrifices. Or let's pay homage to the bad things we've let go of."

There are nods of assent, but I'm confused. We're gathering around a fire to play some kind of "finish the sentence" word game? I feel Joni's eyes on me. I glance over and her gaze is slightly aggressive. This circle is important to her, I realize. I am not to mock it. I am to learn. I feel myself get internally defensive, because I *am* willing to take this seriously. I really don't want to hurt Joni – she's helped me so much.

Her mother makes us all reach out and take the palms of the women either side of us. It's so awkward. I have to hold hands with some Invisible next to me, who grins to reveal a set of slightly-yellowing teeth that make me want to barf.

"Let's close our eyes and really listen to each other's stories. To feel them, to sit with them, to let them become part of our own."

Goodness gracious, this is intense. I try to close my eyes again, but the memory of my mother's heart crashing swarms before my eyes. I shake my head to dislodge it.

"I'll start," Joni's mother says. "And I'm going to start with a positive story, though we don't all have to do that. *When I lost my Mask, I also lost my chains.*"

I wiggle on my cushion, trying not to roll my eyes. Chains? Seriously?

She continues. "When I let go of the Mask, it was the first time I was truly free of the Doctrine. Compliance, insecurity, self-hatred, a drain on my resources – both emotionally and financially. I lost it all. It's like I shed my entire skin, a skin that had never fitted properly. It was the most liberated I've felt my whole life. However…" She gulps. "…I'm not going to pretend I didn't also lose things of actual value that I wish I still had. When I lost my Mask, I also lost my placing in our society. I lost acceptance. I lost my visibility. I lost the feeling of being desirable, of ever being loveable. I lost respect from people. People I thought were my friends. That was the most painful."

I can feel the Invisible nodding to my left. She murmurs in agreement.

"And that is why we fight. Why we're here. I believe we can change this world – make it one where you can give up your Mask and yet not have to pay such a huge cost."

More murmurs of assent. Someone shouts, "Hell yes!" There's laughter. A few cheers. I flutter my eyes open and see the whole circle is smiling with their faces bathed in gold. They look weirdly beautiful, lit up like this. They seem happy.

"So, that's me. Who's next? Speak whenever you feel moved to speak. And, in the meantime, let's sit in a peaceful shared silence."

Joni's on my right and her hand is so warm in mine, as we sit and wait for others to speak. I thought my palm would sweat but it hasn't. There's a cough as a sister signals she wants to speak. The group listens.

"When I lost my Mask," the woman starts. She sounds older, from her voice. Much older. A real elderly. "…I also lost my husband. Things were even worse back when we married, if you can believe it. He always told me what a Natural Beauty I was. He always told me I didn't need to Mask. He'd boast to his friends that he woke up to me always looking perfect. What he didn't know is that I spent most of our Linkship hiding my real face from him. I woke up before him in the mornings to apply my Mask and then pretended to be asleep. I had elaborate excuses to cover how I spent the Finance on Mask products and Empowerment treatments. I really loved him…but then…" I hear her gulp and Joni's hand squeezes mine. This woman's words are doing all sorts of things to me, and it's like Joni knows – my own mother's story seems to be being told in this room. "…it got harder to keep things up. After our children, I was so tired, and I felt like we'd been together so long that I was safe after giving him his children. I thought he loved me but…when I started dropping some Mask rituals, he got annoyed. He complained that I looked tired. When I dared gain some Sin, he poked it and demanded to know what it was. There was this anger in me. This grief at all the thousands of hours of my life I had lost to Masking. The rejection of knowing his love for me depended on this endless charade. And then… just like that, one day he found a New One. Decades of marriage done, because I'd shown him my real face."

I feel vaguely ill. I can't help but feel my own mother's destiny could be the same as this woman's. I start worrying about her again. Her poor face, her poor heart. How Father knows none of this is happening.

More stories are shared.

"When I lost my Mask, I also lost my job."

"When I lost my Mask, I also lost my friends."

Not all of them are sad, though.

One woman says, "When I lost my Mask, I also lost my terribly disappointing sex life and started to truly learn what pleasure my body was capable of having." Everyone cheers and whoops as this woman speaks about how she rediscovered her body. My ears are practically on stilts, as this is the first time

I've ever heard of sex outside the perimeters of the Doctrine, and I really want to hear more. We move onto the next speaker way too quickly, leaving me with many questions and more strange feelings in my stomach.

We go round and around the circle, with everyone sharing their stories of what they've given up in order to be here. I never could have imagined being in this cramped little house, with one of the most despised women in town, everyone breaking the Doctrine and wearing their ugly natural faces, and yet...I can't deny the way I feel in this circle. My shoulders relax and I feel a weird calm and belonging.

"Thank you so much for sharing," Joni's mother says after a final story. "It's so important we acknowledge these losses and truly have our pain felt. It reminds us of the lie we've been told, over and over, the lie that keeps us in shackles of our own making... *It's our choice*... How many times do we hear this part of the Doctrine chanted? But your stories, what they show us is *there is no choice*. Not really. Because if we don't follow the Doctrine, there are significant consequences. We are denied love. We are denied work. We are denied friendship. We are denied respect. We are denied safety. We are denied visibility. It's not a choice and we must remind ourselves of that."

This is when my hands do start sweating, very embarrassingly. I break the circle, whisper an apology, and wipe them on my skirt. It's so uncomfortable sitting on the floor in it. I get a flash of Joni pushing me over the fence – moments from acute danger – because I couldn't climb over.

"*These clothes, these shoes. They're deliberate, to make you weak.*"

Mother felt she didn't have a choice. And today, her heart stopped beating. Only for a moment, but it could've been for ever. And yet...I don't...can't... My brain starts fizzing and I need to breathe, need to get out of these clothes...they are too tight, my head hurts, I want to cry but it will ruin my Mask. The Mask that nobody else here is wearing...and...

"I'm so sorry, I need a second," I whisper to Joni.

I stumble up and I run to the bathroom.

JONI

It's quite wonderful watching someone slowly Awaken, especially when it's the Prettiest girl in school. Belle is quite literally the Doctrine, and yet, half a Sister Circle later, she's not wearing her Mask any more and is making best friends with Destiny – one of our most bold and beloved "Invisibles".

I was worried for a while there that she'd stormed out. Mother certainly didn't hold back, considering the risk of Belle's presence tonight. But she's not rung the Protection Agency yet, and she's laughing, actually laughing, as she paints Destiny's face.

I look over at Belle, delicate paintbrush in her manicured hand, leaning in with a smile as she adds glitter to two lines between Destiny's eyes. The paint looks particularly striking against her darker skin, and I have a mad thought about what it would be like to have Vanessa here too. What would she make of this type of Transformation game with Belle?

"And where did you get these ones?" Belle asks Destiny, filling them in delicately with the golden face paints we bought.

Destiny wiggles her eyebrows, almost jogging Belle's handiwork. "Oh these? These are my anger lines. These might be my favourite actually. These lines represent all the times over the years where my body knew I deserved better than what I was getting. These lines are my self-respect radar. Whenever I'm angry, I feel my *most* powerful, because it's the emotion that creeps up on you when you know you're being swindled. It takes a lot of self-worth to be angry. And it takes a lot of bravery to be angry when you look like me. These lines are my pride and joy."

Belle's eyes widen, and, even I, who have built up a tolerance to Destiny's wisdom over the years, feel a bit tearful. "They're beautiful," Belle says quietly, dabbing at them to give a finishing touch. "Truly." And when Belle says that, I know we are safe. Maybe I didn't need to lie to Darnell, Sita and Hannah, and tell them tonight was cancelled after all? I'd fibbed to protect all of them – my friends from Belle's judgement, Belle from Darnell's snooping. But Belle's actually behaving – acting almost trustworthy.

Mother snaps me away from my spying. "Umm, Joni? Aren't you going to do my laughter lines?"

"Oh, sorry, Mother, I was…"

She follows my gaze and grins. "You can always count on Destiny."

I must say, tonight's activity is inspired. After a rather heavy opening round, Mother has spun the night on its head, saying we have to focus on how all loss comes with gains. She's paired the younger sisters with the older ones, and the task is to use tiny paintbrushes and golden paint to highlight the lines on the older women's faces.

"Let's celebrate these apparent abominations," Mother said. "Let's see them as beauty instead of a failure. Every line we have is a life lived and wisdom gained. Make no mistake – it's entirely deliberate that the Doctrine declares us disgusting and Invisible when we feel our most educated, knowledgeable, proud and angry. They fear what older woman have learned and what we know, so they make the visuals of our life's experience an object of disgust."

Everyone's golden faces are coming along beautifully, and even though it looks bizarre, it's also wonderful. I just love seeing the Elders' faces looking like this, covered in glitter that falls into the grooves of their skin, showing the intricate patterns of a face that has lived and laughed, fought and learned, and been lucky enough to *get* to this age. My mind flits to Belle's mother and how, if today had gone worse, she never would've had the privilege to wrinkle like a peach in the sun. I turn back to Mother and dab my brush in more paint.

"Okay, here come your laughter lines. Talk me through how you got them please."

Mother smiles. "Well, there's all those back-to-back shifts at the Centre, where we all get slightly delirious from exhaustion and everything ends up being hilarious."

Her smile's contagious as I dab glitter into the grooves around her eyes. "I definitely know what you're talking about."

"And of course so many of them come from raising you. You were so funny as a baby, Joni. Whenever I turned my back, you were doing something absurd. Like shoving a carrot up your nose, cutting off your own hair, or wiping Mask product onto the floor and then drawing pictures in the cream."

"I can only apologize."

"Never. Raising you is the best thing I've ever done."

We share our first bonding moment since that letter landed on our mat. We hold our smiles as we tune into the room around us, the tales being told, the stories being passed down. I wish I could bottle the energy the Sister Circles create and put it into a sprayer and douse everyone at school. Belle's still laughing at something Destiny's just shared. A wide, open laugh where her whole face scrunches up and I swear she looks prettier like this. Raw, open, unguarded. "I'm starving," I hear her say, and the two of them stand up mid-Transformation and make their way to the buffet. Belle piles her plate high and seemingly eats with abandon as they return to painting Destiny's face. I've never seen Belle eat until today.

I turn back to Mother, aware that I was staring, and see Mother has been watching me watch Belle with an almost-knowing smile. I turn red and load my brush with more gold. "Right, Mother. Now, hold still…" I carefully trace the creases between her nose and top lip and fill out the feathery branches that stem off them. It's like a tree's growing from her mouth. Mother holds still until her face is in full bloom.

"So, these lines, tell me the story of these ones."

She leans back from the paintbrush. "These ones? They aren't so happy, Joni, I'm afraid. These are the lines etched into my face from worry about what your father was going to do next."

"Oh." My brush freezes in my hand. We're going there then. Right here, with everyone around us.

"These lines are from when I was too scared to sleep. From the times I had to hold in my sobs until I took you on a walk, hiding us under a willow tree so I could cry without anyone seeing. These are the lines he found so repulsive, saying I'd let myself go…"

"I know," I say quietly. "I remember."

She meets my eyes. "I can't believe you're even *thinking* of meeting him, Joni." Her eyes fill with tears. "It's painful. When you know the stories. You lived them with me."

"I know."

"And yet?"

I can't look at her any longer. I push my brush into the paint and swirl it around, swilling some over the edges, which slides like golden teardrops down the side of the pot. "I haven't decided anything yet," I say. "I know he's a monster. But he's also…my father. And he wants to see me again after abandoning me. It's…I don't understand how I feel."

"I'm sorry he's put you in this position."

"I'm sorry too."

Though part of me isn't sorry. Parts of me miss him, even though I hate him. It hurt so much to know I was so easily abandonable and forgettable. That I must've meant so little to him he was able to leave for a decade. But his letter shows he hasn't forgotten. That he's been thinking of me all this time. That I mean something. That I'm still his daughter. And I'm so relieved by that, wrong as it is.

Mother plasters a smile to her face, almost like it's a Mask, and gets out her loud voice.

"Right, ladies. Let's see how gorgeous you all look. Can the younger sisters present their works of art to the rest of us, and tell us of the stories you've learned? And make sure everyone eats. I don't want to be left with food. I'll find it positively insulting."

And so the evening concludes with an array of decorated women presented to the circle. It is, quite simply, glorious. I look over at Belle, who's holding Destiny's withering arm and laughing at something she's whispered to her. Are we breaking through to Belle? Have we? *Wow*, with Belle on our side, how many more people could we set free? I think of Belle's perfectly healthy mother. How today, a supposed *doctor* was willing to cut into the healthy tissue of a healthy body and hack away that healthy tissue and inflict pain…and yet *dares* to call themselves a *doctor*. Today Belle's mother could've died, and yet, this evening, numerous other women will be missing dinner, stopping their drinking at seven p.m., preparing themselves for their own Empowerment surgery tomorrow. And the next day, and the next. A never-ending conveyor belt of healthy bodies willingly ready to be sliced up and cut to size, all in the name of Empowerment. It makes me so sick. I want to scream. I want everyone around me to wake up. But I'm only a seventeen-year-old Objectionable. What can I do? Unless I get this Scholarship, I'll be stuck in this town and with this anger, and with very limited resources to change any of it.

Belle laughs with Destiny again and I can't not look over.

She's never looked prettier than she does tonight. I've never seen her so soft and relaxed. How do I compete against this girl? I want her to join my cause…and yet, she's the one standing between me and my path to real change. Plus, she's shown time and time again that she's willing to throw me under several buses to get what *she* wants and needs out of life. Even tonight, I know I'm being used somewhat, because she has nowhere else to go.

She catches me looking and smiles, the candlelight making her eyes wide and dewy.

"Thank you," she mouths, with what I can only describe as true sincerity.

"You're welcome," I mouth back.

But I'm not sure if she is…

BELLE

Okay, so it's an actual nightmare getting ready for school in this house. How do they live like this? There isn't one Halo! Not one. And I forgot to bring mine. Thank God it's another sunny day. I cannot imagine what my Mask would look like if I'd had to do it under one of their pathetic halogen bulbs.

"It's still the middle of the night," Joni grumbles, as she waits outside the bathroom which I've been locked in for the last hour – opening the window as far as I can to try and apply my Mask by natural light. "What the hell are you doing up so early? Oh my God, you've got your Mask on already?" she says as I emerge.

"It's seven," I say. "This is a restful morning for me. I haven't even done Body Prayer."

She glances me up and down and pulls a pretend disgusted face. "Jeez, you can really tell. I didn't know it was possible to gain so much weight in twenty-four hours, but you've managed it."

"Shut up." I know she's winding me up, but it works. I'm panicking at how much I let myself go last night. I don't think I've ever eaten like that. It was like I drank a magic punch and

193

fell into a different universe or something. I've never slept so well, despite being delirious with worry about Mother. With a full stomach and a warm heart and this strange feeling of safety and belonging…I melted into my unfamiliar pillow. But I jerked awake this morning, feeling like I was going to be sick, remembering everything that happened with Mother…and I now feel an urgent need to be Pretty again, in control again, Belle again.

Joni gestures to the bathroom. "Am I allowed in? Or do you need to perform some kind of head-to-toe body skin scrape?"

I step to one side. "I'm done. I need to do my hair, but I'll do that in my room."

She peers at my hair and I put my hand to it, self-consciously. It's still wet from the stripping and hangs in drabs around my face. Nobody but Mother has ever seen my hair in its natural state before.

"Well I'm going to have a shower, and then, you know what? I'm going to wash my face with a bit of soap, and that's it."

She laughs when she sees my shudder, thinking I've done it as a joke.

"Is my skin that bad?" she asks.

To be honest, her skin really isn't. Which is a miracle if she only uses soap. She has a small blemish on her chin, but then again, so do I…and my skin regime takes at least half an hour, twice a day, and costs a fortune.

"It's…fine."

"Almost like it's a healthy organ that's entirely capable of looking after itself."

She shrugs, then pads into the bathroom and closes the door behind her.

I fight with my hair in the tiny guest bedroom mirror. The end result is fluffier than I wanted. I try to put together a Look, but all my clothes are crumpled from my squished bag, and I don't want to wear anything too tight after all of last night's Sin. I attempt to take some images for the Ranking, but without a Halo they all come out terrible. I flinch when I see my image on the Device. I look drawn and tired, despite my sleep, but simultaneously puffy and flabby and ergh. My Device flashes and I pick it up, hoping for an update from the Centre. They don't take calls until nine a.m., but maybe they'll tell me Mother's ready to be picked up.

Vanessa: Where have you gone? You weren't at school. You've not been on the Ranking for 24 hours. Are you dead?

I'd totally forgotten about everyone at school. I never fall off the Ranking like this. It's important to upload daily and get consistent Validation. If I don't, I could quickly become irrelevant. Totally foolish of me with the Ceremony coming up in only a month. What are people going to think, and… Yikes…Joni. How am I going to explain *Joni*? She's an Objectionable, yet I'm living at her house? If people see us walk in together, I'm going to get annihilated. I've hardly thought of an excuse to protect Mother, let alone myself.

Belle: Sorry. Got a sick bug. Think I'm better to
come in today though.

Vanessa: Lucky! The Sin always drops right off
with those. Come in and give it to me. I'm
freaking out about the Ceremony and fitting into
my dress.

My stomach's reknotted itself by the time I head downstairs
tentatively for breakfast.

"Belle, how did you sleep? We've got eggs again." Joni's
mother greets me, and in the bright light of day her face is
gross again. Her deep creases, her sagging neck. They're no
longer painted with gold and glowing from candlelight.

"Oh, yes. I slept great. Umm. I'm not hungry though,
thanks."

"Ridiculous. You've got to eat something."

"I'm alright."

"You're not leaving the house until you've had at least one
slice of toast."

She stares at me like she really means it and I get a rush of
hate for her. This gross woman trying to make me as flabby and
foul as she is. But I'm staying in her home, so I munch on some
dry toast that turns to sludge in my stomach. I almost cough it
back up.

She calls up the stairs, "Joni, you're going to be late," just as
Joni arrives. She's also stripped her hair, which is a miracle, but
she hasn't bothered drying it properly. It hangs either side of

her Maskless face, and she's wearing a baggy pair of dungarees.

"Any update on your mother?" she asks me, piling her toast with eggs from the pan, without even measuring how much she's taking. Just dollop dollop dollop, like it's nothing.

I struggle to take another bite of toast. "Not yet. I can ring at nine."

I watch Joni chew and I no longer want to be close to this strange family, no matter how kind they've been. I can't handle the association. What will Vanessa say? The other Pretties? Damian? These friends that I was too scared to call yesterday in a crisis – I'm now worrying what they think of me more than the family who is supporting me. I know it's totally fucked, but the panic in my throat cannot be ignored.

"Thanks for taking me in again," I say. My gratitude sounds hollow. Joni's mother may not notice it, but Joni does. I see her eye me over her eggs and I know then that she knows. She knows I'm scared of us going into school together. Breakfast finishes in a heavy silence. Then our bags are packed and we're out the door, walking like we're friends or something.

"Christ, you're slow," Joni complains. "I'd hoped, after last night, you'd ditch the stupid shoes."

I get another stab of anger. Yes, it was lovely of her to take me in, but is it really fair to be using my lowest moment to recruit me to her underground cult?

I deliberately slow my pace, a plan forming. "You don't have to walk with me if I'm slowing you down." I feel I've said it innocently enough, but nothing gets past this girl. She stops, and I clop to a halt next to her.

"Look, Belle, if you want to pretend you're not staying at my house, I don't mind," she says, rubbing her eyes. "You're going through enough as it is without having to declare our acquaintance to your bunch of judgemental, terrible friends."

"I…" Shame and relief tumbles in at the same time.

She holds up her hands. "I mean, it would be nice if you didn't torture me at school today, what with me literally giving you somewhere to live and all. But I get you have your limits…"

"No, Joni. I don't…"

"It's okay. I don't care. I feel sorry for you, if anything. Look, I'll make this easy. You're too slow to walk with anyway."

She strides off, just like I hoped she would, but now it feels terrible. "Let me know how your mother is getting on," she shoots over her shoulder. Again, showing kindness when I'm being my most awful.

What a terrible day it's turning out to be. Not only am I freaking out about Mother's health, I'm failing at being Pretty. I find Vanessa in the recess room and she shrieks like I've been away at war. She tries to run over to hug me in her insane shoes.

"Belle, I've missed you. You poor sick thing. You still don't look right, bless you. So pale."

Pale? She may as well tell me I'm an Objectionable. I want to go back to my house with all its Masking equipment and proper mirrors and lighting. Joni's house just isn't up to scratch. But the thought of being alone makes me feel even sicker.

"Hey, Nessie. Yes, I still feel a bit rough."

"Damian was talking about you all day yesterday," she says, linking my arm and dragging me over to our spot. We pass Joni and her drippy pals, who are all reading in the corner like a bunch of losers. She doesn't even raise her head as I pass, which should be a good thing but feels like a stinging rejection.

"What?"

"He's so into you, especially now you guys are Linked for the Ceremony. He kept asking if I knew where you were."

"I'm surprised he didn't send me a million images of his penis to be honest."

"Well, he *was* missing you. But the boys were busy yesterday." She lowers her voice to a conspiratorial whisper. "Did you see the pictures of Carrie on the Ranking?"

"What? No?"

Carrie was one of the chief Try Hards, with elbows as sharp as her big jaw (thus her Try Hard status). She generally hung around us like a smell we couldn't air out. She was annoying, but harmless.

"Oh my God, it's been so intense. So, anyway, you know the party she threw over the weekend? The one she kept asking us to come to? Well the boys decided to go for a laugh, and she got way too excited and ended up drinking too much, chucking herself at boys like James. She even asked Damian if he'd go to the Ceremony with her. Can you imagine?" Vanessa shakes her head, almost in disbelief, while I try to remember more about Carrie. She's in some of my classes and I sit away from her as she's quite obsessed with me, constantly complimenting me on my Looks and asking me what products I use. She spams my Ranking a lot with gushing praise.

"I can imagine actually," I say. "She's…er…quite determined."

"I know. Such a shame about her jaw. I think she could be quite Pretty otherwise. Anyway, she ends up passing out upstairs, and…well…look at this." Vanessa takes me into a corner and gets out her Device. She opens the Ranking, clicks onto Damian's profile, and there, uploaded for all to see, is a shoot they've done with Carrie's unconscious body. I initially grin, as the first few shots are relatively harmless. In the first, they've just put bunny ears over her head, then in the second, somebody has drawn on a fake moustache. "Keep going," Vanessa says. Her voice is questioning, like she's waiting to see my reaction before she reveals how she feels about this. "The boys were going mad for this yesterday. It's all anyone can talk about." In the third photo, they've added the words *Try Hard* to her forehead, and I wince at the bluntness of it. Then, in the fourth, my hand shakes a bit. "Are they…pulling her clothes down?"

"Yeah. See? They've written *Try Harder* across her stomach."

"Woah, okay."

"I know. It's a lot…and then this."

I gasp at the final image. James is posing with his hand openly up her skirt, giving a thumbs up with his free hand as he mimes touching her. Or maybe he's touching her for real. It's hard to tell.

"Oh my."

"I know, right?"

"Umm."

Vanessa clicks off the images and I can tell they've upset her a little, though she's pretending they haven't.

"Ben says she's going to make a killing as a Smut actress some day, if she can get some Empowerment on her chest. Ben always says his favourite type of Smut is *They Had It Coming*."

"That's a genre?" My mind can hardly keep up with all the awful incoming information.

"Yeah. Jeez, I forget how Vanilla you are. It's, like, one of the top categories. Alongside *Before They're Legal*. Ben says this is a wonderful debut. The boys couldn't leave her alone yesterday. They whistled when she came in. Most attention that girl's ever gotten."

I…I…why am I finding this so hard to digest? It's not so out of the ordinary, and yet I feel totally sick. The Doctrine makes it very clear that if a girl gets too Intoxicated, that's a clear invitation to receive this sort of attention. I'd previously have rolled my eyes, thinking Carrie planned the whole thing out. But it all feels off today. Maybe it's just the stress of Mother?

"Don't you feel a bit sorry for her?" I find myself saying.

Vanessa widens her eyes. "What?"

"I mean…it must be a lot…to find all of this has been done while you're asleep."

She's quiet for a moment, then Ben strides into the recess room, chest puffed out, waving as he sees us. Pure adoration flushes through Vanessa's face followed by an instant conflict. Her eyebrows draw down as I watch her struggling with how she really feels about Carrie versus the part her Linked one played in the drama.

"Nessie!" he calls over. "Get your hot ass over here now."

She blushes and puts her Device back in her tight denim pockets. "Carrie's not stupid, she knows the Rules." Her voice has the same robotic quality I've often found myself speaking in, especially when I'm trying to defend myself to Joni. "Ben says she did it on purpose. It's quite clever really. I mean, nobody's ever even *thought* about her until yesterday."

"I…guess…"

She nudges me with her shoulder. "It's alright for us. We get attention wherever we go. But some of the less fortunates have to be more inventive. I mean, you don't want to be Invisible in your Just Right years. This is probably the best it will ever get for Carrie."

"I suppose so."

And she's right. I know Vanessa is right. Carrie should be happy with the attention. It's all she's ever wanted and yearned for.

And yet, I can't help but notice Carrie isn't in my classes later.

The day continues to be ghastly. I ring the Centre the first chance I get, and manage to get through to Mother's nurse.

"Is she okay?" I clutch my Device to my ear like I'm trying to embed it into my brain.

"Oh, Belle. I'm afraid things haven't improved quite yet."

"What?"

"It's nothing too serious. She's just, as suspected, developed an infection around the stitches. We're pumping her with Antis but she's going to be here a while longer."

"Is everything going to be alright?"

"Oh, sure, eventually. She's very worried about the healing, of course, but we've been discussing how we can Tweak any issues with the results of the Empowerment Procedure."

"I don't mean just alright with her face! Is *she* going to be okay? Like, is she healthy?"

"We'll keep an eye on her, don't worry. Look, this happens, Belle. All Empowerments come with risk. It's just nobody thinks the risk will happen to them." She lists this off with an almost-bored voice.

"Can I visit? Later today?"

"Yes, of course. She may be a bit out of it. Her body has been through a lot." *Because you've put it through a lot,* I think. "But she's been asking for you."

My heart grows thick and heavy in my chest. "She has?"

"Yes. I'll tell her you're coming. It will cheer her up."

I lean against a wall when I hang up, hardly able to take any of it in. An infection. I have no idea what that means, other than it doesn't sound good. My Device goes – a helpful distraction from all the scream-crying I want to do.

Joni: Hey, how did it go calling the Centre?
Is your mother okay? Xxx

I look up and over at Joni in her Objectionable Corner and as our eyes catch one another's, she tips her head in subtle concern. Such a small movement that her little band of friends don't notice.

I fire a message back.

Belle: She's got an infection. Doesn't look great.
They say she has to stay in a while.

Joni: I'm so sorry, Belle. That must be really scary.
You're welcome at ours as long as you need xx

I catch her eye again and feel a trickle of warmth run through me, then lower my gaze before anyone notices. I can't believe she's being so kind when I've blanked her all morning. I really do wish I could run away to some quiet, safe place somewhere and sort my head out. It's been like an exploded wasp's nest these last few weeks and I'm struggling to figure out what's up or down, wrong or right, dangerous or safe.

Speaking of dangerous, Damian really *has* changed since we Linked. He greets me at lunch with a smile and a gentlemanly nod, rather than his usual hug and grope.

"Belle, I hope you're feeling better," he asks, genuinely concerned as we make our way to our corner of the recess room.

"Much better, thank you."

"You don't look sick. You look beautiful, as usual." I wait for the inevitable dodgy comment, or for him to call me Vanilla, but he doesn't. He just adds, "I missed you at school yesterday."

I recollect Vanessa's story of what they were up to. "Really? You weren't busy on the Ranking?"

"Ahh, Vanessa told you about that." We arrive at our corner, where Vanessa and Ben are making out. Damian makes no comment, just steers me to sit down.

"Sounds like the whole school knows anyway."

He can't help but smile at himself. "It was very funny."

"Hilarious." I manage to make it sound vaguely authentic, and Damian smiles again. I'm not going to make things difficult. I may be feeling a bit glitchy right now, but I'm wise enough to keep the ship steady. We're so close to the Ceremony and everything I've worked towards. I can't let my brain fuzz ruin everything.

"Anyway, where are you all the time?" he asks. "You're, like, a very beautiful ghost that only haunts us every so often."

I'm starting to feel weak with hunger, after not eating much breakfast. I wonder if there's anything I could get from the cafeteria that won't be disgusting to consume publicly. Nothing that would stain my teeth, or make my breath smell, or bloat my stomach. I don't trust any foods to not do these things, so I resign myself to feeling hungry and manage another smile for Damian.

"I told you, I've just got this Scholarship prep, that's all."

"Pretty and smart. It's not fair, Belle."

"Hey, you're the same."

His face breaks into another smile and he scootches closer to me, almost romantically. Seriously, what *has* got into him? All my instincts distrust him, but maybe agreeing to go to the Ceremony has softened him? And he is very good-looking...

"No Scholarship for me though," he jokes.

"Surely you don't need one?"

"Yeah, but still…it seems unfair." He grins again. "But maybe I only feel like that because all your preparation means we get to hang out less."

"We've got the Ceremony in a month…we can hang out there."

"Indeed we can." Then he glances me up and down and he can't help himself. He licks his lips and the fear kicks right back in again. This is all a ruse, this romancing. We both know what I need to do after the Ceremony, what the Rules are. It's worse, almost, that he's trying to be all Prince Charming about it. "That reminds me," he says, returning his eyes to my face. "What colour is your Look? I want to make sure we complement each other."

Fear courses through my body. Picturing the Ceremony, picturing being with Damian afterwards. How he'll want to touch me the way they touch each other in Smut, how I'll have to pretend to like being touched like that. It's going to hurt, I have to accept that. The pain of losing your Vanilla status, especially, is seemingly an unavoidable part of the process. And yet, just like with Mother's face, I'm thinking, *But WHY does it have to hurt? Why does it have to happen at all?* I force myself to brazen it out, tapping my nose, turning on the sass.

"I'm not revealing my Look to you. What if you tell someone? It's highly classified information."

"You're going to have to tell me at some point. We're Linked. We have to coordinate."

I stand up and decide, screw it, I'm starving and I'm going

to go to the cafeteria and get something to eat.

"I promise I'll be worth the surprise," I say, throwing him a wink and attempting to saunter off. I get to the cafeteria and grab two bags of chips, before hiding in a toilet cubicle to eat them, stuffing them into my mouth like a deranged seagull, wondering what the hell's wrong with me.

JONI

Belle's eyes find mine across the recess room before they dart down again as she messages me on her Device. I wait with anticipation to see what she's going to write, hoping her mother is okay, while Darnell and the others digest the gossip of the day around me.

"I've tried calling Carrie," Darnell's telling Hannah, Sita and Jack. "We were close in Little School, before she got in with the Try Hards, so I thought she might pick up. But she didn't. I guess she still doesn't want to be associated with us, even after...this."

Jack scowls next to me. "It's disgusting," he says, puffing out his chest for us. "Damian and that. If there was any use to it, I'd call the Protection Agency. Someone needs to stand up to boys like him."

You're not standing up to them, though, I think to myself. *You just want points for saying someone should.*

The other three nod with righteousness, and I should join in really, so as to not raise suspicion about my dabblings with the enemy. The enemy I've openly invited to my house. I almost can't blame Jack for not doing anything – it really does feel quite pointless trying to speak truth against the power of Damian. That's why Awakening Belle would be so brilliant. All she'd need to do is sneer at the photos of Carrie, say, "That's disgusting," and unLink with Damian, to get the whole class thinking the situation is wrong, rather than funny.

My Device buzzes with an update and I check it in my lap, wincing when I see her mother isn't doing too well. Without thinking, I invite her to stay longer, and then watch her receive the message and the beauty of her face as relief sinks into it.

Belle: Thank you. That would be really great.

There's this weird energy in my stomach as I wait for her to look up at me again. Even just a glance to acknowledge the messages we're sending to each other. I'm not expecting a public declaration of friendship, but fleeting eye contact would make this all feel less odd. Less like I'm a dirty secret. But Damian joins her and I watch as she openly flirts with him, even seemingly laughs a little as I hear the name Carrie.

What the hell am I doing?

What is wrong with me that I'm happy to help someone who won't publicly acknowledge me? Someone who's laughing at the ruined life of a girl who did nothing but try hard to be accepted in an impossible society with impossible standards?

What's wrong with me that Belle can't be associated with me?

The poison of the Doctrine settles in my stomach – telling

me it's because I'm disgusting and fat and too loud and all wrong. I fight it inwardly, as the others discuss what they're going to eat for lunch.

See the Doctrine for what it is. Don't let Belle poison you. You can change her mind. You can change this world. Believe in yourself. You're not disgusting. You're powerful. You're brilliant. You're smart.

Finally, one small, dark thought that still brings me light.

And your father. Your father still wants to see you. You matter to him.

BELLE

The stench of iodine hits me as the lift doors open. I pause before I step out, as another unconscious woman's body is rolled past, attached to tubes and bleeping machines. Angry bleeding bandages cover her face as she's roughly pushed past by two nurses who treat her like a sack of potatoes.

You know what? I'm starting to think this place isn't very Empowering after all.

"Mother." I run over to her bedside. "Oh Mother, are you okay?"

She doesn't look it. Her face looks like she's been severely beaten, there are staples all round her hairline, and two giant tubes filled with pus run from her face. Mother blinks but doesn't say anything.

"She's very tired," the nurse tells me. "You can't stay for more than twenty minutes. She needs to rest."

"That's alright." I pick up the hand that isn't attached to a cannula and clasp it to my chest. It's boiling hot. Mother's face slumps in my direction.

"I'll leave you girls to it."

The door shuts and Mother's eyes struggle to focus beneath their border of bandages. I can see they're both bruised purple, and I think randomly of Joni's father and the things he did. I think of my own father, and how he'd recoil if he saw this rather than look after her.

"Belle? Is that you?" Her voice is pure croak. I have to lean forward to hear her properly.

"It's me, Mother. How are you? I've missed you."

"It hurts…"

"I know. I'm sorry."

"Infected."

"They told me. What terrible luck. I'm sorry."

I lean over and take in the seeping bandages. There's a smell of decay that the iodine stench doesn't quite cover and I recoil without meaning to. Sensing my disgust perhaps, Mother wakes up slightly. She lets out a groan of pain and struggles to push herself up on the bed.

"Take it easy."

She bats me away until she's mostly upright, then she lolls her head over and really takes me in.

"No need to worry about me. This…" She waves her cannula in the air. "This is nothing."

"Mother, your vitals crashed."

"Just a silly blip. Although, what if it happens again? What if I can't get any more Cuttings done?"

"Shh. Don't worry about that now. Just worry about getting better."

"I am better! I was never sick. This is just a hiccup, that's all.

I hope there's no scars. Oh, Belle, do you think it's going to scar? If your father sees…" Her hand goes to her infected wound and she dabs at it, wincing hard.

"Mother, stop."

"What does it look like? Does it look terrible? They won't let me look in the mirror yet."

"It will be fine. The important thing is you're safe."

"No. The important thing is will it scar?"

"Mother!" I grab her hand. "I thought you were going to die. They say you're going to be in the hospital for at least a week."

She won't make eye contact. She paws at her staples again. "Honestly, Belle, you're being so dramatic."

"Your vitals crashed. I was here. I watched them crash."

"Well, what do you want me to say? What choice did I have, Belle? To just sit around sagging until I become an Invisible, your father leaving me because I'm so gross? Nobody wanting to book me for Mask appointments because my face horrifies them? Losing my business? What the hell else was I supposed to do?"

She slumps against the pillows, exhausted by her outburst, scowling through her swelling. She tries to cross her arms but the tube gets tangled in her hair and I lean over, shushing her, as she thrashes to detangle it.

"I'm sorry," I whisper. "It's going to be okay, Mother. I'm here."

And I could be seven again, cross-legged on our bathroom floor, helping her colour in her hair. I want to reach over and stroke her face, but it's so swollen and bloody and stapled onto her skull. So I just stroke her arm, saying *shh*, trying to calm her down, and trying not to fall apart on the inside.

It was *her choice.*

That's what Mother says. That's what we all say. But what Mother has just said, in a surreal twist, is exactly what Joni keeps telling me.

Choice means nothing if you feel you have no other option than to choose what everyone chooses. Choice means nothing if there are significant consequences for not following the established path. Mother turns to face me, smiling weakly, her eyes watery with love. I know she's calm now. Maybe some drugs just dripped into the hand I'm holding, I don't know. Mother's always seemed so strong, so stunning, so... *Empowered.* But Mother's just revealed she believes she *needed* this Procedure, otherwise she'd lose love, lose her livelihood, and lose the ability to even be seen by people. Those are huge losses to contemplate. And what makes it more painful is that Mother isn't ill. She's not paranoid and delusional...

She's *right.*

I want to weep because Mother is right.

"Belle, my darling?"

Mother reaches out and tucks a strand of hair behind my ear.

"Yes?"

"What's going on with you? Your Look. Your Mask. What's going on with it today? I'm worried about you, honey."

"I've been busy worrying about you. It's been a bad day."

"You can't afford any bad days. Not with the Ceremony looming. Not ever. You know that. I thought I'd taught you better."

I hang my head, wanting to hide my atrocious face. Feeling guilty that I've made her worry like this, especially now. "I'm sorry. I won't let it happen again."

"It's your choice," she says, without any hint of irony, despite everything she just blurted out. "But I'll worry a lot less about you in here if I know you're going out and presenting your best Mask to the world. We don't want anyone to think anything is wrong."

"I know. I'm sorry. I'll go home and get my Mask sorted."

Except I can't go home because I'm too scared of being in an empty house.

Mother winces. "No. Use my bathroom and go sort it now. I'll rest while you do. That way nobody can see you walking home looking like this."

I sigh and stand, my legs hurting from where I've been squatting for so long.

"Of course."

She's asleep before I've even walked the two metres to the en-suite, her hand flopping onto her chest. I turn on the light, and a fan starts humming while my face is greeted by several mirrors. The Empowerment Centre certainly knows its clients. There are two adjustable Halos in here. I tip my Mask products into the sink and get to work.

JONI

I'm not sure it's doing me any good, having Belle stay here. I thought finally seeing behind the curtains would release me of something. I don't know what. Maybe suspicion? I guess part of me's always been worried Belle's Prettiness is totally innate. That maybe she doesn't have to work very hard to look so very good all the time. That the Mask isn't really a Mask at all. And, don't get me wrong, her natural face is a very strong starting point, but, wow… That girl really doesn't sleep. I should know. She's waking me up at five most mornings, flinging herself around downstairs in her Body Prayer. It's a full-time job, being Belle. I see that now. Her Mask application takes for ever, getting her hair perfect takes even more for ever, and she spends the rest of ever having to document it all for the Ranking. Her eyes are always twitching, scanning the room for the best light. I see her stop and examine her body whenever she passes our hallway mirror, frowning as she points a toe to make her tiny leg look slimmer or sucking in her stomach. She's even pulling me into it now. Yesterday, I actually let her convince me to take her Ranking photo in the garden before school and she shouted at me like a crazed dictator the whole way through.

"No-no-no, don't point the camera up. Oh my God, you're going to make my chin look massive. Don't you know anything?"

"Are fat chins a thing?"

"And you've cut off half my legs, Joni. Why haven't you put my legs in? I don't do all this Body Worship so you can cut my legs off."

"Everyone will see your legs in real life, at school."

"The Ranking is real life too, Joni."

I'm disappointed, because I really thought living here might rub off on her, but if anything, her Doctrine obsession is rubbing off on me. Relaxed Belle from Sister Circle vanished as suddenly as she arrived, and Queen Belle of the Ceremony is officially here to stay. Mother says to not bother her about it. "She's going through a lot," she whispered to me, when I was complaining about how long Belle takes in the shower. "She's probably just using Masking as her coping strategy. Be kind, Joni."

"I thought we were supposed to be fighting against all this?"

"We are. But there are times and places."

Anyway, as I was saying, Belle being here is messing with my head. Because even though I can see the hell she puts herself through, and even though I can see she's not happy… still…I can't deny she always looks *amazing*. Her Mask's always perfect. Her Look's always perfect. Her body matches basically all the Official Criteria. And it's hard, living with someone like that. Having her in such close proximity, in what's supposed to be my safe space. I see Belle glide past the hallway mirror, and then, when I have to lug after her, I can't help but compare my passing reflection with hers. My bare face reveals the hormonal blemishes I'm currently harvesting on my chin. My hair just hangs flat around my head. I would look ridiculous in any of Belle's clothes. My stomach would hang out, and I wouldn't even be able to get my legs into her trousers. I mean, I get it. It's not like Belle is comfortable in these clothes either. I see how carefully she has to arrange each limb, so she can sit in her Looks. I see her constantly sucking in her stomach. But… yeesh…she looks so annoyingly good while she does all this.

I can't help that I think this. I *know* I've been brainwashed. Mother exposed me to the truth of the Doctrine years ago. She opened my eyes to how all the women and girls were being pickled in the juices of the Doctrine's Rules and lies. She explained that, even when we have our Awakening, we've still been soaking in all that poisonous juice our whole lives, and therefore we will always be slightly…pickled…indoctrinated. But we can fight it, remain aware. So I up the ante in fighting against the pickle juice and focus on how my body *feels*, rather than how it looks. I focus on the positives of my freedom to counter Belle's triggering presence. I can sit how I like in my clothes and enjoy how my body isn't restricted. I even start a timer for how long Belle spends following the Doctrine, counting up the minutes and hours of her life she clocks up each day, and try to spend the same amount of time preparing for the Scholarship. But it's hard.

What makes it worse is that Belle still ignores me in school, which really hurts and is rude, to be honest. Each day of chatting to her over breakfast and sort of getting to know her and, annoyingly, quite liking her despite everything, but then being totally blanked later is taking its toll on my self-esteem. With that, alongside living with someone so much more attractive than I am, I'm feeling weakened and weary and gross and resentful, and it's not like my shift today at the Centre is doing anything to distract me from it all.

I'm on babysitting duty again, as all the mothers are having a talk about their career and Finance options. Mother brings in an expert every few months to let the women know what Failments they're entitled to, and what career and training options are open to them through the Centre's links. The women are in the main space, chairs scraped close to the front, listening intently and scribbling notes in the provided notepads. Whereas I'm in the back room, trying to keep seven children occupied for two hours.

The boys are okay. They've found the carriage mat and carriages, and are racing each other quite happily, being pretty self-sufficient despite the annoying *brmm* noises. But the four girls are in a collectively clingy mood, all of them hanging off me like jewellery and demanding we play the Ceremony again.

"But we played that the last time I was here," I protest, yanking my T-shirt up from where Dominique's tugged it down.

"And we want to play it again."

I sigh and collect the relevant On The Cusp Mask products and the matching dressing-up box. The girls act like I've

219

brought out a box of rubies – running over and staking their claims on their favourite pieces. There's a huge fight over who gets to wear the gold dress, resulting in one full-scale tantrum.

"Shh, it's okay. You can wear it next time," I say, crouching down to the screaming Delilah, who can hardly breathe she's sobbing so hard.

"But I won't win the Ceremony without it."

"It's just pretend," I remind her, but she's unconvinced, and I have to eventually lull her to peace with promises she can go first with the red lip enhancer.

Half an hour later, the girls are Masked to the max and ready for their fake Ceremony. It breaks my heart to see their pudgy soft faces smothered and clogged, but they are enraptured with themselves. Another fight breaks out over who's hogging the mirror. Now they're Masked, they're not really sure how the game progresses.

"What happens next?" Dominique asks.

"Yes, what do we do now?"

"I don't really know," I admit.

"What happened at your Ceremony?" Dominique demands.

"I've not had mine yet. Anyway, I'm not sure I'm going to go."

"What?" The four girls fall into a shocked hush. "Why not?"

I shrug. "I don't want to go," I say. I'd never been keen on going, and since Belle's prank it feels even less appealing, even if it is a Rite of Passage. Then I'm not sure why I say this next. "Although I have been Nominated," I tell them.

"You've been *Nominated?*"

They crowd around me like I've just announced I'm famous. Dominique even reaches out to touch me, like I'm a holy relic that can give her luck.

"Umm, yes," I say, thinking it will kill the mood if I explain I was only Nominated as an act of revenge. Dominique sees through it anyway.

"But you're Objectionable," she says. "You can't be Nominated if you're ugly."

I wiggle my eyebrows. "Well, maybe the Rules are changing."

Dominique crosses her arms. "They can't."

I see them study my face in a new way. You can physically see their confusion.

"If you can get Nominated, maybe I can Nominated?" Dominique says, hope lacing her voice. "Although Mother says I have too much melanin to ever win." Her face falls as quickly as it lit up.

Delilah joins in with the heart-breaking self-loathing. "My body is too filled with Sin to ever win," she says. "Well, that's what they tell me at school."

I pull a face. "You're only, how old, *nine*? How can you be worrying about Sin?"

She raises an eyebrow at me, almost like she's a sarcastic older aunty. "*Everyone* talks about Sin at school."

"I..." Nine years old. It shocks me. But then, when I remember my own Fledgling years, it was all kicking off at that age.

The littlest girl joins in. "I have Sin too. It's gross. But I'm going to get rid of it and then win the Ceremony when I grow up, because then my father will be proud."

"Me too," Delilah says.

She turns to Delilah. "Do you want to play Body Prayer together?"

I try to intervene. "You don't need to play Body Prayer!" I tell them. "Just play. Run around. It's the same thing."

But they're not listening. They are already shrugging off their fancy dresses, and Delilah starts teaching the youngest girl how to deep-squat to make sure the exercise really attacks the Sin. With all the kids depressingly occupied, I nudge open the door and lean against it, listening in on the speech. Carol is talking through some training opportunities that have worked for previous women at the Centre, for roles that are perfect for fitting around children. She lists off the most popular choices: Talon maintenance, Mask and Hair experts, Simple Empowerment Procedure training.

I feel a rising choking feeling in my throat. Everything Mother has taught me to fight for seems so unimaginable. So pointless. The Doctrine is too powerful. Look at Belle, living with us for two weeks and no change. I thought we could convince her there was another way. But what if living with me has just confirmed her prejudices that what we do isn't worth it? If I stay how I am, if I stay fighting, am I damning myself to a life of being ignored, overlooked, reviled, degraded and hated? I glance behind me and see the girls have all lined up and are comparing who has the fattest legs. My head hurts. I swear I was doing fine until Belle came into my life. I really am starting to feel that maybe I *am* Objectionable and deserve to be shunned. I know they're just children, but their clear judgement of my appearance still stings.

I close the door again and try to distract the kids from hating their young bodies. But their words about their own fathers haunt me. How they want to win the Ceremony and make their fathers proud, even though their fathers are the reasons they're stuck in this Centre. It shouldn't make sense, but it does. I totally understand them, because I can't help but think I *do* want to meet Father and I *do* want him to be proud. Despite everything he's done, I feel this deep urge for him to smile at me, to love me, to tell his friends about how well I'm doing. I want to be seen, acknowledged. By him…by Belle.

At the end of the week, I'm summoned during class and told to head to Ms Blanche's office. I walk the familiar route through the empty corridors, my head still an upturned beehive. Since Belle agreed to Link with Damian for the Ceremony, it's all around school that she'll finally give up her Vanilla status. Apparently he's been bragging to everyone that he gets to be the one who "breaks in Belle", whereas she seems weirdly oblivious. I notice he's being super nice to her rather than sleazy. Putting his arm gently around her in the recess room, laughing at her jokes, telling her she looks Pretty, rather than making his lewd comments. But word on the corridors is that he's going to "demolish" her. He's taking bets about whether or not she'll let him film it. Which isn't an uncommon thing for girls to agree to, although they always get shamed afterwards.

The Try Hards, especially, do it, hoping it will push them up the Ranking, and instead they are ridiculed and told they're now Objectionable because they have no mystery left.

Even though Belle and her Vanilla status is all anyone's talking about, she seems tucked away and unaware. She spends most days after school with her mother, before she comes back to ours – her Mask freshly applied to cover the obvious fact she's been crying.

"Is she healing okay?" I always ask.

Belle's face always goes tight. "There's going to be scarring, unfortunately. She may need some more Empowerment to conceal them."

I'm sympathetic, but that drains out of me when she still lets me walk ahead every day on our way in. I know I said it was okay. That I understood. But I guess I'd hoped she'd…I dunno…feel guilty. Feel grateful that we took her in. But of course not, this is Belle. I need to stop giving her the benefit of the doubt and start seeing her as the adversary she is. Who cares if Damian is going to demolish her? Isn't that her choice after all?

Here she is. Waiting outside Ms Blanche's office, having to tuck her tiny skirt under her thighs. "Hello," she says, as we're the only two here. It annoys me today more than other days. I'm bored of being a secret.

"Hi back."

"Do you know what this is about?"

"I'm assuming the Scholarship."

She rolls her eyes. "Yes, of course that. But what about it?"

"My guess is as good as yours."

I slouch down next to her and feel her eyes land on me. "Why do you always sit with your legs apart like that?" she asks, obviously also in a scratchy mood.

"It's called being comfortable. You should try it sometime."

"You look like a boy."

"Comfortable? Why, yes, they often are more comfortable than us."

She lets out a small laugh. "You never stop, do you?"

I gesture to how awkwardly she's sitting in today's Look. How she has to hold her posture completely right in order to not flash a body part she shouldn't. "And neither do you."

We glare at each other.

The door opens and Ms Blanche smiles at us with a smudged Lip Enhancer. "Girls, enter," she beams.

Belle pushes herself up and pulls all her clothes down, rearranging herself as she trots in. I stride after her and sit even more like a boy to make a point.

"Sorry for dragging you out of lessons but I'm stuck in training this afternoon and I want you both to have the weekend to prepare."

Belle and I share a look.

"The Education just released the interview dates for the Scholarship and they're close. Next week, in fact! They deliberately leave it until late to tell us."

"Next *week*?" Belle squeaks. "That's right before the Ceremony."

"Yes. On Wednesday. Not ideal timing but I'm sure you'll

be fine. We'll organize your travel and put your itineraries together. You go up on the Tuesday so you can see the place, meet some students and get a feel for it. Then, on Wednesday, you'll have your morning test and interviews. You should be home by Wednesday nightfall."

I almost stand up. Woah. This is it. This is it. *This is it.* My chance. My shot. Get out of this town. Get Educated. Get power. I want to tip Belle out of her chair onto the floor. I need this more than her. When I look over, I see she's watching me, and I feel another stab of annoyance.

Ms Blanche leans back and carries on smiling. "Now, it may feel a bit overwhelming, but hopefully we've prepared you as best we can. And at least you girls are going through this together. In fact, they've agreed to put you in the same dorm room."

Great. How do I know she's not going to glue me to the bed or something so I don't make the interview?

"So, girls. I hope that's okay. I have every confidence one of you is going to make our school proud."

Me. It needs to be me. I'm going to drown if I stay here. Whereas Belle thrives here. Belle was built for this place. It's so unfair she's trying to take this from me. She hardly knows why she's applying. Just some vague Doctrine nonsense about wanting to Have It All.

"Thank you, Ms Blanche," she says in her sugary voice. "We'll try to make you proud."

"Yes," I second, annoyed that she said it first.

We're dismissed with a jolly "Good luck", and spat back into the corridor. The school's still quiet and subdued, students busy in classes, the bell yet to ring.

"So..." Belle starts, which is hardly an inciting word, but it's all I need for my temper to erupt. I've spent two weeks protecting Belle in exchange for being totally publicly shunned, and she still wants to take the Scholarship away from me.

"Oh, you're going to talk to me now, are you?" I spit. "As there's nobody here to see us?"

Her perfect eyebrows arch up in shock. "*What?* I just...well I was going to say, this is a bit weird, isn't it? Us having to fight for the same place. I know that's always been the case, but the interview date makes it all a bit real, doesn't it?"

"That's the only weird thing, Belle? Not the fact you actually live with me but pretend not to know me?"

"Huh? Joni, you said—"

"I know what I said." I fling my hands up. "But come on. Don't pretend you care about me when you've been using me for weeks and then blanking me." I sigh. I'm so angry. Just so very angry. "Look, I get you need to be at ours. Stay until your mother gets out, I don't care. I can be NICE like that. But if you're going to ignore me at school, do me a favour and ignore me at home too. It's too fake otherwise, even for you."

Belle's mouth is wide open. Hilariously, she's the one who looks like she's about to cry. "But..."

"Come on. We're adversaries. We're not friends. You're not nice. Stop pretending you can be nice."

"Joni..."

"Joni, nothing. You either know me or you don't. We're

either in this together or we're not. I'm done."

And I storm off, leaving her aghast. I'm going to win this Scholarship. I'm going to beat Belle. I'm going to escape this broken life I'm trapped in.

I am done being nice and thinking of others. Done.

BELLE

Every minute of my life, I struggle not to scream. I can't remember what sleep is. What being rested feels like. What *liking myself* feels like. And I get why Joni has gone all Ice Queen. I really do. It hurts like hell, but she has self-respect. What did I expect, treating her as I do? But ouch. I wish I had her support. I wish I could tell her it's not what it looks like. That the Sister Circle did mean something to me. That I've not been able to stop thinking about it, and how it made me feel, and how she's likely right about everything, but when I start thinking that, it's like my brain short-circuits and I can't breathe and I want to die rather than face up to it. So it's easier just… not to.

Plus, Mother's recovery is a nightmare. Every time I see her I feel like I'm suffocating. The first week she criticized everything to do with my Look, my Mask, my Sin. All of it. She lay in bed and told me I'm wasting my Just Right years, that I'm letting standards slip, that people will worry she's lost her grip on her Mask business. So I've been making even more effort to keep her calm, but now she's upset I'm rubbing her face in it.

"It's not fair," she keeps saying from her hospital bed. *"I can never have a young face like that again. You're so insensitive."*

The nurse says she's in shock still. That once we sort out her heavier Mask products, she'll calm down. Is there enough time though? Mother's due home Sunday, and Father's home Monday, plus now I have the Scholarship interview next week. The house is a state and needs cleaning. Mother can't apply any Mask to her scars until Monday morning, and if there's a reaction she'll have to wait another week. But of course she doesn't want Father to know what's happened. I'm juggling the weight of all this, plus all my relationships at school are disintegrating.

Vanessa: I swear I never see you. Are you getting all high and mighty now you might get this Scholarship?

Belle: Not at all! Things are just so mad right now.

Vanessa: Is the Ceremony not important to you any more or something? We've not even discussed Looks properly. What's happened to my friend, Belle?

Belle: I'm sorry. So sorry. Of course I still care. One of us HAS to win. The universe will go out of kilter if not.

Vanessa: That's better xxx

I've also got Damian asking me on constant dates, despite me reminding him that I don't have time as I've got to prepare for my test and interview. Maybe it's a good thing Joni has totally shut me out? It saves me some time, and time is something I have none of.

And yet I'm spending so much of it staring at myself in the mirror and thinking how disgusting I am. On Sunday morning, I return home, after thanking Joni's mother profusely for looking after me. Our house is a state, and I waste more precious Scholarship prep time getting it as clean as I can. Then, instead of working, I get Vanessa's messages about the Ceremony and freak out about that too. I strip naked and stand in front of the full-length mirror, taking a full assessment. I've been upping my Body Prayer and hardly eating, but my reflection still doesn't show me the body I want. I have pockets of Sin Pox across my buttocks that nothing seems to get rid of. The space between my two thighs isn't big enough. And, sadly, all my restrictions have meant my breasts have deflated. It looks more like I have nipples staple-gunned onto my ribs, and I dread to think of the comments Damian will make when I inevitably have to show him my body after the Ceremony. I briefly consider saving up to get Falsehoods at the Empowerment Centre. Then I remember Mother's arriving home today after two weeks in hospital. Is it worth that risk? Will I be plagued with this flatness my whole life? Vanessa's so lucky to have curves. It's not fair.

Just then, she messages again.

Vanessa: Hey stranger. Wanna go Consume
today? I think I need new shoes for the
Ceremony after all. The pair I have make my
ankles look fat.

Belle: I'm so sorry but I'm stuck doing a family
thing today. Next weekend???

Vanessa: You're literally a ghost! You're going to
miss out. Damian and Ben were going to meet us
after. Be careful B. He's not going to put up with
this for ever.

Belle: I know. I'm sorry! Things been super
relentless! Should be easier after this week.

Vanessa: Whatever.

I start the shower and let it warm up, and take in my face
before the mirror steams and releases me from my obsession.
Without my Mask on, I look hollow and gaunt. Huge gross bags
under my eyes, my skin dry and flaky, eyes red and watery, a
blemish coming up on my chin. Nobody can ever see me like
this. They can never know the Truth of how I really am. Before
I pick Mother up, I'll quickly dash into some stores and treat us
to loads of Wellness Enhancers, and maybe sort a falsehood bra

to counterbalance my weight loss. At least I'll be the thinnest person at the Ceremony. Under the scalding water, my throat closes up again, and the only thing that makes me breathe is thinking about the Scholarship. How, if I win it, I can leave this town, leave this house, this pressure. I was never sure why I wanted it before but now it's all I dream about in the rare moments I manage to sleep.

Mother winces as I help her step into our home. The Centre said her muscles are wasted and weak from so long being in bed, and I feel like I'm taking an elderly relative in, rather than my parent.

"Are you sure nobody's seen us?" she asks, twisting her neck to look back at the street.

"Nobody."

"They can't know, Belle. It will ruin the business."

"I know. I've not told anyone." Well, apart from Joni. But nobody would believe I talked to her or that I'd been living at her house anyway. "Here, take a seat. I'll put the kettle on. I bought some super-detox tea, how about that? Let's rid you of all those horrible hospital toxins."

Mother smiles and squeezes my hand. It seems to be the first thing I've got right since all of this happened. I lean over and kiss her shoulder, making sure I don't make contact with her sore face. Relief tumbles through me that she's finally home. That I don't have to be the grown-up any more. That things can hopefully get back to normal. But then our moment is ruined as she passes our hallway mirror. Her whole body stiffens. Her hand flies to her face.

"No, Mother, no touching, remember?"

"Oh Christ. I really am a mutant." She leans over, her eyes still in shock at her new face.

"You'll be fine once we apply Mask tomorrow. Remember, the Empowerment Centre explained it all when they took off the bandages and—"

"I'm ruined."

"Mother, it will take time to heal. You're going to be okay. Mother, no!"

She reaches out and punches the mirror with her frail hand, over and over. "Disgusting disgusting disgusting! No no no!"

"Mother, stop! You'll hurt yourself. Please."

She's in a trance, her eyes focused only on her bruised, swollen face. A face that looked a lot better two weeks ago, before she tried to improve it. I have no choice but to grasp her hands and force her to stop. She fights me. Batters me. Punches my shoulder.

"Mother. Stop."

"Let me, let me smash it. I can't bear to see."

"Mother!"

Then, in her flailing, she catches my eye. Hard. My face twists back from the shock of it, pain erupting across my cheekbone. Mother gasps. I gasp. My hand goes to my thumping eye and I stare at her.

"Oh my child," she whispers. "I'm so sorry. So so sorry."

"It hurts." My voice sounds like a toddler's.

"I've not bruised you, have I? Not with the Ceremony coming up?"

"I…I don't think so."

Mother stares at her fist, like she's not sure why it's attached to her. Wanting it to be an alien invasion of her body, making her someone who didn't just strike her only daughter. She starts crying. Not even crying. Full-on weeping.

"Not your face too. Not your beautiful, beautiful face. Oh, my darling. I'm sorry. I'm so sorry."

We collapse to the floor together in a pile of shock and tears.

Everything's perfect for Father's return. Mother and I wake up early so we can try out her new Mask products. It's an intense moment, removing her very last bandages and seeing the entirety of the damage for the first time. I know she's watching my face so I try my best to keep it neutral, but inside I'm flinching. There's a lot of scar tissue around her ears and jaw, with stitches still visible alongside all the swelling. I apply a thick paste of Anti-Infect, like the nurse instructed.

"Do let your wounds oxygenate as much as they can," she advised, while Mother rolled her eyes. With Father coming home, it was unlikely her wounds would ever see daylight.

"Does it sting?" I ask, as she jerks back at my finger.

"It's fine. Hurry. I don't know what time he's due home."

"It's five in the morning. He won't come home for ages yet."

"Please, hurry."

Once the Anti-Infect has set, I set up two Halos, so I can

235

work under the best light possible. It's not like Mother to let me do her Mask. "I'm shaking too much, I'll mess it up," she says. "Maybe tomorrow." I follow her strict guidelines as I build her new Mask, and gradually her face becomes hers for the first time in weeks. The products are thick and heavy and will need to be touched up a lot in the summer heat, but they work. Forty-five minutes later, I hold up the mirror and see her eyes collapse in relief.

"Oh, Belle, my darling. It's worked."

"You're as beautiful as ever."

"I am, I am."

She inspects my handiwork in closer detail, turning her jaw this way and that, checking the scars and stitches have been adequately covered. Then she reaches out to touch one, her body wincing as she grazes it.

"Be careful."

"You don't think he'll notice?"

"No, you look perfect as usual."

She nods slowly, letting herself finally believe me. I sit suspended, waiting for whatever will happen next. Will she tell me I look terrible? Or tell me I'm making her feel bad about herself? Does she want me to go to school today after all, or stay here and wait for him? My mother has been so erratic since her Empowerment that I find my heart thrumming with nerves, anticipating an attack. But, when she turns back to me, I see her face has returned to normal. Not just the Mask, but her whole demeanour. Mother is home. In her skin. She's my mother again.

She smiles and reaches over to her giant box of Mask products. "Now, my darling. It's time for me to do you," she says. I return her smile and lean my face forward, ready for her to work her magic. It would all be quite healing really, if my eye wasn't still sore from where she'd hit me.

JONI

Belle's not been in class since our meeting with Ms Blanche. Not that I've noticed or anything. I'm done with her. Done with wasting my time trying to change her shallow little mind. I don't care that I'm nothing to her. She's nothing to me. A strange blip to this terrible last term of Class. It all seems so surreal that she lived with me for two weeks. I wonder often if it really happened – Mother the only one to confirm it.

"What do you mean she's gone?" I asked her, when I came home the other day to find all Belle's mad Doctrine paraphernalia had been packed up and taken back with her. Our house felt eerily spacious now it wasn't being cluttered with all her Empowerment potions and Body Prayer equipment.

"Her mother's coming home. I think she's healed up okay considering everything."

"So she's just left?"

Mother tilted her head at me. "She didn't just leave. She said thank you. She gave me a box of the strangest tea to say thank you. It tasted like punishment more than gratitude, mind."

"She didn't tell me she was leaving."

Why did I want to cry? Why were my fists clenched? Why did I feel so terrible?

"Didn't you tell her to stop talking to you?"

"Yeah, but…"

Mother gave me one of her knowing smiles, and it upset me even more.

I stare at the empty chair in the corner of the recess room, where she usually sits, and wonder why she's not in. Damian and that are lording about, laughing at some Smut playing on his Device, while that poor girl Vanessa pretends to find it hilarious too. It's all rather depressing. The air around me froths with excitement about the Ceremony next week. Whispers of who is Linking with who, who's wearing which Looks and from where, what carriages have been booked, and who might win buzz around. The end of Class is in sight. After the Ceremony, we have a few weeks off to prepare for final academic assessments and that's it. All over. Our futures beckon. And mine will hopefully be at the Education, where the Doctrine won't be as powerful, and I can learn what I need to learn to really change things. I should be feeling energized and inspired, but I feel…empty and sick. Unable to stop looking at Belle's empty chair and worrying about her.

Weirdly…*missing* her.

Darnell, bless her, is trying to hide from us how exciting she's finding all the gossip.

"Did you hear Vanessa has changed her Look five times?" she says to us, eyes bright with intrigue. "Apparently she's telling everyone 'only perfection will do'. It might be really

239

close between her and Belle, you know." Then she sees our unimpressed faces, lowers her eyes and pushes her hair back behind her ears. "It's all so pathetic," she adds unconvincingly when Hannah scowls at her.

As if they know we're talking about them, the Pretties all stand and start walking towards us. Damian's already smiling and my stomach tightens like it's preparing to be punched. Ben's laughing behind him. I take a tight breath and wait for the hit. The whole room does – stopping and waiting to see what will happen.

"Well, if it isn't Little Miss Objectionable," he says, as they pass our table. "Still hoping to win next week?"

"Just ignore him," Darnell whispers to me.

I jut my jaw out at him defiantly and don't say anything. I wish I could say it's because I know it's the best way of tackling him, but actually it's more that I don't have the strength today. And, sensing my weakness like a super-attuned shark, he leans forward and says loud enough for everyone to hear. "You're not actually planning on turning up, are you? Because that will embarrass everyone. In fact, your very existence is an embarrassment for everyone."

There's a collective shock of breath. Even I'm taken aback. I open my mouth but I'm unable to find words, a comeback. He's always been awful, but this is a weird escalation and I'm thrown by it. As I flounder, I'm surprised to hear a male voice to my side.

"I think you'll find you're the embarrassment," Jack says, his voice shaking, but finally speaking up nonetheless.

Even though he's quaking from his bravery, Damian hardly notices him. "Your boyfriend's squeaking," he tells me, a snide smile on his lips. Jack's head falls and Darnell steps forward.

"Leave us alone," she says, sounding whiny and unconvincing. "We're not doing anything wrong."

"Actually, the very existence of your face is all wrong." Damian yawns as the comeback arrives effortlessly.

So much is happening. I should be standing up for myself. I should be standing up for my friends. Why can't I talk? Why is what he's saying hurting so much when I know he's a pathetic cretin.

Surprisingly, Vanessa, of all people, comes to our rescue. She laughs fakely and puts a hand on Damian's shoulder. "Leave them alone, Damian," she says. "Otherwise she's going to think you still want to Link with her. Have some charity."

It's an insult, sure, but it has the desired effect. I see him get bored and want to move on. He yawns again and walks off, like he's forgotten us already, and I swear I see Vanessa wink as she passes.

Our group sit in a stunned silence after the door swings shut.

"I...thanks for sticking up for me," I tell them. "I...wasn't expecting that. A bit random." I reach out for Jack and Darnell's hands, which are also quaking from humiliation. "Honestly, thank you."

"You're...welcome," Jack says. "Not sure I helped much, mind."

Hannah and Sita are sharing a panicked look, probably

241

wondering why they missed the memo on actually standing up for me.

"That was way weird of him," Hannah starts.

Sita nods. "Really random. Like, we were just sitting here. What's his problem?"

Darnell replies quietly. "Maybe he's panicking because Class is ending soon, and he's going to become a bit irrelevant?" There's another moment of silence as we contemplate her wisdom.

When I look down at my hands, I see they're shaking. This won't do at all. I can't show weakness in public. Not when I know the whole room is watching me. I stand up, stretch, act like I'm not bothered. "Well, I don't know about you, but being this Objectionable is really hungry work. I'm going to go get something to eat. You guys want me to bring back anything?"

Once I'm out of that room, I turn the corner, and smash my fist against a locker. I yelp as the pain bleeds up my arms, and I have to go run it under a cold tap.

"You're an embarrassment."

His words find entry points and flood in, strangling any self-esteem they find in my body and letting it drop to the ground.

I'm an embarrassment.

I'm so gross that Belle lived with me for two weeks and won't even publicly acknowledge me…

It hurts. Sometimes, on bad days, being me is really hard and really hurts.

And in my darkness, with my hand slowly going numb

under the cold flow of water, I think of one person who doesn't think I'm an embarrassment. Who changed their mind. Who wants to know me again. The power of it pushes aside all the other things he has done.

Before I leave school that day, I write a reply to Father, carefully copy his new address onto a fresh envelope, and post it on the way home.

BELLE

Every part of the house gleams as we sit and wait for him. His favourite foods line the cupboards and fridge. His favourite dinner is on the hob. The place is perfect, but Father is still not yet here. I sigh as I watch Mother plump various cushions and take a million photos of herself to upload onto the Ranking. She's planning her perfect *I'm back from my mysterious illness* post, and though we did a full shoot this morning in a practice Mask, I sigh again, annoyed. I could've gone to class today. Joni will be in, and at our additional prep class for the Scholarship, while I'm stuck here, hungry and weirdly nervous about Father coming back. My Device goes and I feel my blood ice slightly as I see it's Damian. But I can't afford to dodge him now, not when I've been so absent. People may forget I'm in the front running to win the Ceremony.

"Hi, gorgeous," he says when I pick up. His voice is honey, but I feel prickles staple my skin. I head upstairs to my room.

"Hello, yourself," I manage. "How are you?"

"I'm fine. It's you I'm worried about. Where were you at school today?" He seems genuinely concerned, and I still can't

244

match this new Damian with the old one.

"Sorry. My mother hasn't been well, I think I caught what she's had."

"You keep getting sick. I feel like I never see you, Babe."

"I know. Sorry. It's just been a mad time. Preparing for this Scholarship thing, and Mother under the weather."

"Your obsession with this Scholarship is hilarious. Nobody as beautiful as you needs any help getting by in the world."

I force myself to smile so it comes through in my voice. "It's something to fall back on if being a Chosen One doesn't work out." I fake laugh. "You never know, I might get my face burned off in a fire or something, then what I would do?"

"You'll fall back onto me, easy," he says. "I'll catch you."

I fake another laugh. "Even with a melted face?"

"Yeah, it would be great. Nobody else would want you."

I can't bring myself to fake laugh at that one, and maybe sensing me bristle, Damian changes tactic. I perch on the bed, feeling weirdly unsafe lying on it, even though he's only on the phone. "Anyway, my poor sick Belle. Even though *you've* been very distracted, I am focused on giving you the best night of your life at the Ceremony. So, I'm ringing to ask what colour dress you're wearing, so I can order the right Ownership Flower. I asked Vanessa but she said to ask you myself."

I raise my eyebrows. Yikes, I really have pissed off Vanessa recently. I make a note to call her, but then wonder where the hell I'll find the time.

"I haven't actually decided on a final dress yet," I admit. Mother and I had planned to spend the last few weeks

245

narrowing down my potential Ceremony Looks, but, for obvious reasons, that hasn't happened.

"What? Surely that's the most important thing in your life right now."

I can't tell if he's being sarcastic or not.

"Yes. Screw the life-changing Scholarship," I blurt out. "I just need to make sure my dress doesn't clash with a flower. That's the real clincher."

I shouldn't have said that. I'm breaking all the Rules. I should be giving the Ceremony my full sincerity, but Damian laughs, which I'm not expecting.

"How about I go with white?" he suggests. "White goes with everything."

I watch myself in the mirror and hold out my palm, pressing it into the reflective glass. "White would be perfect, thank you."

"No worries. As I said, I want to give you the best night of your life."

"I…"

"It's been rubbish not seeing much of you," he continues. "I'm even finding myself jealous of Joni of all people, for getting to do those sessions with you. Can I get a Scholarship too? So we can hang out more?"

It's still so jarring. This morph from Smut fanatic to kind and caring. I don't trust it. I know what he's been saying about me when I'm not there. I'm going to get "destroyed" and "broken in" apparently. I know it's somewhat just talk, but still… Who wants to get *destroyed*? Most girls, I guess, if Smut

246

is anything to go by. It's me who's the problem, I know, and I've put it off for far too long. I need to get it over with. Enjoy it, even. And yet...yet... My throat tightens, heart constricts. I laugh my way through it again.

"Sadly this one's only for girls."

He lets out a whistle. "Jeez, that's medieval. But, anyway, I'm going to get looking for the perfect white flower for my perfect white flower."

So much innuendo... I know I should find it charming and clever, but I just feel sick. "Oh, Damian, thank you."

"I'm really excited, Belle. It's going to be great. Are you in class tomorrow?"

"No. Well, sort of. I've got some morning prep for the Scholarship and then I have to travel to the Education. I have my test and interview on Wednesday."

"Well, absence makes hearts grow fonder," he says, then pauses. "And, well, other things grow harder too..."

I actually do laugh at this. "That's the Damian I remember." He laughs too, admitting he's broken form, and I find this is a bit more relaxing. Him being like this. It's definitely more authentic than this strange trying-to-be-a-Nice-Guy thing. I find an excuse to hang up because I physically can't handle thinking about the Ceremony right now. Not when I'm still anticipating Father's return. I step onto the landing and peer downstairs. Mother's snoozing on a chair, sleeping upright so she's not crumpled when he gets here. I return to my bedroom and go through the motions of trying to catch up on the work I've missed that day, getting out all my notes. But, though I

247

desperately need to, I can't get Damian's call to stop haunting me. The Ceremony's only a week away. *A week*. I've been so busy with Mother and the Scholarship that I've not prepared – not physically, not mentally…not for what I know I need to do after. I take a deep breath and perch on the end of my bed, my Device in my hand, wondering…

I never watch Smut alone. I know that makes me super weird and a huge Frigid, but I never watch it alone. Of course, I can't avoid it at school. Damian regularly sends the "funniest" clips but I always click off.

Now, with the Ceremony looming, I need to know what's expected of me. I type in the most popular Smut outlet with shaky hands and even the homepage is overwhelming. Everywhere I look there are women being "destroyed", bodies slamming into them. Weird grunts of half pain, half pleasure echo out and I quickly turn the volume down so I don't wake Mother. I don't even read the title of the main video, I just click play, sit back a bit, and tell myself I'm going to watch the whole thing. That I *have* to watch at least five all the way through. Exposure therapy. I'm almost eighteen, I should be WANTING to look at this stuff, wanting to recreate it. I can do it, I can… It may even be sexy.

Fifteen minutes later, I feel hollow. My body doesn't know what to do with itself. I'm sweating my Mask off. My stomach's a whirlpool. It's not just my hands shaking but my whole arms. The rest of my body is rigid, my legs crossed, almost a frozen block of marble as I subconsciously make myself impenetrable. I've never felt more sick.

I can't believe this is what I have to do. What I'm supposed to *enjoy*. What I saw…how it looked…I don't understand how…it must hurt. In all the videos, the women just accepted whatever happened to them, whatever was put where, compliantly, and seemingly enthusiastically, when surely it must be agony? The things being done to their bodies looked humiliating and painful. Really painful. I collapse on a chair in front of my large dressing mirror, taking in my grey reflection. I beam the Halo at me, so every part of me's fully lit up. I look haunted. I look…*hunted*. I lean over and take in my face. My eyes are wide with dread and I widen them more. That's how the women in the Smut look. Their eyes so big they look like bugs, as their bodies struggle to comprehend what's happening to them. I stare at myself once more as I put both hands around my neck and mime choking myself. In almost every clip the Smut actress got strangled. Does that mean I'll get strangled? Is that an essential part of Copulation? Will it hurt? How will Damian know when to stop? Will it leave a bruise? In one Smut clip, the woman passed out and the man continued doing what he was doing anyway. Will Damian do that? Will I become Unvanilla while unconscious? And my face… What's the point of giving myself the most perfect Mask for the Ceremony when, from what I've seen, my Mask is going to get repeatedly spat on. Three times I saw Smut women get spat on. I watched them blink away saliva landing on their face. Moaning and making it seem like they enjoyed it, while also, I noticed, trying to wipe it away as quickly as possible.

This is what's expected of me.

My body is to be pummelled in whatever hole of mine the boy chooses to inhabit. Alongside that, I should expect to be smacked, slapped, spat on and strangled. Called a dirty whore and a slut and told that I like it. I need to accept whatever Damian wants to do, and enjoy it.

You need to learn how to find this sexy, I tell myself, still holding my neck. *You only have a week to make yourself desire this. Make yourself like this, Belle. Make yourself want this. What the hell is wrong with you?*

Then a tiny voice finds its way inside me; a memory replaying from that night at the Sister Circle.

"When I lost my Mask, I also lost my terribly disappointing sex life and started to truly learn what pleasure my body was capable of having."

Was there a different way to Copulate? One that women who went to the circle had found? One without pain and humiliation?

But, then again, I'd be so humiliated if Damian told everyone I was a Frigid because I didn't do what he wanted. Nobody would ever want me then, no matter how Pretty I was…

I load up another Smut and I'm about to press play when I hear the door. My father's voice.

"Hello? Is anyone even bloody home?"

"Father!"

I turn off my Device and run down to meet him, trying to shake off what I've just watched. "I've missed you." I reach out to give him a hug. I can feel the heat from outside on his body; his back is sweaty. He hardly hugs me back but pats me roughly.

250

"I was only gone a few weeks."

His eyes are red and he smells stale, though he often does after a long shift. It's hard to shower when he drives the distances he does, and the summer will be making it worse.

"Welcome back, my darling." Mother's in the doorway, looking bright and glowing and not like she's just woken up from a painkiller-induced nap. She moves to say her own hellos, but he holds up a palm, stopping her.

"I just tried to buy drink on my way back," he says. "Can somebody please explain why my Finance was declined?"

I turn to Mother, whose face has whitened even under her heavy Mask. "Really?" she says. "How very odd." Her voice is way too high, and we all notice it.

"It got declined twice. So I checked our account balance and it's zero?"

He leans against the door, arms crossed, fuming. Mother struggles to compose herself.

"Oh, darling. That might be my fault. You see, I've not been very well. I didn't want to worry you, but I've actually not been able to do any of my Masking while you've been away, so things are a bit tight."

"Tight?" Father throws his hands in the air. "I couldn't buy six units."

"There must be a muddle up. Let me look into it. We have drinks in the fridge already. Cold ones."

"Hmm." He's appeased, at least for now. I hover, awaiting his next instructions. Mother keeps touching her scars, and I worry she'll draw attention to them. "Well, anyway," he concedes, "other than that awful scare, it's nice to be home."

Mother beams and goes over for her kiss. "Let me get you a drink," she says. She escorts him through to the living room, sits him in his favourite chair, and goes to fetch him his alcohol. I follow them, still panicking about what Father's just revealed. How can we have NO Finance?

"Come here, beautiful one." Father opens his arms and I climb into his lap. "Have you missed me?"

"Of course."

And I have and I do. It's always more tense with him around, but still. The way he treats me, like I'm a gorgeous human sunbeam. It's nice to have a compliment or two after Mother's incessant bitching.

"You're looking as beautiful as ever. How's the prep going for the Ceremony?"

"Okay. I haven't decided on a dress yet."

"What? I thought that would be the only thing you two thought about while I was away."

"Well, she's been sick…"

He interrupts me and calls out over my shoulder. "Did you hear that? We need to finalize Belle's Look. We didn't call her Belle so she could come *runner-up* in the Ceremony."

He's not enquired about Mother's illness. In fact, he's shown no concern whatsoever.

"She has been very unwell," I remind him.

Mother arrives, cradling his favourite glass. "I really have, my darling. But don't worry, I'm fighting fit now. Belle, we can go through your Looks tomorrow maybe?"

I bite my lip, and clamber off the chair so Father can drink properly. "I can't tomorrow. I'm going to the Education for my interview, remember?"

Both of them half nod. "Oh yes, that. I forgot."

Father doesn't comment at all, only downs half his drink in one. It's not that my parents mind me applying for an Education, but they've never really cared about it. Like Mother's illness, it's something to ignore. Irrelevant, really, to what my family finds important. Having It All is a great Doctrine achievement, but it's not the priority for us. Father wants to boast to everyone about me winning the Ceremony. That's an achievement he understands. One our friends and families understand too. Whereas, if I win this Scholarship, I'm not sure they realize what a big deal it is. They'll be a lot more embarrassed by me failing to win the Ceremony than me failing to get this place at the Education.

We sit together and allow Father to tell us the things he saw on his Big Job. The air in the house relaxes, like all the atoms around us have stopped holding their breath. For the first time in weeks, things feel normal. Mother's scars aren't showing. Father seems content to be "back with his girls". He gets another drink and says, "Go on, let's do this now, show me some options." And, eager to keep us all united, I spend the evening putting on Look after Look. I saunter downstairs in various options, while he applauds and Mother laughs and tells me which Masks options would work with what. They reignite and glow in the light of my Just Right years. Father softens, turns to Mother, and starts reminiscing about some of his favourite Looks she's done over the years. She blooms under the compliments. The sun sets outside, the drinks in the fridge get drunk, I do literally no preparation for my interview. But at least we decide on a dress. We settle for a striking red one that hangs off my shoulders and clings to every part of my body. I guess if I'm going to un-Vanilla myself, I should really just fully go for it.

"You'll need a really strong Mask to get this Look to work," Mother says. "But I can sort that. And you won't be able to dance much. It's too tight. But that's not important."

I can hardly breathe in this dress, let alone dance. I have to crab-walk up and down the stairs. But I can't deny I look almost religiously good. A goddess. So many girls in school wouldn't be able to fit into something like this, let alone pull it off. I will be beyond envied. My Look will invoke insecurity and jealousy and, I can't help it, I feel good about that. With my life, and brain, careering so thoroughly out of control, it's calming to feel powerful in this one small way.

Once it gets dark, the cooler air streaming through our windows, my parents retire for the night, giggling their way up the stairs. I go to my room and wiggle out of the insane dress. I take my Mask off, enjoying the feeling of the cool breeze on my face, being able to recline in my Sleep Wear. I never used to enjoy taking my Mask off before, but I feel free away from Mother's scrutiny and my skin can feel the world on it. Eager to make amends with Vanessa, I shoot her a message.

Belle: FINALLY decided on my Ceremony look.

Phew! Won't be able to dance though, or walk.
Worth it, I'm sure.

Vanessa: I'm PAINTING my Look on. Walking is
overrated :)

The smiley face makes me know I'm temporarily forgiven and that's one less thing to worry about. I check the clock. Almost eleven. I know I should try and be well-rested for tomorrow, but I also need to be well-prepared. So I turn away from my bed and head to my desk instead and get out my books. At midnight, I hear the squeak of the landing floorboards, and peek out to see Mother tiptoeing to the bathroom. I watch as she reapplies all her Mask products again, flinching as her fingers graze her scars. I close my bedroom door quietly and turn back to my studies, but I'm no longer able to concentrate, reminded of our total lack of Finance...

Once I'm sure they're both asleep, I creep downstairs and stand in the hallway, unsure where to look and what I'm even looking for. I open the cupboard door, finding Mother's bag from the Empowerment Centre inside. Clearly she was too busy making the house perfect to unpack and stuffed it in here. I settle on the ground, cross-legged, and pull the bag over, unzipping it slowly so it doesn't make a noise. The smell of disinfectant hits my nostrils, the stench of illness in her folded pyjamas. It brings back a horrible flash of Mother flatlining on the bed and I blink it away. Alongside her pyjamas are some healing creams, a toothbrush – and a huge wodge of papers

255

stuffed to one side. I tug them out and flatten them, my eyes scanning them.

They're bills. All of them.

It appears she's only paid for the initial Procedures at the Empowerment Centre, but since her crisis they've been adding the extra care onto the bill. The costs are astronomical. Every meal she didn't eat was practically the cost of an expensive dinner out. Every time they washed her body, every millilitre of medicine they injected to keep her alive – all of it's been costed up and charged back to us. I don't know how we'll ever repay it. It didn't occur to me they'd charge us for all of this. I thought surely they'd cover the cost of keeping Mother alive, but no…it's on us. Our family. Mother has bankrupted us paying for a Ritual that almost killed her and has made her look worse. I can't… How will we ever pay this back? The walls around me squeeze in as my throat constricts. We've never had enough Finance, I know this. It's why I've always tried to help with my Chosen One work. Why Mother flogs herself with her business when Father's away. We have to do it quietly, as he's too proud to acknowledge our help, but this amount is insane. Too much. I flutter through the papers again, wondering if there's anything I can do to help. Anything to undo this. To make it go away.

Then, in a gasp of grief, it comes to me.

Don't go to the Education, I think.

Make it work, really work, as a Chosen One.

The pay is good, if you make the most of your Just Right years. School has always stopped me doing it properly, but when I finish I can start earning right away. And if I win the Ceremony, that will certainly be logged on my booking profile and get me more jobs.

I push the papers back and lean my face on a step, feeling nothing but dread and disappointment and confusion. I really have started noticing how relaxed I feel when I'm away from this home, away from Mother, and the pressure she puts on me. That's when parts of myself feel like they're budding and unfurling and could really bloom. Parts of myself that I'm finding I quite like. Being around Joni made me realize I'm more than just Pretty – that I'm funny and sharp, that I can get on with people I never thought I'd have anything in common with. I'm missing her since I left…missing how she made me feel… But Mother needs my help…and Joni…Joni deserves the Scholarship more than me anyway. I wipe away a threatening tear. This could be the start of me being less selfish and vain – a better person. A nicer person. Helping my family. Helping the girl who has helped me so much. Stepping aside and reducing the competition is probably the best way I can repay her kindness and make up for my absolute failure to be nice in return. I should back out now. Call her. Tell her. Take the pressure off.

Then I have a thought.

If I don't go tomorrow, I won't spend any more time with Joni ever again. Once our interviews are over, that's it. No more special lessons, no more living in her house. And, for some reason, I don't want this to be the abrupt end of us. I can't sacrifice our last chance to spend time together. Not when I feel the dead weight of sacrificing my chance to get away from here. I put my hands on the step and push myself up. I'll go, but I won't try. Not really. The space is hers. I'm out. This trip is only about making amends and saying goodbye. I need to surrender to my fate of being Just A Pretty Face, until time inevitably takes that from me too.

JONI

It's quite hilarious, really, the Look Belle has put together for this trip. I mean, who needs to be comfortable on a three-hour train journey? Why *not* assemble a Look that includes knee-high socks, a tiny kilt, a blazer, and shoes you can hardly stand in? It's not like we're going to be walking miles today once we get to the Education and are shown around campus. It's not like it's way too hot to be wearing socks that go up to mid-thigh. We nod at each other on the train station platform but stand apart. That's fine with me. Well, it slightly isn't. She hasn't been in school for days and, with her no longer living with us and all, I've weirdly missed her. I'm an idiot, but I know better than to be friendly. We can stay away from each other these next two days.

School has other plans, however, because when the train pulls up and I go and find my seat, Belle's already there after joining the train from the other door. She's trying to push her huge suitcase into the overhead compartment, and she's basically flashing her knickers to the whole carriage in her struggle. She's putting the case right above my head, so I guess we're sitting together. This won't be awkward. This won't be awkward at all.

I hold up my ticket. "Fifty-nine A," I say.

She dusts her hands now the case is tucked away. "Fifty-nine B."

"Well, isn't that cute? Don't worry. I don't think anyone from school is on this train."

She twists to let me past to the window seat, and, as she does, she almost vanishes, she's so thin. "You're hilarious."

We arrange ourselves in a rather awkward silence as the train slowly drifts away from the station, revving up until our town is well behind us. I let out a sigh and lean my head against the window, enjoying the feeling of the space between me and where I live increasing, watching the world rush by. Mother says the Doctrine isn't so powerful everywhere, especially in the city with the Education, and I'm looking forward to experiencing this for myself. My stomach burns with anticipation. I want to get in so much. Everything I've sacrificed growing up has been because of this, and now it's my shot. My chance. Like Belle, I've hardly eaten in days because I feel so nauseous.

I wish everything wasn't happening all at once. Father wrote back and I managed to intercept the letter before Mother saw. He wants to see me. He's delighted I got in touch. He doesn't live nearby but can come visit in two weeks' time. I've felt sick in both excitement and dread at the idea of meeting.

The carriage is practically empty but Belle makes no move to change to a different seat. I bet she's one of those people who literally can't handle not sitting in her allocated seat, even if there's plenty spare.

"Did I miss much at the last prep session?" she asks finally, once a good half-hour has passed.

"Oh, it was great," I lie to wind her up. "They told me exactly what questions are going to come up in the interview AND the exam."

"Seriously?"

"No. I'm joking. It was just another run-through of interview technique. Don't worry. You'll ace it. You're good at being fake."

"Joni…"

I widen my eyes in confrontation and she holds up her hands.

"Never mind."

The world keeps flashing on by while I stew in my awkwardness and guilt for being mean. It takes me only ten minutes before I ask, "Is your mother okay?"

"She's…yeah, she's alright. She has some scars, but her new Mask products are working well."

"Well that's…good."

"Yeah."

"You've not been in school much."

"I needed to get the house ready for Father coming home, and for Mother. It's been intense. Thanks again, though, for letting me stay."

I bat my hand. "It was nothing."

She grabs my hand and squeezes it, surprising me. I look up

at her with wide eyes. "No, Joni, it was everything. Thank you."

The intensity's too much, especially with everything that's coming up that day. I shrug her off and mutter it's nothing again, wondering if this is a ploy. Is she trying to disarm me for tomorrow?

"I better do some last-minute studying," I say, reaching between my legs to get out a book. I settle back with it, reading the chapter on Internal Policy for the third time, trying to commit it fully to memory. After about ten minutes, I notice Belle hasn't done anything other than stare at her Device. She's on the Ranking, refreshing to see how much Validation she's got for her Kilt Look that morning. I catch her refreshing at least five times.

"Don't you want to revise?" I ask, feeling a bit embarrassed for her. I know the Ranking's important to her, but we only have a few hours left until the life-changing interview.

"I'm okay," she says, jabbing the refresh button again. "Not much point this late, is there?"

"Well I'm going to cram."

"I'll test you if you'd like?"

I hold up a hand. "No, I'm good. Thanks."

The train journey passes with me reading two more chapters, and Belle winning the school's daily Validation competition. Once, when I glance over, I see she's zoomed the screen in on her own face and is scanning every centimetre of it, basically using a magnifying glass on herself. She's completely absorbed as she analyses each pixel of her face, like it's a tranquillizing spell. As we get closer, the train slows, tugging us both out of our concentration. I can smell Belle's scent as she leans over me to look out the window.

"Wow," she says. "The city's beautiful."

"That it is."

I've never seen anything like it. It's so vastly different from our town, where everything is grey and uniform and drab. The train weaves us through old architecture cast of golden brick and each building looks like it's some kind of elaborate sandcastle created by the gods during their childhood. We go over a river on a stunning bridge held up by gargoyles and I smear my forehead against the window to get a better view. Boats float through the water, filled with people who look our age. It's idyllic. I feel my shoulders relax, excitement tingle in my gut.

I could live here. I could belong here. This could be my town, my life.

I'm so excited I forget to be mad at Belle. I whistle as I help her grab her giant suitcase down, yelling "Timber!" as it lands on our heads, and she laughs her first laugh of the day. I've forgotten how good it feels, making Belle laugh. We steer our way through the station, taking everything in. There are students everywhere, but it couldn't be more different from school. I notice it right away. Hardly any girls here are wearing Masks. Faces. Naked faces. Of young women. It's practically unimaginable where we're from. When we step out into the city, trying to find the carriage queue, I actually say "Wow" out loud. It's a different world. I wind down the window as we're driven to the Education and lean out like a tongue-lolling dog while Belle quietly complains the wind is ruining her hair. Oh, I can taste the opportunity in the air. I can feel the way my blood changes. It senses…the possibility of this place.

I let out a further "Wow" once we reach the Education, and Belle joins me. She stops dragging her giant suitcase along and we just stand on the perfect lawn and stare up at it. This palace of beauty. I notice the change in atmosphere instantly. There are no boys here. They're not strictly forbidden from the grounds, but they clearly don't bother hanging around this campus. It's just girls walking around, again almost all minimally-Masked or Maskless, clutching books, laughing in groups. Some are wearing Mask products but in a different way from back home. They've decorated their faces in creative designs, rather than covering them and ensuring they follow the regulations of the Doctrine. I'd never seen Mask worn that way before – it looks quite…fun. And the girls walk with a delicious mixture of relaxation and a sense of purpose. I want to be them. For the first time in my life, outside the Sister Circle, I don't feel like a disgusting sore thumb. I blend in. Nobody is wincing as they pass me, shuddering at my Objectionable ways. It's like the world has reversed and, as we start walking towards the main entrance again, it's almost Belle who looks Objectionable. Her tiny kilt, teetering shoes and heavy Mask draw a few glances, especially as the wheels of her suitcase roar against the cobblestones. She notices it too. She hunches her shoulders and hides behind her perfectly waved hair.

We get to a welcome desk, and Belle's so hunched over that I step forward and introduce us to the enthusiastic girl wearing a lanyard.

"Hello, hello, and welcome," she says, her voice bright, looking genuinely pleased to see us. "Have you come a long way?"

I tell her the name of our town.

"Wow. You're from the proper Land of the Doctrine. Cool. I can't wait to hear all about it."

Belle and I share a look.

"Anyway, welcome. Here are your orientation packs. They have maps and a timetable and stuff. We'll show you to your dorm and you'll have some time to rest before we take you on a tour. Then, tonight, we've organized a little get-together so you can chat to some students here, see what the place is about." She tilts her head. She's wearing no Mask whatsoever and it really is jarring, even to me. The sun is so bright that every pore of her face is lit up and it's like staring into an alien landscape. Pores. Never in my life did I think I'd see pores in broad daylight. "Now, no doubt you guys are totally stressed about tomorrow. I remember I was. But, please, try to enjoy yourself and relax. There's no point in doing any extra cramming. Just drink it all in! The professors love it when you show real enthusiasm for the Education in interview anyway."

"Wow, okay," I say. "Thank you."

Belle stays silent the whole time as we follow some friendly guide called Aniyah to our dorm. She huffs as she carries the suitcase over uneven stone surfaces, across grass, under stone arches, and eventually all three of us have to carry it up three flights of stairs.

"All books in here?" Aniyah asks. "Is that why it's so heavy?"

I know it's more likely to be filled with Belle's daily Mask requirements, but Belle nods before hiding behind her hair again.

"This will be worth it when you see your room," she says. "The view is fantastic from the top floor." Her smile is so welcoming that I beam right back at her, noticing her incredible Afro that's like a volumized halo around her head. I've not seen anyone our age wear their hair like that back where we live. I find myself thinking of Belle's friend, Vanessa, and how cool she'd look. "Here it is."

We step into the stunning dorm room.

"Wow," I say, for the third time that day.

Aniyah smiles again. "I'll leave you two to settle in. There's a Device number if you get lost, and you've got maps for the orientation later."

I drop my bag and walk straight to the window, taking in the view. You can see the spire and turrets of a nearby building, glowing gold in the sunshine, while girls lounge on the manicured lawn below us, stretched out reading books and laughing. The room's so impressive. Everything's made from oak beams, with old iron windows and a slanted roof. Two single beds lay made up, separated only by a small side table. I flop belly first onto one and let out a floomph noise of happiness. Oh yes, I could live here, I could do this, I could thrive here, I am meant to be here. Learn here. This is where my story truly starts.

Belle finally speaks behind me. "I take it that's your bed then?" When I twist around, a tiny bit of her has returned. She raises an eyebrow at me, smirking.

"I didn't think about it. It just looked so comfy I couldn't deny the urge to flop."

"I'm joking. I don't mind which bed I have. Anyway, you getting the one by the window is the least I can do."

She pulls her suitcase to the end of the other and she too flops onto it, backwards, and lets out a sigh.

"I can't believe we're here," she tells the wooden beams of the ceiling. "It's so surreal. I feel like I've been building up to this for years and now it's here, and it's happening, and it's weird…"

"Very weird."

I hear her shift in the bed to face me. "I'm glad I'm not doing this alone. I'm glad you're here. It's all quite overwhelming."

I blink several times at the ceiling, not wanting to get sucked in. "It is."

"I'm sorry, Joni. I know I've been awful."

I still won't look at her. "You've been…how I expected you to be."

"Ouch."

"Look, please don't be nice to me just because we're somewhere alien and you feel out of your depth and want to cling to something that reminds you of home, especially when we're going back tomorrow and you'll still pretend not to know me at school."

"Ouch again."

"I know that's what you're doing."

"It's not…I… Okay, I can totally see why you think that. But it's not the truth, I promise."

I can't help it. I turn over and look at her. She is so Pretty it's ridiculous, even though I can see she's got Mask all over the clean pillow already. She smiles, acknowledging I've given in. So, to get my power back, I point at the stain.

"Marking your territory, are you?"

Her eyes follow my finger and she notices the mark and lurches up. "Oh Christ. How embarrassing. Where's the bathroom?"

"I think it's through that door."

She returns from the en-suite with a wet tissue and tries to dab the stain away. "Stop laughing."

"I'm not."

"I can feel you doing it in your head."

"Yikes, okay, Thought Police. Calm down."

She finishes dabbing at it. "I think I got it in time. Christ, this place is weird. Have you seen how nobody's wearing a Mask? I didn't even know that was legal."

"Societally, it isn't, no."

"I've never seen anything like it. You seem MUCH less mad here, it has to be said."

I smile. "That's why I want to get in so badly."

The air sours. Belle looks away and starts twisting her hands, and I notice them sweating.

"Yeah, I can tell," she finally replies, biting her lip. "I really want to get in too."

* * *

We make a silent pact to ignore the fact we're competing from now on. After lying down and chilling for an hour, we scan the map together and make our way to the orientation lecture. The walk there is simply stunning and we crane our heads around, bumping into people, blushing and apologizing, but being unable to stop gawping.

"So, this is our competition," I say, once we arrive at the right hall. Waiting for the giant door to open is a crowd of other girls our age, chatting to one another nervously, or determinedly reading their intro packs to avoid making small talk.

Belle looks around and her face relaxes a bit. There are a lot more Masks to be found in this group. At least eighty to ninety per cent of them have, like her, really gone for it with their Looks today, and I morph from feeling free and excited to feeling like I'm in school again. "I wonder where they're all from," she muses. Belle really does stand out as the Prettiest, even with this new competition. I see the other Masked girls glance over at her, grading her, their shoulders collapsing a bit when they see her clear advantage.

"Nowhere towns like ours, I guess."

The doors open of their own accord and we all rattle through into a giant and beautiful lecture theatre, pushing to try and sit at the front to make the best impression. This hall is something else. The lines of desks are carved out of gorgeous wood, the ceiling stretches up into eaves of oaken boughs, supported by stone pillars. The air smells of concentration and achievement.

My mind sharpens just from the collective historical energy that's accumulated within these walls – of the generations of girls who have sat here before me, their minds filling with powerful information every hour that they're here.

A Maskless professor sits at the front, waiting for us to settle. She's smiling and trying to make as much eye contact with everyone as possible. She'd definitely be considered an Invisible out on the streets, but, to be a professor here, she must be in the top one per cent of the smartest women in the country. I feel vaguely better that she's also Maskless. After the parade outside, I did worry that tomorrow's interview would be judged on looks, even if it is subconsciously.

The Professor claps her hands. "Welcome, ladies, welcome," she says. Her voice is pure gravity. So commanding I feel like I could fly over my desk, attracted to her like a magnet. "It's wonderful to have you all here today. You're sitting in history right now. This college has been educating and inspiring women for hundreds of years, and our alumni include some of the most powerful women in the world." She pauses. "Of course, none of them are as powerful as if they'd been men, but we do our best."

I let out a belt of a laugh but realize I'm one of few to do so. Many, Belle included, look a bit thrown and confused by what she's just said. The Professor notices my laugh, however, and looks over at me and winks. *Winks!* "Anyway," she says. "I'm lucky enough to be interviewing some of you tomorrow and I can't wait to meet you. But, for today, I want to introduce you to the college and what to expect, to see if it will be a good fit for you."

The lights lower and she does a whole presentation about how great and prestigious and wonderful the Education is. I find myself leaning forward in my chair, practically dribbling, as she talks us through the study options, the extracurricular activities, and the general way of life there. "We aim to make our girls critical and independent thinkers, who don't let society's expectations and gender inequalities hold them back."

"Inequalities?" Belle whispers to me. "What gender inequalities?"

I shake my head and pat her hand.

"The Education has been called radical, and we've had to fight to preserve it and its way of life. But we believe what we've always believed, and we will not be swayed by propaganda. Come be part of our community, part of history, part of a path to change."

Once the lecture is over, we spill out, people discussing things excitedly. I overhear snippets of conversation. "*If I don't get her as my interviewer tomorrow I will officially die.*" "*Oh my God, I love her so much.*" I smile at the Professor on our way out. I've never felt surer that I'm precisely where I need to be. Belle, however, seems less certain. She's hiding behind her hair again as we follow the trail of girls making their way over to the "Induction Social".

"I didn't understand half of that," she admits, her voice thick with self-hatred. "Did you?"

I put my arm around her. "Yes."

"Coming here's made me feel like I've been wearing my left shoe and my right shoe the wrong way around. I'm...well,

I'm not going to get in, am I? Not if I don't even understand the orientation."

"Don't be so sure. They want students who are willing to learn. That's all. They're looking for potential. A willingness." I'm not sure why I reassure her.

"A willingness for what?"

I squeeze her to me. I'm not sure why, yet again. "A willingness to admit things in this world aren't quite what they seem."

If the orientation lecture was amazing, then the social is even more amazing. We're led through to this grand dining hall that looks like it's been carved out of the inside of a wooden whale, where existing students wait for us with drinks and snacks. There's an initial half-hour of awkwardness but I drain my juice, determined to make the most of the opportunity, and drag Belle over to an approachable-looking girl with auburn hair who smiles at us.

"Hi, I'm Joni, this is Belle," I say. Belle waves and squeaks. "We're from the same town."

"Hi, I'm Lottie. I'm a second year." She shakes both our hands and I take her in. She's Maskless, like me, her face pink and slightly sunburned from the day's sunny weather. "Where are you from?"

We tell her our town name.

"Never heard of it," she laughs. "Just like where I grew up. I'm so excited for you girls to get in. You're going to love it here! It's so much better away from a small town. I mean, it makes going home for the holidays hard and weird..." She scratches her peeling nose. "It's tough coming from those places that still really buy into the Doctrine."

I glance sideways at Belle, who's looking at us like we're both speaking fluent Latin or something. She's tilted her head and is biting her lip. "Is that why so many of you don't wear Masks?" she asks suddenly. "Do you all reject the Doctrine?"

Lottie takes in her perfect face, her Look, and her eyes widen in kindness. "Yes. When I first came here, I used to wear a Mask every day and found it mad that people didn't. But it's such a freeing place. Everyone really looks after each other. And, away from male students especially, you just start feeling less pressure to Mask. It seems pointless when nobody else is. But I'm not going to lie, it's hard at first. Jarring. And I always wobble when I go home."

Belle jabs out a finger, like she's desperate to talk. "But being here has made you better? *Happier?*"

"Oh, a million times yes. Getting in was the best thing that's ever happened to me. I really hope you girls make it. Let me know if you have any questions about tomorrow. I'll see if I have any tips."

We speak to Lottie a while longer, and I stay to ask specifically about Political Sciences as that's her Major too. When we're done, I try to find Belle in the throng. The ice has well and truly shattered and the room is noisy with small talk, as everyone clambers to speak to the existing students. I wonder if Belle's maybe gone to re-Mask or something, but I find her in quiet conversation with a girl in the corner.

"So…yeah…being a trans girl here has been amazing. All the other girls are so great. I thought I'd have to Mask more than ever to fit in, but, if anything, I've learned I don't have to Mask so much to Pass, you know?"

Belle nods with understanding. "That makes sense, actually."

The girl reaches out and takes a strand of Belle's hair. "I mean this in the nicest way, but you're very Pretty…and yet, if you come here, you'll realize you won't need to do this as much. That's the most powerful thing I've learned. We *all* Mask to try and pass these impossible tests. Being here helps you see it's beneficial to focus your energy on other things. To challenge all of it. I sometimes worry what would've happened if I hadn't got in. It was quite controversial when I was accepted…"

I hold my breath as I stand behind them. For some reason, I expect Belle to say something dreadful. We have no trans girls in our school. Or in our town really. Not out ones anyway. Everyone who doesn't match the Doctrine's ideals tends to flee to cities like this one. I take a step forward, reaching out almost to protect this girl, but Belle shakes her head.

"That's ridiculous," she says, "why would it be controversial? It's about a safe place for girls to learn, isn't it?"

"It's definitely that."

"You know what's weird?" Belle continues. "I've only been here a day and I already feel safe. In fact, I feel like this is the first time in ages I've ever felt safe. And, like, shouldn't we feel safe when we, like, fucking *learn*? Isn't that fundamental?"

They nod and beam at each other, already firm friends. "Exactly, exactly."

"I'm scared to go home now," Belle says. "I don't want this feeling to go away."

It's then I realize she's not noticed me standing behind them eavesdropping, and she may not want me to hear this. I start stepping backwards, to give her some privacy, retreating back into the hall.

"Well, I hope you get in then. I'll keep everything crossed for you."

Belle sighs. "I doubt it. I'm up against the cleverest girl in my town, and she deserves it more than me…" My breath catches as I realize she's talking about me. "…she's smarter and braver and kinder, and to be honest, these two days just feel like I'm along for the ride. But…it's going to be hard, going back now. Not feeling safe. I thought I could cope with not coming here, and now I'm not sure."

That's all I overhear before I'm swallowed by the hall.

I network a while longer but can't stop Belle's words from refluxing on me. She *never* feels safe? I mean, none of us do, I guess, but I certainly don't feel it as strongly as she seems to. I guess I've learned, day by day, that you can challenge what's expected of you and mostly the worst doesn't happen. People hate me and sneer at me, but my way of life is still vaguely tolerated, and I know where I truly stand. Whereas, someone like Belle, her whole existence has always depended on her playing and looking a part. Yes, she's not lumped into the Objectionable pile at school, but it must be quite scary, knowing everything she is depends on her literally never letting the Mask drop. I glance over while stuffing some canapés into my mouth and remember what Damian's been saying about her. Another part she apparently feels the need to play – Linking with him for the Ceremony and "losing her Vanilla", like that's even a thing. Just accepting her fate that night, the way she accepts how he talks about her, and the foul things he will do to her. The canapé turns to sludge in my mouth and I spend a while struggling to swallow.

The party calms down pretty early. Everyone's keen to get back to their dorms and get enough sleep for the interviews tomorrow. I make my way over to Belle, who's still in conversation with the same girl, and cough. Belle breaks into a giant smile at the sight of me.

"Joni! You must meet Becca. Becca, this is my rival, Joni. She's great."

I shake Becca's hand. "You guys are mighty pally for rivals," she comments, raising an eyebrow at me, noticing the stark differences in our appearance.

"We're not usually," Belle laughs. "Joni hates me and thinks I'm shallow and terrible, and she's mostly right, but we're sharing a dorm."

"Well you don't seem shallow and terrible to me," Becca says.

Belle bats the comment away. "I'm not at home right now. I can afford not to be."

"Belle? I'm going up. Wanna come?"

"Yes. I'm exhausted." She stands and readjusts her kilt. "Thanks for being so friendly, Becca. I'm happy you're so happy here."

"It was lovely to meet you. I'll keep everything crossed."

They share a brief hug and then it's just Belle and me. Alone again. Climbing up the mountain of stairs to get to our room. I flop on the bed, unsure what to say, as Belle gets out a variety of potions and starts to take her Mask off in various steps. I thought she would hide this process from me, squirrelling away in the bathroom like she did when she stayed at mine, but today seems to have emboldened her. In fact, she's holding herself totally differently than she was on the train this morning; shoulders relaxed, humming under her breath, chucking cottons chock-a-block full of mask cheerfully into the bin to her side. It's quite something to watch how many tries it takes to remove her Mask fully, but slowly, gradually, Belle's natural face re-emerges and I try not to gasp. This isn't the same face I saw few months ago, after her Mask came off running away from that guy. This face is gaunt, stretched, the bags under her eyes heavy, black and sunken. She brushes out her hair and it hangs limply. She turns her back as she undresses, lifting her arms to put on Sleep Wear, and I can see every single bone of her ribs. Then I do gasp and she hears, twisting around with her top clutched to her.

"What is it?"

"Belle…are you okay?"

She laughs at my question rather than ducking it. "You know what? No. I'm not. I'm really, really not." She laughs again.

"And that's funny?"

"Yes. No."

She finishes getting dressed then turns to face me. Her Sleep Wear is unsurprisingly tiny and matching, while I'm just wearing a baggy T-shirt and shorts.

"Do you want to go to sleep?" she asks. "Or shall I go down and bring us up a hot cocoa?"

I raise both eyebrows. "You'll go out looking like that?" I gesture to her. "No Mask on or anything?"

"Yes. Why not? Isn't that the point of this place?"

"Well, then. Okay. A cocoa before bed can't hurt."

"Brilliant." She leaps up, ties a dressing gown around herself, and makes for the door, while I sit back against my pillows, my head still reeling. Just as she's about to turn the knob, she pauses. "Joni?"

"Yep?"

"I know you don't owe me anything. And I know we've got a big day tomorrow. So it's fine if you say no but…" She dances from foot to foot, her eyes darting around the room. "…but will you explain it all to me? Tonight, I mean?"

"Explain what?"

"The Truth. About the Doctrine. I…I want to know."

I shift my weight forward. I wasn't expecting this. Not at all. Especially *now*. "You actually want to know? Really?"

She nods resolutely. "Yes. I promise I won't get mad or defensive like last time."

Wow. I never thought I'd see the day. I never thought I'd succeed in Awakening Belle, of all people.

"Are you sure you're ready?" I ask, almost wanting to delay it – unsure I'm up for the giant responsibility after a long day. I'd basically given up on this whole stupid campaign, and now Belle's falling into my lap.

I expect her to waver. To say, *Sorry, let's get some sleep*. But she juts out her jaw.

"Oh yes, I'm ready," she says. "In fact, I think I'm long overdue."

BELLE

I stand by the cocoa machine in the downstairs corridor and lean my head against the cool metal. Everything's changed today. I feel it in my DNA. I smile at girls as they patter past me. This place feels so right. For the first time in weeks, months, years, my breath is reaching my stomach.

I bring up the drinks to Joni, having to push my back against the double doors so I don't spill. The chocolate smells divine. I know it's full of Sin but I don't even care. I want to know. I'm ready to learn. Ready to change. Home seems far away. Mother. Father. Damian. The Ceremony. Vanessa. My whole life. It's a dot in a different place. And, without it, I can be this person I feel beating inside of me. Someone strong. Someone curious. Someone who wants to understand. I'm starting to think I was too hasty to let this Scholarship opportunity go. I'm worried about my parents, of course, but this feeling, I can't run away from it. It feels too good. Too vital.

Joni's sat cross-legged on her bed when I get back and eyes me suspiciously as I present the drinks with a "Ta da". She doesn't believe I want to know. She doesn't believe I'm ready.

She's bracing herself for my typical behaviour of one-eighty-ing and being a total bitch, which is fair enough.

"Thanks," she says, taking the cup, and looking increasingly anxious as I join her on her bed. It's mad how, after only one day of being around Naked faces, Joni's is already less jarring. In fact, without her coming up short to every Masked girl around, I can see parts of her that really are quite beautiful. Like the deep hazel of her eyes and the perfect frame of her eyebrows, which I know for sure aren't Tamed. I gulp my drink, feeling it scorch about ten million taste buds, then lean over to put it on her bedside table.

"So," I say, sitting up.

"I'm not sure I'm the right person to tell you all this," she says, weirdly uncertain for her. "Mother's so much better at Awakenings than me."

"You're the perfect person." I squeeze her hand and little licks of electricity run up my arm as I do. "You're the one who got me this far."

"It's hard stuff to un-know," she warns. "It will be easier for you, and your life, if I don't Awaken you."

I shake my head. "You know, I think that's where you're wrong. It's actually not very easy being me."

"I can see it's very hungry being you, to be fair."

I flinch, but know it's a concern rather than an insult. It's strange. Joni's the first person who's ever expressed *concern* about my body, rather than envy or praise. "It is VERY hungry being me," I admit. And I can't tell you what it releases, admitting it. My stomach relaxes more at finally having this acknowledged. "Honestly, I can't remember a time in my life when I wasn't hungry."

It's Joni's turn to take a too-hot slurp of her drink. She blows on it with pursed lips, but comes to the same decision that it needs a while and puts it to one side. "Well, that's part of it. The purpose of the Doctrine. Keeping you hungry. Keeping us weak. It's all part of the Big Lie."

Shudders roll through my body. I can feel myself standing on the edge of the cliff, the wind whipping my hair, knowing that once I jump I can't get back up again. I can only fall and hope I'll learn how to fly rather than crash into the rocks. Outside our dorm window, the sun is setting and gold nudges at the drawn curtains. I feel bathed in light and warmth. The truth is coming. "And what's the Big Lie?" I ask.

"That we won," Joni says simply, shrugging. "That women and girls did it. That the fight is over. The Mask you wear every day, that most women wear every day, is evidence that the fight *isn't* over."

"But…the Bad Times are over. We're all equal now. Everyone says…"

She shakes her head gently, cutting me off. "No, they're not. They're still here. All the Bad Things are just more hidden, and everything we've gained has come at a cost. And this cost we wear on our faces every day. Both metaphorically and literally."

I bite my lip. "I'm still not sure I understand."

Joni smiles, lit by the gold. "I'll try my best to explain."

And as the air outside turns dark, she tries her best to wake me up.

"So," she says, clapping her hands. "The Doctrine says that the Bad Times are essentially over, right? That we achieved equality."

I remember history lessons of women marching in the street. Of them waving placards, coming together, going on strike, fighting to end the Bad Times. "And we did," I say. "We can do anything men can do now. We even had that female Leader."

Joni rolls her eyes slightly. "We've achieved a lot, sure," she says, "but there's a limit to what we can achieve for a number of reasons. Mainly, our society, how it's built, cannot function if women are given true equality. The survival of how things are literally depends on women being less, earning less, thinking they are less…despite being told everything is equal now."

My nose wrinkles without me meaning it to. "What do you mean?"

"I mean girls and women often take on the most essential roles we need to keep our society going. Whether that's by having the children we need and raising them, or nursing sick people, or nursing elderly people. Whether that's keeping homes running and clean, and keeping everybody fed and nurtured. Even if women go into the Industry, they provide their labour for less Finance. They are almost always paid less for the same Industry work." She smiles wryly and takes a sip of her drink. "The truth is, if we started actually paying women for all the vital jobs they do…well…where would the Finance come from? How do we even *begin* to start paying for these things we expect women to do for free, or insultingly cheaply? The *entire financial system* needs to change. Men and boys need to *give things up*. Give up their easier way of life, rather than relying on our free or cheap vital labour. They need to share their income with us. Take on their share of raising children. Be willing to take on those caring jobs too, or at least properly pay the women who do them."

I wrinkle my nose again. I have no idea why Joni is banging on about *Industry*. What's Finance got to do with anything? Also, this is all covered by the Doctrine. Women *choose* to do these things. They *prefer* the caring roles. We are better designed to do them. We choose to have children and shouldn't judge other women's choices. Part of the Bad Times ending was celebrating the choices we make.

Joni, sensing my discomfort, tilts her head. "What is it?" she asks. "Where have I lost you?"

I tell her everything I've just thought and how the Doctrine covers it all. "And what's it got to do with Masks and stuff? All of this?" I ask. "What has *Industry* got to do with being Pretty?"

Joni stretches out both palms. "Well, this is the important link actually. Basically, your Awakening is all about opening your eyes up to the multiple ways in which girls are deliberately tricked and pressured to think less of ourselves. To hate ourselves. To make ourselves weak. To essentially not have the self-esteem to *really* fight for true equality. To really demand the giant overhaul of the systems required for things to be actually equal. The Doctrine exists to make us truly believe we are *less than*." She takes another sip. "There are all these invisible beauty pressures to make us scared and miserable, and they're so time-consuming and impossibly hard to keep up, so we don't have the strength or time to truly fight to overthrow everything. To believe we *deserve* to overthrow everything. And Masking, and Ceremonies, and Chosen Ones, and literally every single thing associated with what we look like…how we're all groomed to worry *constantly* about what we look like…it's a deliberate pressure. It's designed to keep us down. To limit us. Divide us. Masks…Beauty…it's all about weakening and dividing us." She smiles sadly. "Once you see it, you can't unsee it."

My drink's forgotten. My head swimming. "See what?"

"That being Pretty is a trap," she says, "because we *need* girls to hate themselves so they accept less. And wanting to be Pretty isn't a choice. It's something you want out of necessity. We have to be Pretty in order to get anyone to see us in this supposed-equal society we are so lucky to live in. You have to be Pretty in order to be liked. In order to be loved. We're groomed to be terrified of showing our faces – literally just showing our natural faces to the world, because we're told natural girls' faces are plain and ugly, and artificial Masks are what make you Pretty and Visible. What does that do to us? That fear? That pressure? It's a constant distraction to undermine us." She laughs cynically. "And what makes it so hilarious is it's sold to us as being Empowered, and wanting the best for ourselves, as aspirational. Who can look the least like a real girl? She wins! But at what cost?"

I shake my head, struggling to take it in. My whole life,

I've been told by the Doctrine that it's a choice. Our choice. Her choice. My choice. That we are free, and are therefore free to make whatever choices we want.

"So it's not about getting girls to look Pretty?" I ask, still not sure I get it.

Joni shakes her head so hard her hair flies around her face. "No. Absolutely not. It's NOTHING to do with our appearance, and ALL to do with behaviour. The more we achieve, the stricter the Pretty Rules of the Doctrine get. Not so we're prettier to look at, but so *we feel worse about ourselves*, and are therefore weakened. The escalation is deliberate to cancel out any rights we've won. They up the ante so we dedicate more time and more energy and more Finance to trying to chase the impossible Pretty."

I cross my arms. "And, what? A bunch of evil people just decided this one day, as a secret plan?"

She shakes her head again. "It's not that simple. If it was that obvious, I could point it out and people would listen. People would fight against it. The power of it is that it's mostly invisible, the power of it is that we believe we have choices, the power of it is that girls totally buy into it. Adopt it. Make it their Doctrine too. Women will fight you for even *daring* to suggest there's other reasons why they dedicate endless amounts of time, energy and Finance to make themselves look like some impossible version of woman, other than they enjoy it and they actually want to."

I pick up my cup again, needing a slight pause. The drink's cooled now, and I glug down three sugary slurps to try and steady myself. It hasn't occurred to me that looking Pretty is anything other than looking Pretty. That there are other reasons to do it – the main one being my life would be much harder if I didn't.

"Think about it." Joni's off again, her hands stabbing the darkness as she explains. "Think about how impossible it is back home to think you're actually Pretty. Just take a face – any human girl's face. Then list all the things the Doctrine has told us that can be wrong with it. There's your skin. No blemishes, no pores, no dryness. Must glow. Must emit light, even though that's physically impossible. No redness. Have the right amount of melanin. Then there's the size of your forehead. Can't be too big or too small – if it is, cover it with Mask or your hair. Eyes. I could talk for ten minutes just about everything that the Doctrine says should be happening with our eyes. Is the shape of them right? Big? Small? Almond, circle? Not too googly? Or close together? What are your eyelids like? Are they hooded? They shouldn't be hooded. How long are your eyelashes? They need to be long. Not only long, but thick. And dark. At the top as well as the bottom. Are there bags under your eyes? Dark circles? Are the eyeballs themselves too red? Must spray something in them to make them white. Are there wrinkles around them? Must prevent them, or get rid of them, even though they're a scientific inevitability for all of us. Ignore that and delete them with creams, and Empowerments. Inject yourself with Immobilizer every few months so it looks like your face never lived, that your eyes never crinkled in laughter, that the years never passed. Lift them away. And hang on, I

287

almost forgot the eyebrows. They have to be perfectly shaped. Bushy and full and arched. They must be sculpted in a way that suits your face shape. This requires essentially near-constant maintenance and expense. Are we ready to move onto the nose? Can't be too big. Can't have a bump in it. Slim it down with Mask techniques. Get an Empowerment surgeon to shave actual bone off your face. What if your nostrils are too big? That can ruin everything too. Shall we move onto cheeks? Well, your cheekbones have to be sculpted – to look constantly slightly flushed and full, but also high and arching. Mask up, Mask up. You need at least three different products to achieve that. Then MOUTHS. Mouths! Lips can't be thin. Must inject them at the Empowerment Centre to make them full. Line them, colour them in. Plump them up but not too big. That's ugly too. There has to be the perfect amount of bigness. Now smile. Do you have dimples? Oh, we do like dimples. Don't have them? Have some carved in. And, oh, teeth. *TEETH.* They must be straight, and big, and whiter than freshly fallen snow – despite the fact hardly anyone is born with teeth like this. Are your front teeth too big? Are some teeth too pointy? How about your gums? Too much gum on show? Yikes, don't smile if that's the case." Joni took a giant breath and kept going. "The shape of your chin, of course, is worth consideration. You want a nice, defined chin, but not a pointy witchy one. And your neck. Can't be too fat, or too short. Your ears? Well, make sure they don't stick out too much, and that they're not too big or too small. Shall we move onto hair? Where do we even start with hair? It must have volume and look healthy but controlled.

Not too flat. Not too greasy. Jeez. Not too fine, either. Here's a list of all the different ways you can and should wear your hair. Each of them involves using at least five different products, and will take, on average, at least twenty minutes to achieve. Get it cut regularly so it's not straggly. It's boring to have hair that's all the same colour. Here's a list of all the different time-consuming and expensive ways you should colour it. You will need to repeat this process about every six weeks. And, yikes, losing pigment? No. That will instantly make you an Invisible. Fear it more than you fear death. It *is* death, in some way. As what's the point of being alive if nobody sees you?…" She runs out of steam eventually, and she drains her cocoa to revive her scratchy voice. "I could continue with everything else from the neck down – all the body parts and body image stuff – but I think you get my point," she says.

I keep blinking. I'm exhausted by her monologue. Nobody's ever spelled out all of this to me, but it's all true. I've worried about literally every single thing she's just mentioned. Whenever I look in a mirror, I'm seeing my face as the list she just listed, not just "My Face". It's a cut-up list of all the wins and losses I've managed. It's a to-do of how to improve myself. It's weird that she finished on hair. My mind flits once more to that night Mother found her first unpigmented hair. It was like a death, the way she behaved. The terror, the shock, the denial, the mourning. And now look at what she's gone through to try and keep delaying that death. The Empowerment Procedures, the pain, the infection, the debt. I don't want to think about home, not here, not now. I feel like this trip away is a gift – just the gift I needed, exactly when I needed it. I was about to resign myself to living the life my parents want, but coming here, meeting the girls, seeing what life could feel like, what *I* could feel like…I feel hopeful for the first time in my living memory.

"You've not even got into Masks," I add. "How the fashion of Masking and Looks changes all the time. Even the way I cover my face is something I can get wrong. Vanessa and I, we…" It's hard to admit this. "…we laugh about the Try Hards at school because sometimes their Looks aren't up-to-date."

Joni nods and doesn't tell me off for being a terrible, shallow person. I guess we both already know that. "Yep. The bar needs to be constantly raised, and changed, so we never have time to relax, no time to question it, to not be exhausted by it." She points at my face. "And think about it. You're one of the lucky ones. You're an actual Chosen One. Just by luck of how you came out of the womb, the way you look naturally already ticks so many of the Doctrine's boxes. And yet…are you happy, Belle? You follow the Doctrine to the letter but how do you feel about yourself?" She stares at me, curious.

My throat closes. I'm quiet for a very long time. I turn my head away from her gaze and stare at the beams around the curtained windows. The words fall about on my tongue, not wanting to be said. I don't want to admit this.

"I'm not happy, no," I say. Saying it unleashes something. Tears fall from my eyes. My shoulders sink. It hurts so much to say it out loud. It makes it real. I've been pretending it's not real for so long. "I…don't like how I look. I…it's exhausting, how hard I try. How much I need to be the best. I'm not even sure why. Because I know I win the Ranking most times, but it only feels good for a moment and then I feel scared that the next day it's going to be taken away from me. I'm so hungry. All the time. I'm so tired. All the time. My brain never stops. It's always time for a New Look, or my next Body Prayer, or a top-up treatment, or to take new images. There is always something wrong with me that needs fixing. I…I'm so tired." I really start crying then, huge pealing sobs. And Joni's up immediately, sitting next to me on the bed, pulling me to her.

"It's okay," she shushes. "Of course you're tired. That's the whole point of it. To feel like this. To be stuck in this. To hate yourself and exhaust yourself trying to be more beautiful. To feel too tired and distracted and lesser than to realize you're being exploited and should fight against that. This is the whole point."

"But *you* don't care," I wail. "You're so much better than me. You don't Mask or anything. You're so free."

She laughs. "And it comes with huge consequences," she admits. "I'm an Objectionable. People hate me. Ridicule me. People find it actively hard to look at me. Look at how Damian treats me. Nobody listens to me. It hurts me too. I reject it because I want to be free…but it hurts. To see how you're admired. How you're noticed. How people listen when you speak." She sighs and pulls me closer. "I hate seeing you like this," she says…then she pauses, with my head on her shoulder, making it wet. "And yet I'm also quite relieved. To know it hurts you too, in a different way." She sighs once more. "The

291

pain is what connects us. Mother always says it's the pain that reminds us that this is real, that there is a huge problem, that we're not imagining it. The pain means there's something we need to fight against."

I snuffle and twist my head to look up at her. "Pain?"

She nods, her eyes dewy, like she's catching my tears. "Yes, pain. The physical and the emotional. It's everywhere, in our lives, every day. Maybe it's the pain we've totally normalized from Empowerment Procedures – we don't think twice about cutting open perfectly healthy bodies with literally nothing wrong with them other than they look like a natural body, and we hardly mention the pain these Procedures cause and how long it takes to heal. Or the pain of walking in shoes that twist our feet into deformed pretzels. Or the pain of hunger gnawing at our stomachs. The pain of having our hairs ripped out. Girls accept a huge amount of daily physical pain, to try and save us from the emotional pain of rejection. You're not irrational, Belle," she says, stroking my hair, almost to soothe herself as much as me. "You're not shallow to want to avoid that pain. The pain of nobody noticing you, or listening to you, or thinking you're someone they could fall in love with. The losses that come with rejecting all this are huge, and they are painful. But the one thing Mother always reminds me of is that the whole point of this is to pull us apart, so we don't unite to fight back against it. We're united by our pain, but the Doctrine aims to divide us. It teaches us to look at every girl we meet and see them as a threat, rather than a sister to fight alongside. It teaches us to be terrified of women older than us, who may have learned some important things, so we don't listen to them when they try to warn us. Think about our Just Right years, Belle. Soon, they're over. You're only just waking up to all this, but soon you'll be considered past it, you'll be less visible. People won't listen to you when you try to talk to them about it. The girls below us will come up and take our spots and look at us and feel a bit sorry for us, but also smug and disgusted. All of it is here to divide, rather than unite. Remember, it's absolutely nothing to do with being Pretty, and absolutely everything to do with being compliant and placid."

I find my head on my knees. Everything she says makes sense but accepting it…accepting what she says as true, what does that mean? My whole life has been about embracing the Doctrine. My mother's life too…

Joni carries on, regardless of my discomfort, answering my question. "It means we'll get to the point – in fact, I believe we are at this point – where so many girls and women buckle under the pressures of the Doctrine, and try and transform themselves to meet impossible standards, that it *is* obligatory. No one needs to enforce it, because *we* enforce it. We're all so blindly buying into it that any girl who doesn't go out with a completely non-human face is called an Objectionable. It's seen as a lack of self-respect. It's so disgusting to us that we don't listen to why anyone would do it. Think of how much you hate my face the way it is. How much it upsets and irritates you to look at me…"

I open my mouth. "I don't."

"You do. I can see you do. My face looking like a face

horrifies you. So, until recently, you've never listened to me. I'm a monster. I'm something to fear, not actually be inspired by and follow."

The shame I feel is so potent I gain weight with it; it sinks me into the bed. I push myself up and wipe my eyes and turn to her. "I know I constantly need to apologize to you," I say, "but I am sorry." I stare at her through my falling tears.

Joni smiles. She's always been too kind. I've never deserved her friendship. "I'd rather you listen to me than apologize," she replies, "and it sounds like you're starting to do that."

"I am. But…it's a lot. I…I don't know what to do with it all."

She takes my hand and the warmth from it makes my heart start buzzing. "Just knowing it is the first step," she says. "And it's often the hardest one."

JONI

Bloody hell, I think I've broken Belle. I did it. I actually did it. We're just sort of lying here, in the dark, holding each other on her bed, while she stares at a wall.

I know I went too far. I've probably short-circuited her. Did I even explain it properly? I bet not. And I've missed loads out, and also probably sounded like a deranged bitter conspiracy theorist. Whatever I did, it's rendered her speechless for at least twenty minutes. Our room's completely black now and I'm not sure when to reach over and turn on the bedside lamp. Tingles of worry dance around my mind. I have the biggest interview of my life tomorrow, yet here I am, up late with my enemy, trying to get her to understand a whole lifetime of learning in an hour. Or are the tingles coming from holding her so close? I have this weird urge to smell her, to put my nose in her arm, to lean in closer. Instead, I find I'm stroking her hair to keep her calm, rubbing its buttery smoothness between my fingers.

Eventually, she twists to me, and I can just about make her face out in the moonlight.

"Joni?"

"Yes?"

"If I'm not Pretty, then what am I?"

I let out a small laugh in the dark. "You're Belle Gentle."

"But if I'm not thin, what am I?"

"You're a person, living in a body that enables you to have a life and do the things you want to do with it."

"If I don't win the Ceremony, what does that mean?"

"Nothing."

"Then why is it all so scary?"

"Because you've been trained to think it's life and death. And, in some ways, it is. As I said, it's not easy being me. Being my mother."

"At least you can eat food with Sin in it."

We both laugh in the dark, the bed shaking gently beneath us. Then Belle stiffens next to me. "I'm so scared of the Ceremony," she tells the darkness. "Damian. The Rules. I've been putting him off for so long, but I can't once it arrives."

I gulp, wondering how much she really knows about his boasting.

"I know what he's been saying about me," she says, reading my mind. "He's being so kind and sweet to my face, but I know he won't be kind and sweet when the time comes. Not if the Smut he watches is anything to go by." She buries her face into the cover and my urge to protect zings through me like a bolt of lightning. The quiet way she's just accepting the prospect of terrible, painful sex... I can't take it.

"You know that Smut is part of the Doctrine too?" I say,

being careful with every word I pick. This is such a delicate conversation already, and now it's turned to the thinnest of glass. I could get it wrong. Make things worse. Though nothing seems worse to me than Belle's body being used by some terrible guy just so he can boast about it. I realize I'm starting to care about her. It's not just about changing her mind any more. I've got to know Belle and see why she is the way she is, and now I have just this giant instinct to protect her. Alongside something else…another unfamiliar feeling.

She lifts her head, her eyes curious. She wants a way out. I can feel it. Sense it. "Really? Christ, is there anything that isn't part of the Doctrine's Big Lie?"

"It's the same thing really. Smut is used as another way of numbing women to violence, of thinking that's all they deserve. Smut is made to convince us we actually *want* to be hurt. That it's our choice. Smut is our payback for everything we fought for sexually in the Bad Times. We can protect ourselves from pregnancy now. Copulation lost its biggest consequence, its biggest inequality. If you look at the dates when they made Smut legal, it's almost *exactly* the same time we won all our fertility rights."

The whites of her eyes widen in the gloom. "No way."

I nod. "Yes. Think about how Smut makes you feel. How it *really* makes you feel. How it's everywhere. How every boy we know spends most of his time watching Smut. Watching girls like us in pain. In actual pain. Watching girls like us pretend to enjoy this pain."

"So they don't enjoy it?"

I pause, sensing the glass grow thinner. "The sex you see in Smut is, yes, usually physically uncomfortable for most girls. It's very different from the sort of sex that can feel great for us. Do girls still enjoy Smut sex even if it hurts? Hmm... I think the Doctrine has made us want to be desirable so potently, that we get *some* enjoyment out of the pain. The Doctrine teaches us that being picked and desired by boys is so inherently important that many girls think the being-picked-ness is worth the discomfort of what the boy does to your body. Also, because Smut actresses pretend it doesn't hurt, that it's actually enjoyable, we pretend along too because we don't want to be seen as 'wrong' or well...Frigid."

Belle goes very, very still.

"Are you okay?"

"Yes," she says eventually. "It's just...it reminds me of something Vanessa said. She said it hurts with Ben but she doesn't seem to mind."

I close my eyes. Vanessa is very low down my list of favourite people but it's still horrible to hear this. To know she's normalized pain to her body...intimate pain to her body. I feel my head clouding as I get overwhelmed with how awful it all is. This happens quite regularly, but it's stronger tonight, with Belle's head on the pillow next to mine, psyching herself up for something she clearly doesn't want. I feel how shocked she is by the simple truths about our lives under the Doctrine. The layers and layers of it. They all feel too much. Too hurtful. Too invisible. Too hard to fight. That's why I wanted to come to the Education. To get more power so I can fight against all this, but I do worry I can't. That it's too big. Too beyond any of us.

Belle shifts her weight and turns towards me again. "Are you okay?"

"Yeah. I'm just…poor Vanessa. I don't normally feel sorry for her, I must admit."

"She's a nice person. I'm the horrid one, mostly. Anyway, with Ben, she's so in love with him. She doesn't seem to mind whatever they do together. I mean…maybe she's lying, but she does seem okay."

"Of course, it's her choice too."

And this is the first time I ever hear Belle laugh at this phrase. "Yeah, right."

"Woah, have I converted you?"

"I don't know. Maybe… With Damian…I don't feel like I have a choice."

I reach over and pat her back. "You *do*. You really do. I know there are Rules, but they aren't official. You do actually have a choice. The choice to reject any bits of the Doctrine that you want."

She throws her hands up. "You know that Smut terrifies me? I can hardly watch it. I tried to watch it the other day, and I felt physically sick. Is something wrong with me?"

"No! Something is wrong with *Smut*. And what's wrong with it is deliberate, remember? The way girls are treated in it, and the way the violence against us is so normalized, it's part of how they brainwash us. Brainwash boys too. Even if you avoid Smut yourself, you can't avoid the effects of it, because practically all men and boys watch it. Every boy you meet and try to have any kind of relationship with, Smut has infiltrated that relationship. Whether that's falling in love with them, being their friend, trying to work with them on a Science project…hell, even the teachers educating you about the Science project are affected. You are interacting with boys and men who are being conditioned by their Smut habits into thinking girls want, or deserve, intimate pain. Violent Smut shows naked women being hurt and tells us that's sexy and normal, which makes them believe that to pleasure a girl is to hurt them. That our bodies are things to be violated and used for their pleasure. That impacts every interaction you have with them, even if it's not a sexual one. Yes, there's some Smut that is nicer, more gentle, but that's not the Smut everyone watches."

Belle sighs. "You're right. Gah, you're so right. I hate it, I hate…" The mattress wobbles as Belle turns her weight fully towards me. I sense a strange energy shift. A tingling in the air. "You know I've never had a nice kiss," she says, her voice hardly a whisper. "Every time I've kissed a boy, it's always been wet and aggressive and, like, they're doing to my mouth what they want, rather than thinking about how it *feels* for me." She stares up at me. "I'm scared that's what Copulation will be like. On a much bigger scale."

Why is my mouth dry? Throat tight? I gulp. "That's what's so sad about it. Mother always told me that our bodies are wired to be able to experience this amazing pleasure. But we're so often deprived of this, because Smut has made violence and being degraded the 'right' or 'healthy' way to be with people,

300

and it treats…tenderness, softness…as if it's deviant or 'unmanly' to want to Copulate that way." I gulp again. "Like, kissing can be so gentle. Quiet. Slow. Electric. So can Copulation. But so many of us never get the chance to experience that."

"Like me?" Belle says sadly.

"I guess."

"How about you?"

My mind flickers back to two summers ago, to this boy I met at one of Mother's training summer stays. He was one of the Good Ones. One of the few good ones. He'd lost his sister to Voluntary Starvation and had come to spend the summer trying to understand it. He was the first boy I'd met who wasn't disappointed by how I looked, but seemed to find it beautiful. *Theo…*

My mouth un-dries itself at the memory of Theo and the things we did together. "I've had some good kisses, yes. And I've Copulated with someone too…"

"You have?"

I laugh smally. "Don't be so surprised."

"But…"

Who would want to? I can imagine her thinking. Who would want to kiss me, let alone Link with someone who looked like me? Oh, Belle, if only she could realize the pleasures out there in the world that she deserves, even if she gives up being Pretty.

"It can be amazing," I say. "With the right people. I was lucky I met someone to learn this with I guess."

There's a quietness between us. It really is almost pitch

black now. I guess Belle's shocked that anyone would find me attractive enough to kiss, let alone touch me in a way that feels good. She's probably assumed I'm just a toad who lives under my ugly rock. Then her face is so close I can feel her breath on my lips, and something strange is happening to my body again. A jolt of electricity. This strange pull.

"I want a kiss. A good kiss." Her voice is both cracking and husky at the same time. Her lips are almost on mine. I have no idea what's going on. What to do. I am so, so thrown. By all of it. The day, this evening, Belle... We're not...are we?

I attempt a joke. "Well then, stay away from Damian... Oh—"

Natural as anything, Belle's kissing me. Belle's mouth is on my mouth, nudging my lips open with hers. She tastes of chocolate. There are a few seconds of being stunned. Utterly stunned. I've never kissed a girl. I've never thought I'm someone who wants to kiss girls. I never thought Belle was someone who wants to kiss girls either. I'm not sure...but oh my, I forget it all. My body sighs with how good this feels and I let myself go with it. So much has happened in one day that this may as well happen too. I kiss Belle back, and I don't even have to think about what I'm doing, or whether it feels good, because kissing her is like dancing a dance we both already know all the steps to. It's everything she's never had before. Tender. Gentle. Delicate. Yet my whole body is lit up by it, and the way she's leaning into me, the little sigh she lets out, lets me know she's lighting up too. The room goes hazy. Time slips down some mysterious magical drain. My life, my reasoning,

302

fades to nothing, and we both stay lost in how good this feels for quite some time. Before, finally, Belle pulls away. Her face is hardly visible, it's now so dark.

"Okay," she says, and she's giggling. "So that just happened."

Now she's stopped the kiss, reality has caught up with me fast, tapping me on the shoulders, out of breath from the chase. What just happened? What did we just do? And why? "It did," I manage.

"I…I'm sorry."

"No, don't be."

"I'm not a…I don't think."

"Neither am I…"

"But we just…"

"We did…"

Belle pushes herself up and leans over to turn on the bedside light. The room comes into glaring focus, and I scramble up, disorientated, like I've just woken up. She raises her knees up, and I worry she's about to freeze me out. Leave me with this and what's just happened. But she doesn't. She looks right at me. "I'm so confused," she admits, with pure honesty in her voice. "I don't want to hurt you. I have no idea why I just did that. This whole night, this whole trip…I feel like I'm unravelling."

I budge over to comfort her, and I feel the electricity between us leave. Something different…stronger…emerging to take its place. A bond. I'm not sure if it's friendship or something else. "Hey, it's okay. It's not like I've been secretly lusting after you and you've broken my heart."

303

"But I'm so Pretty! How could you not?"

We both laugh and the air fully defuses around us with her joke.

"I'm such a mess," she says, throwing her hands up. "My head's all over the place. Since my mother's Procedure, she's now got all this debt. I'm thinking of giving up trying for the Scholarship so I can stay at home and work to help repay everything, but I don't want to. And then there's everything with Damian. The Ceremony. And now you just sit me down and tell me that everything I've ever known and believed is wrong and a ploy, and I have no idea why I do anything I do, or what I want, or what to do next, or anything… So of course, why not kiss the girl who has only ever been nice to me, and who I've only ever been horrible to. Way to go, Belle."

I giggle and realize I don't mind. I don't mind that she kissed me. I don't care that she doesn't know why. Because I don't know why I returned her kiss. I'm just as confused as she is. It felt amazing. I sort of want to do it again. I sort of want her to want to do it again and I have no idea what that means. But I don't mind that I'm confused. It just feels vaguely hilarious. I just kissed Belle Gentle. That's *hilarious*.

"I'm okay," I tell her. "It doesn't have to mean anything."

"I'm not sure about that."

Our eyes lock and I'm so glad she's just said that. "Okay, how about it doesn't have to mean anything right this moment."

She throws her hands up again. "Stop being such a good person all the time! Why are you so wise and clever and bigger than me in every way?"

I shrug. "I have a lot more time than you to practise. I don't spend three hours a day painting a fake face over my real one."

She laughs again and mock-thumps me. Then she leans her head into my shoulder and I lean my face into her hair.

"Yes, well, maybe I want to stop doing that."

"Really?" I ask her hair.

"Yes. I want to stop. I want to escape my life back home. I want to fight. I want to change. But I don't know how…"

I smile against her head as the perfect plan lands effortlessly into my mind. "I know a really good place to start."

BELLE

It's today. It's here. The day we've all counted down to. School is finished until we return for our final assessments, and there is just one thing anyone cares about in the meantime. The Ceremony. *My* Ceremony. I look in the mirror and everything's perfect. It's taken for ever. In fact, this reflection is the result of two days' solid and intense work but, wow, is it worth it. The Mask's perfect. Dewy, glowy, radiant. Every detail of the face staring back at me is totally transformed. Perfect. The hair falls beautifully, rippling down the back, while parts of it are pinned up to give volume. The dress couldn't fit better, and the whole accompanying look is one of pure Princess. A worthy winner of the Ceremony. Beauty. Royalty. I bite my lip as I take it in.

"You look so beautiful," I tell Joni, who's standing next to me, an exquisite vision. I tuck my Mask brush behind my ear. "Totally and utterly beautiful."

"I know," she laughs. "I hate it. What the hell have you done to me?"

And we both watch ourselves burst into giggles.

My own reflection is a stark comparison to Joni's. I wear not a scrap of Mask. My hair's stripped but hangs down naturally, curling in an annoying way at the front and frizzing a bit at the back. I have two blemishes on my chin from stress, that radiate redness and anger like sirens. My eyes are small, tired. My lips are pale. I feel slightly sick whenever I look at myself, wondering if this plan is worth it, if I'm brave enough to follow it through. My whole life, I've been building towards tonight. And now I plan to throw it all away, to break every Rule I've ever been taught.

"You look beautiful too," Joni says, sensing my anxiety. She squeezes both my shoulders, still looking at ourselves in the mirror.

"Yeah right."

"Honestly, you've never looked better."

"I think literally everyone tonight is going to think the complete opposite."

"I won't."

"Yeah, well, you're a weirdo."

"I feel like a weirdo with all this crap on my face. Seriously, how do you cope? I can feel my skin gasping for breath. And my hair is crispy. *CRISPY.*"

I laugh again. "You've not even gotten into your shoes yet."

"Don't remind me. I've written a memorial speech for my ankles in preparation."

I'm grateful for the laughter to distract me from it all. It's been such a mad week. We both had to get through our entrance exam and interviews totally sleep-deprived, although, to be fair, I'd never felt more awake my whole life. I actually had my interview with the Professor from the induction lecture, and the hour with her cemented the knowledge that I wanted nothing more from life than to get this Scholarship. Even with my woeful lack of preparedness, I felt I aced it. I spoke honestly and frankly about the pressures I was under back home, how I saw this Scholarship as the start of a new life, the first step on an important journey. She kept nodding and saying, "*Yes, this is what we love to see here. One day within our walls, and look what's happened to you.*" I came out beaming, knowing I'd done my absolute best. It was then Joni's turn, and she'd come out equally ramped up, excited and saying she thought it had gone "really well".

"All we can do is wait," she'd said. "And not let this get between us."

"Never in a million years."

"If I don't get in, you getting in will really help take the edge off that pain."

"Ditto."

We hugged and jumped up and down and, on the journey home, hatched our plan. Joni was so wonderful, talking everything through about my family, making me realize it's not my responsibility to be everything my mother needs me to be. That I've got to do what's right for me, not her. I cried multiple times, but was soon distracted by our master plan to disrupt the Ceremony. Since then, I've been working my arse off getting Joni ready for it. There was quite a significant amount of work to do. Finding her a dress, ripping all her hairs out, putting her Look together, working out how to emotionally prepare my mother for the fact I was about to erode our life's work. The only upside of the debt was I could encourage her to not do my Mask.

"You need the Finance too much," I'd told her, whispering one night so we didn't wake Father. "I can do my own Mask, and you know you'll get about a trillion clients if you're not focused on me."

"Belle, I can't. It's your Ceremony. It's the most important night of your Just Right years."

"Yes, but we need to pay the bills. I've got a plan for a different look anyway."

Her head snapped around. "What? Belle, it's quite late in the day to be changing something so important."

"Mother, it's fine. It's in the bag. This way, you can book at least four Masking appointments, charging top price." I reached over and kissed her face, careful not to press on her scars lurking beneath their thick Mask. "You know it makes sense."

The plan was weaving itself together. Belle would *not* be the belle of the ball. I would not win the Ceremony. Instead I would totally disrupt it, with the simple act of showing my natural face. The face I was born with. The face that has been hidden most of its life. It shouldn't feel like an act of gross sabotage, but it sort of does. I'm breaking everything the Doctrine tells me to do tonight. And I'm not only "letting myself down", but my family down too – and Damian, hilariously, to some degree, who's showered me with lovely messages all week, saying how excited he is and asking how the Scholarship went. The utter relief I feel about not having to

Copulate with him tonight is so strong I can't stop laughing – I feel light with it. I glance up at our reflections again, and it's so jarring. Her, the Pretty. Me, the Objectionable. She looks so Pretty but I keep overriding my brain and telling myself she doesn't look Pretty, she just looks compliant. Her appearance is relaxing to me because it's finally what's expected, rather than the jarring aggression of what she normally looks like. I glance at her lips, which I've sketched perfectly, and a slight tingle runs through me as I remember that night in the dorm. How gentle they were. We seem to have made an unspoken pact not to mention our kiss as there's so much going on, but I think about it a lot. How good it felt. Unlike what Damian has planned for later. Oh, Damian, I'm going to let you down in so many ways tonight and I don't even care.

"Right, I better go," I say, looking down at my Device. It's been pinging all day as everyone uploads their Looks to the Ranking. Many girls couldn't get professional Maskers for the good slots, so got painted way too early and are keen to capture their efforts and get Validation before their Masks start to droop. Before Joni, I would've spent today scrolling through them, obsessing over them, zooming in on them, scouting out my competition, worrying I wouldn't win, that someone would outdo me at the last minute, anticipating posting my own Look. How I've *dreamed* of the moment of posting my Ceremony Look. How I've imagined the Validation coming in, the thrill of it, as I check and check, seeing more and more. But I know I'd feel empty afterwards. I always feel empty afterwards. Tonight is all about trying to feel full.

Joni struggles to stand up to hug me goodbye. She tugs the top of her dress about five times. "I'm so uncomfortable," she complains. "And hungry. But, if I eat anything, I think the dress will split."

I wrap my arms around her. "But you look so Pretty."

"That's all that matters."

We laugh and hug once more. I spot her checking her Mask for damage from the hug and giggle to myself at our total role reversal. "Are you sure you're okay facing your parents yourself?" she asks.

I gulp. "Yes, it's better I'm alone. It's going to get nasty."

"Remember, you're not doing anything wrong. Your life is for you, not them. I know you love them, but you're allowed to be who you are, rather than who they need you to be."

I gulp again. "I know."

"And you're alright walking home?"

I shrug. I feel so much less scared than I did only a week ago. "It's only two blocks, and hey, what hair and make-up am I going to ruin? None."

"I literally can't imagine walking to yours in these shoes."

"Well, it's a good thing you don't have to."

She shuffles alongside me to her bedroom door, her dress making rustling noises from the tight fabric. We hesitate on the threshold.

"Are you sure you want to do this?" she asks yet again.

"I'm sure."

"You're being very brave."

"I'm not. I'm literally just not putting a Mask on."

"It shouldn't be brave. It shouldn't be revolutionary. But it is. I'm…proud of you, Belle. I'm proud to be your sort-of friend."

I feel my eyes well up and I wipe the tear away comfortably, knowing it won't ruin my Mask in any way. Whereas Joni's panic-dabbing at her face with a tissue. "I'm proud to be yours too. Yikes, who could ever have imagined it? Us? Friends?" I grin at her. "And tonight will be fun, you know," I say, wanting to convince myself. "Hey, you may even win the Ceremony."

"And then the world will end."

"It won't. But it would show everyone just how ludicrous this whole thing is if we're able to switch social standings practically overnight. Anyway. I'll see you there."

She takes in as deep a breath as her dress allows, and I realize she's having to be brave too. It's not the easy option, what she's doing. She's playing with a dangerous fire, and she knows it. "See you there, gorgeous."

When I get home, I run up to my room before Father can see me. Then I stay holed up in there, waiting for Mother to return and everything to get awful.

"I'm busy getting ready," I call when he knocks on my door.

"Okay, my darling. Make sure you leave enough time for photos though."

He's been in a jolly mood all week, with the Ceremony approaching. Our whole family is invested in the importance of this and what it means for our collective and individual identities. He is the Husband to one of the Prettiest women, and Father to one of the Prettiest girls. My father has collected compliments about us and used it as oxygen since as early as I can remember.

My beautiful girls.

That's all we've ever been.

His beautiful girls.

His.

There's not much longer to wait, but I really don't have much to do. I go and have a quick armpit wash in the bathroom as I got sweaty from the walk. But that's it. Nothing else to do but sit and freak out about how I'm letting my family down and ruining everything I've spent my whole life working towards.

Vanessa's sent me a thousand messages.

Vanessa:
How's it going?
Oh God, my Mask. It's not going to plan.
Why haven't you uploaded on the Ranking yet?
Is everything okay? I'm not sure when to
post mine.
Are you excited about DAMIAN tonight?
NO MORE VANILLA
Okay, seriously, where is your upload? I want to
see your Look! You've been so cagey!
Fine then. Be like that. Carriage is coming to
pick me up at six, so we'll be at yours by six
twenty-ish.

I CAN'T BELIEVE THE CEREMONY IS
FINALLY HERE

I type out a million replies but none of them make sense. None of them will prepare her. I have no idea what her response will be tonight, how me doing this will impact our friendship. I sit at my dressing table and take in my appearance once more. I've never spent so much time looking at my natural face like this. This "starting palette" is something I cover up the moment I wake. It's not the finished product. It's not my face as I've known it, since I started Masking aged eleven.

But it is my face. It is. It is. And my face is enough.

I hear the front door click open and shut. Mother's excitement pours up the stairs. "I'm home! Where are you, my beautiful girl? Oh I can't wait to see you."

My whole body tightens. This is it. What am I doing? Why? What's wrong with me? It's almost six o'clock. It's too late to backtrack. And I want this. I want to be this person. I want to let go of old Belle. But, Mother. I'm sorry, I'm so, so sorry.

I take in a breath, smooth down my plain, comfortable dress, and I make my way downstairs.

"There she is." Mother's voice is more screech than voice when I pause at the top of the stairs. I don't see their faces at first. Instead they are both giant camera lenses, flash-flash-flashing away at their stunning daughter, the likely winner of the Ceremony, their precious...

"Oh my, Belle, what's happened?"

I make myself breathe as I waltz down the stairs, holding

my head high, like I'm proud of how I look. It's so easy to walk down stairs in flats. Everyone should totally try it.

"I'm ready," I say, coming to a stop in front of them. I smile widely and spin around, just as Father lowers his camera too. I do really like this dress. I wore it last summer, during the heatwave, and it's baggy and short but breathable and super comfortable, with pockets.

"What's going on?" Father asks, puzzled but not panicking yet. "Why aren't you dressed?"

I hold out the skirt of my dress. "I am dressed."

Mother's mouth is hanging open like she's stuck that way. Utter and complete horror widens her eyes. "Belle, honey, this isn't funny."

"I think I look nice."

"You don't have a Mask on! Your hair. Your dress! Where's your beautiful dress?"

I make myself twirl around like an excited bride. "This dress is more comfortable. I can actually dance in it."

They still think I'm winding them up. They're still in disbelief. I glance at the clock ticking on the wall behind them. Only ten minutes before the carriage arrives. How do they expect me to get all Masked up in ten minutes?

Father's looking me up and down, eyebrows furrowed. I have to fight the urge to cover my chest with crossed arms. I want to appear confident and free, not scared and scrutinized, but it's hard.

"I don't understand," he says. "Belle. I don't understand."

"There's nothing to understand. This is how I'm going."

"But you look so…"

"What?" I demand. "I look so what?"

"You look like an…"

"Objectionable?"

"I don't even know. I just know you don't look like yourself, poppet!"

"This is literally what I look like. I couldn't look more like myself if I'd tried. This is essentially the most me I could ever look."

Mother reaches out and takes his hand. "I think she's being serious." She says it gravely, more and more horror widening her eyes.

I throw up my arms. "I AM being serious. I don't want to do it any more. Being so hungry. Wasting hours of my life each day applying a Mask over my face. Only caring if I'm the Prettiest, or getting the most Validation, or how much Sin I've eaten that day."

Mother takes a step forward and I worry for a second she's going to slap me. "It's the Rules, Belle."

"Says who?" I almost yell back. "It's not the law, is it? I'm not going to be arrested tonight for going like this."

Her face is starting to go pink and it highlights the scarring by her ears, even through her heavy Mask. "Well you certainly won't win the Ceremony."

"I don't care. What does winning mean anyway?"

"These are your Just Right years." She's trying to calm me, plead with me, win me over. "You only get them once. And winning will help your Chosen One work. Don't do something you'll regret."

I throw my hands up to the air. "Don't you see how nuts that is? That I get, what, two to three years *tops*, to feel like I have any power? To feel like I'm Pretty? Then what? As younger girls come up behind me, I just feel more and more Objectionable? What sort of way to live my life is that? Also, guess what? I AM in my Just Right years, and I WAS going to win the Ceremony, and yet I never once felt Pretty. Or happy. So what's the point? Really? What's the point?"

Father's walking off, shaking his head, acting like the sound of my voice is an irritating barking dog. It hurts watching him drop his camera to the sofa. Not wanting to document his daughter's face. The face that came from him. The face I was born with. He only wants to celebrate me looking like non-human girl. Like a societally constructed obstacle course of a girl. And it hurts. I remember what Joni has told me, time and time over. It's not a choice. Because you risk losing love if you don't play by the Rules.

Mother watches him walk off, and when he's clearly not listening she twists back to me, her face even redder. "Look, Belle, I don't know what you're playing at, honey," she whispers urgently, "but this has got to stop. We can still fix this, okay? We'll delay your carriage, and there's a lot I can do very quickly. Don't make the worst mistake of your life."

I laugh. "Going outside without a Mask on will be the worst mistake of my life?"

"When did you suddenly start hating Masks? Masks ARE this family. If it wasn't for them, there'd be no roof over your head, no food in your stomach. You think your father's job

317

gives us enough Finance to live off?" She shakes her head, her face a full sneer. "Not at all. I carry all of us with my Masking business, and if we didn't have such great Masks ourselves, nobody would book me. You owe your whole life to Masks! Now, please, let's go upstairs and fix this."

I shake my head. "No, Mother. I don't want to. I'm sorry. I really am."

She lets out a grunt of frustration and shakes me. Actually shakes me. "You're so ungrateful. I would KILL to have my Just Right years back. To win the Ceremony. To feel like that again. You're so ungrateful. So...I don't...I can't...how dare you waste this? How dare you?"

"Mother, stop." I push her back just as I hear the carriage pull up outside. There's a loud honk and Vanessa's voice as she leans out the window.

"Belle, get your stunning butt out here, it's time for the Ceremony." Followed by whoops and cheers from my friends. Well, people who may no longer be my friends in five minutes' time.

I turn my attention back to my mother. My mother who I love so deeply, even with everything she's saying. I see the scars by her ears, the thick paste on her face, the fear and jealousy in her eyes and I wish so much I could make her happy. Could help her free herself from this place. But she's not ready.

"I love you," I tell her, my voice tripping on withheld tears. "I'm so grateful for everything you've ever done for me and this family. But I want to do this. I need to do this. I don't want to be scared any more. I want to be happy. I want to be free.

318

Please, Mother, try and understand…"

And before she can drag me back, and before I can change my mind, I take a deep breath, check myself one last time in the hallway mirror, and step out to meet my carriage. Just as I leave, I upload the picture of my Look I took upstairs onto the Ranking.

JONI

So, okay, this is clearly how the trap works. Christ, it's powerful. I literally cannot stop looking at myself in the mirror. I want to marry my mirror. I have, at least twice since Belle left, reached out and *stroked* my own reflection.

For years I've been tempted by this. Have wondered about this. Have, in my weaker moments, fantasized that, yes, maybe I am Pretty after all. I've pictured this Transformation in all its glory. Now it's happening, at the most fairy-tale time, the night of my very own Ceremony, where I'm Nominated to potentially win. It's like being on drugs. The drugs of my own reflection.

A reflection, I remind myself, it took two days to create.

Mother hasn't seen me yet. She's downstairs, lost in some new legal document that she wants to campaign against. She hardly acknowledged Belle and her transformation when she came bounding down the stairs, vibrating with nerves. I still can't believe she's doing it. Going through with it. I feel so unbelievably proud of her, it's almost sickening.

"Mother?" I call, watching my mouth in the mirror. Wow, this colour really does suit me. Belle has drawn around my lips in this strange tattoo pen, making everything defined, and then also added stuff that plumps them up too. I never knew my mouth could look like this. "I'm ready."

"Brilliant," she calls back, half distracted, half still punishing me. It's not just Belle who's been having a tricky time recalibrating with her parents. I eventually built the courage to tell Mother I'm meeting Father next week, and she's been basically non-verbal ever since. Will hardly make eye contact with me, she's so betrayed. It feels completely wrong, us being like this, but her behaviour has made a strange part of me grind my heels in and stay determined to go. He is my father. That means something. It's not strange for me to want to see him, maybe get some answers, an apology, a hug…

I pick up the heavy skirt of my dress and take one last look at myself before I descend the stairs. I'm nervous too, it has to be said. I know I get off lightly in this experiment compared with Belle, but still. What if I'm laughed at? What if people call me a Try Hard? And, the most dangerous outcome yet…what if I can't come back from this? What if tonight ruins me? Makes me like Belle was? Obsessed, addicted, competitive? I'm drinking poison because Belle says it's important to know what it tastes like, but what if I like the taste too much?

It takes much time to descend the stairs as I'm very wary of tripping and dying. I remind myself of this, to help counterbalance the poison. I note how restricted my body is. How I have to think about the placement of each foot, and I'm not even in my stupid heels yet. *This is control*, I remind myself. I look Pretty, yes, but it's not about looking Pretty. It never has been. It's about control…

I come to the bottom and feel my heart ramp up at the close proximity to Mother. She's going to turn and see me any moment now and I'm not sure how she's going to handle it. I shuffle to her desk, where she's still lost in a stack of paperwork, her unpigmented hair pulled on top of her head, her eyes red and tired as she reads the small print. I…I hate this, but I can't help but compare myself to her. Now I'm Masked, now I'm as perfect as I can make myself get, her juxtaposition to me is huge. I feel the distance. I feel the weird sour taste of superiority on my tongue. *Look at the state of her.* Look how tired and saggy and old and past-it she looks, compared to me, with my youth and glow and Just Rightness radiating off me. I shake my head to dislodge the poison and cough to get her attention.

"Sorry, honey, I'm so distracted today. It's just this awful bill. It's going to make it legal to…" She turns and her face freezes. "What the actual hell have you done to yourself?" Total horror latches onto all her features, and her eyes scan me frantically like I've been shot multiple times and she's trying to work out where to stem the bleeding.

I curtsey and laugh a weird dumb laugh. "All ready for my Ceremony."

She stands and then crouches before me, reaching out with both hands, almost as if to shake me. "Joni? What is this? I… who did this to you? I…I…"

"Mother, it's fine. Belle did it…"

"What? Who? I should've known. I never should've let her into this house. Oh Joni…"

"Mother! It's not what it looks like, I promise."

She's standing again, pacing back and forth, unable to look at me. I feel shame bloom through me, even though I know it's not what she thinks.

"Mother? Mother! I'm not trying to be a Pretty. Well, I am, but just for tonight. It's this experiment I'm doing with Belle. She's not what you think. We got through to her! She's Awake. She's going to the Ceremony tonight totally Maskless. Can you believe it? She says it's the best way to wake everyone else up. To get them to question everything. And, she said, if we're going to fight this together, it's worth me seeing what it's like from the other side. If we show how easy it is to switch societal standing, it may get everyone at school to think how fragile and pointless it all is. This is just one night, Mother. One! Think of it as me going undercover."

I'm not sure if she's listening. She's still pacing, muttering to herself. I knew she'd likely be reactionary, but I wasn't anticipating this...this...free fall almost, into some dark place. She stops and turns, stares right at me.

"I can hardly look at you."

You've hardly been able to look at me all week anyway.

"It's just for one night, I promise."

"You think that. But, oh, Joni, this is a dangerous game you're playing."

"I know what I'm doing. And isn't it important? To understand what it's like on the other side?"

She bites her lip. "Honey, we *know* what it's like on the other side. Don't you remember? Life with your father?" She sighs. "Oh, I forgot. You obviously don't as you're happily going to see him again. You're forgetting everything I taught you, everything we've been through together."

I wince. "Mother, I don't think these things are the same."

"Aren't they? Don't you remember how he used to speak to us? If we weren't Pretty enough? You should take some photos tonight. Show him when you meet up with him. He'll be very proud."

"Yeah, well, maybe it's not totally mad to want my father to be proud of me. To want to see him. Maybe that's a totally natural thing to want." Her eyes redden. I can see it's hurting her too much to talk again. Guilt makes my stomach heavy and there's no space for that in this dress. "I know what I'm doing, Mother. About everything. And, tonight, it's just an experiment."

She's shaking her head, walking away from me towards the kitchen. "The Doctrine's pull is too strong. You're walking into a trap. I know you think you know what you're doing, but you don't. It took me years to wean us off, Joni. Years. And it can all be undone so quickly. The whole system is there to drag you back in. Just you wait and see. Tonight…you'll see. Go out like that, and see how it feels to have everyone tell you how much worth they see in you now, and how it feels…and then tell me you won't find it hard to wake up and be Objectionable again tomorrow."

I throw up my arms, which is quite hard to do in my tight dress. "But what if there's nothing wrong with wanting to be Pretty? I look nice. It feels good to look nice. What's wrong with that?"

"Because you know it's a trap! You're in over your head here. That stupid girl has been such a bad influence."

"I'm not in over my head! I just want to try it. For one day. And I just want to give my own father one chance. Why is everything so black and white with you?"

"Because it is. But, hey, why are you going to listen to me? I'm an Invisible, aren't I?"

I feel my eyes prick with tears, and yet I can't wipe my face because I'll ruin my Mask. "Mother, you know that's not true."

"Why listen to me? I'm old and gross and bitter and jealous."

"Mother."

"Oh, just go. Enjoy it. God knows it won't last. You. This. It gets taken from all of us. Though it feels so much better when we've chosen to give it up beforehand."

"Mother, it's just one night."

And it is.

What can go wrong in one night?

BELLE

Breathe. Just breathe.

Which is easy to do in this dress, so that's something.

My Device is already going mad in the bag I've got hitched over my shoulder. I put my best smile on. I must lean into this. I must try and enjoy this and inspire others. It's going to be hard, but I'm ripping off a plaster...

The windows of the carriage roll down and I wave as Vanessa, Damian and Ben's stunned faces greet me on the other side of it.

"What the actual hell?" Vanessa's almost smiling in her shock. She looks at me in total amazement.

"Hey, guys," I call, acting like nothing's different. "The Ceremony starts here!"

I yank the door open, keeping my smile on, then lean over. "Do we want some photos before I get in?"

There's a collective silence, apart from Vanessa's quiet laughter. I think she's totally stunned. Damian's eyes are red, and he's scanning me up and down, a white Ownership Flower frozen in his hand.

"What's up?" I have a huge urge to hide my body, to turn away and shelter behind a bush. But I fight it. It's just a body. My body. My face. It's a beautiful thing, just as it is.

Vanessa manages to get something out. "Belle? What's going on? You look…why aren't you ready?" She starts giggling again. As reactions go, she's not been horrible yet.

"I'm ready. I just posted my Look on the Ranking."

Damian's nostrils flare at this additional information. That's when I feel the first hum of danger from him. "Other people have seen this already?" His voice is calm, but everything about his face has turned red. If it's on the Ranking, it can't really be undone.

I shrug and keep up my pretend breeziness. "Yeah, I guess. So, photos? *Photos?*"

Vanessa clambers out of the carriage awkwardly. "Why not? I mean…this is…something…let's document it." Once she stumbles out on her heels, I hug her fiercely, loving her for embracing this, even if I'm unclear if she's taking the piss or not. The boys get out too, looking confused but following her lead, while Vanessa asks the driver to take some group shots. She arranges us in order and gets us all to smile.

"Don't your parents want to take some?" she asks, as we're huddled together. The driver asks Damian to put his arm around me, and I feel a tight squeeze on my shoulder, one that makes me wince. When I glance over, I see the red has moved to his ears.

I grin at Vanessa and pretend everything's normal and fine when, inside, I'm terrified and hurt, yet also exhilarated.

"Oddly enough, no. They don't like this particular Look."

Between shots, she leans over and whispers in my ear. "What the hell is going on? Are you going mad? Do I need to perform an intervention? I'm quite…freaked out to be honest. I'm worried."

"I'm fine," I insist, still facing forward and smiling as we're told to say cheese. "I appreciate you worrying, honestly. But I'm okay. This is just…this is something I want to try."

Damian overhears and pinches my shoulder like an angry crab. "And you thought *tonight* was the best night to try something like this?" he growls. "The Ceremony? When you're Nominated to win?"

"Ow." I take his hand off my shoulder. "What's wrong, Damian?"

"You…you don't look like you."

"On the contrary, this is exactly what I look like."

"You know what I mean."

I sigh. "Shall we just get in the carriage already? I've not got an explosive tied to my chest. I'm just not wearing a Mask…"

The driver hands Vanessa her camera back and shoos us into the carriage. We start climbing in. Both the boys cannot stop staring at me. In fact, Ben's eyes are almost glued to my face.

"I never knew you got blemishes," he says, practically in awe.

"So do most people."

"But not you."

The engine starts and the driver starts reversing out of my driveway.

"And…your eyes…they look tired."

"It's been a busy week."

"I…this is so weird."

"It's not weird, it's just my face."

We all jump as Damian thumps the side of the carriage, the driver yelling at him to stop. "Oh, this is just stupid," he says, snarling and coiling up into his suit like a snake. "Absolutely stupid."

I twist in my seat as we leave my road, looking at my home getting smaller. My parents didn't wave me out. They didn't take one photo. Damian looks like he wants to murder me. I really hope I've made the right decision.

The ride to the Ceremony is tense. Ben won't stop staring at me and asking me questions.

"So, your hair? It's not naturally all lovely and wavy?"

"No. It takes about an hour to make it like that."

"So, when you wake up in the morning, your hair is like this…all flat?"

"Yeah."

"Woah." He takes me in again. "And your nose. Why does your nose look different?"

"Because I blend three different shades of Mask products together to make it look slimmer."

"You put Mask on your nose?"

"Yes."

I try to catch my reflection in the window to see if my nose really is that bad, while I hear him turn towards Vanessa, who's still using giggling as her coping strategy. "Nessie?" Ben asks. "Do *you* wear Mask on your nose?"

"No," she says, while I keep staring out the window. "I wake up every morning looking exactly like this." I suppress a laugh and turn towards her to see her wink at me. I smile back in relief and it's the first time I fully take in her Look. I know tonight is just as important to her as it is to me, and she's been preparing for months. And, woah. I'm blown apart. Vanessa looks utterly stunning. Every part of her Look works, from the neon yellow dress she's wearing, to the flawless Mask teamed with a hot pink lip. She is perfection. Utter perfection, and I beam at her again while she wiggles her eyebrows at me – taking it all in her stride, while Damian glowers to my side, his ears still tinged with red.

Vanessa holds up her Device. "Belle, your Ranking is going insane. Everyone's liking it."

"Really?" A tiny thrill dances in my veins. The taste of poison on my tongue. Maybe people think I'm Pretty regardless? Isn't that the ultimate dream?

"Yes, it's your most popular one to date."

Ben nudges Damian. "You hear that?" he half whispers. "People like it."

"They're being ironic," Damian replies, his voice gruff and dismissive, still staring out the window.

I try to ignore how the Ranking makes me feel. How it gives me a false hope. We're almost at the Ceremony and I feel my armpits and palms start to sweat. I distract myself by taking in

Vanessa's perfection again. "You look amazing." I reach out and squeeze her hand.

"Really?" Her voice is shy, modest, but I can also sense she knows how brilliant she looks. That she's quietly thrilled with herself.

"Honestly, Nessie. I... Well done. I'm sorry I've been so AWOL and such a bad friend recently, but clearly you don't need my advice. You really do look absolutely flawless."

She smiles, revealing her gleaming white teeth. "Thank you. And, yeah, you really have gone missing recently. Looks like you're going through something..."

"Something ridiculous," Damian mutters, ruining our moment.

That's when I lose my temper. "Excuse me, Damian," I say, tapping him on the shoulder and breaking all the Doctrine's Rules on placidity. "But I can't help but notice you're being a total dick. What's your problem?"

He turns away from the window and snarls around like an escaped bull. "You," he spits. "You're my problem. I could've taken any girl tonight. *Any*. And you repay me for choosing you by turning up like that?"

I put my hands on my hips. "And what's wrong with me looking like this?"

"You're a mess. You're a total mess. You look like an Objectionable. At the Ceremony! Even *they're* trying tonight, for fuck's sake. Even they understand the importance of the Ceremony."

"I don't look like an Objectionable," I say, hoping lowering my voice will calm him down. I'm quite scared by his rage, it has to be said. "I look like a human girl. There's nothing objectionable about looking like a human girl."

"I can't believe under all of it, you look like this." He grimaces. "Talk about false fucking advertising."

I blink and try not to flinch. Am I really so disgusting without my Mask on?

"Oh, you can talk about false advertising," I say, refusing to let the poison sink in. "*Mr I'm Suddenly Being Really Nice to You So I Can Screw You.* Do you think I'm deaf? Or stupid? I know what you've been telling everyone about later tonight."

The carriage slows. We're here. At the Ceremony. Outside, there's crowds of everyone from school, revealing their Looks, showcasing their efforts, posing for photographs with their carriages. The silent grading is beginning. We've counted down for years to this moment and now we're here. I can't even see the venue, it's so packed.

"Yeah, well," he says, "if you think I'm going near you tonight looking like that, you can think again."

I fake-clutch my hand to my heart in sarcasm, while Vanessa and Ben gawk at us. "Oh no! You mean I don't get subjected to sexual violence tonight?" I say. "I don't have to re-enact one of your awful Smut clips? Poor me! Here I was, so looking forward to you…what is it you've been saying…*destroying* me?"

He lets out a hack of a laugh. "I knew it. I knew you were a Frigid." He chucks his Ownership Flower at me and it smacks me in the chest. I gasp, and watch him storm out of the carriage, his face turning from monstrous to charming the second his polished shoe hits the pavement. The three of us watch him, gawping, as he stalks through the crowds, cheerfully greeting everyone.

There's a moment or two of stunned silence, us all watching him, before Vanessa turns to me and I can see in her face that she's unsure how to proceed. "I really hope you know what you're doing," she says, picking neutrality, before holding out her delicate, manicured hand to be escorted out by Ben.

Vanessa, too, is transformed when she steps out of the carriage – acting calm and regal. Everyone stands back to take in this main event. A potential Queen arriving at the Ceremony, looking like every fairy tale come true. Playing the part. Living the dream. Fulfilling the Doctrine. There are gasps as people see her perfected Look. She doesn't look back, and I realize that was the extent of her friendship tonight. She's offered me all she can offer. She hasn't scorned me, but she isn't going to be associated with me either.

I'm on my own.

JONI

Okay, so it's actually mad how being a Pretty changes literally everything right away. Darnell's reaction is my first indication of just how screwed everything is.

"Joni, oh my," she says, when I hop out the carriage and knock on her door to pick her up. We're meeting the others there, as attendance at the Ceremony is a Rite of Passage that even Objectionables are loathe to miss. "Oh my, oh my. You look...*amazing*. I don't understand." She steps out into her front garden, twisting an ankle slightly in her low heels, and can't stop gawping at me. "What's going on?"

"It's just this experiment I'm doing," I try to explain, crossing my arms, hating the scrutiny. "Belle and I decided to swap places for the night. To try and learn from each other and make everyone think."

Now her mouth falls fully open. "You guys are in on this together? Have you SEEN her Ranking? I can't believe it. You knew? And you..." She throws out her hand to me. "And... you're able to look like that."

I turn and try to steer her back towards the car. She's

practically star-struck by me. It's weird. I don't like it. It's not how our friendship is supposed to be.

"Darnell, it's taken *two days* to look like this, with Belle's expert help. And literally every part of my body is uncomfortable."

We open the carriage door and shuffle inside. It's just a regular carriage, rather than one of the hugely fancy ones most of the students are getting to the Ceremony. The driver's playing the radio and hardly acknowledges us as we slam the door behind us. Darnell's still gawking as she puts on her safety belt. "But you look amazing," she states. "Completely amazing."

Oh, how the compliment lands. How it nestles into a deep part of me, unlocking a sense of joy and relief and validation.

"I look like a fake person," I remind her. "I look like a business model for how to make Finance out of controlling and subordinating women."

I want Darnell to nod and air-punch and give me a high-five, but instead she looks down at her feet. "I wouldn't look like that, ever. Not even with Belle's help."

I gulp, unable to take in this sudden hit of sadness. We drive without saying anything for a moment, and I take in Darnell's Look. It's clear she's made an effort for the Ceremony tonight. Everything about her screams of time and dedication. She's put on some Mask, to cover the worst of her blemishes, as well as tinting her lips and lashes to make them stand out a bit. Her hair has been carefully stripped and pulled into a clumsy up-do that must've taken her ages. And I can tell she's picked out this dress especially. It's an emerald green, which has been her favourite colour the whole time I've known her, and it's long and ruffled and been carefully pressed. I bite my lip and endure another jolt of sadness at the state of this awful place we live in where this upsets someone as wonderful as her. I like Darnell because she's a loyal friend, and super smart, and brave enough to hang around me and put up with all my constant furies – how she looks is irrelevant. But I see now that it matters to her. Secretly. Quietly.

It's the pain that unites us.

As we turn onto the road of the Ceremony, the carriage slows as it gets caught in the clog of everyone else's. I crane out the window to take it in. The school's Ceremony takes place in the same Function Centre each year some way out of town. A former grand house and garden converted into a place where people can find reasons to dress up and fulfil the Doctrine. There are way too many carriages on the giant gravel driveway, and some students are choosing to spill out, rather than wait to get closer. We watch as the girls totter out on their heels, or struggle to get out without showing their undergarments. I reach out and take Darnell's hand and look at her, really look at her.

"You're beautiful," I tell her.

She can hardly look at me. "Stop being stupid."

"No, I promise you. You're beautiful. And you're an amazing friend. I'm so lucky to have you in my life."

She lifts her face. She's unconvinced. But some of my words have gotten through. Oh, how much I want to be in a world where this wonderful girl doesn't hate herself. Doesn't think less of herself because of the placement of her bones under skin, and the condition of the skin on top of them. My mind flutters once more to the Education and everything I could do for my friend, if only I can get in.

"Everyone's going to stare at you the second you step out of this carriage," she warns.

"That might be so," I say. "But they're going to be staring at Belle more."

BELLE

I've never had so many people stare at me all at once, not even
when I've looked my absolute best. It's like I've wiped excrement
over my face and I'm dancing around naked. In fact, I reckon
people would understand that more because it would be so
obviously "crazy", whereas what I'm doing here tonight is just
confusing.

Why would the Prettiest girl in school do this? Break all the
Rules? Reveal her real face? Tonight of all nights?

I love that I'm making them think, even though the collective
gaze is almost suffocating. I stride up the driveway and into the
Ceremony, where I'm greeted with twinkling fairy lights, music
playing, and Linked couples swirling on the polished dance
floor. Whispers follow me wherever I go, as I'm greeting friends
who aren't sure how, or even if, to greet me back.

"Belle. Wow. You look so…different."

I've plastered a smile on my face, determined to show how
happy and confident I feel in my own skin, even though I'm
very nervous. "Thanks, it's a new Look I've wanted to try for
some time."

I still can't believe I'm here. At my Ceremony. Now I'm here, even with all the drama of what I'm doing, it's vaguely anticlimactic. In essence, we're just in a hall, with some food in the corner, and music playing. That's it, really. Yes, the hall has been decorated, and yes, everyone is Masked within an inch of their lives and dressed in their smartest attire…but come on… it's not like we're in a castle, it's not like any of this is actually that special. It's just school, but in a special hall with some topiary hedges outside.

I cannot believe how not a big deal this is.

And realizing that makes me braver.

I'm chatting to some Try Hards, who are determinedly telling me how "great" I look, when I hear more whispers. More gasps. Then one of the Try Hards lets out a shriek, and points behind me.

"Oh my, she looks amazing," she says, and I know, before I turn, that I'm about to see Joni.

My eyes, like everyone else's, turn in her direction as she shuffles into the Ceremony with her friend, Darnell, who is neon red from all the second-hand attention. It's like the whole room inhales when they see her, and I grin, so proud of my handiwork. She really does look like a Pretty. Her essential Joni-ness takes the edge off a bit. She clearly cannot walk in those shoes and is wobbling more than she walks, and her posture is hunched and crossed, but still… She's living the ultimate Ceremony fantasy. And I can't help it. I run over, wanting to be close to her. Even with everyone watching, I launch myself at her in a big hug.

"This is so surreal," I say into the crunch of her hair. "Are you okay? Everyone's staring."

She hugs me back hard. "I literally feel like I'm having an out-of-body experience," she says, before letting go and introducing me to Darnell. I say hello, and she looks like she's about to faint.

"Hi," she squeaks. "Er... Hi."

I feel everyone's eyes on us as we make our way to the bar to get a drink. Not only are Joni and I throwing people with our Looks, I guess nobody knew we were friends. Well, World, Objectionables can be friends with Pretties, don't you know? And they can even swap places! That's how meaningless and surface-level the whole thing is.

"Are you okay?" Joni asks, as we sip punch from our golden goblets. "You seem weirdly fine. In fact, you seem more comfortable than me."

I smile. "I am weirdly fine. Weirdly good, in fact. I mean, my parents were so upset that they essentially disowned me. I reckon that's going to hurt when I allow myself to think about it. And Damian was AWFUL in the carriage here, but I'm getting used to the stares. It's going to be worth it."

Joni raises both eyebrows and takes a careful sip, trying not to smudge her lips. I grin at the hassle she's going through to fulfil this basic task of drinking. "Damian? Awful? What a huge shock. Hang on, I may need a few minutes to digest this super surprising information."

Darnell and I laugh. "Yeah, and Vanessa's been okay. Have you seen her? She looks beyond incredible. And she's not been

340

judgemental at all, she's just not standing too close."

"I mean, you *are* contagious."

A popular song comes on and a few students whoop and make their way onto the floor, awkwardly throwing themselves into dance shapes, highly aware that most people are watching them. I spot Vanessa and the rest of my group in the corner, not dancing. They won't until the end. Not until after they've won. Dancing will make them too hot and sweaty and ruin their Looks. My feet involuntarily tap. I do love this song. Normally I'd be having the same reservations they are. I'd be worrying about how to move in my dress, how much my heels would hurt my feet, how sweat would ruin my Mask and hair, how my body would look as I danced. It's always better to sit there, looking perfect, rather than ruin it by looking human. But I look human already, and I really do love this song, so I find myself step-tapping a bit. If I've ruined my future and my relationship with my parents, I may as well try and enjoy myself.

"What are you doing?" Joni asks, noticing and smiling.

"Dancing."

"I can see that."

I reach out and take her hand, pulling her with me. "Come dance with me."

"I can hardly walk."

I throw back my head and laugh. I drag her and Darnell with me, and then I'm lost. Totally lost in the music. I raise my arms in the air, I feel the beat pump through my body, I sing along with the words. I love the next song that comes on, and the next one. People dance around me, some even cheering me on, but I hardly notice them. I've never felt so free. I'm doing it. I'm being everything I've ever feared. Looking like myself, acting like myself, being myself – the self I've carefully zipped up every morning to stop it coming out, before painting that zip with so many layers of Mask that I can't even see it. I spin with my arms above my head, making myself dizzy, and I bump into Joni, who clasps me. "Careful," she says, before complaining about her feet again. It's so fun to dance with her, to lose myself with her. I notice people staring, but already I'm noticing my Look isn't getting much disdain any more. I was almost convinced I'd get rotten fruit thrown at me, but everyone's already over the shock. So I've turned up looking like a human, with the sort of face we all hide each morning, but that we know we all have. So what? Yes, I've broken every Rule there is, but Joni's right. They're not law. I'm not going to be arrested. And so I won't win tonight. Who cares? I feel like I'm winning already, because, now I'm over the worst of everyone's reactions, I feel so free. So totally free. Not just in how I dance, but in everything. The music feels like warm rain and I dance and dance. Joni tells me she has to sort her foot out because her shoe's filled up with blood, but still I dance. Alone, I dance. And, yes, people are staring, but there's an awe in it. They are still envying me, I tell myself. Because, though I'm totally Objectionable tonight, I'm so clearly having the best time. I'm so clearly enjoying my body. I am *IN* my body rather than imagining other people observing my body. It's existing for me – for me to have fun in it for the first time in for ever. I've had nothing to drink, yet I feel drunk. Darnell's still gallantly step-tapping to my side, looking mildly shell-shocked from the evening's developments. I lift my arms and twist and turn and twist and turn and twist and sing along to the chorus…

…until I'm stopped. With hands on my waist. Rough, fat hands.

Damian.

"Hey, can we talk?" he yells into my ear.

I wiggle away so his hands aren't on my waist. "Aren't you embarrassed to be seen with me?"

"Look, I was shocked. I didn't behave well. But come on. We're Linked. And you've chosen the Ceremony to make this point. That's hardly fair. It's my Ceremony too, not just yours…"

I stop dancing. He's right, of course. I don't feel particularly sorry for him because of all the gross stuff he's said about me, but I have twisted the ending of his big night.

"It's nothing personal," I yell back into his ear over the song, my feet still tapping.

"What?" He cranes in.

"I said, it's nothing personal."

"I can't hear anything. The music's too loud. Can we step outside for a moment?" He takes my hand and leads me off the dance floor, and I'm taken aback by that. By this public acknowledgement of me, when I'm looking like this. What if I win over Damian tonight? Wake him up? I mean, miracles can happen.

"It's still too loud," he shouts once we're standing in front of the buffet. "Shall we go outside for a moment?"

I nod. "Okay. I'm boiling anyway."

He tries to lead me away, but I pull back. If he thinks I'm going to walk past this table groaning with gorgeous food without eating any of it, he has another think coming.

"Hang on. Let me make a plate."

It's almost a test, to see if he gets impatient and starts being a dick again. But he laughs as I put a small sausage into my mouth whole, almost like he's finding it charming. Wow, this sausage is great. So spicy and juicy. I add four more to my plate, alongside some pastry-covered things. I don't even know what the pastry is covering and, to be honest, it doesn't matter. The pastry is the important bit. I shove loads of those on, and then some crudités.

"I'm ready," I say, holding up my spoils, beaming. He laughs again, and I feel a strange sense of safety. Like, because I'm being me now, I'm safer. Rather than Compliant Belle, ready to be used and abused. I feel high...untouchable.

He steers me away, and I feel everyone's eyes on us. Triumphant, I shove a pastry square into my mouth, chewing as the cooler outside air hits me. There are a few other couples out here – the girls in their long dresses and Masked faces, cuddling up to the boys in their simple suits. They all look up as we step out, and Damian's mouth tugs downwards.

"Shall we go around the side or something? It's not very private."

And I'm too delighted with the second pastry square in my mouth to wonder why we need privacy. We wander around the corner, into the grounds of the Ceremony, and it's truly beautiful outside the hall. Rolling green lawns, marble statues, little benches. It's strange to be able to keep up with Damian as he takes us to a bench surrounded by privet hedges. It's so easy to walk in these shoes, to not have to worry about sinking into the lawn, to not be tottering behind him like a wobbly useless decorative doll. I drop onto the bench, my skirt whooshing out under me, and let out a little sigh. Damian laughs.

"You're so happy," he comments.

"I am. I really am."

"What's going on? It's like you've had a brain transplant as well as a Mask transplant."

"God, is my human face really that terrible?"

He gently cups my face, making me jolt in surprise. The tenderness of it. The way he's looking at me. I can't not look back. Damian really is a beautiful boy. Every part of his face exactly where it should be. "You know what?" he says. "You actually look quite beautiful. I was shocked at first, yes. But if anyone can pull this off, it's you."

I don't know what to say to that. The old part of me is melting at the compliment. Isn't that the ultimate win, according to the Doctrine? To still be considered beautiful, by somebody like Damian, with literally no effort made whatsoever? But a newer part of me ripples with irritation. I don't want to be told I'm still beautiful. The whole point is that it *shouldn't matter*. That how I look should be totally irrelevant to how people view me, or like me, or listen to me.

"I know you're trying to be nice," I say, moving my face away from his hand and shaking my head to get my hair off my neck. "But I don't care what you think I look like."

Damian's eyes redden. His nostrils flare. I see an internal fight play out on his face. Then a side wins, and it must be a good side, as he smiles at me. "You really are fiery tonight. Who is this Belle?"

"I've always been like this," I tell him. "Inside, I think. I'm just tired of holding it in."

"I quite like it. I always knew there was something about you. I sensed something underneath..." He lowers his face to mine, his lips gently brushing against my own. It happens so quickly that it takes a moment to pull away, as my lips respond to the kiss by kissing back before the surprise sets in. I yank back, and I see his nostrils flare again.

"Why are we out here?" I ask, straining around to take in the little hidden garden we're in. "What did you want to talk to me about?"

"I wanted this..." He gestures between the two of us. "You and me. We're Linked. I've been waiting for you for months. I've been so patient with all your Scholarship stuff. I've tried really hard to make the Ceremony perfect for you, and yet you turn up all...well...different. But I'm here saying I still want to be with you, Belle. I still want you on my arm tonight."

"I...but...my blemishes." I point to my chin.

He laughs. "So?"

"You're so confusing."

"I could say the same about you."

Then, for the second time in a week, I find myself kissing someone I wasn't expecting to. Initially, part of me runs away with the fantasy of having the perfect Ceremony, and kissing the most handsome boy there, like the Doctrine tells me I should want to. Damian's kissing me gently. He cradles my face in both hands, lightly stroking my chin with his rough thumb, his tongue gentle and probing. It feels nice, kind of, in a detached way, but it also doesn't feel like anything. Not like it did when I kissed Joni and I felt *everything*. And I find myself remembering kissing Joni and imagining it's her I'm kissing now – the thought coming into my mind like sinking into a warm bath. The unexpected electricity, the rightness, the most wonderful of surprises that maybe I do like being touched after all…but by Joni, not…well…*boys*. So, yeah, I kiss Damian at the Ceremony, like I was always supposed to, following the Rules, but, in my mind and in my heart, I'm kissing Joni. And it feels nice…

…until, of course, it doesn't.

Damian's demeanour changes and I'm flung back into reality. He lets go of my face and pushes me backwards, down onto the bench, his weight shifting so it's slightly on top of me, pinning me down. My eyes bulge open. His tongue pushes into my mouth, not giving me much room to breathe. He lets out a groan that I can only really describe as half groan, half war cry. It's an alert, to let me know he's passed to some other part of himself.

"Damian!" I push his face away. "What are you doing?"

His red eyes are back. And he's not fighting against them now, he's embracing them. There's a strange calmness about him, one that prickles my skin. *This is planned*, I realize. This moment has been planned and prepared for with the same clinical coldness of the man who tried to drag me into his car.

"Come on," he says, trying to keep up the pretence, but his eyes give him away.

"What does that mean?"

"Belle, it's the Ceremony."

"Yes, and?"

"And I've told you. I'm happy for it to go forward."

He's not leaning back. He's not taking his weight off me. I try to shift under him, the wooden slats suddenly rough and hard under my back. A tiny drop of panic lands in my stomach but I try to keep calm. It's Damian. This isn't out of control... yet.

"For *what* to go forward?" I ask.

"You know. Tonight!" He shrugs. "Come on, it's time to stop being Blue Balls Belle."

I reach out and push him back again, speaking clearly. "Damian, that's not going to happen tonight. I don't want it to."

His face, then, when I say that. I know then I'm in danger.

"Excuse me?"

"What I just said."

"But I've just told you...I'm happy to. Even when you look like this."

He is still not shifting his weight and I know I should play this cautiously but I'm prickling with anger. "Oh, lucky me." I roll my eyes.

"Belle..."

"What? I've not signed a contract. I don't want to. I know what you've been saying about me, how you want to treat me like a Smut actress. Why would I want that?"

He's breathing heavily through his nostrils. He's still pinning me down. He's not going to… No…we're only metres away from people…though we are hidden by a hedge.

"Damian. You have no interest in me, you just want the prize of me. To tell people. To hurt me and tell people about it. Why would I sign up to that?"

"Because everyone will think you're a pathetic Frigid Vanilla otherwise?"

I notice how he's not denied any of what I've said.

"I'd rather be Vanilla than let you use my body, for what? To recreate some Smut scene? Because you think it's something you're owed? Getting off on the thought of it degrading me. If you feel you're owed that…well, that's totally fucked and now please let me go."

I push him hard in his chest and it works. Taken by surprise, he falls backwards. Relief seeps through me as I untangle my limbs and stagger upwards. I turn to leave. They'll be doing the crowning any moment now. I may as well go watch. It will be good for me to witness my not-winning. For everyone else to witness it too, and see I don't care. Tonight's important to me in a new way now and I don't want a stupid boy to ruin it. I shuffle into my shoe, which had come a bit loose, and take a step away from the bench….

But Damian's hand snatches my wrist.

JONI

So, from the outside, I'm basically living the dream, but I'm not having much fun, it has to be said. Every part of my body is uncomfortable. My shoes hurt so much that I actually had to spend a full ten minutes on the toilet, with them dangling off my feet, groaning. Every step is painful. My toes are so squashed I fear they'll fuse for ever. And this dress. Even going to the toilet is a nightmare. It takes for ever to roll everything up and twist around to unzip and make sure I'm not peeing on bits of it, and then there's the whole hell of getting back into it again. My face feels so hot and uncomfortable under all this Mask. I just want to wash it off, to feel air on me rather than a clogging layer of product. Every part of me is suffocating, and yet everyone can't wait to tell me how brilliant I look, when the truth is I've never felt worse.

Once I get out of the toilet, I'm hounded by people I've never spoken to before. At least three boys come over to tell me how "hot" I look, trying to put their sweaty arms around me, winking, like they are a million per cent sure I've done this for them.

"Never knew you had such good boobs under there," a boy, Sam, says, genuinely beaming at me like I'd be glad to hear such a thing.

I growl at him. "I mean, they will likely lactate if I ever decide to have a baby," I respond. "That's always been the case."

He winces at the word "lactate" and shakes his head. "Should've known you'd still be weird."

"*Weird?* You're a person I've never once spoken to, who's approached me to tell me my mammary glands suddenly meet your approval. What's weird is you thinking I'd care."

He stalks off, face red. "Don't dress like that if you don't want attention." He throws the comment over his shoulder, muttering out the Doctrine.

Other people are nicer, but it's still really irking me. A bunch of Try Hards scuttle over in their teetering shoes, crowding me and littering me with compliments and questions, stopping me from finding Belle and Darnell.

"Joni, you look amazing."

"How did you do your Mask so well? What did you use?"

"Your hair? Who did your hair?"

"I always knew you were Pretty."

That has come up a lot since I stepped out of the carriage this evening. "I always knew you could be Pretty." Everyone can't wait to celebrate this Transformation. This final twist, this end-of-school revelation that I can be Pretty after all. I'm hot. I'm one of them. I can comply. It's strange how happy it makes them. Many of them seem positively *moved* by what I've done. I've been told I'm "inspirational" at least twice. Which is mad, as I can hardly walk. Whereas, behind the crowd, on the dance floor, I catch glimpses of Belle dancing. She's never looked happier or freer. She's spinning, her arms in the air, able to move in her flowing dress and comfy shoes, having what appears to be the best night of her life. Dragging poor bewildered Darnell back onto the dance floor whenever she dares leave. And yet people are actively keeping a few metres between her and them, like she's going to contaminate them. With what? Her happiness? Her joy? She's the inspirational one – this free and natural body. Not me. Confined and dolled up and suffocated.

I go get a drink, every step I take hurting. It takes for ever due to all the well-wishers and perverts. I think I've found the antidote to the poison. The compliments are no longer making me feel good, but irritated. Yes, a tiny part of me likes what I see in the mirror. Yes, I can imagine I will think about tonight for the rest of my life, always having this knowledge of how "good" I can look, if only I'll follow the Doctrine. Of how life has got nicer in one night – if you discount how long it took to make me look like this and the fact navigating this world in constant pain is quite difficult. But look at how people are welcoming me, wanting to speak to me, include me, *praise me. Is the trade-off worth it?* I wonder, pouring out a glass of punch. Would I achieve more, change more things, if I paid the toll of following the Rules? Could I wake more people up about the Doctrine if I fit into its requirements? *Probably*, I realize. If I'm Pretty, people are more likely to listen to me when I tell them what's wrong about being Pretty. Oh my, it's so fucked! So depressing. I down my drink, then another, aware that my stupid Lip Enhancer has probably come off and I need to schlep back to the toilet to touch it up. How does anyone live like this? I scan the dance floor for Belle. I want to go outside and debrief with her. See how she's doing. Complain to her. But she's not there any more. Maybe she went to the bathroom while I was downing my drink? Well, I need to go there to make my lips look like they are naturally a juicy perfect artificial red still, so back I go. As I push through the crowd again, I spy my friends for the first time. Sita, Hannah and Jack had always planned to turn up late and for the smallest time imaginable, and from the looks on Sita and Hannah's faces, they are stunned at the sight of me.

I hobble over. "Hi, you guys made it," I say.

I expect a hug hello but it doesn't come. In fact, Hannah's crossing her arms, looking me up and down with the sort of face Pretties used to save for Objectionable me, while Sita looks practically tearful.

"What the hell are you doing?" Hannah asks, her lip curled.

"Oh, this?" I shrug, not sure how to explain it all quickly. "It's just this experiment I'm doing with Belle. I've been... we've become friends. I've finally woken her up to the Doctrine, but she said it's worth me seeing what it's like on the Other Side."

Both Sita and Hannah have committed to rejecting the Doctrine, even at the Ceremony. Sita's wearing baggy jeans and a top, no Mask on. And Hannah's also totally bare-faced and wearing a short T-shirt dress with flat shoes. They both shake

353

their heads at me. Jack, sensing conflict, shuffles off into the crowd after squeaking hello.

"I have to say," Sita starts, "I feel really let down by you. Like, I'm genuinely upset."

"What?" I step back and my dress rustles.

Hannah nods. "Yeah, you've been an inspiration to us for years. You gave me my Awakening. You said you were *proud* to be Objectionable, and now look at you...selling out..."

My mouth drops open. "I'm not selling out...I'm just trying out—"

"At the Ceremony of all places. You're such a hypocrite." She lets out an angry huff and shakes her head again. "Here I was, thinking you were inspirational, but secretly you've wanted to be a Pretty this whole time."

"That's not tru—"

"Look at you." Sita points at me, her voice almost quivering with betrayal. "You can hardly walk! You can hardly breathe. You're doing everything you've told us is bad, everything you've told us you're against."

Hannah's practically snarling. "And you can't get enough of the compliments, can you? You're loving it. Being embraced by the Doctrine. I can't believe—"

I hold up my hand to stop them. Anger races through me, my pulse rocketing. "Enough now," I say. "Honestly, listen to yourself."

"Well, it's better than listening to you. You hypocrite—"

"Oh my God. I'm not! And so what if I was? The way you're talking about me...how is that not wrong too?" I glance over at the dance floor again, looking for Belle. It would be nice to have some backup around now, but she's still nowhere to be seen.

"What do you mean, how we're talking about you?"

"You're *objectifying* me too and it sounds like you've been doing so for ages."

They're stunned into temporary subordination. "Huh?" Hannah crosses her arms more tightly.

"Look," I say. "If you've been using my Objectionable face and body to feel *better* about yourself, then you've totally missed the point of everything I've tried to teach you. Sorry, Sita, but if you feel 'let down' by me being Pretty for one day, then you've still been seeing me as a fucking...*body* all this time, and not a *person*. You've been using me. Reducing me, and my body, to a Thing. A *cause*. Something to hold up and use. How is that different to what Pretties do to each other?"

"But..." Hannah gapes like a fish. "But..." Whereas Sita looks like she's going to cry.

"What I've been trying to do all this time is get girls to stop seeing themselves and others as *things* that either look right or wrong, based on the Doctrine." I clench my fists. "We dehumanize all girls if we contextualize them based on their looks." I throw my fists in the air, which has limited effect as this dress is so damn tight. "You have no idea why I'm doing this. You're making assumptions, based on how I look. That's literally everything I've tried to get you not to do."

I'm quite proud of all this, pouring from my mouth. I wish some classical music was playing, to make it more triumphant and dramatic. I finish, shrugging and smiling to let them know I come in peace. I'm expecting applause. An apology. But no. Hannah's face is still sour and Sita still looks totally betrayed. They haven't heard any of it. Just like Mother… And I feel that horrid pain again. Nobody sees me. Nobody listens to me…

"You're selling out and you know it," Hannah says. "Dress it up however you like. Put as much Mask on it as you like. But part of you wanted to know if you'd ever pass as a Pretty, and part of you is smug as hell that you have. Don't pretend otherwise. Don't try and make it some grand statement."

"Yeah," Sita says, nodding along furiously, siding with Hannah. "Until the Doctrine is totally overthrown, being Pretty is endorsing it."

I shake my head. "So you're saying nobody will listen to me if I'm Objectionable because we don't listen to ugly girls, but nobody will listen to me if I'm Pretty because it means I've sold out and I can't be trusted?"

"Er…yeah…"

I throw up my arms again. "Great. So nobody is going to listen and therefore nothing is going to change. How *inspiring*. I'm done with this. Have a good night."

I squeeze past them to the bathroom and kind of want to cry. Their words have left an impact. I'm not sure if I'm angry at them because they're wrong, or if I'm angry at them because they're right. It's such a mess. The whole thing. It's such an overwhelming and totally confusing mess. Which I guess, Mother would say, is the point. To be drained by it…silenced by it…never able to pin it down. The Doctrine weakens and diminishes, but it's invisible, and there's no obvious monster to kill. Just different girls to attack for different reasons.

I need Belle.

I feel so alone in this. Weirdly, she's the one who gets it. Just before I push it to the bathroom, I check the dance floor again to see if she's out dancing. I also want to make sure Darnell's okay, as she's taken to this evening's shocks very well. I smile when I see her dancing with Jack and looking very happy about it indeed.

Belle's not in the toilets, and that's when I start to worry. I push back out, leaving my Lip Enhancer undone, and cram myself into the heaving Ceremony. It's hard to look for her amongst the crush. The dance floor's packed now but she's nowhere to be seen. An awful feeling blobs through me. I make my way over to Vanessa, who's still sitting with her gang of Pretties, surveying the scene, sitting up straight, looking like statues. I'm expecting her to snarl with disgust when I talk to her, but I'd forgotten I'm covered in Mask and she greets me in quite a friendly way. I have to say, she looks absolutely stunning…

"Hey, Joni, isn't it?" she asks.

"Yeah, hi."

"You're Belle's friend. The one who put her up to tonight, I'm taking?"

"That was Belle's choice."

She smiles, and her teeth are so perfect, lips so perfect, face so perfect. "She has changed a lot. It's kinda funny. Watching her nuke her own life."

I raise both eyebrows. "Or maybe save her own life? By rejecting all this gross Doctrine nonsense?"

Vanessa's friendliness fades. "You're so smug, I can't stand it sometimes," she lets out. "Where do you get off, thinking your way is best? Not considering what it might be like for girls not like you?"

I stumble back in my heels. "Excuse me?"

"If I win tonight, that's important. Girls who look like me, we've had to fight so hard to be considered beautiful rather than beastly."

It takes me a second to realize she's talking about her skin. "I…" I start but she holds a hand up.

"Enough. I'm really not interested. You do you, and Belle can do whatever the hell she's doing too. But leave me out of it, please. If I win the Ceremony, that's huge. If I win, it might help me become a Chosen One, which is even huger. It could really change how girls like me are perceived. You know nothing about what it's like to be me, so stop judging. Now, you wanted Belle?"

She tilts her head, finished and impatient, and I'm temporarily silent. Digesting what she's said, knowing I'll need to stew it over for a while. Just as I think I understand the complexity of the Doctrine, it reveals another layer.

"Umm, yeah. Have you seen Belle at all?"

"She went outside with Damian." Vanessa says it casually enough, waving her hand dismissively, but the words shoot rockets through me.

"Thanks," I call behind me, already pushing through the crowd to make sure she's alright.

"You look great by the way," she calls after me. "Love the Look. Genuinely."

It's so refreshing outside, with circulating air and fewer people. I can breathe a bit easier, even if my dress is still incredibly restrictive. A few heads glance in my direction. There are many couples milling about, but no Damian and Belle. I take off my shoes, my feet sighing, and pick my way around the gravel, around the corner, looking everywhere. They aren't that couple on the bench. Nor are they that couple necking against the wall. I search and search and see nothing apart from a bunch of hedges. I'm starting to panic. Then I hear a muffled shriek coming from the hedge and I run over, realizing it's hiding a little garden, and there, being pushed against the privet, is Belle, with Damian's hand over her mouth, her dress straps down. She's crying and trying to pull his hand away as he holds her pinned.

I stand for a second and see only rage.

I run over and smash my high heel into the side of his head. He lets out an ooph and stumbles backwards, releasing Belle, who gasps out a scream. Damian's balance is recovering, though his forehead's bleeding. No. I lean back, try to lift a kick, but I can't. Not in this stupid dress. It's too tight. I lose my balance and fall backwards and Damian lets out a laugh. His face is quiet – the scariest of angers. I try to get to my feet, but this stupid dress literally makes it impossible. I don't know how I'm going to get up. I don't know how I'm going to help Belle. Or myself. Because Damian's walking over slowly, assessing me. I struggle harder to get up... What's he going to do?

Dooph.

Damian lets out a startled yelp and falls to the ground before me. Belle stands behind him, fists clenched, looking like some kind of warrior princess. She's kicked him right in the groin, in her sensible shoes, and he's down. Before he can scramble back up, she kicks him again and he lets out a cat-like scream. He folds in on himself, unable to do anything but crumple, totally neutralized.

"Are you okay?" she asks, reaching out and yanking me up.

"Are you?"

"No." Her face is sodden with tears. We both assess Damian as he struggles to get onto all fours, groans, and fails.

"You fucking bitch," he yells. "Both of you."

"I can kick you a third time," Belle says, holding up her leg and he flinches.

"You're...you're supposed to be with me tonight."

"I owe you nothing. Nothing."

"You're an ugly little bitch anyway."

"Oh shut up, Damian. As if I care."

She takes my hand and starts to pull me away. She's pale and shaken but also radiating strength. She's never looked more beautiful. "Come on," she tells me. "I was having fun in there. I refuse to let this stop me."

I look back at Damian, who is, once again, trying and failing to stumble up. "Are you okay?"

"Yes. No. I just don't want to be near him."

She starts stalking off, forgetting I can't walk as fast as her. But, even on the grass, Damian has some parting shots. "You're over," he yells, twisting onto his side, his face a portrait of pure hate. "You know that, right, Belle? I'm going to tell everyone what a scared little Frigid you are. From now on, you are totally over."

She stops. I worry at first his words have gotten to her. She's prepared her whole life to be with him tonight – winning, not finished. Then I see rage flare across her face like fireworks. She turns and surveys him on the ground.

"Good," she says quietly.

Damian's eyebrows rise up in confusion. "*Good?*"

"Yes, good," she says louder. "I want it to be over. I don't want to be that Belle any more. Because, you know what? She may be nice to look at, but she's starving and she's weak and she's exhausted and she's terrified. And no matter how much she wins, she still hates herself and worries she's not good enough and doesn't live a damned fucking day inside her body, enjoying her life, and instead watches herself like she's having some kind of freakin' out of body experience." She stands closer, as I marvel and wonder if she's going to kick him again. I sort of want her to. I mean, if I hadn't come…hadn't found them… "That Belle would've been more harmed tonight than I am now, even though you've assaulted me anyway, you disgusting, pathetic waste of oxygen. So, yeah, I'm over. Great. Where's the party? I'll join you in the celebration. Now, I'm going to go back inside and have the best Ceremony of my life, if you don't mind."

Then, Belle – my darling, timid, feminine, delicate Belle – spits on him.

Spits on him.

Damian.

"You like that, don't you?" she says innocently, as his face scrunches and he frantically wipes away her spit from his eye. "It's in all the Smut you watch. So I figure you'd like that."

Damian's too stunned to get off the ground.

"Oh, you weren't expecting it was going to be *you* who was spat on? What a surprise. Not so sexy now, is it?" And Belle laughs before turning to me. "You coming?" she asks.

"I'm coming."

I'm desperate for breath – reeling from everything that's just happened, but Belle is undeterred.

"Are you okay?" I ask, with practically every step we take back towards the hall.

"I'm fine."

"But are you really okay?"

"I refuse to let that boy ruin tonight for me." Her face is set, eyes almost steel-like in their resolve. "If I need to cry, I'll cry tomorrow."

"If you're sure?"

She reaches out and gives my hand a quick squeeze, letting sparks dance up my forearm. "Come on, let's see who wins."

As we re-enter the Ceremony, we find a crowd has packed around the main stage. The music's stopped, Ms Blanche is clutching the microphone, and anticipation hangs thick in the air.

"Looks like they're about to reveal it," Belle says.

"Looks like it."

People notice us arrive and make space for us. I can see Vanessa and the rest of the Pretties waiting eagerly to the side – their faces painted, perfect, but tense. Too consumed with the upcoming moment to notice us, with Belle's tear-streaked face and ruined hair.

"Do you still want to win?" I ask her under my breath, looking at the two crowns perched on cushions onstage.

"Of course," she says, surprising me, her eyes greedily on the crown. "I've wanted to win ever since the day my mother told me I should."

Ms Blanche is delaying the agony, thanking all the people who helped organize the Ceremony and boring us senseless.

Then Belle surprises me again. "How about you?" she asks back. "Do *you* still want to win?"

"I…"

She grins and winks. "Don't pretend you don't."

I sigh and let out a laugh, admitting I've been rumbled. She's so clever, this girl, on the sly. I think I knew this would be the case if she gave it all up. Belle with all her energy focused on kicking ass rather than worrying about the size of hers – she's going to be such a force. And she's right – of course I've wanted to win the Ceremony. I've fantasized about it for years, though it's hard to admit that to myself. This may be the first time I ever have. It's what we've been fed in the Doctrine since we were girls. Go to the Ceremony, be the Prettiest, then you have achieved the ultimate goal. Every girl in this crowd secretly wants their name to be called, even if they haven't been Nominated. They will go home hurting a little because it wasn't them, no matter how much fun they've had otherwise. They still weren't enough, no matter how hard they tried. That's the power of the Doctrine in action. To make us feel less, so we accept less. To push us down and keep us there. So clever. I marvel every day at how clever it is. However, tonight, for both Belle and I, winning isn't a pipe dream, something to hold us down. Winning is literally possible. We've been Nominated. Our names could be called. The ultimate goal is in our sights. We could win. We could feel amazing.

"And now…" Ms Blanche cranes her neck up, knowing she's got to the good bit. "It's time for the announcement you've all been waiting for. The winners of tonight's Ceremony." Another teacher gets onstage and picks up the crowns waiting on purple cushions. The room's eyes fall on them. She coughs. "And without further ado…"

If Belle wins, it will be a fairy tale. The girl who showed who she truly was and was still the most beautiful. And if I win, I guess it will be a fairy tale too. The ugly girl who discovered she was beautiful after all. We squeeze hands, smile at one another, the poisoned dart in me making me dare to hope…

"Vanessa Parker and Ben Ferguson."

…and the dream dies. As it was always going to. As the Doctrine demands.

Squeals from Vanessa. Applause. Cheers. We watch as she glides up onstage, practically crying, saying, "Thank you, thank you", with Ben beaming after her. They are the Prettiest. They are the most compliant. They keep the order. So, of course, they win.

Because we're living in a nightmare, never a fairy tale.

Although, as I watch Vanessa bow her beautiful head to receive her crown, I reflect on what she said to me. How this win means something profound to her, something I could never understand. And I find myself smiling for her for a moment, despite myself.

"What a surprise," Belle deadpans next to me, trying to make a joke but I know she's disappointed. I am too.

Remember how strong the poison is, says Mother's voice in my head.

She's right, she's so right. In fact, I need to get out of here, to stop breathing it in, to wash it from my face, before it infects me irreversibly.

Belle, reading my mind, turns around.

"Come on," she says. "It's time to go."

And as we walk away from the most important night of our lives, her hand's so warm in mine.

ONE
WEEK
LATER

BELLE

What's so mad is, the Ceremony didn't change anything. Not for any of us. The next day, the sun rose, and Vanessa had won, and I'd thrown away "everything we worked for" (according to Mother), and it was all over, and none of it meant anything at all. We were done. School was over. And as my class woke up with throbby heads, aching feet and a lot of photos for the Ranking, memories were all we were left with. It was time for the class behind us to worry about their Ceremony. To be preoccupied with it to an obsession. A *distraction* – I see it now for what it is. All of it a huge distraction.

I don't think Mother will ever forgive me however. It took two days before she'd even look at me, and even now it's with utter distaste.

Father's parting words this morning, before he went on another long trip, were, "I hope you're proud of yourself. Your mother is a hysterical mess," before not kissing me on the head, like he usually does and driving away without even waving goodbye. As I watched him leave out my bedroom window, I reflected on that transformative Sister Circle that I went to, and all the women sharing what they lost when they found their inner liberty. I sniffed up a tear, worrying that I'll never get my parents' love back, worrying about them and their Finance situation. The anxiety gnaws at my stomach like a hungry guinea pig, but it's infinitely more manageable than the years of hunger gnawing at my stomach, of the itchy feeling everything about me is wrong.

It still hurts though. So much. It really, really hurts.

I've spent the days with Joni, which has helped, enjoying the summer sunshine. Lying sprawled on our backs in a clearing in the woods, the warmth baking my face without me having to worry about my Mask sweating off, trying to talk about anything other than, a) the kiss we shared and what it means, and b) the giant verdict that's awaiting us any day now. Which of us will win the Scholarship? What will I do if I don't get in? How will I feel if I get in over Joni? We've become so close but, since the Ceremony, there's a lacing of tension. Instead, we debrief about the Ceremony, like everyone else is.

"Vanessa has uploaded over two hundred images to the Ranking of her being crowned," I tell the warm air, as I sense Joni's belly jiggle with laughter next to me.

"Good for her." She sounds like she genuinely means it.

"I can't look at any images of myself," I admit. "Is that bad?"

"No. Give it time. I can't look at any images of myself either."

"Why not?"

"I'm scared I'll like them too much."

We both giggle again. What I don't admit is I've looked at loads of the images posted of Joni. I find myself going through them in the evenings, while Mother is downstairs doing Body Prayer without me and scowling if I come down for a glass of water. It's this strange compulsion, wanting to see her face, how it makes me feel. A small, unfurling part of me knows this means something. That people don't behave this way about someone who is just a friend. Images of her at the Ceremony are the only ones I have and I really can't stop looking.

There's something else I can't get out of my head since that night.

"Joni?"

"Hmm?" Her eyes are closed against the sun, freckles erupting one by one across her nose.

"Thanks again. For finding me in time. Damian…"

She turns onto her side, reaches out and pats my hand. "Don't worry about it."

"If you hadn't come…"

"But I did."

"I can't believe Damian tried to…and that man in the car… why do they? I wish we could do something to stop it."

She pats me again to calm me. "Me too."

"We can't though. Can we?" I ask. "The Doctrine's very clear on this. *If a girl tempts a man to lose his control, it's only her fault.*"

"We can try," she says. "We can report Damian to the Protection Agency, but, well, the Protection Agency is quite into the Doctrine."

"I know." I sigh and clench my fists. "I just hate that he gets away with it. That they *all* get away with it. It makes me feel so angry and powerless, and, well, really, *really* unsafe. All the time."

Joni's quiet – letting there be space in the sunshine for what I've just said. What I love about her is she doesn't say it's okay when it isn't. She doesn't pretend things aren't screwed when they are. I feel so safe around her. That honesty.

"He didn't completely get away with it…" she muses finally, shielding her eyes from the harsh light. "I mean, you did spit on him…"

We both lose ourselves to hysterics at the memory of me spitting on Damian. I tell her to stop.

"I mean, Belle of the ball, I never thought I'd see the day you literally *spat* on someone."

"Don't, don't. It's too gross. It just happened. I didn't know what else to do."

"No. I love it. It's my favourite thing to ever have happened. And, hey, he definitely would've done it to you. And worse."

"That's true." I shudder, like I always do when I imagine the alternate universe that exists where I wasn't brought together with Joni. Where I am still the Prettiest who did everything she was supposed to do.

I'll never get bored of these comfortable silences with her. We lie in the heat, both thinking about everything that's changed. Not with the world, but between us, and I feel so good.

"I'm scared too," she says after a while, almost as a prayer to the clouds.

"Huh?"

I turn onto my side, the lawn tickling my nose, but Joni stays facing the sky, her face guarded. She doesn't elaborate, so I ask. "About getting into the Education?"

It's the first time we've named it in days, and her face scrunches up.

"Yes, that. Also, seeing Father. It's tomorrow. I'm…not sure what I'm doing. Why I'm seeing him."

She'd told me she's planning to meet him and it doesn't seem like the best idea at all, but I don't think I can judge. After all the ways I've bent myself to get something back from my parents. It's a very powerful force to ignore.

"You don't have to do it," I remind her.

"I know. I'm just weirdly desperate to see him. Even though it's upset Mother so much."

"Join the 'My Mother Hates My Life Choices' Club." I grin through our shared pain. "I guess you're just going on your instincts. Sometimes you have to do that."

"Maybe…he's my dad. That's all I can think. *But he's my dad.*" She sighs. "At least it's a vague distraction from waiting to see if I've got into the Education."

She trails off and our silence is far from comfortable now. Here we are, naming the elephant in the room. Another reason why I like her. She aways names it. It makes me feel safe. Her sincerity. Joni's making me feel all sorts of things I never knew were in me – most of them, about her.

The Scholarship though. Who will get it? One of us? Neither of us? We both have so much riding on it.

…and just like that, both our Devices chime.

We sit up in unison, instinctively knowing. My whole body trembles as I open a message from Ms Blanche.

Can you and Joni please meet me in my office at 9am tomorrow morning?

I look up at Joni, who's just finished reading hers too. She holds up her Device and I see her identical message.

"What does it mean?" she says.

JONI

It must mean we've both got in. It has to. Oh my, can you imagine? Last night, while I was definitely not sleeping, I pictured us hugging and squealing as Ms Blanche officializes the incredible news. They were blown away by both of us, couldn't decide and want to offer us both a place. We will travel there together and become our best selves and learn what we need to know to overthrow the Doctrine and Mother will forgive me for daring to be a Pretty for one day and for seeing my father.

She actually smiles at me this morning, as I scatter around the kitchen, unable to eat breakfast properly. She puts both hands on my shoulders to steady me.

"Whatever happens today, it's going to be okay," she says, kissing the top of my head. She doesn't know I'm meeting Father today too as I couldn't face telling her. But it's reassuring to hear, nevertheless.

"I want it so much, Mother."

"I know."

"It's a good sign, right? Them asking us in at the same time? It *must* be a good sign?"

When I look up at her, she's biting her lip. "I don't know," she admits. "Let's hope so."

I feel beyond queasy as I leave the house, my knees wobbling about. Why have both these things fallen on the same day? It seems most unfair. I'm a mixture of frantically worried and hopeful about both situations. Obviously, the best outcome would be that Belle and I both get in, dance around like lunatics in celebration, and then I go meet Father and he's loving and apologetic and we figure out a way to be in each other's lives again. But he could be awful, or only one of us could get in. Or neither of us.

I meet Belle at the end of the road. It's still a shock to see her Maskless and dressed in ordinary clothes. Much easier to walk with her places though. It's the first day she looks, according to the Doctrine, "proper rough" though. She has giant dark circles under her eyes and the gaunt look of someone whose whole future hangs in the balance.

"I've gone to the bathroom twelve times already," she says, greeting me with a stiff hug. "And I still may soil myself on the walk in."

I fake a laugh. "Let's do this."

We get to school in silence. Announce our arrival at reception in silence. It's strange to be there now we've left. The school is still in session, the noise of classes being conducted seeping from behind doors, each room stuffed with students waiting to spill out like the contents of a freshly opened champagne bottle when the bell rings. Last week, this was part of my life, but now I'm detached from it. We return only to do our final assessments and that's it. It's over. I'll never be part of this disgusting forced ecosystem ever again. Belle's head is down as we wait outside Ms Blanche's office. Her foot is tapping like mad, her fingers twisting like a combine harvester in her lap. I try to pull deep breaths into my lungs. I can't believe I'm putting myself through this on the same day I'm seeing Father. But it will be good news. We are going together. That's why we're here together. To be honest, the thought of only one of us getting in creates a pang just for the fact it means we'll be apart.

We must both be going. We have to be.

The door opens and I swear my heart's on the ceiling.

Ms Blanche's face is neutral. "Girls. Good morning. Come in."

I can hardly move my legs into the office. It's like someone's pointed a stun gun at them and turned them to pudding. Belle's equally wobbly, like a baby deer on ice trying to get to the chair. Ms Blanche is already sitting at her desk, hands clasped in front of her like a barrier, watching us struggle to get into our seats. I plop down, and find myself holding my heart through my top.

"Thanks for coming in, girls," she says. "I appreciate it's untraditional to have you in at the same time, but today is a day all about breaking traditions."

Oh, my heart's soaring. We've both got in! We have. Belle senses it too. She flicks me a look of such joy and hope that I think I may cry. I think I may *like* her...

Then I notice Ms Blanche isn't making eye contact. In fact,

she's staring at the desk. "Now, what I'm about to say won't be easy to hear but…"

My ears are ringing. There's a loud humming in my head. I can hardly keep up. She's saying phrases like, "behind the scenes of your applications, a lot has been going on," and "we wanted to protect you from it while we decided what to do," and "our commitment to total equality is paramount and we've had to address this with balancing what's best for our students."

Belle's standing. "Please tell us. Please tell us what's actually happening," she yelps in desperation. And I see Ms Blanche look at her – really look at her. At this prized pupil who used to be so beautiful and compliant and follow the Doctrine so wonderfully, who's now angry and demanding and looking like that. She sours. I visibly see Ms Blanche's face sour, and that's when I know. It's bad. It's bad. Everything's really bad.

"Please sit down and calm yourself, Belle. Honestly. As I said, we've been dealing with a serious allegation from a fellow student that your application to the Education is a breach of equality. A male student believes the school has discriminated against him by not allowing him access to the Scholarship. His legal team have convinced us of our error, and we have no choice but to withdraw you both from the process in the interests of protecting everyone's rights…"

Every atom of my body turns cold.

"You're kidding," I interrupt. It must be a joke. It must.

"I'm afraid I've never been more serious."

"So *neither* of us has gotten in?"

"I'm sorry, girls. We've been forced to withdraw your

applications for fear of legal action. We appreciate how hard you've worked, and you're welcome to apply to the Education next year independently. I hope you can see this decision is for the benefit of everyone."

I can't. I don't. I...I...I have no emotions, only shock. My Future starts draining from me, like water swirling down a drain. I won't go to the Education. I will be stuck here. My hope of escape gone. My hope to better myself and change things gone. All my hard work, for nothing. That place. I felt so safe and myself in that place. I belonged there. I felt it so strongly. And now, no. Door closed. Future closed. Hope closed. For what? *Equality.* I realize it's quite hard to breathe. My lungs are hardly taking anything down. I'm gulping for air. My heart is shattering. I'm totally malfunctioning, unable to fight, lost in a mist of despair...

Then I hear Belle's voice cut through.

"Who?" she asks. I've never heard a voice with more ice in it.

"Excuse me?" Mrs Blanche says, looking hugely uncomfortable and like she wants us to leave.

"Who complained?"

"That's confidential."

"It was Damian, wasn't it?"

"As I said, it's confidential." Her eyes give her away, and we both know it immediately. I'm still struggling to digest it all. Still feeling my heart break in slow motion. But Belle...Belle... her eyes are on fire.

BELLE

There is nothing but rage. White rage. Blinding rage. A rage that surges through my body like I'm being super-charged with it.

"You're a disgrace," I tell our head teacher.

"Excuse me?"

"You're a complete disgrace. You're supposed to be educating us! Protecting us! And instead you are complicit in this damaging...bullshit. You let your girl students deal with totally normalized violence every single day, and then claim you believe in equality. You're a total disgrace."

Ms Blanche stands up – defensive. She must know this is bullshit, but can't say so. I sense her own temper breaking. Oh, I can fight rage with rage.

"I appreciate you're disappointed, Belle, but that is no excuse to speak to me like this."

"Have you heard how Damian speaks about girls?" I snap back. "Your beacon of equality? Do you know how he's allowed to behave in your school? Do you know he openly plays Smut in lessons? That he regularly calls us all names. Do you know he assaulted me at the Ceremony?"

Ms Blanche's face is pinched. "I saw you at the Ceremony, Belle. You were certainly bringing a lot of attention to yourself."

"Oh my, listen to yourself! You know this is wrong. Why are you pretending it's not wrong? Have you forgotten what it's like, trying to learn alongside a boy like Damian? You have, haven't you?" Joni's watching us, her mouth wide open. She looks quite broken. I know I'll break soon too, but for now the anger is all I can feel. It's got the steering wheel and is driving me right towards Ms Blanche. "You're an Invisible after all," I add.

"That's enough, Belle." She leans over the desk.

"Is this punishment for us? Because you're jealous? Because we're seen and leered at and in our Just Right years, and you're ignored and frumpy and resentful that—"

"Stop it right now. Stop it. Or you'll be expelled before you can take your exams, and then you won't get into any Education."

"I can't go to any anyway. My family can't afford it. You think I'm applying for a Scholarship for laughs? We're too poor to go and you know this."

"Belle, I'm *disgusted* by this behaviour. I knew you'd be disappointed, but you must see, these opportunities are unfair." She's using that same robotic voice that I used to, like the Doctrine is controlling her voice box. "We've moved past the Bad Times," Ms Blanche insists. "Things need to be readdressed. This was just a hangover from history."

"The Bad Times are still here," I yell, so loud I'm surprised the ceiling doesn't fall down. "I'd call them *the Worse Times*. Because at least back then we acknowledged things were bad.

381

We were fighting for equality, not torturing ourselves and calling it our choice... You...you..." Uh oh, the pain is rising, pushing away the anger like it's blocking a path. Tears hurtling into my eyes. Voice breaking. Everything I worked towards vanishing. My family hating me, for what? No triumphant reason. Stuck in this broken place. "You should be helping us," I say, tears falling, my voice no longer a shout but a whimper. "Surely you'd want to help us?"

She's blinking each word I say away. She's dug in. And my dreams are broken, shattered, messed all over the floor. Joni's too. It would've hurt not to get in, but I also would've been so happy for her. But neither of us gets to thrive...because of Damian... Damian.

"Belle! Belle? Where are you going? You can't just storm off."

The rage is back. I stalk out of her office, running past the Invisible at the reception desk even though she's been instructed to stop me. Joni's on my heel, keeping pace with me. I don't even know where I'm going, only that I have to run. For years and years these feelings have been building and squashed, building and squashed, as I overrode all my instincts that told me to get mad, that told me things weren't safe, that things weren't right. Now they're overflowing like a hose left without anyone holding it – spiralling into the air, cartwheeling, getting mess everywhere.

"Belle? Are you okay? Belle? Belle."

I push into a bathroom and start pacing back and forth, while Joni stands watching, concerned, crying.

Damian.

I let out a piercing scream, and oh my, it feels good. Like my body is finally matching how it feels inside. I scream and scream, not caring who hears, or if it disrupts the school. Then I catch sight of myself screaming in the bank of mirrors on the wall, and I jump at how deranged I look. A plain, empty, blotchy face with sunken eyes and flat hair and no effort made, just screaming like a mad woman. I am an Objectionable. I truly am. I see it in this moment. I am a disgrace. I am foul. I am repulsive. I am everything we shouldn't be. Screaming and ugly and letting my rage out and not making an effort, and I can't bear it. How broken it all is. How the Doctrine is so powerful, even in my darkest moment, that I'm judging how ugly I am as I'm crying in pain.

I scream again, and find myself ripping a toilet paper holder off the wall.

"Belle? Belle! No."

I smash it into the mirror and the glass shatters, falling into the sink below it. My reflection fractures and splinters and I can no longer see myself. Good. These mirrors have taunted and controlled me my whole life. I smash the next one, and the next. There's glass everywhere, shards of it falling around me. Joni gives up and watches me, stunned, as I ruin every last one. I don't want these mirrors here. I don't want girls to come in and look into them and list every single thing that is wrong with them just before they go out and try to learn. I don't want them to see their faces as something to disguise in order to get by in this world.

"Belle, we should leave. They'll send security. We need to get away."

"I hate it. My whole life. I hate it. I hate that they told me it was good."

"I know, I know. But, come on. Let's get out of here. Calm down. Before the Protection Agency comes and you do something you regret."

"They never protect us! They only protect the Doctrine."

"I know, that's why we need to get out."

I'm staring at all the different fragments of myself in all the mirrored shards on the floor. Dozens and dozens of versions of me. The parts who want to win. To look the nicest. To be the Prettiest. To Have It All. To make my family happy. To go along with it. The part that feels good when she looks in mirrors and knows she's got it right. Then the other parts. The part who finds the problems, all the bits of myself that aren't good enough. The part who is tired and angry. The part who feels helpless, like there's no choice. The part who spat on Damian. The part who is awake to everything now, and can't go back to sleep again, no matter how much easier that would seem. These pieces of me are broken inside me and scattered and can't be put back together again, just like all these pieces of me I see on the floor. I reach out my foot and grind the glass into dust. Then I turn to Joni. Oh, wonderful Joni. Who is looking half terrified and half proud of me. She reaches out her hand. She always reaches out her hand to me, no matter how little I deserve it.

"Come on, let's go."

And I run with her, away from it all, leaving my reflection ground to dust on the floor behind me.

JONI

I'm not sure how to handle what Belle's doing apart from running her away from it. So we flee from school, sweat beading down our backs, and we run and run, putting distance between us and it. Us and our disappointment. Us and our betrayal. Us and Belle's behaviour, which they'll no doubt take more seriously than that of a predator like Damian, sabotaging our futures just because he hated that we dared to think we deserve one. We run until we end up in an alleyway, our lungs and legs unable to take the strain any more, and we grind to a halt, bending over on ourselves, coughing, panting. I fall to the dusty ground, holding my chest. There's still so much to take in. I still can't believe we're not going. That all my hard work has come to nothing. That there's no escape tunnel. My future feels so empty, so devoid of purpose, I can't even...

That's when I realize where we are.

We're in the alleyway where we first "met" – as it were. We're at the exact point where we jumped over the fence to escape that man. I can see our scuff marks on the wood. And I see Belle realize it too, as she leans over on her knees, panting.

She stares at the fence, and I see the past play out across her face, the memory dancing and taunting her. The rage finds her once more and I watch her fists clench and Belle screams again, and starts hitting and thumping the fence, yelling all the swear words, imploding and exploding at the same time. I let her get it out. I'm too broken myself to offer any support. Then she slumps to the floor behind me and lets out giant yelping sobs. I reach out my arm and she falls into my shoulder, and we cry together. We cry, and we cry, and we cry, sitting in our past, with our future taken away from us.

"I still can't believe it," she says eventually, after at least half an hour, when it seems like there's no crying left.

"I know."

"Damian. He's been secretly fighting our Scholarship the whole time. If I'd gone to the Ceremony properly with him…if I'd…and he'd been…"

"I know."

"And I can't believe Ms Blanche. Like, she's smart. Surely she can see?"

"So many people don't want to see. It's easier not to see. It's easier to think the Bad Times are over."

Belle starts quietly sobbing again. "I really wanted to go. I wanted to go so much."

I pat her, join her in her crying. "Me too."

"I really thought I'd found my place, my future. Now my parents hate me. For nothing."

"Not for nothing. We'll…we'll think of something."

But as our breathing calms and the sweat dries onto our

bodies, neither of us can come up with one good plan. There is only sorrow, loss and rage. There is only a question mark where our future is. How do we get out of here? How can we make our lives into something important again?

There is also another very pressing matter.

"My father," I say, almost laughing at the ridiculous timing. "I'm supposed to be meeting him in twenty minutes." It's beyond absurd. An unimaginable bolt-on to this car crash of a day.

Belle sniffs and wipes her nose. "Are you okay to do that?"

"I guess so."

"I mean, you really don't have to. I've never been sure it's a good idea."

"He's travelled all this way."

She raises both shoulders. "So?"

"So…I can't not go."

Why are you doing this? a voice whispers. *Why?* I still, this close to doing it, have no idea.

Belle reaches over and pats my shoulder. "Do you want me to come with you?" Her voice is motherly, calming.

I lean my head on her head and pull her tighter. "Yes, thank you. That would be amazing."

We shuffle up in the heat and wipe ourselves down. I feel like I'm in some strange dreamscape. It cannot be happening that I'm about to see Father for the first time in ten years. Not when I'm such a mess. I'm still not even sure if I want to see him. If I can bear it. Will he look different? He must look older. What will he be like? Will he be nice to me?

387

We get a lot of second glances as we get into the busier area of town. Two Objectionables, covered in dust and with cried-out faces, holding hands and hobbling towards the cafe where I said I'd meet him. Belle's practically holding me up, steering me there, telling me it's going to be okay. When did she become the rescuer? When did we switch? Or maybe it's about taking it in turns. I glance over at her set, determined face, and I get my first flash that everything might be alright. That maybe we're not both doomed to be trapped here. This girl met me and listened to me, and now look at her. Look at what she's been able to become. I helped with that. She spat on Damian… I mean, he deserves a lot more, but at least we'll always have that. And I helped start her engine and, my, look at how fast she's driving. There's something in that…

Maybe we don't need the Education after all?

Maybe we can still fight? Still change things? Still carve out a happiness for ourselves, even from deep inside this broken place?

The cafe gets closer and my legs weaken. He's in there. My *father*. I just want him to smile at me. To clasp my hand. To say how well I'm looking. We're almost there. We're across the street, and the cafe has a giant wide window, people perched at high tables looking out. And there he is. My father. Sitting. In real life. At a table. Waiting for me. His daughter.

My legs stop. We jolt to a halt.

"Are you okay?" Belle asks. I hardly hear her.

Because I'm looking at this man who has half my face. This man who has aged ten years since I last saw it. He's glancing down at his Device. He hasn't seen us. The blood in my body quickens, like it can sense similar blood nearby. It rages through me, wanting to drag me back to him. But something else is happening. Memories are crowding into my brain like they're rabid dogs with a scent to chase. Mother using Mask to cover her black eyes. Mother cowering on the floor while he told her all the ways in which she was Objectionable. The way he jeered and pointed at her face creases and said, *"Where is she? I can't see her. She's Invisible now."* Mother frantically pulling me into Pretty dresses that would make Father happy. How scared she was if I dared muddy my clothes, or let my hair get tangled. Putting Mask on me when I was very young, so my cheeks and lips looked redder, because otherwise he'd tease me for looking sickly.

I stare at this man from across the street and know instinctively that if he was to look up and see me now, his face would drop. He would not be proud. He would look at me with disdain – my knotted hair, sweaty face, lack of Look, no Mask. Just me. My face. His daughter's face.

And just in time, sense finally finds me – though it breaks my heart.

"I'm not going in," I tell Belle.

"What? Is he even there?"

"I can see him."

"Who is he? Which one?"

"It doesn't matter."

I take him in one last time, this haunting of a person. A dangerous hope. Something I clung to when I lost myself –

forcing myself to forget the unforgettable because I was so desperate to be seen. Forgetting all the things my brave, brilliant Mother taught me about who to give power to.

I turn away, I walk away from my father.

Let him wait. Let him keep checking his Device. Let him wonder. Let him feel slightly powerless.

I will never contact him again.

I will never see him again.

And, most importantly, I won't give him the chance to see me.

Because he won't see the real me. He'll see the difference between the real me and his disgusting idea of what the real me should be based on the Doctrine. He will judge how much he loves and misses me based on how well I fulfil a foul criteria of how girls should look. I refuse to give him that power. I refuse for him to be disappointed with how I look while ignoring all I've *done*. What I've achieved. How I've not crumbled from the trauma of what he did to us. How I've been able to grow up and be strong enough to fight against this world that wants to make me feel as small as he did. How I help other girls and women feel safe and themselves.

But I know him. Even after ten years away, I know him.

And he wouldn't want to see any of that.

Belle's hand is still in mine. She asks no questions. She trusts my decisions. We walk away and keep walking and walking, until town is behind us, until houses make way for meadows and trees, until it's a spot in the distance. We walk for over an hour, in silence, the sun baking our faces, the movement helping us process today's huge disappointment. Not needing words, just each other. We eventually climb a hill, and somehow we both know it's time to stop. We collapse into the grass littered with beautiful daisies and we stare back at the town we've both grown up in, the town we have lost our escape tunnel from.

It seems less scary when it's small like this.

Belle speaks first. "I want to fight still," she says. "I want to fight to stop future Damians forming. I want to fight to end the Doctrine. I want to grow in the ways I would've grown if we'd gotten in."

I swallow. "Me too."

"I don't need to be there to feel how that place made me feel. I can make myself feel that way without them."

I swallow harder, tears wanting to arrive again. At just how proud I am of her. "Me too."

"I want to look at myself in the mirror and see only a person. A person who can do extraordinary things."

I nudge myself closer to her. "I want to make it so every girl looks at their reflection and feels like that," I add.

"Yes," she says, picking up my hand again. It's like we can't stop touching each other. "Yes, I want that too." With her spare hand she picks up a small rock and weighs it in her palm. "Do you know what my mother said to me this morning?"

I raise both eyebrows. I can imagine it wasn't very nice.

"She said, 'Belle, what are you doing to yourself? *You could be so Pretty.*' Like that's the most important thing to be." She looks down at her rock. "I wish it was the reverse. I wish she could be looking at my Masked face, my fake face, my face that doesn't look like a face at all, and I wish she could say, 'Oh my darling, you could be so *free*…'"

Free.

Her words bury in. Her wisdom. Her strength to feel them and say them.

And that's when I realize it.

We may not have everything we want right now. We may feel like we're losing. Like we've lost. Like it's not worth trying any more. That there's no hope left. But there *is* hope, because, Belle and I, we are free. So awake and so free.

And free feels so much better than Pretty.

I look over at this girl, feelings pouring into my stomach. Feelings I'm sure we're going to have to address soon. That could further unravel how the world sees us, and how we see ourselves. Feelings I'm sure are felt back, however unnerving that is for us both. Yet, together, we've shown ourselves to be so much braver than we could've ever thought.

I pick up a rock too, and hold it out to her like we're about to clink glasses with them. "Here's to freedom."

She smiles. "To freedom."

Belle holds her rock to the skyline, aiming it at our town, squints with one eye, and thrusts her arm back. She chucks it high into the sky, where it soars and smashes over the horizon.

THIS ISN'T A DYSTOPIA

This isn't a fiction.

This is now. Normal. Our world today.

We watch the two girls, throwing rocks across the sky, aiming at their ordinary town, in this ordinary world. Well, this world we've come to accept as ordinary. A world where girls must paint over their entire faces with make-up before leaving the house in order to look "normal", let alone beautiful. Where they check the altered faces of others on their phones almost constantly. Face after face that make them feel disgusting and terrible, but faces that aren't real faces. Faces that have been injected and cut, smothered and well-lit, and then tweaked and altered before posting...all to win a game where the winners are weaker not stronger. To be the best at having a face, for a short period of time, before time itself will make that face offensive, and not worth listening to, or noticing...so you chase the face you used to have.

You chase and you chase and you chase.

The girls laugh as they keep throwing the rocks. These girls who go to school every day, trying to learn, and yet spend their time trying to stop their bodies being touched, groped, commented on, assaulted. Porn sent to them, porn played to them, porn that tells them, *This is what sex is, what pleasure is.*

It will hurt for you. Accept this. Embrace this. Or there's something wrong with you.

Alongside these girls' official education, they are taught invisible lessons about how their body should be. How much space it should take up. The hunger involved so their body can look the "right" way. Then blamed when their body looking that way means boys cannot help but assault them.

So ordinary. So perfectly ordinary. Not a dystopia. Just normality.

But it doesn't have to be normal.

One of the girls gets up, still laughing, and starts running further up the hill, the other following her.

"I need to let it out," she says.

They pelt up the hill, casting a silhouette against the sky, chasing one another. Today they've not been given the escape they wanted. They weren't rewarded for their bravery. It's a bitter pill to swallow, and it's one they'll have to get used to the taste of, but in the way they run, you can see they've learned the most important lesson of all.

The escape tunnel they craved was always there, and they'd already found it. It was inside them the whole time.

These girls, running, playing, so free, opened their eyes and they saw it. They saw everything for what it was, and you know this is only the start. That they will go to the places they want to go, do the things they want to do, change the minds that want to be changed. They're at the peak of the hill now, the summer breeze lifting their hair. One throws her arms back and starts to scream out towards the horizon. The other girl laughs and joins in. They scream and scream, taking breaks only to laugh and hug each other, before launching their chests open and screaming some more. The war cries of freedom.

And they look so pretty. *So pretty.*

THE END

If you have been affected by the issues
raised in this book, the following
organizations can help:

Samaritans are available round the clock, every single day of
the year. You can talk to them any time you like, and in your
own way, about whatever's getting to you.

Call, free, any time, on 116 123

Or email jo@samaritans.org

Visit – find your nearest branch on

samaritans.org

The Mix is here to help under 25s get to grips with any
challenge they face. Anywhere and anytime,
online, over the phone or via social media.

Helpline: 0808 808 4994

themix.org.uk

ACKNOWLEDGEMENTS

Everything changed for me the year I wrote this book, which seems fitting as this book is quite different from my others. Firstly, I want to thank Maddy, Rebecca, Sarah and Chloe for totally getting it when I pitched this idea. I will always fondly recall bombarding you with my endlessly-depressing research, and finishing with, "So this will be a contemporary novel, just like my others, but I'm writing it in dystopian language because we are actually already living this nightmare, sorry." I was so nervous to try something different but you have all believed in me right from the start, giving me the confidence to create the world of The Doctrine. Thank you.

And thank you to Fritha, Emily, Hannah, Jessica and everyone behind the scenes at Usborne for your amazing campaign for this book. Thank you also to Will Steele for his absolutely bombastic cover that is so iconically and ironically GORGEOUS to behold.

Speaking of Usborne, I was devastated when Peter Usborne, the founder of my beloved publisher, died unexpectedly in March 2023. Truly there was no man like him, and I owe him so much for championing my career since my very first novel. Peter read every book his authors wrote before publication – one of the endlessly amazing things about him – and it breaks my heart he'll never get to read *You Could Be So Pretty*. He will be missed and remembered for his dedication to children's literacy, his incredible sense of humour, and for building a family more than a publisher – a family I feel very privileged to be a member of.

Writing this novel meant exploring the pressures of some beauty standards I haven't personally experienced and I'd like to thank Helen and Hannah for their advice and guidance.

I also want to thank all my wonderful friends and colleagues who I love and adore and who have guided me through this book and year of incredible change. Sara, Tanya, Nina, Katie, Alwyn, Samantha, Krystal, Lucy, Sophie, Josh, Emily K, Kat, Rachel, Becky, Lexi, Christi, Emily S, Louie, Maartje, Emma, Clare…I don't know where I'd be without the group chats and epically long voice notes. Thank you, as always, to my supportive parents and sisters.

And, finally, the biggest thank you of all to my new family. W, you are my rock, my everything. And, little C. You grew in me as this book grew on my laptop. Every day I'll fight to make the world a better, brighter and safer place for you.

ALSO BY HOLLY BOURNE

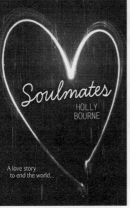

HOLLY BOURNE

is a bestselling and critically acclaimed author. Inspired by her work with young people, and her own experiences of everyday sexism, Holly is a passionate mental health advocate and proud feminist.

#YouCouldBeSoPretty
🐦 **@holly_bourneYA**
📷 **@hollybourneYA**
@UsborneYA
hollybourne.co.uk

**For discussion questions about this book,
scan the below code**